A Contradiction
to His Pride

A Contradiction to His Pride/Leanne W. Smith

A Contradiction
to His Pride

LEANNE W. SMITH

Scripture references are from the Holy Bible, King James Version, public domain.

Published by Leanne W. Smith; printed and distributed through Ingram Content.

ISBN: 978-0-692-12579-3
This book is also available as an e-book, ISBN: 978-0-692-12582-3

Cover design by Shelby M'lynn Mick.
Cover model, John King (@itsjohnking).
Cover photo of John King by Falk Neumann
(www.falkneumannphotography.com), used by permission.
Cover photo of town from the Denver Public Library, Western History
Collection, Call # X-6370, used by permission.

To Miss J,
who grew wings
and was strong to face
what lay before her.

CHARACTER LIST

- *James Parker* — Hoke Mathews' younger, former riding partner
- *Hoke Mathews* — Helped lead Colonel Dotson's wagon train in *Leaving Independence*, married to Abigail

THE BALDWYNS

- *Abigail (Baldwyn) Mathews* — Left Marston, Tennessee with her four children to join Colonel Dotson's wagon train in *Leaving Independence*, married to Hoke
- *Charlie Baldwyn* — Abigail's older son
- *Corrine Baldwyn* — Abigail's older daughter
- *Jacob Baldwyn* — Abigail's younger son
- *Lina Baldwyn* — Abigail's younger daughter
- *Mimi* — Abigail's friend and former cook in Marston
- *Rascal* — The Baldwyns' dog
- *Thad Walstone* — Abigail's brother in Marston

FORMER WAGON TRAIN MEMBERS NOW LIVING IN BAKER CITY, OREGON

- *Emma Austelle* — Corrine's friend and Charlie's sweetheart
- *Charles & Melinda Austelle* — Emma's parents
- *Clyde & Cooper Austelle* — Emma's younger brothers

- *Colonel George & Christine Dotson* — Leader of the wagon train in *Leaving Independence*, and his wife
- *Gerald & Josephine Jenkins* — Dotson's brother-in-law, and his wife, Christine's sister
- *Harry & Tam (Woodford) Sims* — Preacher, and his spunky wife
- *Marc & Nelda (Peters) Isaacs* — Doctor, and his wife, who helps at the mercantile
- *Caroline & Will Atwood* — Doc's Isaac's widowed sister, and her son
- *Tim & Bart Peters* — Father and son who own the mercantile
- *Michael Chessor* — Young adventurer

NEW CHARACTERS

- *Sam Eston* — Baker City Sheriff
- *Bennett Solomon* — Newspaperman who takes tintypes
- *Duke Walden* — Notorious outlaw and father to four sons
- *Marquis Walden* — Duke's oldest son
- *Earl Walden* — Duke's middle son
- *Viscount & Baron Walden* — Duke's twin sons
- *Hannah* — D&J Hotel cook
- *Chancey* — Saloon owner
- *Collin Mears* — U.S. Marshall
- *José* — Hispanic man who lives remotely
- *Carlina (Bitty)* — Former slave who lives with José

- *Pearl Parker* — James' grandmother, a midwife who lives in Silvertown, Colorado
- *Tom Burleson* — Silvertown doctor
- *Sairee Adams* — Girl who knew James as a child
- *Harold Pickens* — Silvertown attorney
- *Buford Starnes* — Silvertown sheriff
- *Mrs. Spencer* — Woman from Silvertown hotel

A Contradiction to His Pride/Leanne W. Smith

PROLOGUE

A cold wind rustled the leaves of the evergreens west of Baker City, building like the crescendo of a symphony. When the wind unfurled and swept into town, it lifted the top layer of a twenty-inch snow that had fallen the day before, sending icy sprays swirling over several residents who rushed to stand in the drifts and on the boardwalk following the gunshots.

James Parker wanted to give Corrine Baldwyn a day to remember him by, not a day to curse his name.

Now, as she thrashed while he tried to hold her, the blood from her hands raking stains over the sleeves of his coat, James squeezed his eyes shut against the wind, the ice, the snow and the slaughter, and wondered if she could ever forgive him.

A Contradiction to His Pride/Leanne W. Smith

CHAPTER 1

Smoke curling up

The day James Parker helped Hoke Mathews hang the final door on his cabin was the same day he decided how he'd sweep Corrine Baldwyn off her feet. James was standing on the ground he and Hoke had packed hard with their foot traffic — arms crossed, admiring the work of their labor — when the idea seeded and planted in his mind.

The Baldwyns' dog Rascal sat on his haunches between the two men, his black tail thumping contentment.

James nodded toward the cabin. "Think it'll hold in a hard wind?"

He watched Hoke's eyes fan over the trees closest to them as the early December wind teased their branches up and down, making them look like they were host to an army of hopping squirrels.

"It better."

Hoke pulled two wooden sticks from his pocket, handed one to James, then put the other in his mouth and turned back to the cabin. They used to gnaw on hickory sticks, but had taken to chewing sugar maple out here in Oregon.

"Think it's got enough windows?" Hoke pointed to the eastern side of the cabin. "I'll put Abigail a flower garden there, come spring. That's where the mornin' sun hits."

James raised an eyebrow. "You sure you don't want to go ahead and break the ground right now? Set the fencerow? Build the barn and stables while we're at it? I know you don't like to sit while there's still half a sun peepin' over the horizon."

Hoke shot him a sideways smirk, then turned his attention to the smoke curling up from the chimney. James followed his eyes. How many nights had he and Hoke watched the smoke curling up from a campfire on the trail?

Six years' worth of nights, that's how many. Standing on the worn knoll of his former riding partner's new homestead, looking at the house they'd labored to build and knowing that the women they'd built it for now stood inside it cooking them supper, flooded James's heart with mixed emotions.

James Parker liked to think he was soundly in charge of his own mind. Like he had been eight months ago, when he joined a wagon train headed northwest along the Oregon Trail. No one made him do that, not even Hoke.

True, Hoke had been the first to decide to join Colonel George Dotson's group. James remembered standing outside the livery in Independence, Missouri, and hearing Hoke mutter around the edges of the hickory stick he was chewing then, "George Dotson's been after me to join his wagon train. I believe I'll do it."

When James asked why, Hoke said he didn't know. And therein lay the attraction of the notion. Wasn't it he, James

Parker, who — being clearly in charge of his own mind — had responded, "We better do it then. When you start making decisions you can't explain, things always get interesting"?

Yes, that had been him.

And it was he, James Parker, who had known the moment he met Corrine's mother, Abigail, that here was Hoke's reason for joining the group, whether Hoke was ready to admit it or not. What James hadn't seen coming was how the woman's feisty daughter would capture his own free-ranging heart.

His affection had started innocently enough. He played the same game with Corrine he played with every female he ever met: see if he could get her to smile, or better yet, to blush. The game was made all the more exciting, of course, with her being such a sharp-mouthed beauty.

But then the game had stopped being a game to him.

James ran his eyes over the outside walls of the cabin. It gave him a solid feeling to survey the logs he'd helped hew and place, knowing he'd done it beside the most capable man with whom he'd ever ridden a trail. But it also made him restless.

It was time for James to stake his own claim. Only, he had a job to do first.

Hoke leaned over to stroke the top of the dog's head. "You're coming in, aren't you?" The look he gave James was a fond one. The fierceness in Hoke's eyes had grown softer since he married.

James nodded. "Corrine promised me biscuits."

The men walked up the steps to the wide porch, Hoke running his black boot against the side of each stair, testing the strength and smoothness of the boards. James turned back to the setting sun.

"My God, Hoke. What a view." A lump the size of a walnut formed in his throat. With Hoke's marriage, a chapter of James's life had come to an end, just as the year—1866—was about to come to an end. What would the next year and chapter hold?

Hoke leaned against the porch railing. "I still don't understand why you haven't filed a land claim."

James leaned opposite him. "I told you why."

"We made good off the sales of that herd from Texas."

James avoided Hoke's eyes, concentrating instead on the orange sun sliding below the horizon. "I sent the better portion of that money to my grandmaw."

Hoke crossed his arms. "What women got the other parts?"

James didn't answer.

"I don't understand why you do that, James. Never have."

"I know you don't. It's none of your business anyway."

"It becomes my business if you involve members of my family."

His *family*. Hoke had never had a family before. James started to ask, *What does that make me?* but stopped himself. He liked to think he'd been something like a brother to Hoke, the bond between them born of hardship shared.

"None of your family is involved, far as I can tell."

A flame blazed up in Hoke's eyes. "What are your intentions toward Corrine, James?"

James looked back out at the sunset. "I see you're taking this father business seriously."

"Don't skirt the issue. What are your intentions?"

James turned to face him. His intentions were simple. First, win Corrine Baldwyn's heart. Second, head back to Kansas to round up the large herd of horses he and Hoke had seen while riding from Texas to Independence, before they'd joined the train last summer. And third, return to Baker City with his quiver full of horses and his pockets full of gold, to claim Corrine's hand with honor.

Then again, maybe the third thing was that he'd get out on the trail and realize it was only proximity to a lovely girl that had briefly clouded his judgment. He needed time and distance to gain clarity and control of his mind.

James and Hoke had a six-year, running argument over whether it was a man's heart, head or gut that served him finest. James always argued heart, while Hoke insisted the gut was a man's most reliable source of strength. Both his gut and heart were telling James now he would never find a better life's companion than the budding woman who lived inside this cabin. But his mind still wanted convincing.

Hoke's questions about his intentions didn't sit well with James. It rankled him to have been supplanted by family so newly acquired, even if the family did include the girl who held his interest. "I believe I'll discuss my intentions with her before I discuss them with you."

Just then the door swung open, revealing the prettiest sixteen-year-old ever to come to Oregon. How could any man think straight when beholding her? James had known plenty of girls her age to marry men his age or older. Still, the ten-year gap bothered him. Much as he wanted her to be crazy about him, he wanted to know her feelings were solid and not likely to change.

Corrine's eyes flickered from James to her stepfather, and back again. James's blood stirred as her gaze traveled up from his knee-length boots, paused on the Walker Colt hanging on his right hip, then got caught in the thick of his beard. The lift of one eyebrow as she pulled her eyes back up to his was slight, but enough for him to detect it.

She tapped her heel against the porch made from sturdy poplars James had planed himself. "Are you two coming in?"

James considered the young lady standing before him. How could she have gotten in his head so strong at such a tender age? Yes, she was lovely—Hoke's new role as stepfather would no doubt be challenging—but it wasn't just her looks that drew him to her. She was whip-smart, too.

James had felt he had the upper hand with most people he ever met. Not Hoke, of course. Hoke was more than James's equal, being nine years older and not inclined to care what anybody thought of him. And now there was Corrine Baldwyn. Even at sixteen short years of age, she stood pretty solid on her feet. She had a way about her that kept a man humble, and yet James felt a thrill each time she sassed him. He wondered if that might be what was causing him to lose his upper hand.

James removed his hat as he stepped through the cabin door, thankful that Hoke had seen fit to make it a tall one. "Darlin', I didn't think anything could outshine that sunset yonder, but you just did."

Both her eyebrows lifted this time. "Mr. Parker, words roll off your tongue so fast, I can't help but wonder if you take proper time to consider them."

Abigail stepped around her daughter, took James's hat and held out her hand for his coat. "Corrine, don't be smart with Mr. Parker. Without his help, we'd still be living out of a wagon."

James kissed Abigail on the forehead. "Lovely, as always, despite your slave-drivin' husband. I hope you don't get callouses on your hands like I have."

Corinne's sister Lina ran to hug James's legs. He reached down and scooped the angelic four-year-old into his arms, rubbing his beard against the bend of her neck.

Giggles filled the cabin.

"Will you sit by me?" he asked.

"Yes!"

Lina wiggled from his arms and ran to push their chairs together. She climbed up in one and pushed her plate until it clinked against his.

He took his seat and looked across the table at Corrine who refused to look back. "I'm glad somebody loves me." He winked down at Lina.

Corinne refused to take the bait, but James was undeterred. Throughout the meal he made a game out of winking across the table. "I believe your biscuits are gettin' even better, Corrine." He cracked one open and stuffed first one half, then the other in his mouth.

"It's the butter." She pushed a small plate of it toward him. "The cow's milk is richer now that we're not making her walk twenty miles a day." She pushed the long narrow bowl of biscuits toward him next.

James reached for another. "You don't think it's this bowl?" This time he slathered the cracked biscuit with melting gold before stuffing each half into his mouth.

Corrine looked at him with level eyes. "It's a beautiful bowl and I'm grateful to have it, but I don't see how that changes the nature of the dough."

From the corner of his eye James could see Hoke grinning into his plate. He knew Hoke enjoyed Corrine's ability to take the starch from James's chest.

James would have sworn when he made Corrine that bowl during the wagon train's journey west that he'd done it only to encourage her cooking. He'd never carved a useful item out of wood before. But James's grandmother who'd raised him made her biscuits in an old wooden bowl, so when James spied a fallen oak at Ash Hollow, he'd followed a strong urge to see if he could carve one like it for Corrine. He discovered he liked making things out of wood.

He ran his hand over the top of the table. "This holding up okay for you?"

Abigail squeezed James's wrist. "We love it! It's beautiful. And I'm so grateful you made it this large. I've talked Hoke into letting me invite everyone here for

Christmas dinner. What's the news from town? Is the hotel finished?"

"Nearly. Prettiest hotel I ever saw. They painted it white."

"They never let on they were going to build a hotel," said Hoke. George Dotson and Gerald Jenkins, leaders of the wagon train they'd all traveled west with, surprised everyone by building a hotel in the heart of the Oregon town where the group had settled.

"Dotson says they didn't think about it until they got out here and saw one was needed. Jenkins has experience, since he owned one in the east."

"Have they decided on a name for it?" asked Abigail.

"The D&J."

Abigail's eyes brightened. "The D&J Hotel...how perfect!"

"Has a nice ring, don't it? Tim Peters finished his mercantile, too, and Harry Sims has been preaching at the church every Sunday since the old preacher packed up and moved to Oregon City. Doc Isaacs built a house near Harry and Tam with a side room for doctorin."

"Is Nelda doing okay?" asked Abigail.

It wasn't customary to discuss the condition of a woman expecting a child, but everyone from Dotson's wagon train was concerned for Nelda Isaacs, formerly Peters, who had lost both a husband and a baby on the hard journey to Baker City. Doc Isaacs and Nelda had married shortly after Hoke and Abigail, and Nelda already in the early stages of another pregnancy.

"Seems to be doin' fine, just fine." James winked across the table at Corrine. "Doc's going to have a houseful." His widowed sister, Caroline Atwood, and her young son, Will, also lived with them.

Charlie, a year older than Corrine and oldest of the four fair-haired, blue-eyed Baldwyn children, spoke up from the far end of the table. "You seen the Austelles lately?"

James grinned. "Thought I'd swing by there on my way back if there's anything anyone wants to send." The Austelle family had claimed land closer to town.

"Oh!" Corrine smiled for the first time. "I have a letter for Emma."

James laid a hand over his chest. "I'd be honored to deliver it."

She mumbled her thanks.

James smiled, thinking how his grandmother said the sassiest women made for the warmest if you knew how to melt their protective layers of ice.

Taking courage from the thought, he decided he had nothing to lose by implementing his newly formed plan. Christmas was in three weeks. That would be the perfect time to set the first part of his strategy into motion.

CHAPTER 2
More slate gray than blue

Corrine wrapped twine around the envelope of her letter to Emma Austelle and double-knotted it before laying it into James Parker's long outstretched hands. But her fingers were reluctant to let go of the package. "You won't read it, will you?"

He looked down at the parcel and back up into her eyes. "Sweetheart, I would die before I took advantage of your trust in me."

James had such a natural way of letting sweet words fall that it was hard for Corrine not to let them soak in like sunshine on her neck. But sometimes she wondered if he was just pulling her marionette strings. She didn't want to be the brunt of a secret joke James Parker had going in his head.

Then the corners of his lips slid into a mischievous grin as his fingers closed over hers. "Did you write about me?"

"Why would I write about you, Mr. Parker?"

Self-conscious, she snatched her hand away, leaving the letter behind.

"It's just a silly letter between girlfriends, but it's private. I wouldn't like to think you were of such low character that I couldn't trust the contents of my heart in your sneaky, curious hands. That's all."

James burst into laughter. "Darlin', the contents of your heart couldn't be safer than with me."

He put the letter in his shirt pocket and reached for his coat and hat. "If you ever want to write *me* letters, you go right ahead. I'd enjoy readin' those. I surely would."

Then he was gone. Three weeks passed before she saw him again.

*   *   *

On Christmas morning Corrine rose early. Not since their former cook Mimi had lived with them back in Tennessee had she known such baking and preparations. Though her mother had come a long way since they'd left Independence, Corrine was still better in the kitchen, and Abigail depended on her.

Abigail's gifts were sewing and gardening. New lace curtains swung from the tops of the windows, an embroidered cloth graced the large oak table, and a blue and yellow woven rug hugged the floor in front of the fireplace, rescued from the home the family lost back in Tennessee.

Cloth sacks that once held supplies inside Abigail's wagons had been transformed into Christmas stockings for each member of the family. Abigail had stitched initials on each one and fastened them to the walls on either side of the hearth. Her rocking chair, with the same colored fabrics woven into its seat, sat in one corner by the butter churn.

Corrine's brothers, Charlie and Jacob, had been sent on expeditions for mistletoe and pine boughs, and she and Lina poured thick wax candles. Abigail arranged the fruits of their labors until the whole house wrapped its occupants like the warmest of blankets. Everything was ready. The Dotsons, Jenkins, Harry and Tam Sims, Doc and Nelda, Caroline and Baby Will, and the Austelles were all coming to dinner.

And James...James was coming.

Corrine grabbed the egg basket and slipped out into the cold, making her way through the barn to the henhouse behind it. She could hear Charlie mucking the stalls in the stables over the clucking of the hens as they reshuffled from her prying hands. Then Hoke's ax began to ring.

She came back into the cabin with a blast of cold air. Hoke came in behind her, his arms full of wood for Abigail's stove and the fireplace.

"Jacob!" he called up the ladder to the loft. "Come gather the rest of the kindling. Stack it by this wall so we'll have plenty for the day. Sweetheart...." He turned to Abigail. "I'll be out here with the smoker if you need me." Hoke had hollowed out an old tree stump and been smoking strips of venison with cherry wood chips for days.

He stopped at the door.

Abigail, who was pressing butter into a wooden mold with Lina, looked up and saw him watching her. Hoke smiled.

Wiping her hands on her apron, Abigail went to him. They stepped outside and must have thought they were hidden behind the door, but Corrine could see them through the window, kissing. Hoke's arms wrapped around her mother's waist, and his hands lingered on the ties of her apron until Abigail finally opened the door and came back inside.

Her mother was in love.

Unlike James, whose tongue flowed with praises, Hoke rarely complimented Abigail. But Abigail didn't seem adversely affected by the absence. In fact—it hurt Corrine to admit this, she had wanted so badly for her own father to be alive and return to them after the war—Abigail had never seemed happier.

For all the group's hardship on the journey west, a lot of love had blossomed. Harry Sims, the preacher, and Tam Woodford had been two of the first to get eyes for one another. More gradually, so had Nelda Peters and Doc Isaacs. Corrine knew Emma Austelle had captured Charlie's heart, too. With all this love in the air, she couldn't help but wonder…what about her? Were her growing curiosities about James Parker the same as love? Or was Corrine just curious about love itself?

When James had given her the wooden bowl, he said he liked the idea of eating her biscuits when he was old. He said he aimed to court her. Just when did he aim to start then? And what did courting entail, exactly? She longed to put these questions to someone, but the only person she trusted was Emma Austelle.

Back in Tennessee, Corrine had friends, but never one to call her closest. After five months of visiting with Emma on a wagon seat by day and dreaming into a campfire with her at night, now she did.

Charlie was guarded with his feelings—he always had been—but it was easy to see he was smitten with Emma. And what man wouldn't be? Emma kept an ever-present smile on her lips, and drew smiles from all around her.

Having a friend like Emma and enjoying the flirtations of a man like James Parker should have been plenty of reason for Corrine to feel lighthearted and hopeful about the future. So why didn't she? What was this unexplained restlessness she felt instead?

Her restlessness was often worse when James was around. His words were filled with honey, but how much stock should she put into the honey-coated words of a man ten years her senior? Was James Parker serious about his intentions to marry her? And if he was, was it what *she* wanted?

Emma seemed more than ready to marry Charlie, as if she had no other ambition in the world. But Corrine's heart yearned for something...she just couldn't put a name to it. Now that the cabin was built and James's reasons for hanging around the ranch had ended, what would happen next? If she was reading the future right, he'd be riding back down the trail soon and she'd be holed up in a cabin. Corrine missed the heart-thumping thrill of overland travel, of not knowing what was around the next bend in the trail. She hated to think she had come to the end of all that mystery and adventure.

*   *   *

James pulled the borrowed wagon into the side yard. When he unhitched his horse and led it into Hoke's new barn, he recognized several of the other horses standing amidst the generous stockpiles of hay. Hoke was never one to do a halfway job for his horses.

James stroked the noses of Hoke's black stallion and white filly before letting Rascal walk him to the door.

The Dotsons and Jenkinses were sitting at the broad oak table when James stepped inside. The main room of the cabin was large. Hoke had walled Corrine and Lina a private room on the left, behind the fireplace, and him and Abigail a room to the right, past the table. The kitchen lay between them. The boys slept in an open loft above the girls' room, and the family's food was stored in the loft above Hoke and Abigail's, at the opposite end.

Dotson rose to greet him. "James! Welcome." Dotson pointed to the table. "Hoke said you made this."

"That's right." James kissed Abigail on the cheek when she came to get his coat and hat. He nodded to the women at the table. "Feel that wood under the cloth. Like glass. Sanded it myself." He caught Corrine's eye as she stood at the potbellied stove across the room and winked at her. She blew a strand of fallen hair from her eyes and raised her chin.

Colonel Dotson lifted a corner of the tablecloth to inspect James's work. "We need tables at the D&J."

Abigail brought a basket over and motioned to Harry and Tam Sims who were standing by the fireplace with Hoke. "You're just in time, James. Harry and Tam, come to the table and get a slice of bread while it's hot."

James nodded at Tam as she approached, then looked at her more closely. "You expectin'?"

She swatted him with her hand. "What a thing to ask! Married life's just making me fat."

"I see it hasn't made you any more proper. Harry, can't you do nothin' about that? A preacher's wife ought to be silent."

Tam picked up a fork. "Don't make me tong you, James."

Dark-headed and hardworking, Tam had arms and grit so strong most men would have thought long and hard before marrying her. But not close-lipped, stocky-shouldered Harry Sims.

"The next platter comin' to this table is Christmas turkey," Tam told James with a swell of her chest. "One I shot myself."

James winked at Corrine again before teasing Tam. "Did you make Harry cook it?"

Tam waved her fork at him again. "I can hunt *and* cook, thank you very much."

Abigail laid the turkey platter on the table and looked across the room at Hoke, who stood with one foot on the stone hearth, watching her. Charlie and Jacob had dug those stones out of the creek that ran the perimeter of the hill while James and Hoke had felled the trees.

If Hoke was ever still from working these days, he was watching Abigail with a little grin. Much as James liked looking at Corrine, he hoped *he* didn't watch *her* with a silly grin.

Lina tugged Hoke's sleeve. "Are you going to say the prayer, Papa?"

Hoke scooped her up and took a minute to speak. James knew Hoke was choked up because Lina had called him Papa. Rascal started barking in the yard. "Let's give the others a chance to get inside," Hoke said thickly.

Presently the door swung open and Marc and Nelda Isaacs stepped in along with Marc's sister, Caroline Atwood, and her baby boy, Will. "Hope we haven't kept you waiting." Doc held up a pie in each hand as Will turned loose of his leg and ran to hug Corrine. "These women have been cooking for days. The Austelles are right behind us. By the looks of it, Melinda and Emma have been cooking for days, too."

Folks got in the house, coats and hats were removed, and food was added to the table. James sat at one of the table's benches enjoying the friendly banter.

"How're we goin' to fit all this food in here...much less eat it all?"

"Oh, we'll eat it all."

"Good thing it's a big table."

"James made it. Didn't he do a fine job?"

"You ladies have outdone yourselves."

Hoke asked Harry Sims to offer grace and the feasting began. As the meal wound down, one of the children suggested, "Let's play hide 'n' seek after lunch!"

James saw Charlie and Emma exchange a look and a grin.

When the men got up to go admire Hoke's new barn, the women stayed inside to make candy and swap gossip and recipes. James caught some of their conversation when he eased back in a little later to look for Corrine.

"I still plan to work for Mr. Peters behind the counter in the mercantile even after the baby comes," Nelda was saying. "He'll need help since Bart's planning to go with James back to Kansas this spring."

Christine Dotson turned to Abigail. "You've got to come see the D&J, Abigail."

"Gerald has promised me a piano for the parlor," said Josephine Jenkins. "And we're looking for a cook. You know any good cooks?"

James would have joined their conversation, but right now he had more pressing matters on his mind. He caught Corrine's eye and motioned her over. "Come out to the yard with me. I want to show you somethin.'"

She lifted her gray flannel shawl from a hook by the door and wrapped it over her shoulders. As she stepped out on the porch James said, "Close your eyes. You got 'em closed good?" He laid his left hand over them to be sure.

She caught hold of his wrist. "I can't see where I'm going, Mr. Parker."

He put his right hand on the small of her back and steered her where he wanted her to go. "Here are the steps. Count four."

He watched over her as she went down each step, loving the way her long lashes brushed against the palm of the hand he held over her eyes, and loving the way her skirts brushed against his pants legs as he came down the steps beside her.

"Turn left." He slid his hand to the side of her waist, nudging her in the direction he wanted her to go, marveling at how trim her hips were.

"You ever goin' to call me 'James'?" He nudged her again. "Say it. Say 'James.'"

He felt her cheeks stretch underneath his hand from smiling, then watched her bite her lower lip as if she was trying hard to keep from it.

Finally, she gave in. "James."

They stopped and he gazed down at the top of her golden hair. "That didn't hurt a bit, now did it?"

James had her directly in front of the buckboard now. He looked from the blue of Corrine's dress collar to the gray of her shawl, trying to decide which was closest to the color of her eyes that still lay hidden beneath his hand. Steam rose from between her smiling lips in the chill December air. He was just leaning over her right shoulder to taste that steam and brush those lips with his own when she pulled his hand off.

Her eyes cut over to the rough boards of the buckboard before she looked back up at James. "Why'd you bring me out here?"

It was the shawl. Her eyes were more slate gray than blue, fringed in the longest lashes he'd ever seen. And they weren't afraid to look a man level in the eye. That might be his favorite thing about her.

James pointed to a wooden chest that sat in the buckboard.

Corrine blinked. "What is it?"

"What do you think it is? It's a hope chest."

"Who's it for?"

"For you!"

She bit her lower lip again and ran her hand over the end of the chest nearest to her.

"Smooth as glass," he said with pride. "It's cedar. I made you that bowl out of oak, but that was before I knew how much easier it is to work with cedar and poplar."

She looked at him with those level eyes again. "Why do you keep making me things out of wood, Mr. Par—James?"

He shook his head. This was only the first part of his plan, but he wasn't ready for her to know that yet. "Can't seem to help myself."

Her eyes fell and she hesitated. Then she pulled a small package from her pocket, wrapped in paper and twine. "I made you something, too. It's not nearly as fine as a hope chest."

James took it from her hands and started to open it, but she stopped him, her fingers warm on his.

"No! Don't open it until you get back to your place."

"Why can't I open it now?"

"Because. I just...would rather you wait."

It pleased him that she'd thought of him. He hadn't expected it. And it pleased him to see her acting shy. That was a hopeful sign.

"All right then."

As well as James thought he could read most women, it was hard to read Corrine Baldwyn. He was pretty sure she liked him – genuinely liked him – and he had tried to make it plain he had feelings for her. But she was prideful, and a prideful woman didn't like to let her feelings be known, not if there was any chance of getting them trampled. At least, that's what his grandmother used to say.

He smiled and put the package in his coat pocket.

*   *   *

Corrine helped stoke the fire in the stove. Food was warmed and served again. As another blessing was offered, the door opened and Charlie and Emma slid inside.

Jacob hopped up as soon as the 'amen' was uttered. "Where have you two been? We searched everywhere!"

Charlie's face reddened.

Emma laughed and squeezed Charlie's arm. "Your brother was showing me around your land, Jacob."

Later, as the Austelles prepared to leave, Corrine and Emma walked outside arm-in-arm. "What were you and Charlie *really* off doing?" Corrine whispered.

Emma giggled. "Stealin' kisses."

Corrine studied the frozen ground beneath her boots. "What's it like?"

Emma's mouth fell open. "You mean to tell me you've never been kissed? Did the boys in Tennessee have no courage? I bet Paul Sutler was planning to steal him a kiss that day at Chimney Rock, but you never gave him a decent chance."

"What am I supposed to do?"

"I don't know. Put a few signals out there. Button your smart lip, for one."

Corrine elbowed her in the side. Emma elbowed her back.

Emma's voice dropped. "Your brother, now, he's a shy kisser. But...he's very good at it."

"Emma!"

Even as she scolded her friend, Corrine thought how perfect Emma was for Charlie—for any man, for that matter. Emma was a girl who could build a man's confidence. Corrine, on the other hand, felt like she needed to keep every man in check.

"I imagine Mr. Parker's kissed plenty of girls." Emma elbowed her again.

Corrine pushed Emma toward her waiting family. "You need to go home and practice being chaste-minded." But the comment left Corrine wondering just how many girls James Parker *had* kissed. She bit her lip as she thought about the note she had included with his gift.

As the Austelles' buckboard rolled down the hill, James came out and unloaded Corrine's hope chest and took it into the house for her.

Corrine wasn't sure she liked what a hope chest implied—a life of domesticity, everything a woman was supposed to want—but she buttoned her lip as Emma had advised, not wanting to seem ungrateful.

She was helping her mother clean the dishes when James came and stood at the door, signaling that he was ready to go. Should she walk with him out to the buckboard? Might he kiss her if she did? She wanted to find out, but self-consciousness wouldn't allow her to move her feet in that direction, even when her mother nudged her with a wooden spoon.

"Thank you for the hope chest, Mr. Parker," she said instead. "It's very nice."

James tipped his hat, laid his hand over the pocket where Corrine's present lay and turned to her mother. "Abigail, thank you for a lovely day." With a final wink to Corrine, he was gone.

She could hear him through the plaster that lay between the wooden logs as he softly yawed his team and drove the buckboard away.

* * *

It was a two-hour ride to town in the wagon. The sun was beginning its descent, but a bright moon hung overhead stationed for its evening watch. As soon as James was down the hill he reached in his coat pocket and pulled out Corrine's package.

He held it to his nose, drinking in the scent of her along with what smelled like soap. Tearing back the paper, he found a soap bar in a small stone dish with a lather brush. He smiled. When he picked up the soap to look at the dish more closely, he found a folded note beneath it. There was still enough light to make out the words.

I would like to know what your face really looks like before you ride back down the trail.

He smiled again. She had nice handwriting.

CHAPTER 3
Smooth as glass

A thick blanket of snow lay over Baker City throughout January and February. The white expanse surrounding Hoke's homestead was broken only by the tracks of the white filly and black stallion made when he and Charlie ventured out in search of game.

It was March before the snow melted and another week before the road to town was dry. Then, just as Corrine grew hopeful about the prospect of seeing other humans, more snow clouds rolled up and dropped twenty inches. She was sitting melancholy at the oak table the next morning, wrapped in her gray shawl and finishing a letter to Emma, when she heard Rascal barking on the porch.

Abigail looked out the window. "Children! Come see."

Jacob got there first. "A sleigh!"

Lina scooted a ladder back chair to the window and climbed up to peer over the windowsill. "Like St. Nicholas," she breathed. Colonel Dotson had read "A Visit from St. Nicholas" to the children at Christmas.

Standing at the window with the others, Corinne watched as the driver stopped the sleigh in front of the cabin. The sleigh was painted white to match the snow, but sported a red cushion seat and red curved runners. The driver climbed down, stepped tall through the deep snow then up the steps, and stamped his feet on the porch. Corrine ran to open the door. When she flung it open, James Parker's brown eyes twinkled at her above a wool scarf wrapped around his neck and cheeks.

"Hello, darlin'." He winked at her.

Her heart flipped over.

"Can we ride in it?" begged Jacob and Lina, hopping up and down as James stepped inside.

"Why do you think I brought it out here?" He pulled off the scarf and Corrine's eyes widened. She hardly knew him.

"You shaved!"

James grinned. "That's right. And my face is freezing off, thanks to you." He took her hands and put one on each of his cheeks. "Feel that. Smooth as glass."

Corrine snatched her hands back, embarrassed to have touched a man's face. To have touched *James Parker's* face…cool as silk against her fingers. Teasing James about his beard had been something of a game. But what did she care whether he had a hairy face or not? What difference did it make to her what lay beneath that beard?

Ever since James had made her the wooden bowl Corrine had felt she owed him something. Then on a trip to town before Christmas, she saw the shaving set in the newly opened Peters's Mercantile. Corrine didn't have any money of her own, so she'd sketched a drawing of the new store in trade. And that's what she'd given James: the shaving set, along with a soap bar made with a few fine chips of the cherry wood Hoke used for smoking meat, because James always smelled like wood shavings.

She had written the note at the last minute, but never dreamed he'd follow through on her request. Who knew he had such a strong jawline? Or that the absence of his beard would make his eyes stand out, all liquid brown?

"Why James!" exclaimed Abigail behind her. "What a pleasing face you were hiding under all that hair!"

"Does it make me look younger?" James asked Abigail. Then he turned to Corrine. "'Cause I don't want to look older than I really am." Corrine tried to think of something smart to say, but couldn't. He seemed pleased by that and winked at her again.

"I came to take you for a ride, Missy."

*   *   *

"Where'd you get the sleigh?" Hoke wanted to know when he and Charlie came in from hunting.

James cradled a hot cup of coffee in his hands, enjoying the feel of the steam on his chin. He'd forgotten what that felt like after sporting a beard so long. "From a man who owns one of the saloons. He loans it out to people he likes."

Hoke shot him a sideways grin. "How much did you have to pay him to make him like you?"

"Come ride in it, Hoke! Let me take you, Jacob and Lina out while Corrine gets ready to go to town with me."

Hoke looked to Corrine then back at James. "She's not going with you by herself. Not with that new face you got."

James feigned innocence. "What does my face have to do with me being a gentleman?"

Hoke crossed his arms and glared at James.

James countered, "Then how 'bout Charlie coming with us, and we'll pick up Miss Austelle on the way." That had been his plan all along.

Corrine beamed with joy. And *that* of course was the real goal. The plan he'd hatched prior to Christmas was about to enter its second phase.

*   *   *

Abigail piled them with quilts a short time later, along with a basket of food. "I want them home by dark, James."

James, liking the feel of Corrine seated so close to him under the heavy tuck of the quilt, tipped his hat and wrapped the scarf around his cheeks. "Yes, ma'am." His response was to Abigail, but he winked at Corrine.

On the way to the Austelles', James discovered that when he steered the horses right, it brought Corrine closer to his side. He kept urging the horses to the left just so he could turn them sharply to the right again and send her shoulder bumping back into his.

Once they added Emma to their group and reached town, James had another surprise. "There's a man here takes tintypes. At the newspaper office."

They sat as a straight-backed group twenty minutes later, watching the newspaperman set up to take their picture. The man fluttered behind a large contraption: a black cloth coming off the back of two square wooden blocks, fastened together in the center by what looked like a long accordion.

"Is that a telescope on the front there?" James eyed the machine. He was eager to inspect what kind of wood was in the blocks.

"No. But it's a similar concept. How many types did you say you wanted? I have to prepare the plates."

"Four," said James.

Emma beamed. "We'll all get one to keep? Oh, Mr. Parker, thank you! I've never had my portrait made."

James smiled at Emma but his mind was still on the camera. He pointed. "And what's that folded piece in the middle?"

"Cloth on a wire frame," said the man.

Corrine twisted her brow. "You're asking a lot of questions, James. Why don't you let the man concentrate on what he's doing?"

He grinned at her. "You think I'm distracting him?"

"I do."

James considered teasing her about the "I do" she'd just uttered, but decided against it. He quit asking questions as they watched the photographer prepare several small plates then stick his head under the cloth.

A moment later he pulled his head back out and looked at Emma.

"Most folks don't smile," he said.

"I can't help it, I'm so happy!" Emma nudged Corrine with her elbow. "You're smiling, too, aren't you?"

"Should I?"

"No," said the man.

"Why not?" James reached for Corrine's hand. "Smile as big as you want to."

The man shook his head and ducked it back underneath the cloth. "Guess you're paying for it. Just hold real still. You can move when I switch the plates."

They sat like statues four times, then a fifth when the man said he wanted an extra.

"How soon can we see them?" asked Charlie.

"They'll be ready within the hour."

"You're sure it's not too expensive?" Emma asked James with a worried wrinkle in her brow.

James waved the question off. It was all part of his plan, after all, and well worth the cost to see the girls so happy.

The photographer put out his hand to James as the group stood to leave. "Name's Solomon, by the way. Bennett Solomon, like the king." He offered his hand to Charlie next, but his eyes were on Corrine. "You folks come in with Dotson? I heard there were some pretty young ladies in that group."

James put a hand to the back of Corrine's waist. "You're looking at 'em." He steered her toward the door, hoping they would run into the surly young sheriff next. It was all part of his well-thought-out plan.

First, James wanted every bachelor in town to see that Corrine belonged to him. Next, when Corrine and Emma went to the mercantile, Nelda would ask Corrine which fabric she liked, just as he'd instructed. Later, James would encourage Charlie to take Emma for a stroll. That's when he'd walk Corrine up the slope to the little white church and kiss her.

The church stood out against the dark hillside. After their kiss, any time she visited town, Corrine would see it and think of him. The church implied marriage, of course, though James didn't intend to make the formal offer yet. He needed to take his trip south first. He just wanted to tie her heart up in a tidy little bow before he left, as neat and secure as he could make it, because a girl like Corrine Baldwyn was bound to draw notice. A man about to leave Oregon for a year would be a fool not to tie her heart up, if he wanted a chance at winning her hand when he returned.

Then in a few weeks, just before he was to leave town, James planned to ride out to the cabin, kiss her again, and give her the fabric she liked. That was the third and final stage of his plan. While he was gone, she could think back on the taste of his lips and be surrounded by his thoughtful gifts, which he rather hoped she'd work into something pretty for her hope chest. And she'd have his tintype to watch over her every day until his return.

Yes, sir. It was a mighty fine plan.

Sure enough, while they were having lunch in the D&J Hotel, the new sheriff walked in, looking sleek and handsome in a dark, gray duster.

Emma's eyes popped. "Who is that?"

"The sheriff," said James, flatly.

Corrine looked at James. "Why don't you like him?"

"Don't care for his type." James couldn't keep the disdain from his voice.

Corrine raised her brows. "I thought *you* were a former lawman."

"I wasn't like him."

A young auburn-haired woman came to the table to serve them coffee. Freckles speckled her cheeks and her voice was chirpy as a bird's. "Everybody who comes in here brags on these tables, James!" The woman's eyes rolled over Charlie, Emma and Corrine, resting on Corrine the longest. "Who you got with you?"

He introduced them and turned back to her. "How's the new job going, Hannah?" James saw Charlie give him a quizzical look.

"I guess you'll tell me when you get your plate! The Dotsons and Jenkins are about the nicest people I ever met, I'll tell you that much." Hannah glanced around the room and when her eyes landed on the sheriff, the smile drained from them.

James reached for her hand. "What?"

"Nothing. A badge always makes me nervous, is all." She squeezed James's shoulder and smiled at him. "I'll have your food out shortly. Extra biscuits for you."

*   *   *

So, the tables explained what James had been doing the past three months. But...had he been eating this woman's biscuits?

Corrine tried not to feel irritated, but couldn't help wondering how James and this woman knew one another. She wasn't about to ask. After all, she didn't want to give James Parker the wrong impression. She didn't want to make him think she was silly over him, clean-shaven or not.

During lunch, Corrine felt the sheriff staring at her. Once, she looked back at him. He *was* strikingly handsome. He smiled and lifted a hand. Corrine returned his smile awkwardly and looked away. As her group stood to leave, he walked over.

"Parker. Introduce me to your guests."

James glowered at him and put a hand to Corrine's waistline. "Miss Emma Austelle, Charlie Baldwyn...Miss *Corrine* Baldwyn." He put unnecessary emphasis on her given name.

"Sam Eston." The sheriff's eyes swept over Charlie and Emma before locking on Corrine. "I've met Charles Austelle. Haven't met any Baldwyns. Y'all just get to Baker City?"

"We staked a place west of here. Back in September," said Charlie.

The sheriff's eyes, hazel as a cat's, stayed on Corrine. "With that Mathews fella? I heard he married an upscale lady with some older children."

"What are you so nosy for?" asked James.

The sheriff turned to James, irritation showing in the hard set of his mouth. "I'm the law here, Parker. It's my job to know." He turned back to Corrine. "I'll ride out there sometime."

"That's just great," muttered James, taking Corrine's elbow and steering her toward the door.

When they stepped out on the boardwalk, Corrine shook her arm free.

"You were rude to him, James Parker!"

"It won't hurt his feelin's."

The food she'd just eaten suddenly sat heavy in Corrine's stomach. She didn't like the way James was acting, the way he kept putting his hand to her waist. She had initially loved the feel of his strong, masculine hand resting comfortably at the dip of her back, as if God had specially purposed it for a handhold. But she wasn't some prize horse for him to steer around Baker City!

She took a step back, away from his hand, and hooked her arm through Emma's. "This might be a good time for you and Charlie to go take care of that saddle for Hoke," she told James. "Emma and I are going to see Nelda."

As she and Emma walked away, Corrine heard James say to Charlie, "What's she so heated about?"

Corrine started to ask Emma if she thought James was acting strange but decided against it when Emma said with a giggle, "Have you ever seen a more handsome man than that Sheriff Eston? You think he's married?"

Corrine was suddenly sorry she had come to town. She felt irritated with James. She felt irritated with Charlie for letting James boss the group around. And now she felt irritated with Emma, too. Why would Emma act interested in the sheriff when she was supposed to be smitten with Charlie?

As they reached the mercantile Corrine tried to shake her mounting frustration. She and Emma both carried lists from their mothers. Corrine looked at hers now, grateful for the distraction.

Nelda Isaacs helped them pick out supplies. "Come look at this new cloth, Corrine." Nelda waved them over to the fabric table. "Show me which is your favorite."

*   *   *

James was still muttering about Corrine when he and Charlie walked back toward the edge of town with the repaired saddle he'd promised to pick up for Hoke. He laid it in the bed of the sleigh that sat in an alley near the newspaper office, just as he caught sight of Corrine and Emma stepping out of the mercantile at the opposite end of town.

Charlie pulled two letters from his pocket. "I'm going to run these over to the post office before the girls get here." He grinned down at his boots then looked back up at James. "One is to Mimi, from Mother. But this one," he ran his hand over the letter on top, "is from me to my Uncle Thad."

James looked down the long row of clapboard buildings to Corrine and Emma, who were slowly coming up the left side of the boardwalk, back to where he and Charlie stood. The girls kept stopping to talk to people they passed.

"My grandmother promised me her wedding ring before she died." Charlie looked toward Emma. "I'm going to see if Thad'll send it to me. Don't say anything, all right?"

James clapped Charlie on the shoulder. The boy was only nine years younger than him—same age difference as between James and Hoke. "I won't say a thing. I'll just step in here and see if those tintypes are ready while you're at it, so you'll have her likeness to look at while you wait on that ring."

James had just stepped back out of the newspaper office, tintypes safely tucked inside his coat pocket, when he heard yelling and gunshots. Palming the Walker slung low on his hip, he leaped off the boardwalk and threw himself against a wall in the narrow space between the news office and the post office, where Charlie had gone.

As he peered around the corner, two men with kerchiefs over their faces came out of the bank, guns drawn, and ran down the boardwalk at the far end of town. James saw the sheriff take position across the street.

Where were Corrine and Emma?

The mercantile stood on the corner opposite the bank. When James had glanced at the girls before going in to see Bennett Solomon, they were midway down the boardwalk standing in front of the D&J.

Had they gone inside it? Or moved on past?

As people scurried from the boardwalks James scanned every open space, but he couldn't locate Corrine and Emma. They must have ducked inside.

The two men ran down the right side of the boardwalk toward James, shooting behind them at the bank and across the street, where the sheriff crouched.

He heard a horse whinny in a nearby alley. Guessing it belonged to the bank robbers, seeing as how they were headed straight in that direction, James stepped up on the boardwalk then into the street and raised the Walker.

He put two quick shots into the man holding the moneybag, then took aim on the second thief. The first man shot at James as he toppled off the boardwalk, but the bullet flew wide. The second man's fire came closer. James heard the sound of bullets ricocheting off the wooden buildings behind him. Then for one moment, silence, as if one bullet, instead of striking the wall, had sunk into something soft. The silence was broken by a woman's startled grunt.

Whipping his head to the left, James saw Emma Austelle fall as he squeezed off a shot that should have gone through the second man's chest, but instead dropped low and hit his upper thigh.

An instant realization that Emma and Corrine had taken shelter on the opposite side of the newspaper office—and that James had drawn gunfire in that direction when he stepped out and tried to stop the men—hit James full in the heart.

He was vaguely aware that the second man was now hobbling toward the waiting horses, that he now flung himself over one and slapped its rump, that the sheriff was running toward them, but he was frozen in the moment wishing he could pull it back. He stared, mute and horrified, at the widening pool of blood that encircled Corrine, who held a dying Emma in her arms.

Corrine didn't scream. She didn't cry. Those would come later when Mrs. Chris, Mrs. Jo, and Nelda Isaacs all ran to her side. But she looked up at James with the biggest slice of hurt he ever saw in slate gray eyes.

James had drawn the gunfire that killed Emma Austelle, and they both knew it.

CHAPTER 4
Over snow covered hillsides

Corrine would remember every detail of that day for the rest of her life. She would remember how light her heart had felt as she rode in the sleigh between James and Charlie, over snow-covered hillsides. She would remember how pretty Emma had looked when she ran out of the Austelles' cabin, jumping on the porch at the prospect of a trip to town. She would remember the sound of her and Emma's squeals when James flipped the reins to make the team go faster, so fast the runners lifted off the ground when they went over a dip in the land.

The smell of evergreens in the winter air, the taste of cream in her coffee at the D&J, the sound of her and Emma's boots clicking on the clean-swept boardwalk, and the hot slick of blood pouring over her hands and seeping through the layers of her skirts, then into the white snow, staining it crimson.

Corrine thought back to the time her mother had been shot in an Indian attack outside Fort Laramie. That was her first look at what a bullet could do to human flesh. With shaking hands, she helped Doc Isaacs cut her mother's clothes away that day so he could get to the wound that had torn a hole through her side. But that was only a small hole, the size of Lina's smallest finger.

Without Doc Isaacs or anybody else telling her, Corrine knew Emma's wound came from a bigger gun. Because when she looked down at the fading light in Emma's eyes, she could see in her peripheral view a hole in her friend's stomach large enough to hold a fat man's thumb.

Corrine looked up into James Parker's eyes as he stood in the middle of the blinding white street, and knew Emma could not live. Not with that hole. And neither Corrine, nor James, nor Charlie — now running toward them with Doc Isaacs and the sheriff close behind — could change it.

Emma was gone by the time Charlie fell to his knees beside her, a soft smile frozen on her face as he reached for her hand.

Corrine looked past Charlie and saw the sheriff kneel to inspect the fallen man in the street, pulling down the kerchief that covered the man's face. When the sheriff straightened back up, James grabbed the front of his duster with both fists. "Why are you still here? Get after him!"

"Do you know who that is?" The sheriff pointed. "That's Duke Walden's son you just killed!"

"Who the hell is Duke Walden?"

James shouldn't be cursing, thought Corrine. *He's upset. Did the sheriff say James killed that man?* She looked past James's feet and saw another widening circle of blood. Snow was supposed to be clean— clean enough to scoop up and add to milk and sugar. Mimi taught her that.

"He's well-known in these parts. Has a huge bounty on his head." This was the sheriff talking.

"Well if that was Walden, he's hit! Get after him, if he's wanted!" James flung his arm in the direction the man had fled.

"I need a posse."

"Posse, my ass! There's only one of him. Do your *job*!"

A crowd was gathering. The sheriff walked away, presumably to go after Duke Walden. Corrine wished everyone would go away. Who were all these people staring down at them? Couldn't she, Emma, Charlie and James just get back in the sleigh and ride out over the snow again? And laugh like they had that morning?

Charlie kept squeezing Emma's lifeless hand. "Doc, help her!"

Isn't that a beautiful smile, Charlie? Corrine wanted to ask, but she seemed to have misplaced her voice.

"She's gone, son," Corrine heard Doc say, his voice tight and cracking.

"No." Charlie began to stroke Emma's hand, as if doing so might restore her life. "We're going to get married."

That's when Corrine found her voice—when the screaming and the tears started. And once they started, she wasn't sure if she could ever make them stop.

*   *   *

When Corrine started screaming, several women in the crowd rushed to her side. James's heart burned in his chest as they tried to move her away from Emma's body, but Corrine kept fighting to hold her.

"Don't disturb her! Can't you see she's happy to have me holding her?"

Christine Dotson looked in his direction and said one word.

"James."

James swallowed his hurt and bent down to hold Corrine while the others pulled Emma's body from her arms. She fought him like a wounded cat, slapping and screaming so loud he thought she'd damage her windpipe. He couldn't stay upright on the slippery snow with her flailing at him, so he locked his arms around her and sat down with a crunch. He set his back to the boardwalk steps and held her as she kicked her legs, sending snow in every direction, and cried herself out.

"Go on," James instructed the others hoarsely after they'd lifted Emma's body off the ground. Charlie insisted on being the one to carry her. "I'll bring Corrine to Doc's directly."

Everyone left but James and Corrine.

It felt like a long time—a whole lifetime—and it tested every ounce of strength in his arms, not to mention his will, but James held tight. Corrine's hands raked blood over the sleeves of his jacket as she tore to get loose, until finally, *finally*...she started to quiet.

James felt tears slide off the end of his nose and into the top of her hair. "I'm sorry," he whispered. "I wanted to give you a special day."

But the day had been more for him than her; he knew that now.

The hope chest...the fabric...he had wanted her to think of him every time she ran a needle through it. He had hoped she would put his picture by her bedside, think of him every night when she laid her head down and every morning when she opened her eyes.

Men were selfish bastards. He'd never known it more certainly or felt it more keenly.

James held Corrine in the snow a long time—long enough for his backside to go past numb. When she stopped screaming, she cried. He'd never seen so many tears...dropping on his sleeves like water from a pump...turning to ice in the blowing wind.

Finally, she turned and buried her head in his shoulder.

He opened his coat and tucked her cold, blood-soaked hands inside, then stroked her hair, vaguely remembering a woolen hat she'd worn earlier that must had fallen off.

When her hands thawed, she wrapped them around his body. This wasn't the way James had wanted to get her in his arms. There would be no walk to the little white church, no sweet kisses to signify a promise. And Emma would never smile for another picture or celebrate her own love, now. James winced as he realized Emma's first and only tintype lay inside his coat pocket.

Corrine lay still, until James whispered into her hair, "Aren't you cold?"

Her voice came back raspy and low. "Maybe I'll freeze to death."

James flinched at the thought. "I don't want you to."

Corrine put her hands on his chest and raised her head. She stared long and hard at the trampled red snow then turned to him with swollen eyes.

"Take me to her."

*   *   *

James sat with his head in his hands in Doc Isaacs' parlor, trying to get the events of the last two hours to stop replaying in his mind. Charlie was circling the rug. Doc Isaacs brought them clean shirts and jackets.

Taking the articles offered to him, James stood. He peeled off his jacket and shirt stained with Emma's blood and Corrine's tears. He could hear water being poured in the next room as the women bathed Emma's body and continued to softly cry. Remembering the tintypes, he slipped them from his pocket and handed over the soiled garments, cupping the photographs in his large hands so nobody would see them.

Colonel Dotson stepped through the door and laid a hand on James's shoulder. "Christine and I are going to ride out to the Austelles to break the news."

James looked across the room at Charlie, who was still circling the rug, and tucked the tintypes into his pants pocket. He pulled on the borrowed shirt. The sleeves were too short.

"We'll do it," said James.

"*I'll* do it." Charlie stopped pacing and began to peel off his own stained garments. Tears hung in his eyes, but his voice was clear and true. "I'll do it."

Dotson gave him a nod of approval. "We'll follow behind you, then."

It was a long ride to the Austelles to break the news, and a longer ride still to Hoke's cabin on the hill. A bright moon hung high overhead as Rascal started barking to signal their return.

Hoke met James and Charlie in the yard. "Where's Corrine? What's happened?"

Charlie jumped out of the sleigh and ran for the barn.

James hung his head, unable to look Hoke in the eye. "There was a bank robbery."

James felt Hoke grip the side of the sleigh. "Corrine?"

"She's fine. She's at Doc and Nelda's. But...." James looked up at Hoke then, remembering Hoke's initial pronouncement that Corrine couldn't go. If only they could go back to that moment, James wouldn't ask again. How he wished he could undo the events of this day! He swallowed and got the words out. "Emma was shot by a stray bullet."

Hoke's jaw tightened. "She survive it?"

James shook his head.

Hoke grimaced and looked over his shoulder toward the barn. "Abigail will want to be with Corrine. And Melinda. Will you take her? Someone needs to stay here for Charlie."

*   *   *

Abigail quickly packed up Jacob and Lina and rode back to town in the sleigh with James. Moonlight bounced off the snow.

After watching them disappear down the hill, Hoke stepped into the cabin, gathered an armful of blankets, and walked out to the barn with Rascal. He could hear Charlie spilling his grief into the hay in one of the stalls.

Sliding down, Hoke sat with his back just inside the barn's opening, out of the cold wind gliding over the frozen land. He touched Rascal on the head to signal for him to keep quiet...to not disturb the young man they both loved.

Then he waited.

Hoke thought back over the hurt he'd felt when each of his parents died. When he'd been duped as a fifteen-year-old into killing a man to help a woman. When he'd left Independence and sat on a snow covered hill on a night as cold as this one, watching a family and their neighbors, listening to them laugh and sing, while tears froze to his cheeks.

When the sobs of the boy's broken heart finally grew quiet, Hoke eased into the stall where Charlie lay half buried in the hay, and covered him with blankets. Then he went back to Rascal, pulling the dog in close under the woolen wrappings that remained.

Eventually both dog and man dozed, Hoke's hand resting on the back of Rascal's neck.

As the sun began to light the sky the following morning, Rascal raised his head. Hoke's eyes flew open. Charlie stood looking down at them.

"You been out here all night?" A blanket was wrapped around Charlie's shoulders. His eyes were puffed nearly shut.

Hoke didn't answer. He didn't know any words to speak. Instead he stood, feeling stiff in every bone, while Rascal jumped up to lick Charlie's hand.

They walked in silence to the house and sat on the porch steps to watch the sun finish rising, bright and brilliant, over the white-capped hillsides.

"Your mother took Jacob and Lina and rode with James to town last night, to be with Corrine and check on the Austelles."

Charlie nodded. Presently, he said, "I wanted to marry her."

Hoke looked at him a long minute. "You'd have made her a fine husband."

Charlie's face crumbled then and Hoke pulled him into the crook of his arm.

*   *   *

The whole town turned out for Emma's funeral, thanks to Bennett Solomon, the newspaperman. It wasn't every day that a brunette maiden got shot outside his office.

Not only had he snapped Emma's picture in the last hours of her life, he'd snapped a couple more from the window after the shots were fired, testing his new Petzval lens for the first time from such a distance. He'd even gotten an image of James holding Corrine by the boardwalk.

By the day of Emma's funeral at the end of March, after the heavy snow melted and the ground had a couple of weeks to thaw, everyone in Baker City and most of the neighboring towns had seen Solomon's pictures and read about Duke Walden: about how he was wanted for several bank robberies, how he had evaded Sheriff Sam Eston's posse, how it was speculated he had rejoined his criminal family, how James Parker was to be awarded money by the bank and the Federal government for the bounty on Earl Walden's head, and how an innocent bystander had fallen. They had also read how her young lover and his sister had grieved, and how everyone in Colonel George Dotson's tightly knitted group had come together to support the family.

Emma was dressed by her mother in a pink calico dress, laid in a pine coffin, and buried beside a stand of evergreens at the edge of her father's land.

*   *   *

Harry Sims delivered a fine service. James watched Corrine from the opposite side of mourners. He longed to stride over and take her in his arms, but instead stood with them hanging loosely at his sides. Their normal strength had never felt so useless.

As Harry finished, James crossed his arms to keep from reaching out and grabbing a shovel from one of the men scooping dirt and filling in the grave. He wanted to whack the man with the shovel for moving so slow, dragging out everybody's pain. He knew the ground was still hard from the recent snow, but hadn't the temperature begun to rise right after Emma's death?

James wondered if the ice block that had formed inside his chest would ever thaw.

*   *   *

Corrine studied James from under the safety of her hat's brim. Even from a distance the regrowth of beard on his jaw was evident and his eyes, which glared at the man shoveling dirt into Emma's open grave, held pain.

A memory came to her of James's strong arms holding her as she flailed in the snow. She hadn't seen him since that day. Still, hadn't she and James shared something sacred? At the lowest moment of Corrine's life, James was the one who had come to her—who held her as the unwelcome grief torrents pulsed through her body.

Though she hadn't acknowledged James's tears with words, Corrine had felt them fall into her hair. Selfishly, in quiet moments, she replayed and cultivated the memory, tucked it away like a secret treasure, knowing he had shed those tears on her account and not his own.

Corrine wanted someone to talk to—someone she could trust with one particular regret gnawing at her memory—and James's face was the one her eyes kept returning to. James was safe. He would understand. But...why had he not come to see her? Why was he not standing beside her now?

Once the grave was finally filled, Corrine took a step toward him, but Hoke reached him first. She stopped. She wanted to talk to him privately. Then Corrine noticed the cook from the hotel standing near James, too, as if *she* was waiting to talk to him.

So Corrine walked over and stood by her brother, but she couldn't talk to Charlie about what troubled her. Charlie had been the most hopeful of the Baldwyns about coming west. She and her siblings learned their father was dead only seven short months ago, and now the girl Charlie loved was gone forever, too.

Charlie had been too wounded already.

*   *   *

Hoke stood by James, his hat in his hands, for several minutes before he spoke.

"Beautiful coffin."

"Least I could do." James had made it like Corrine's hope chest, without nails save in the hinges on the lid. It took precise notching in the wood pieces at the corners.

"Why don't you come stay at the house a few days? I could use some help on a fencerow."

James looked at his former riding partner with heavy eyes. "Is *work* your answer to everything, Hoke?"

Hoke twisted his hat. "It's one way to take the edge off."

James wasn't sure he agreed. He must have grown more like Hoke than he realized, for since Emma's death he'd thrown himself into a flurry of woodworking. But the effort hadn't yet dulled the sharp ache in his chest. James saw Hoke glance back toward the young woman who stood several feet away.

James nodded his head toward her. "That's Hannah, the new cook at the hotel."

"She here with you?"

"She's not here *with* me, but I gave her a ride out here. She met Emma. Served her coffee. Wanted to pay her respects."

Hoke shook his head. "Let me guess what her livelihood was prior to becomin' a cook."

"It might have been, Hoke. But she's a cook now."

Hoke's eyes heated. "Why do you have to get mixed up with women like that in every town you ever visit?"

"I'm not mixed up with her."

"You tellin' me none of your money's rattlin' in her pockets?"

James scowled. "How's Charlie?"

Hoke looked out over the crowd of mourners toward his older stepson. "Not sayin' much."

"How's Corrine?"

Hoke shook his head. "Never heard her cry 'til this. Goin' to take some time."

"I can't believe that sorry Sam Eston let Duke Walden get away with a heavy snow on the ground. And the man shot and bleedin.'"

"They said he got in a creek and Eston never could find where his horse came out."

Hoke's face betrayed his disgust. James knew what he was thinking: Walden had to be a mean one to freeze his horse's feet in cold weather. Hoke never could stand for a man to treat his horse ill.

"Look," said James, "I don't mind helpin' you build a fence, but I'm not sure Corrine wants me around right now."

Hoke's eyes narrowed. "Why's that?"

"It doesn't have anything to do with the cook over there." James shuffled his feet. "I'm the one that drew the fire, Hoke."

"James—"

"We wouldn't be standin' here mournin' Emma Austelle if it weren't for me." His throat was so tight James could hardly get the confession out. "If it weren't for my selfishness and stupidity."

There, he'd finally said what had clawed at his heart since Corrine turned those hurt-filled eyes on him.

Hoke's eyes softened. "James, I didn't know you were blaming yourself for this. This is not your fault."

"Yeah, well…what do you know about it?"

"You didn't ask those men to rob the bank, did you?"

James winced. "If you want to know the truth of it, I had an elaborate plan to try to make your step-daughter fall in love with me. I only invited Charlie and Emma because I knew I could send them off and have Corrine to myself. I had a number of charms planned."

Hoke pointed his hat at James. "I see what you're doing. You want somebody to smack you and make you feel better, but I'm not makin' a scene here, out of respect for the Austelles."

James didn't say anything.

"You been to see Harry?"

James shook his head.

"Go talk to Harry."

"What good is that going to do?"

"Always helps to talk to a preacher, James. If that don't work, come set this fencerow with me." Hoke put a finger in the middle of James's broad chest. "And stay away from women with questionable backgrounds."

CHAPTER 5

Long and deep

Six more weeks passed, slow and painful, as March rolled into April and April into early May.

James went to see Harry like Hoke suggested, and Tam started feeding him on Sundays after church.

"I reckon you were right," said Tam between bites, on his sixth Sunday.

James looked up from his plate. "Right about what?"

"I know it ain't standard for women to talk about such things with an unmarried man, but I ain't never been too standard." She glanced down and brushed food crumbs from her apron. "I *am* expectin'."

James slapped the table so hard the dishes rattled. "I knew it!"

Tam punched his arm. "How'd you know it, 'fore I knew it?"

"Well...don't be offended now, but that baby's stealin' part of your beauty." James picked up his fork. "That's not what normally happens right after a woman marries, her looks fadin' and all—not if a woman's happy. But if she's

67

carryin' a baby girl?" He pointed his fork at her. "That girl starts stealin' her beauty."

"So what you were really thinkin' at Christmas wasn't that I was fat, but that I was *ugly?*" Tam punched him in the arm again, and Tam didn't punch lightly.

"I didn't say that." James rubbed his arm. "I said I could tell something was siphonin' your good looks. *You're* the one said you was gettin' fat. But that's how else I know it's a baby girl. Carryin' a girl makes a woman's cravin's tend toward sweet things, and eatin' a lot of sweet things adds extra weight."

"You really think I'm having a girl?" Tam smiled at Harry then. "Would you mind that, Harry? If we had a girl?"

"I'd love to have a little girl. Long as she looks like you."

Tam's brow furrowed. "What if she *acts* like me?"

Harry's lips twitched below his handlebar mustache. "Even better."

A pink flush rose to Tam's cheeks. For all her blunt talk and manly ways, Tam Sims had a mighty tender heart.

"Don't worry," said James, scooping up the last of his food. "She ain't stole *all* your beauty."

He moved his arm away when it looked like Tam might punch him again, but she didn't.

"I want to know how you know so much about it," she said. "Or think you know so much."

James pushed his plate away and reached to pour more coffee in his cup. "My grandmaw was a midwife—*is* a midwife. She raised me, so I was around it."

"You never said anything when Nelda was expecting on the trail! Or when Audrey Beckett had her baby."

"No need. Doc Isaacs was there." James gulped down the coffee. "That was right fine, Tam. I really appreciate you feedin' me. And you, Harry, for lettin' me talk things through."

"I saw Charles Austelle yesterday," said Harry. "He mentioned you'd been out there."

Tam laid a hand on James's arm. "Melinda told me again this mornin' I should try to get you to stop blamin' yourself. And she said you ought to ride out and see Charlie and Corrine, for your own peace of mind. They don't blame you, neither. Nobody does. The only ones to blame are those outlaws. You were just tryin' to stop 'em."

If only I had stopped them, thought James. *Not just one, but both of them.*

He had walked the boardwalk of the town every day for six weeks, going back over what happened that day. He stood in the alley and mentally laid Hoke's saddle in the sleigh again. He turned his head toward the bank. He stood in the street in front of the newspaper office.

If only he'd stepped this way instead of that. If only he'd shot the second man first. If only he'd fired a little sooner and taken them both down, before either man could get off a shot.

If only...

As if reading his mind, Harry said, "God controls the order of things, James, not you. Not me. Not anybody. I don't believe it would have mattered if Emma Austelle had gone to town that day or not. That was her appointed day. Doesn't mean God's mean, just means life is life, and part of life is death. You know that as well as anybody, living hard like you have."

"Best we can do is live so we might join her someday," added Tam.

James ran his hand over the wood of Harry and Tam's tabletop. If he'd made that table, it would have had a smoother finish.

"I appreciate all you're sayin' – both of you. I do. My grandmaw used to say sin and guilt were poison, and the best one could do with poison was to let it out. So thank you, Harry, for helpin' me let it out." James stood, sorry to know his Sunday meals with the Sims had come to an end. "Me and the boys have decided to head out tomorrow. I need to ride out to Hoke's now and let them know."

"So this is it?" Across the table from him, Tam stood. Sure enough, her belly had a slight swell to it under the fabric of her apron. James guessed she must be four or five months along. The extra weight looked well distributed, which wasn't surprising with her being so strong and active. "We won't see you until you get back?"

"That's right."

"How long do you think it will take you?" asked Harry.

"Don't know...at least a year. That herd we're after in Kansas is twice the size of the one Hoke and I brought back to Independence, so it'll take longer to move 'em and break 'em. And we're not traveling the same way this time, so we won't be familiar with the route. That'll add some time. We'll drop south of the Oregon Trail after Soda Springs, head to Fort Bridger then east through Colorado country. I have some business in Colorado."

"What kind of business?" asked Tam.

Harry put his arm around his wife. "James may not want to say, Tam. His business is his own."

James nodded at Harry. The two of them had done some private talking in the past few weeks. In the six years James had known Hoke, he had never known his friend to talk to a preacher, but Hoke was right. Hoke was right about most things, which was one of the reasons James had ridden with him so long. Harry had proven to be a good listener, and over the course of talking with him, James's heart had eased a bit.

Harry had also helped him gain clarity about how to move forward concerning other burdens. Now, James was taking Harry's advice, but that was just between him and Harry.

Harry stuck a burly hand out. "Have a good trip, friend."

James took it, pulling him in for a hug. Then he hugged Tam and kissed her on the cheek.

"She ain't stole *all* your beauty," he whispered again.

*   *   *

James walked out of the D&J, where he'd said his good-byes to the Dotsons and Jenkinses and the teary-eyed cook, then slowly walked down the boardwalk to the spot where he had held Corrine in his arms. Would he ever hold her again?

Pulling out the tintypes he carried every day in his pocket, he looked down at them. Would Corrine ever smile like that again? The memory of the pain in her and Charlie's eyes at the funeral haunted him.

As sorry as James still thought the sheriff was, he had to admit he'd put together a first-rate posse to go after Duke Walden, one that included Michael Chessor, Bart Peters, Dotson and Jenkins. But after searching for days, they'd come home empty-handed.

As James put the tintypes back in his pocket and turned to leave, Bennett Solomon stepped out of the newspaper office.

"How long are you going to keep making this trek, James Parker? You've just about worn a hole in that spot where you're standing."

James scowled at him. "You don't want to make me mad, Solomon. I already got a bone to pick with you for all that stuff you wrote."

"I may have played it up a little, but it *was* heroic, what you did."

In three quick strides, James was on the boardwalk, nose-to-nose with him. "If I'd been shot and died in the snow that day, you could have made me sound as heroic as you wanted. But don't paint me that way when I got to live with the memory that a girl died. Heroic would have been savin' her, not gettin' her shot!"

Solomon squirmed under James's dark scowl. "I understand."

"I doubt that's right."

James glared at him, but Solomon was persistent as a gnat. "I've heard some other things about you, Parker. Things I'd like to ask you about."

"I'm not takin' questions today." James turned to leave.

Unfazed, Solomon stepped in front of him. "I heard about some things you did during the war, and while you were marshaling."

"That's all over and I don't want to talk about it."

"Not only that, but a woman in town here — "

James wheeled on him. "I'm surprised anybody's willing to talk to you, Solomon, the way you twist things!"

"What did you do with your reward money?"

James reached into his pocket to feel the edges of the tintypes. He thought about punching Bennett Solomon in the gut the way James felt punched in the gut every time someone came up to thank him for saving their bank money, or to ask what he was going to do with his reward.

It wasn't anybody's business what he did with his money.

But because he valued Solomon's skill for making tintypes, James decided not to punch him in the gut. He put his hat on and turned to go. "Don't worry, I won't be botherin' you by makin' this trek anymore."

The heaviest snows were over. It was time to head back down the trail.

*   *   *

Answering the knock, Corrine swung open the door. There stood James…finally. His eyes fell from her face to the infant in her arms and widened in surprise.

"Doc and Nelda's baby girl," she explained. "She came early. They've named her Emma and wanted me to meet her." She could feel tears in her eyes and blinked hard to keep them from spilling over.

James's face relaxed. "Oh." He was clean-shaven again.

Corrine stepped back from the doorway. "Won't you come in?"

James leaned his head inside and waved. Doc's nephew ran to the door and flung himself around Corrine's leg.

"That's a fine-lookin' baby girl, Doc…Nelda."

"Come in, James," invited Abigail.

"Thanks, but I really just came to talk to Corrine." James looked down at the boy clutching her leg. "I didn't know she was all tangled up in children."

Corrine's cheeks grew warm. "I can get untangled."

After she'd handed the baby back to Nelda and sent Will back to his mother, Corrine lifted her gray shawl off the hook by the door and wrapped it around her shoulders. "Come on. Let's go for a walk."

*   *   *

Before stepping off the porch, James drank in the view. A body could see for miles from the top of Hoke's hill. A smaller hill sat below it to the south, ringed by evergreens. James could see a hawk flying over the valley and marveled at what the bird's view must include. He had finally gotten some good views of his own—some clarity. He knew his next steps, or at least thought he did. Last time he'd laid down plans they'd slapped him cold.

He turned toward Corrine and offered her his arm. Surprisingly, she took it. She didn't remove her hand as they walked toward the slope of the hill, either. It felt good to have her hand resting in the crook of his elbow.

She was different...changed. Older in her eyes. James's heart tightened. He was the cause of it. He put his free hand on top of hers and silently prayed he hadn't lost her.

They walked down the hill, out of sight of the house, and were headed toward the creek that ran along the base of it before James got the words ordered in his head. "I'm sorry about what happened. I wish I could go back and change that day."

"Me, too."

He turned toward her, hope rising. "Do you blame me for it?"

Corrine shook her head. "No, James. I don't blame you for it."

James.

Relief shot through his veins. He pulled her to his chest and hugged her long and deep, cupping the back of her knotted up hair, taking care not to mess it. How good it felt to hold her again! How good it felt to know he might still have a chance. He tried to say "thank you" but his voice no longer worked.

She pushed herself back and looked up at him.

"Are you still going to Kansas?"

The question caught him off guard. "Leaving tomorrow."

Corrine's face fell and she wriggled from his arms. "Tomorrow?" She backed away. "Why did you wait so long to come see me if you're leaving tomorrow?"

James shook his head, trying to get a handle on the way the air between them had changed so swiftly. "There were things I had to see to. Things I needed to work through." James's heart tightened again to see her brow twist. The last thing he wanted to do was cause her more pain.

"I can't believe you haven't come to see me in all this time, James Parker. You didn't even talk to me the day of Emma's funeral! But I saw you talking to the cook from the D&J. Help me understand why you would talk to her and not me."

James's throat grew as tight as his chest. "I was giving you space, Corrine. I thought you blamed me for what happened."

"I've been hurting." Her voice cracked. "I could have used a friend."

Well…if that didn't shred what was left of his heart.

He watched her fight to get her voice back as she lifted her chin. "All kinds of other people have ridden out here to check on me and Charlie." She looked him straight in the eye. "Bennett Solomon…Sam Eston, the sheriff."

James knew he had some heart left then, for it stoked up hot and mad. "That sorry Eston! He better not be sniffin' around here."

"What is it to you?"

James clenched his jaw. That look in her eye...he didn't like it. "Don't ever try to pit men against one another, Corrine. That's playin' with fire! And it's not becomin' of you. And don't ever encourage a man like Sam Eston, either, whether you're trying to rile me up or not."

She lifted her chin again. "How is Sam Eston any different than you?"

Was it only moments ago his voice wouldn't work? It was working just fine now. "I should hope to God I'm a better man than Sam Eston."

"What makes him worse?" Her hands went to her hips. "Fact is, Bennett Solomon suggested that a Christian woman might not ought to be alone with *you*."

James stepped nearly to her nose and said, just above a whisper. "Then why are you alone with me right now?"

Dropping her chin, Corrine took a step back.

By God, he wouldn't lose her to a man like Sam Eston — not so long as he could breathe!

"Come on, Corrine. You know me. You really think I'm a scoundrel? Solomon painted me as some kind of hero just so he could sell some newspapers, but I ain't no hero. Never claimed to be! I'm not surprised people are tryin' to set Solomon straight. But that don't make me a bad man."

Her expression changed as she tried a new tactic.

"Why do you still have to go to Kansas when you got all that reward money?"

James crossed his arms and turned away from her, not liking where this line of questioning was headed. "I just need to."

"Is it only the horse herd you're after?"

"No. I got some other business."

"What sort of other business?"

Had Hoke put her up to these questions? Uncrossing his arms, James swept his hat off his head and turned back to face her. "I'm not ready to talk about it. You know, if I didn't know better, I'd think you're just looking for a way to pick a fight with me."

The hands came off her hips then. "I'm not trying to pick a fight with you, James. I'm trying to put your mind at ease about what happened. But I don't understand why you've still got to go all the way to Kansas when you were given that reward money."

James stared up at the hawk that was flying overhead again. He wasn't ready to tell her everything. Not yet. "I don't feel right using that money for myself."

*   *   *

Corrine's brow twisted in confusion.

James didn't want to use the reward money? Not even if it meant staying in Oregon? With *her*? If James had really intended to marry her, that money would have given him a good start toward claiming land and building a cabin.

"Look." James squeezed his hat in his hands. "I didn't come out here to quarrel with you."

"Then why did you come?"

Maybe James meant to ask her to marry him after all. Was Corrine prepared to answer him if he did? Was she ready to give her life over to him—or to anyone—now that she knew how quickly it could all be spilled out over the snow? Or maybe James had changed his mind about marrying her. What if, during all the time he'd spent in town, he had grown fonder of the cook instead?

Was Corrine about to get her heart broken? Emma's death had shown her that life could take sharp, unwelcome turns without warning. She braced herself for the worst.

"I came to say good-bye," said James.

Good-bye.

Corrine's eyes burned.

For how long? She was afraid to ask.

Corrine didn't want James to go. She had missed Emma so badly in the last six weeks it ached—it tore at her gut and kept her awake at night, tears springing to her eyes all the time at the least little things, where it used to take a lot to make her shed them. But she'd missed James, too.

Ever since they arrived in Baker City last September, James had been around her family. He stayed with them at the ranch while the house was being built, lived out of his and Hoke's old wagon, and only moved into town after the D&J was finished, for the coldest part of winter.

Before Emma's death, Corrine hadn't gone more than a few days without seeing James. He had grown on her. James had a lightness of heart she lacked—the same kind of lightness Emma had.

There were times Corrine had actually thought Emma a little silly. She felt so guilty for remembering that now. But the void left by Emma's death had made Corrine realize how much she wanted — needed — someone in her life with an easy smile and ready laughter.

And...it felt so good to think she might be another person's most prized companion.

On the journey west James had begun to act like he liked her — said that he wanted to marry her. Corrine's heart had begun to bank on that.

Before Emma's death, Corrine hadn't been sure how she really felt about James Parker. But the absence of his compliments for a six-week stretch had shown her how much she had come to depend on the flame he ignited inside her chest. She hated to think she was staring at a yearlong drought without him.

"Good-bye, then," she muttered, turning back to the house. She would have to close her feelings off if she was going to survive this. Might as well start now.

"Don't leave, Corrine." James reached for her hand. "I want to kiss you before I go."

She wheeled to face him. "*Kiss* me before I go? Why, you arrogant man! Everyone for miles around thinks we're engaged, thanks to that newspaper story. And the whole time, you're cavorting with other women!"

James's eyes darkened. "I resent that. I am *not* cavorting with other women."

Corrine clenched her fists. "Quit toying with me, James! Quit treating me like a little girl."

She turned again to leave and he tried once more to take her hand. Jerking it free she swung it up to slap him, but he caught it and arced it down instead, moving her into his arms once more.

"I have *never* treated you like a little girl, Corrine." James's expression was so pained that Corrine's anger melted. "And I want a kiss before I go," he whispered.

CHAPTER 6
An early education

James braced himself for a stiff-lipped kiss, seeing the kind of mood she was in. But no sooner had his lips touched hers than Corrine's whole body melted. One minute he was holding an angry female with stiff arms, and the next, he had to catch her or she would have fallen.

He drew back to look at her, surprised at her reaction, but she reached up to each side of his clean-shaven face and pulled his head back down, kissing him softly and slowly at first, then with more boldness…eager to learn.

James had only meant to give her a light peck on the lips, never dreaming she would take such a rich interest in the matter. Who knew a peck could grow so quickly into a hot, roaring fire?

James Parker had kissed a woman or two. He had even kissed a few who were green at the outset. But, *mercy*! Corrine Baldwyn was a fast learner, and she lit his blood.

As her hands wrapped around the back of his neck, his went to her knotted hair, deftly pulling out the pins that held it. As the golden silk cascaded down, his hands followed it along the curve of her back. Her spine ran strong and perfect. And her front...her front was pressed up against him.

His mouth ventured down to her upturned chin — how he'd wanted to explore it for months — then traveled hungrily down her throat and back up to the tender space behind her left ear. He heard her breath catch as her body pressed in closer against his.

Corrine followed his lead, her lips beginning to explore his throat, but he couldn't take it.

James pulled back, struggling for breath, trying to shake free from the fog in his brain. "I thought sure I was going to be the first man you ever kissed."

"You are." Corrine eyed his lips again before stopping herself. "Am I not doing it right?"

"Oh no." His voice was husky, even to his own ears. "You're doin' it too right. You set those lips on a less experienced man and he'll lose his head. Then your virtue's goin' to be compromised."

"My virtue?" Her brow twisted. "What about *your* virtue?"

"I've got virtue. You think I don't have virtue? A woman's virtue is just more precious, that's all I'm sayin'."

Corrine scowled up at him. "You're awfully bossy, James Parker."

She twisted to get out of his arms, but he wasn't ready to relinquish her.

"Wait? What did I say now?"

"Give me my hair pins!" Corrine slapped at his hand. "How did you know how to remove those, anyway? Men aren't supposed to know how women put their hair up."

He held them out to her and she snatched them from his hand. "You said 'a less experienced man.' Just how experienced are you?"

James lifted his hands. "I got an early education!"

"What does *that* mean?"

James was still trying to get control of the situation that had so quickly slipped out of his hands again. "It means I've had a chance to make a study of women. You won't ever be sorry you chose me."

Corrine broke lose of his hold and reeled on him.

"I can see how this is going to go—you'll be instructing me for the duration of my life because you're older. You think you know so much more than I do. It makes me want to go against you just so you won't sit so smugly on top of your high horse."

James's lips slid into a grin. "That's all right! I like a woman with a healthy dose of sass. Some men...*most* men...would see that as a contradiction to their pride, but not me. That'll keep me humble through the years."

He couldn't resist letting his eyes trace down the lines of her dress and back up again, his gaze resting a moment on her chin then stopping on the pleasing pout of her mouth. He felt his heart dancing wildly. "I know for a fact we'll be a good fit."

*   *   *

Corrine wanted to stay mad at him, but staying mad at James wasn't easy.

She crossed her arms and sat down on the side of the hill, hugging her knees, embarrassed by her display of passion. Emma had made it seem like kissing was fun, and Corrine now had to agree it was. But...she hadn't known it had the power to stir such deep feelings or turn a girl into someone she wasn't normally.

Would James think her low for letting him see that she liked kissing him? She felt certain most others would think her low if they could read her mind. Society gave men grace when it came to such activities, but a Christian woman was expected to remain unschooled.

Just one short year ago, Corrine thought she knew things about the world. Now she was finding that much of her comprehension had grown murky. "I don't understand men at all," she muttered, thinking, too, that she didn't even understand herself. How she longed to have Emma to talk to about it all! And how her heart pulsed painfully at knowing she'd never get the chance.

James sat on the ground beside her. "I'll teach you everything you need to know," he said with a playful bump of his knee.

She shot him a look and he smiled again, winking at her. "Or maybe you'll teach me."

Yes...an easy smile and ready laughter. That was her favorite thing about him, although he really did have a nice jawline, too. And eyes. And his kisses had been so warm.

James reached in his pocket and pulled out a tintype. "I gave Emma's copy to her mother, and before I saw you at the house, I gave Charlie his." James held it out to her. "This one's yours."

Corrine swiped at her eyes as she took the picture from his hand. Her fingers grazed his. James's fingers were long, strong, well shaped and masculine. She had loved the way they felt sliding down her back, had loved the feel of him holding her in the snow that day, despite the painful circumstances.

She hung her head. "I feel guilty going on with a normal life when Emma's has ended."

James reached over and lifted her chin to its normal position.

"Don't you owe it to her to live every day as if it were your last? Greeting the sun with that raised chin of yours, and those gray-blue eyes? Loving the people around you? Making all the difference in one man's life?" He swept a fallen strand of hair from her cheek. "I want to be that man, Corrine."

James Parker was pulling her heart in every possible direction. Corrine had feared for a moment that he had changed his mind about her, but it seemed evident now that he did intend to marry her.

"What are you saying, James? Are you asking me to marry you? Strangers think we're engaged, but if we are, I sure don't know it."

James leaned over to pick up his hat that had dropped to the ground and ran his hands around the rim. "I'm not officially asking. Not yet. You won't have to wonder when it's official; I'll make it clear. And I can see now the engagement's goin' to have to be short, hot little pepper you are." He flashed her another grin.

He had nice teeth, too. Corrine had never really noticed that before. Had she just not seen them, distracted by the thick of his beard? Or did she have a new fascination for his mouth now that she knew what his lips felt like on hers?

"I just want you to promise you'll wait for me," said James, growing serious again. "Give me a decent chance. Not take up with some fool like Sam Eston while I'm gone."

She nudged him playfully with her knee this time. "What makes you better than him?"

James looked out toward the creek where a sycamore grew over the bank. "Most men are pretty selfish, Corrine, includin' me. But at least I know when I'm bein' selfish."

She tried to keep the whine from her voice. "I think it's selfish of you to leave tomorrow." Corrine needed a confidant. If James left, who would she have?

"Aw, darlin'."

Corrine loved it when James called her *darlin'*.

"I wish you wouldn't see it that way," he said. "I've got to take care of somethin'."

Corrine bristled. She might love being called *darlin'*, but she was still mad at him for leaving. "And you want me to sit here and wait for you, not even knowing what that 'something' is?"

"Yes."

If James couldn't tell her what it was, then she wasn't making him any promises.

Corrine looked up at the hawk that flew over again. "Maybe I'll be here when you get back, and maybe I won't."

"Corrine."

He reached for her again, but she ducked under his arms and scrambled to her feet. She had loved kissing him. If she did it again, she risked turning into a fool. Corrine didn't want James or any other man to have that kind of control over her.

She started up the hill.

*　　*　　*

James stood, still shaken from the unchecked hunger of her mouth. He wasn't sure he'd accomplished his purpose for the day.

"I'm leavin' tomorrow, Corrine," he called after her. "Are you sure you don't want another kiss?"

He threw out the offer lightly, half expecting her to turn and come running back to him. He even steeled his nerves for it, knowing it was a dangerous proposition if he really intended to head back down the trail at sunrise.

But she never slowed.

"Have a good trip."

With her face pointed toward the top of the hill, her voice floated back to him only faintly.

*　　*　　*

James, Michael Chessor and Bart Peters were already three miles out of town when they saw Hoke on his stallion, waiting on the trail in the middle of a morning sunbeam.

"Is he coming with us?" asked Peters.

James shook his head. "No. He promised Abigail he'd never leave her. He's just come to see us off."

When they stopped in front of him, Hoke tossed James a tied up piece of cloth with something wrapped inside. "Corrine sent you biscuits."

James caught the bag, wondering if it was meant to be a peace offering. He looked closer at the material the biscuits were wrapped in. "Where'd she get this fabric?"

"I don't know. From Nelda, maybe?"

James looked again. It was the cloth she'd picked out the day Emma died, he was sure of it. Nelda had eventually showed it to him, but he'd lost the heart to buy it for her, figuring it would only serve as a painful reminder of that day.

Had Corrine sent it to him on purpose? Was this her way of saying she would wait for him, after all?

"Do me a favor, Hoke." James hugged the cloth bag to his chest. "Don't let that sheriff court her while I'm gone."

"All right, but you have to do me a favor in return." Hoke stepped his black horse closer to James's chestnut colored Palomino and held out a book. "Take this."

James reached for it. It was Hoke's father's Bible. He turned it over in his hands, thinking of all the times he'd seen Hoke reading it by the light of an evening fire, and of all the times Hoke had read or quoted him passages from it. A lump rose in his throat. "I know how much this means to you."

"Always felt like it was what got me out of scrapes. I marked some passages for you." A sideways smirk spread over Hoke's face. "Some of your favorites." Then another look settled on Hoke's countenance. He started to say something but stopped at the sound of an approaching horse.

Charlie came galloping into view, then slowed when he saw they were stopped. The brown horse he had claimed for his own was loaded with a bedroll and bulging sidesaddles.

"What are you doin' here?" asked Hoke.

Charlie nodded toward James and the others. "I'm going with 'em."

*   *   *

Hoke knew it as soon as Charlie came into sight, but his heart still knotted at the boy's words. He already had a bad feeling about James riding off. Maybe this was the reason. Abigail's heart would be affected, and what affected her heart, affected his.

"Your mother's not going to like this."

"I know. But I've got to get out of here, Hoke."

Charlie was hurting and Hoke knew it, but there was something mighty tender that had passed between them the morning following Emma Austelle's death. It had meant more to Hoke than he knew how to express. The opportunity for tender moments with his own father had been cut short, and he'd never had a son. It wrenched his gut to think Charlie was going to ride off from home, even though he understood the need.

Still, he couldn't resist asking, "Why didn't you say anything before now?"

Charlie's eyes dropped. "I didn't decide until I saw James yesterday. These men could use another hand, and I could use a reason to get out of Baker City."

Hoke scowled in spite of his best efforts not to.

James said low, "I'll look after him." Then loud enough for Charlie to hear, "Be good to have another strong back along."

Hoke studied Charlie's horse and rifle. He dismounted and unwound an Army Colt from his own pommel holster. "I see you've got your father's Henry. Take this, too." He wrapped it around Charlie's pommel. "In case you need it. You got that knife I gave you for Christmas?"

"Yes, sir." Charlie pointed to his belt where the knife was sheathed.

"Good." He patted Charlie's leg. "Get James to show you how to throw it."

Hoke looked deep into Charlie's eyes. "Trail's a good place to heal, son, but don't let it keep you from the people who love you. I made that mistake and let it stretch out twenty years."

Charlie nodded. "Yes, sir. I'll be back."

As Hoke stepped toward the stallion, he clapped a hand around the ankle of James's knee-high boot and held it there a minute. Then without another word, Hoke mounted and rode back toward the cabin.

CHAPTER 7
Miles from home

Duke Walden had given all four of his sons names taken from English nobility. Marquis, as the oldest, was flighty and unpredictable. Because Marquis hadn't been born with a predisposition to meanness, Duke had tripped, mocked and withheld food from the boy until he'd toughened up.

Every year on Marquis's birthday, starting when he was five, Duke had ridden him out an equal number of miles from where they lived—five miles the first year; six, the next—and left him at dark.

"Claw your way back by mornin' without gettin' killed and you can live with us another year."

He never left the child a gun or a horse, but he did give him a sharp knife.

Duke Walden had chosen a careful hideout in the craggy mountains of northern Utah, careful hideouts being essential to the survival of any outlaw. It was centrally located near developing western towns along the California, Oregon and Mormon trails. Wild animals that shared those craggy mountains included antelope, beavers, bears, bobcats, coyotes, rabbits and mountain lions. Rattlesnakes often lay coiled between the rocks and on cooler days crawled out to sun themselves.

When Marquis turned fifteen, his father stopped leaving him miles from home and took him on a bank robbery instead.

"Kill you at least one man today, and that'll earn you another year."

Marquis killed two, drawing his knife deep across their throats, the way he'd learned to kill animals that stalked him when he was a child.

Baron and Viscount, the youngest Walden sons, were twins. Like Jacob and Esau from the Old Testament, the first one born, Baron, was the larger and stockier of the two. Viscount, younger by eight minutes, had grown up lean and crafty, taking pleasure in outwitting his stronger brother. The twins *had* been born with predispositions to meanness, doubly so since they had each other to out-do, so they were never left miles from home on their birthday.

Since the day of their birth was also the day of their mother's death, it was never acknowledged, anyway. As a result, the twins weren't sure how old they really were. Marquis knew. He'd been six when they were born and found their birth something of a miracle, but having learned early to keep his mouth shut, never shed light on the question of when they had come into the world.

Marquis was twenty-seven, the twins twenty-one, and a fourth son, Earl, was twenty-five when James Parker shot him on the street in Baker City. Earl was his father's most favored.

Marquis, Baron and Viscount, for all their fancy names, had proven themselves throbbing disappointments to Duke Walden. He'd have borne the loss of any one of them—all three—in a hold-up, and never shed a tear. But Earl was his heart and soul. From the time Earl could walk, he had followed his father across the crags of their mountainous hideout, growing into a picture-perfect, younger version of Duke Walden, himself.

Earl brought a woman home once, when he was twenty-three. He'd been robbing a bank in eastern Utah when he spotted a pretty, young Mormon with her family. He took out a handful of gold coins from one of the bank's bags, handed them to her father and scooped the girl up over his shoulder. She never fussed until Earl rode out of the crags and she saw the house with four more men—all unsmiling—standing in the scratched-up yard.

She lasted four weeks.

Riding her out from the hideout like his father had done with Marquis, Earl dropped her from his horse, threw a knife in the dirt beside her, and said, "If you can make it back and stop your bawling when you get there, we'll let you stay."

When he and Duke rode out to check on her three days later, they found her body precisely where they'd left her, drained of its blood, both wrists cut, the knife lying in the dirt beside her. Earl shook his head. "I thought Mormons were against that sort of thing."

Back in March, when Duke Walden rode out of Baker City with his leg shot—his beloved son, Earl, sprawled in the snow—he vowed he'd kill the man who shot him, if it was the last thing he ever accomplished. So when Baron and Viscount rode back to the hideout in early May with a newspaper tucked in their saddlebag, Duke Walden took the paper, smoothed it out across the bed where he lay recovering, and smiled.

A man named Bennett Solomon told him everything he needed to know: James Parker, a former U.S. Marshal, had killed his son and been richly rewarded for it. Emma Austelle had been shot, died, and buried, grieving the whole town. And two people named Charlie and Corrine Baldwyn were linked somehow to Parker. One photograph showed all four of them, the girls smiling sweetly. Another portrayed Parker holding the Baldwyn girl by the boardwalk.

"Pretty girls," breathed Baron over his father's shoulder. "Prettier than the one Earl brought home that time. Shame you killed the dark-haired one."

Viscount grinned and pointed a wiry finger at Corrine. "That one ain't dead."

Duke folded the paper and said in a strained voice not much above a whisper, "Boys, get your gear ready to go to Baker City."

"What about your leg, Pa?" asked Viscount. "Don't it need more time to heal?"

"I've traveled with worse."

Duke Walden's hatred toward James Parker out-burned the pain.

*   *   *

Corrine sat next to Emma's grave, the packed dirt on top still soft from a mid-May rain the night before. Early morning damp seeped through the layers of her split riding skirt, but she was beyond caring about such things.

Smoothing out a piece of paper, Corrine read aloud.

"'Charlie misses you something awful.'"

She'd skipped over the date she'd written at the top. This was the reason Corrine had felt compelled to slip out and visit Emma's grave: the date—May 22, 1867—was Charlie's eighteenth birthday. And Corrine would be seventeen tomorrow. She and Charlie had never spent their birthdays apart.

"'He's gone with James to Kansas. I'm jealous men get to ride off on adventures, Emma. It's been two weeks since they left, and two months since I lost you. It's hard not to feel abandoned.'"

The branches of the nearby evergreens were still moist with dew. Corrine wished she'd brought her charcoal pencil. She would have enjoyed trying to capture the way the rising sun reflected off the damp, feathery pines. Sketching brought her more peace than almost any endeavor.

Corrine's heart caught suddenly. Her face crumbled. "I'm sorry I was irritated with you, Emma. That day." She shook her head at the memory. "I wish..." She looked up at the sunlight on the pine branches. "I wish none of this would have happened."

It was a pointless thing to say. It did happen. All of it. And now nothing was the same.

She folded the note, having strayed from its contents. "Want to know something ironic? I envied your peace and contentment. Your future seemed so clear, and your joy in the hope of that future, so full. Then, in a single moment, everything changed."

Wiping at her eyes, she opened the note to read again. The paper shook faintly, the swelling of her heart affecting the steadiness of her hands. "'I am more fully aware of the fragility of life than I have ever been. I suddenly want to reach out both my hands and grasp it, Emma. Really grasp it! Taste it. Touch it. Experience it. But the people I most want to experience life with are no longer here with me.'"

For some reason, Corrine now felt truly free to share even her deepest thoughts with Emma. Why hadn't she spoken this honestly to her friend while she'd been living? She wondered how Emma might have received her words, if she had.

"'I've been searching through my father's Bible to try to discover where you've gone. Did your soul instantly go up to heaven, or are you sleeping here until Christ comes back? I've asked Mother and Hoke, Tam and Harry, Doc Isaacs and Nelda, and opinions are divided.

"'No one can tell me if you have any continued awareness of our lives, or if you can hear me if I read my letters aloud to you. But it gives me comfort to believe you might.'"

She'd written more on the page, but Corrine's throat had begun to tighten, so she folded the letter again and laid it under a wilted flower. The limp, pink petals were soft as the morning dew on her fingers. She tucked one in her pocket to sketch later. She wanted to see if she could capture the silky texture.

Corrine nudged the mound of dirt with her elbow. "I know what it feels like to kiss now."

Her heart swelled with a sharp ache again. More tears.

After a while, she stood and shook out her skirt before turning to untie the gray dun. With a jolt she realized a man sat on a brown horse with a splotched neck several yards away watching her. He must have seen her start because he raised a hand and called out, "Don't be frightened, Miss Baldwyn! Sam Eston."

He kicked his horse toward her. "I was just leaving the Austelles' and noticed you out here. Are you alone?"

Yes, she was alone. And Hoke and her mother weren't going to like it when they found out, but two months without Emma and two weeks without James and Charlie had stirred her soul to action. When she'd awakened that morning, the moon still overhead, she'd known her heart would burst wide open if she didn't saddle the dun and ride. She had to see Emma...or her grave, at least. She needed to be near her. She needed to talk to someone.

"It's not that far," she said.

Corrine started to raise her foot to the stirrup, then felt self-conscious because the sheriff had nudged his horse closer to her. In spite of her long, split riding skirt and tall boots, she feared Sam Eston would see part of her leg when she hiked her knee.

"Let me help," he offered.

As he swung down from his mount with his face turned away, she stuck her foot in the stirrup and swung her leg over.

"That's alright. I can manage." She pointed the dun toward home.

Eston was quick to remount and fall in step beside her. "I was coming out to your place next. You don't mind if I ride along, do you?"

What could she say? "No, I don't mind."

But she really did. She felt flustered at having been watched while she talked to Emma. It also made her wary that James hadn't liked the sheriff. *Why was that?*

"Do you often go riding this far alone, Miss Baldwyn?"

"No."

"Just needed to visit your friend?"

The compassion in his voice made her turn to study him. His question seemed genuine.

"Yes."

The sheriff was wearing his black duster again. He made a dashing image as he sat on his horse. "I want to tell you again how sorry I am about what happened. I didn't mention this when I rode out to your place several weeks ago, but I saw you and her that day, with your arms linked, going to the mercantile."

Corrine didn't say anything. They rode in silence for a bit. "I'm sorry," she said at last. "Emma was better with conversation than I am. She could make conversation with a tree stump."

"I've been called worse."

"I didn't mean — " Corrine felt heat rise to her face.

He laughed. "I know you didn't. I'm just teasing." He smiled over at her. "Your friend James Parker struck me the same way. I believe he could make conversation with a tree stump, too."

Corrine smiled. She wondered again why James didn't like the sheriff. He seemed harmless enough, pleasant even. She remembered when the sheriff had stepped into the D&J in his long black duster. Emma had whispered, "Who is that?" And it was no wonder. He was a handsome man—not as tall as James, but stockier, with dark hair and dancing cat's eyes. And a neatly trimmed mustache framing a mouth that seemed equally comfortable bestowing smiles or barking orders.

"Ah." He was grinning now. "I've been wanting to see that."

"See what?"

"Your smile…in person. The one in the newspaper was nice, but I wanted to see it for myself."

Corrine felt her face heat again. She had just been considering his smile, and now he was commenting on hers. Corrine wondered how old Sam Eston was.

"My wife had a smile like that. It lit up the sky."

The dun stepped in a dip and its shoulders rolled, forcing Corrine to grab the saddle horn to keep her balance. *The sheriff was married?*

She turned to him. "'Had'?"

He smiled again, nudging his horse around the dip hers had stepped in. "She died the year we married. Fever."

"I'm sorry."

"Me, too."

He kicked his horse in front of her dun suddenly, forcing her to stop and look him in the eye. "I know what it feels like to lose someone you care about."

Corrine's eyes burned with tears again. He moved his horse and fell back in step beside her. They rode in silence until he held a hand up, signaling for her to stop. Then he put a finger to his lips before reaching for his gun.

Several yards ahead of them, Hoke nudged the black stallion from behind a stand of cedars, his rifle lying casually across his arm.

"Hoke!" Corrine's face flushed with embarrassment. It didn't help that Hoke's eyes flickered fire and irritation.

"You gave us a scare, Corrine. Didn't tell us you were goin' for a mornin' ride with the sheriff."

Shame rolled through her. "I'm sorry. I should have left a note."

"I saw her as I was leaving the Austelles'," Eston said. "Was coming to see you folks next. There's some news you need to know about."

Corrine turned to him. "You said you were coming this way, but you didn't say you had news. What news?"

Eston looked from Corrine to Hoke then back again. "I'd rather wait and tell it when we get to your place."

It was a silent ride back, as a strong sense of foreboding crawled up the back of Corrine's neck. Had something happened to Charlie? To James? Had there been even more to that *I know how it feels to lose someone you care about* comment?

Abigail met them in the yard. "Corrine! Why didn't you tell us where you were going?"

Corrine dismounted and handed the dun's reins to Hoke. While he and Eston took the horses to the barn, she went inside with Abigail to make coffee.

"He's got some kind of news," Corrine warned her mother. They exchanged worried looks and put cups on the table.

*   *   *

As Hoke and Eston walked to the house, Eston stopped to take in the view. "You sure have made a nice place here, Mathews."

"What's this about, Eston?"

The sheriff moved toward the porch. "I'd rather tell it inside."

Hoke stepped in front of him. "How 'bout you tell me now?"

"Duke Walden's headed this way."

CHAPTER 8

Whatever lies before them

The sheriff was talking.

Harry and Tam Sims, and Colonel Dotson and Gerald Jenkins, having heard the news, arrived shortly after Eston. They all sat at the large oak table in Hoke's cabin, leaning in and listening.

"Chancey said he talked to a man who'd just come through Nevada, where he played poker with Viscount Walden," Eston said.

"Who's Chancey?" asked Tam.

"The saloon owner. The one who loaned James the sleigh."

"And Viscount is…?"

"Duke Walden's son, one of his twins. Earl was the one James killed. There's an older brother, too. Between them they've robbed banks and killed people all the way from California to Colorado."

"So some fella came to Chancey's saloon here in Baker City…." Tam waved her hand for him to continue.

Eston gave her a wry smile. "And he said we better hunker down because all four Waldens are headed our way, gunning for the man who killed Earl."

"You think Walden knows who James is?" asked Tam.

Hoke frowned. "Thanks to Bennett Solomon, everybody knows who James is. And what he looks like."

Hoke and Sam Eston both glanced at Corrine. A pregnant pause swelled and filled the room. Corrine's chest felt tight.

Colonel Dotson turned to the sheriff. "What's your plan, Eston?"

"I respect your military background." Eston looked from Dotson to Hoke. "And your work as a marshal, Mathews. I've sworn Chancey in as a deputy and I'll swear either of you in, too, if you're willing to stay here and keep your guard up while I ride out to warn Parker and his group. I don't expect you to go and leave your places defenseless, but I do think Parker needs to be warned. I'd send a telegraph but the wire's down between here and Fort Bridger. Government men are working to find where, and fix it."

"I'm going with you," Harry said to Eston.

"If you're going, I'm going," said Tam.

Eston nodded. "I plan to ride hard."

"That's fine by us," said Tam.

Harry laid a hand on his wife's arm. "Tam, you might ought to stay here."

"I don't see any reason not to go, Harry. I can ride just as hard, and shoot just as straight as any man. Besides, I think I can talk James into coming on back here. He's off chasing horses, but missing a prime business opportunity right here in Baker City."

Tam looked into the faces around the table. "What about those tables he made for the hotel, and that gorgeous coffin? Some people said it was too pretty to put in the ground. I believe he'd be set on money if he'd come back here and stay put. They *all* need to get back here and stay put. Don't you agree?"

Harry, Dotson and Jenkins nodded.

Tam tapped the top of the table. "Four Waldens can't stand against our bunch if we're all together, I don't care how god-awful their reputation is."

"I want James and Charlie warned as much as anybody here," said Abigail, "but are you sure you should leave town, Sheriff?" Her eyes rested on Hoke's. "Should you go instead?"

Hoke shook his head. "I'm not leaving you, Abigail."

"But Charlie's out there, Hoke."

Hoke looked at Corrine again. Sheriff Eston did, too. They were all looking at her. The dread that had crawled up Corrine's neck earlier that day when Sam Eston said he had news now wrapped around it again and squeezed. Her chest grew tighter still.

"Why are you all looking at me?" she asked.

Eston answered. "The Waldons don't know Parker's left town, that's why they're coming here. When they get here, they won't find him. Or Charlie, either."

The dread popped like a bubble grown too large. Corrine looked down at her hands. "But they'll find me."

"No." Abigail laid her hand on Corrine's arm and shook her head. "Corrine doesn't live in town." She turned to Eston. "Why don't you get another posse together and head them off? Take care of this before they get to Baker City?"

Eston shook his head. "Their place is somewhere in northern Utah, but nobody knows exactly where. I can't take a chance on being out there hunting for a needle in a haystack, only to have them slip in here while I'm gone."

"They're not at their place in Utah if they're coming here," insisted Abigail. "Head them off on the trail!"

"I doubt they'd use a main trail coming into town, and I don't know when they'll get here. There's even a chance they'll get word James has left and never come here at all."

"But you said they were coming here, and you're leaving town!"

"That's true, and I think they are. But Parker and his men are on a main trail and should be easier to find. If I ride after Parker, I won't need a posse, and those deputized men can stay here and protect this town if the Waldens show up before I'm back."

"It's a sound plan," said Dotson.

"I agree," added Hoke.

Abigail rubbed her temples.

"It's possible I can make it to Parker's group and still get back here before the Waldens arrive." Eston looked at Tam. "Which is why I'm riding hard. And leaving at first light."

*   *   *

Corrine could hear the sounds of her mother and Hoke talking long into the night. Once their voices grew quiet, she kissed her sleeping sister on the forehead and eased out of bed. Her mother had taken Corrine's riding skirt and washed it the night before, hanging it on a string in the kitchen along with other laundry. It was still too damp to wear, so Corrine chose a regular skirt.

Dressing as quickly and quietly as she could, she padded through the cabin in her stocking feet, holding her boots in one hand and touching Rascal on the head with the other. Hoke had brought him in last night, knowing the dog would warn them if anyone or anything came into the yard.

Reaching into the larder bucket, Corrine dug out a soup bone and laid it in front of the hearth, hoping it would distract Rascal long enough to let her get out of earshot. She didn't have any weapons of her own save her sewing shears, so she took those and tied them around the calf of her leg with an embroidered handkerchief, knowing the boots would cover the scissors when she got outside and put them on.

She leaned the letter she'd written last night against the bowl James had made for her, now sitting in the middle of the large oak table, then eased out the door and made her way to the barn.

The weather felt as pent up as her emotions. Clouds lay swollen overhead, threatening to give birth to rain. Cold air brushed her face like moist cotton.

In the pre-dawn light she could see branches—some still naked, others with new leaves sprouting, and thick evergreens—swaying in the trees framing the hill. The weather was building...building...but toward what end?

She fumbled to find what she needed in the dark, lifting the heavy saddle to the gray dun's back and reaching under its belly to tighten the cinch, then stopped. What if a bad storm was brewing? What if the saddle slipped and she fell? Or if a snake lay coiled on the path? She could meet a bear foraging in the woods, or bad men—the Waldens, or others.

Then she heard James's words again in her ear. *"Don't you owe it to her to live every day as if it were your last? Greeting the sun with that raised chin of yours, and those gray-blue eyes? Loving the people around you? Making all the difference in one lucky man's life?"*

Today Corrine was seventeen, the same age her mother had been when she married and left home. She pulled the collar of her jacket up around her ears and stuffed her gray shawl in the saddlebag. Hadn't she been just fine the morning she rode out to Emma's grave? Feeling thankful for the bright moon that shone through cracks in the clouds, she stuck her foot in the stirrup, grasped the pommel and swung up.

When Harry and Tam stepped out of their door at daybreak, Corrine was waiting in their yard.

Tam's jaw dropped. "What do you think you're doin'?"

Feeling more alive than she'd felt in months, Corrine smiled and said, still breathing hard, "I'm going with you."

"No, you're not," said mild-mannered Harry.

"Harry, please! I'm a danger to my family if I stay. Those men know what I look like."

"Does your mother know you're here?" asked Tam.

Corrine looked to the sky. "She will any minute now."

"We're going to be riding hard, Corrine."

"I can ride hard. I've been riding all my life." Her confidence had risen like yeast dough after conquering the ride to town.

"Do you know how to shoot a gun?"

"I have a basic understanding."

Tam shook her head. "That means no."

Harry looked at the sky. "Let us take you to Doc and Nelda's. We've got to go meet the sheriff at the jail."

Corrine steeled her resolve. "If you make me go to Doc's, I'll just follow you later, Harry, which would be more dangerous with me traveling alone."

Tam's eyes bored into her. "Why are you so hell-bent — sorry, Harry — why are you so hell-bent on goin'?"

Corrine looked down to the pommel of her saddle. "I'm worried about Charlie."

Out of the corner of her eye, she saw Tam squinting at her. "That the real reason?"

Corrine considered lying, but she didn't think it would do any good with Tam, who was scrutinizing her closely. "And James. James is in danger and I want to help warn him."

Tam squinted harder. "I didn't think he'd officially asked you to marry him."

"He hasn't." Corrine looked Tam in the eye then. "But he's going to."

"Well you can't go in that skirt, Corrine. Get in here and get you a pair of my bloomers. They're better for overland travel. You'll need a hat, too, for God's sake. And tie up that long hair. I don't see a bedroll on that horse of yours." Tam looked simultaneously impressed and frustrated. "I swear, Corrine, you haven't put much thought into this."

*   *   *

Corrine braced herself for another battle with Sheriff Eston when they reached the jail, but he just smiled at her, his eyes traveling the length of her bloomers as the sky continued to lighten.

"Can you shoot?"

Corrine looked at Tam. "No."

"That's okay. I'll teach you." He stepped back inside his office and walked out with a rifle and saddle holster. Moving her left boot from its stirrup and out of the way, he tied the holster on.

Not used to having so few layers on, Corrine couldn't help but feel half-dressed, as if she was gallivanting in public in her petticoats. Her mother would be horrified, and Mimi, their former cook, would have given her a tongue-lashing and called her brazen.

She tried not to think about the sheriff's hands brushing against her leg as he tied the rifle in place. Any minute now, Hoke might charge up on the black stallion and scold her for causing her mother to worry again. But how could she just sit here in Baker City knowing James and Charlie were in danger? And how could she stay put, knowing her presence was putting so many people she loved at risk?

Those Walden men were angry with James, no one else, and the only people they were going to associate with James were Charlie and Corrine. If neither Charlie nor Corrine was in town, surely the Waldens would move on and the danger would pass.

Eston looked up at her. "This rifle's not loaded. But if we get in any sticky situations before I can teach you how to shoot it, just pull it out and act like it is." Then he tucked her foot back in the stirrup and mounted his own horse.

He led the way down the dirt road before them.

Corrine and Tam fell in behind him, and Harry brought up the rear.

*   *   *

Hoke and Abigail had bickered plenty on the overland journey from Independence, but since the day they professed their love and married, hardly a cross word had passed between them. Now, as Abigail stood holding Corrine's letter in her hand, she couldn't find anyone else to blame in her misery.

"Hoke!" Why was he just standing there? "We have to go after her!" Abigail woke Lina then called up the ladder to Jacob. "Get dressed, Jacob! Now!"

She raced to the stove, where yesterday's biscuits were covered with a cloth, to fill them with jam so the children would have something to eat. "Hoke! Go get the horses ready.

Lina can ride with me on the filly and Jacob can ride with you."

Hoke came behind her to stop her arms from spreading the jam. "No, Abigail. Let her go."

Throwing his hands off, she turned, the knife still in her hand. "Let her go? Are you out of your mind? She has no business going with Harry and Tam. It's dangerous!"

"It's no more dangerous than being here."

"If she's here, she's got us to protect her."

"And if she's with Harry and Tam, she's got them to protect her. And if she's with James and Charlie, she's got James and Charlie to protect her. Or maybe she doesn't need as much protecting as you think. She's not a child anymore."

"Yes, she is!" Abigail's hand that held the knife shook slightly.

They both knew it was Corrine's seventeenth birthday. Hoke had helped Abigail shell the walnuts for the cake she had planned to make. And Charlie had turned eighteen the day before. But no matter how old they were, Abigail couldn't bear the thought of Charlie and Corrine being out of her sight, of them living out from under the protective roof Hoke had built for them. She hadn't brought them all this way, hadn't put so much effort into restoring their family, just so they could go riding off within months of having safely arrived!

Love burned in Hoke's eyes, but she could see that his body and mind were rigid—unbending. "She's the same age you were when you left home. Who protected you?"

"I was in Marston, where it was more civilized."

Abigail reached for a biscuit, but Hoke stilled her hands again, slipping the knife from her fingers and laying it on the counter.

"Abby, the law's been scarce since we left Laramie. You know that. And Corrine is strong. She's got your blood runnin' in her veins. She's smart, and she's with good people. Harry and Tam are seasoned, and Eston's got sense, too."

She groaned involuntarily. Abigail's heart and voice trembled with equal velocity. This could not be happening! Why was Hoke not agreeing with her? She looked through the window at the early morning sky, tumultuous through a thickening cloud cover. Menacing. "The Waldens are supposed to be to the south, and Charlie and Corrine's groups went east, but...is there any chance they could meet on the trail, Hoke?"

"They shouldn't."

"Corrine's got no business traveling with an unmarried man!"

"She's with Tam, Abigail."

Abigail felt like her heart was going to burst right out of her chest and onto the floor. "My children, Hoke. *Our* children! Out there, God only knows where."

Hoke reached for her but she stepped away.

"Who better to know, Abby?" he said quietly.

"Hoke." The only word she could groan out was his name, even though her heart was shouting, *Do something!*

He reached for her again and she let him take her in his arms this time. He whispered, with his nose in her hair,

"Look, I'm sorry she's taken off. I am. I love Corrine like she was my own daughter. But we got Jacob and Lina to think about, too." They both looked toward the door of the girls' room, where Lina stood watching them with wide, troubled eyes. Jacob was peeping over the loft above.

Hoke laid his hand on the front waistline of Abigail's skirt. "And this one."

Abigail closed her eyes and groaned against the flood of tears she felt rising. She knew she needed to reassure Lina and Jacob that all would be fine, but first she needed to believe it herself. She turned and buried her face in Hoke's neck.

"I hate feeling so helpless, Hoke. I've felt helpless for weeks, not knowing how to be good for the Austelles after losing Emma. And now I feel helpless, wondering what's going to happen to Charlie and Corrine."

Hoke held her and stroked her back like he was stroking the stallion's coat. He waved Jacob and Lina over and let them know it was all right to wrap their arms around their mother, too.

"Children grow wings, Abigail," he whispered into her hair. "You got to let 'em, or they won't be strong to face whatever lies before them."

CHAPTER 9
A piece of torn paper

Corrine's heart pumped with dread and exhilaration. She waited for the skies to open and douse her with punishing rain, but they never did. Every time she and the other riders rounded a bend in the trail, she expected to see Hoke waiting on his stallion, his heated eyes accusing her for the worry she was causing her mother. But he never appeared.

Mid-morning, Harry Sims said low from the back of the group, "Someone's coming."

Corrine's heart caught. *Hoke!*

Sheriff Eston wheeled his splotch-necked horse around, grabbed the reins of Corrine's dun, and led her toward a clump of trees to the left of the trail. Harry and Tam went right. Eston swung down from his mount, threw the loop to Corrine, and put himself behind a tree. They waited.

Minutes later, the thud of hoofbeats reached their ears. Eston raised his rifle.

"No!" whispered Corrine, afraid Eston would shoot Hoke. If he did, it would be her fault.

Bennett Solomon rode into view.

"Solomon!" barked Eston as Corrine sagged with relief.

The sheriff's shout so startled Solomon, he nearly toppled from his mount—a small pinto not much larger than a pony.

Eston stepped from the brush on one side, and Harry from the other.

"Where are you going in such a hurry?" asked Eston.

Solomon got his horse stilled and threw his hands in the air. "I'm looking for you! Didn't think I was ever going to catch you." His breath came in spurts.

"Why? You got some kind of news?"

"No. I'm following the news!"

Eston lowered his gun in disgust. "You are *not* coming with us."

"But I can help you!"

Corrine stepped the dun out of the brush and Solomon noticed her for the first time. "Miss Baldwyn! I didn't know you were here." A smile lit his face.

*　　　*　　　*

Hoke was cleaning out the stables and Abigail was gathering the morning eggs when a man knocked on the door of the cabin. Rascal, who would have normally alerted them, didn't hear it either. He was close by Hoke's side, inspecting his work.

Lina opened the door.

*　　　*　　　*

Marquis Walden stuck his foot inside. He looked over the contents of the room: lace curtains, wooden bowl on the oak table, large stone hearth, rug, rocking chair and churn. He stretched an arm that held a piece of torn paper in front of the child's nose. "You know this girl?"

She didn't answer; she raised her big blue eyes to the loft instead. Marquis' eyes followed, but no one was up there.

He took a step inside, looking through the open door of the closest bedroom, and spied a small frame on a wooden chest. His foot was raised for a second step toward it when the click of a gun hammer stilled his feet.

"I wouldn't go in there if I was you," said a boy's voice.

This time when Marquis looked to the loft, the barrel of a rifle pointed down at him.

"Lina, step back in case I need to shoot this man."

Marquis cut his eyes back to the girl. She had already slipped beyond his reach, moving closer to the fireplace.

Careful not to move and set the boy off, Marquis only spoke. "Better be glad it was me that came here. I'm partial to little ones. Raised my twin brothers after my mother died."

"I guess you heard me cock the hammer. You might want to take your leave now."

Marquis raised his hands in the air. "I'm leavin'."

He glanced to the bedroom one last time before backing out the door. Having been blessed with keen eyesight, he could tell that the picture on the wooden chest was the same one that was printed in the paper he held in his hand. Plus, the little girl looked just like the older girl in the photo. He also noticed that only one small side of the bed in the room appeared to have been slept on.

Corrine Baldwyn wasn't in this house, and she wasn't in the yard. That's all the information he had needed. He'd been watching the house three days, long enough to know the patterns of the hardworking man and woman. He knew, too, that he needed to make haste if he was to get to where his horse was tied and get away without the savvy man of this homestead hunting him down. It had been key to Marquis Walden's lifelong survival that he know where the danger lay and how to avoid it.

He turned and ran.

*　　*　　*

Abigail was just coming around the corner of the house when she saw a man drop off the hill.

"Hoke!" she screamed. Dropping the egg basket, she ran inside.

She was hugging Lina to her breast, her heart pounding relief, when Hoke and Rascal burst through the door.

"Jacob!" Hoke said. "What are you doin' with the rifle?"

Jacob climbed down the ladder with the gun laid over the crook of his arm. Hoke reached for it.

"I was looking at it in the loft."

"You had the rifle in the loft?" Abigail's eyes widened. "Jacob Baldwyn! You were supposed to be in here helping Lina churn the butter. You know better than to play with guns!"

"It was her turn to churn." Jacob looked at Hoke. "I unloaded the gun before I took it up there. I was practicing sightin' in on targets, like you showed me."

"What happened?" asked Hoke. "Why'd you holler, Abigail? Because he had the rifle?"

"No." Abigail shook her head. "I saw someone go down the hill."

"A man knocked on the door," said Lina, her eyes brimming for a cry. "I shouldn't have opened it."

"Who was it?" asked Hoke.

"He didn't say," said Jacob. "He had that picture from the paper and was asking about Corrine."

Abigail felt the blood drain from her face.

Hoke cracked open the rifle's barrel. "I guess it was lucky you had this, then. What'd you do with the shells?"

Jacob pointed to the wooden bowl covered with a cloth.

Abigail stepped over to the bowl and pulled the cloth back. There lay the shells. "So it wasn't loaded." Abigail breathed relief, then scolded, "That was sneaky, Jacob." She knew he'd hidden them hoping not to get caught.

Hoke reached out and squeezed Jacob's shoulder. "You did good, son." He reloaded the rifle, stuffed his pockets with extra ammunition, and tied his Bowie knife to his thigh. Then he went into his and Abigail's bedroom and came back out with the Navy Colt they kept in the cherry box. He laid it on the oak table.

"Keep this close," he told her. "I'm going to look around."

*   *   *

Hoke finally found where the man had camped. He swore. He hated to think someone had been on his land without him knowing it. And Hoke had been taking precautions, too, wearing his Colt on his hip when he worked outside, bringing Rascal in the house at night, scouting around the hill each day.

But this man had been crafty. He'd moved around.

Hoke couldn't find proof that he'd ever made a campfire. He did discover one patch of dried blood and the hide of a squirrel near a beat down spot where the man must have slept one night, but there was no indication that he'd cooked ...it was as if he'd eaten the animal raw. The pelt had been cut neatly with a sharp knife, the bones neatly stacked beside it.

He also found where the man had tethered his horse. From the deep indentions of the tracks, Hoke gathered he'd ridden out fast.

The stallion could have caught him, but Hoke wouldn't leave his family. He couldn't afford to ride into a trap or leave them unprotected. Still...he sensed more unwelcome change in the air. His gut hadn't known peace since James told him he was leaving.

A cold dread settled in his heart.

*   *   *

The next day, Hoke and Jacob were splitting logs for the fence when the stallion's ears perked up. They still had Abigail's mules, and the mules were best for a job like this one, but Hoke was using the stallion to move the logs because it had the most sensitive ears.

Rascal started barking. Hoke looked up to see two riders still half a mile down the road. He recognized one.

"Go tell your mother Colonel Dotson and another man are coming. She'll want to set two more places."

As soon as the two men rode up, Dotson introduced the stranger. "U.S. Marshal Collin Mears."

"Heard of you." Hoke extended a hand. "Nice horse." Mears had ridden up on a spotted mustang, fast and strong.

Mears took Hoke's hand. "Heard of you, too, and was told you had an appreciation for fine horses. It was our loss when you and Parker turned in your badges."

"Mears is staying at the hotel," Dotson said. "He already wanted to meet you, and then this morning something happened you need to know about."

Sam Eston had deputized Dotson before he left town. He'd wanted to deputize Hoke, too, but Hoke had declined. Hoke's family was his first priority. And while he felt a strong loyalty to the members of Dotson's wagon train, he didn't want to feel responsible for all the other people in the town.

The men went inside and sat at the oak table, where Mears told the story.

"A fist fight broke out in one of the saloons—not Chancey's, but O'Brien's. A fight like that's unusual so early in the day. Someone fetched Doc Isaacs to come tend to one of the men. We think now it was the Walden twins, and that the fight was staged, to get Doc out of his house.

"Doc's wife was at the mercantile, which left his sister Caroline there with her boy and the Doc's new baby. She said she went out to hang wet clothes on a line, and when she went back in, a man was inside standing over the baby's cradle, showing his knife to the little boy. He told Caroline if she screamed he'd cut their throats."

Hoke's eyes cut to Abigail. As expected, her face was pale.

"Then he pulled out a newspaper clipping and asked her where James, Charlie and Corrine had all gone. Said he knew they weren't in Baker City, and that he could tell when people were lying to him. Told her if she lied to him about where they'd gone, he'd take those children and she'd never see them again."

"She was scared, Hoke," said Dotson.

Hoke nodded. The Waldens wouldn't have had to ask around long to learn that Emma had been taken to Doc Isaac's place after she was shot, and that Emma and the Isaacs were all part of the Dotson wagon party. That would explain why they'd target Doc Isaac's house.

"What did Caroline tell 'em?"

"Everything she knew. That James, Charlie, Chessor and Peters left three weeks ago, headed back down the trail. And that ten days ago, the sheriff, Harry, Tam and Corrine rode out to warn them. So did Bennett Solomon."

"I didn't know that. The newsman who wrote that story?"

Dotson nodded. "That's him. He told our new cook at the D&J he was following the news, and she told Christine."

Abigail covered her eyes with one hand. Hoke reached to hold the other one. He told Dotson and Mears about the man who had come to the cabin.

"I bet it was the oldest son, Marquis," said Mears. "Word is, he's an oddity. Made so by his old man. Duke Walden evidently doted on Earl, the one Parker killed. They have a hideout to the south, in Utah. I've been all over those hills trying to find it, but it's pretty well hidden."

Mears gulped down the last of his coffee. "From what I know of Duke Walden, he wouldn't send those boys out here alone. He's with them. And they're looking for Parker."

"Then why are they asking about Charlie and Corrine?" asked Abigail in a low voice. Hoke could hear the fear that lay coiled in her question.

"Because they're in the picture with him. They know that's one way to get to him."

Abigail rose from the table then, pulling her hand from Hoke's. The dread that had settled in his heart the day before now tightened up a notch.

"Excuse me, gentlemen," Abigail whispered. "I'm not feeling well."

After Colonel Dotson and Marshal Mears left, Hoke found her retching near the henhouse. He held her shoulders until she finished, then pulled her back to him, lifting fallen strands of hair from her eyes before circling his arms around her waist.

"Tell me what you want me to do, Abigail, and I'll do it."

He knew without looking there was a twist in her brow from worry. It never failed to amuse him when her brow twisted in irritation, but he hated for it to knot in worry. He fought the urge to smooth it out with his hand, burying his nose in her hair instead.

Oh, how he loved her! There was nothing he would not do for her, even if that meant going against his instincts.

"Is the telegraph still out?" asked Abigail.

"It is."

"Is Mears going after them, then?"

"He is."

"Is he as good as you?"

Hoke hesitated before answering. "I think he knows what he's doing. He's been at it a while."

Abigail drew in a breath and put her hands on Hoke's arms, wrapped around her middle. "I believe the child in a womb can feel its mother's fears and courage. For some reason I still can't explain, I had the strongest sense of peace when I was pregnant with Lina. And hers is a peaceful heart.

"I'm trying to push down my fears and reach for my courage now, Hoke, because I want our child to be brave, not afraid. I keep asking myself what will shore up my courage more, sending you after them or trusting God to watch over them?"

She turned and laid her head on his chest. "You were right when you said Charlie and Corrine are smart and strong. Stay here and help me keep my courage up."

Hoke took a deep breath of relief. In spite of his unease, his instincts were telling him to stay. So...why did the dread linger?

CHAPTER 10
The finer man

Ten days of hard travel led Corrine Baldwyn to two conclusions: she had over-glamorized trail riding in her mind, and James Parker was the finer man.

Corrine had accused James of being arrogant, but now saw that wasn't true. James was confident. *Sam Eston* was arrogant. The Baker City sheriff had assumed leadership from the moment they pointed their horses down the trail.

"We'll make camp here," he announced each evening when he decided it was time to stop. Once Harry pointed out a better location, and another time, suggested they might put another few miles behind them before darkness fell. Both times, Eston was quick to shoot him down.

"We won't find a better location than this one. I'm more familiar with the route." Self-possession dripped from Eston's pores.

Harry didn't argue, not even when Tam mumbled, "It's not like we didn't just come up this route. There's a plenty good spot a mile further on."

But Harry's glance told her it wasn't worth arguing, and this was the sheriff's domain, after all.

Solomon, on the other hand, proved to be an agreeable traveling companion. What Eston lacked in humility, Solomon owned in ample supply. Though he introduced himself, "Solomon, like the king," his height was the only stately thing about him. He was as tall as James, but lankier, and had a similar jawline. At least Corrine thought so, now that she knew what James's face really looked like.

Corrine's body ached worse than she'd ever dreamed possible, but not wanting to be accused of having made a poor decision in coming, she kept quiet about it. No one else was complaining, even though Eston paced the group hard. Tam grumbled to herself, but she wasn't one to whine to others. Corrine wondered if the sheriff was as eager to catch the other group as he claimed, or if he just wanted to prove his own endurance. She could see in his eyes that he knew the ride was taking a toll on her. It seemed to please him.

Corrine's unacknowledged birthday had long ago passed. Tired of their boring food rations, she kept thinking about the bowl of shelled walnuts she'd seen in the kitchen the morning she snuck out of the cabin. Her mother must have planned to surprise her with a cake.

It had been a tradition back in Tennessee for Mimi to make a buttermilk cake with cream frosting and toasted black walnuts for Charlie and Corrine's birthdays, which were celebrated together. Last year on the journey west Corrine and Abigail had attempted to replicate the cake, but it hadn't been the same.

Travel afforded a girl a wealth of time for thinking. So much change had stolen into her life in the past year that it was hard for Corrine not to feel wistful about her losses, even simple ones like a birthday celebration, or the smooth, rich taste of Mimi's buttermilk cake.

One evening, while Harry and Tam were hunting and Corrine was stiffly bent over the fire stirring beans, Eston came up behind her and put his hands on her shoulders. "Let me rub some of that soreness out for you."

She raked his hands off and stepped back from the fire. "That's not necessary."

"Sure it is. It's obvious you need it." He put his hands on her shoulders again and began working his thumbs down the spine of her back.

It did feel good, better than she would have believed, but it made her uncomfortable for him to touch her. She decided she should ask Tam to rub the soreness out.

Eston's hands worked lower...lower down her spine. Corrine bit her lip to keep from crying out, it felt so good.

Solomon watched from the other side of the campfire.

Eston leaned his mouth close to Corrine's ear and whispered, "I used to do this for my wife. She really liked it."

Corrine stepped out of his reach. "I told you, I'm fine." She walked over and sat next to Solomon on a fallen log.

The sheriff laughed. "Suit yourself. What about you, Solomon? You need somebody to rub your back? You look like you're having a worse time than she is."

Solomon had his boots off and was looking down at the holes in his socks, but he raised his head and smiled. "Making it just fine, thanks. It's not my first trail ride."

"Sure fooled me."

When Eston walked out of earshot, headed down to the nearby creek, Solomon turned to Corrine. "People in town said he was arrogant, but I've only lately had a chance to observe it for myself."

Corrine shook her head, remembering the compassion in Eston's eyes when he'd found her at Emma's grave. "He seemed genuine to me at first."

"Well...people's truer colors come through when you're around them every minute of the clock's face."

He was right. She'd learned that coming up the Oregon Trail.

Solomon grinned. "Enough about him. Let's talk about why you came and how you're feeling about the trip so far."

"Are you asking so you can write it into a story, or are you asking because you really want to know? I can fix those holes in your socks, by the way."

Solomon raised an eyebrow. "I can't promise they smell good."

"I have brothers."

He peeled off one of his socks and handed it to her. Catching her staring at his foot, he said, "My toes have always been that way. The last two are fused together...both feet." He raised the naked foot to show her. The line of separation between the last two toes started just at the base of the toenails. "But back to you. I really want to know. I'll leave my quill packed in my saddlebag as evidence of my sincerity."

Bennett Solomon might be a lanky, humble, non-kingly man with strange toes, but he had a good command of words, like James. And he shared James's cheerful outlook.

Corrine dug in her bag for an embroidery needle and part of a woolen skein. Then she unlaced her boot and pulled out the shears she'd continued to tie to her calf each day.

Solomon raised his eyebrow again. "I've heard of people hiding derringers that way. Remind me not to make you mad."

Corrine threaded the needle and tied a knot in the end with a quick roll of her fingers. "I doubt you ever make anyone mad."

"On the contrary!" Solomon peeled off his second sock. "I make people mad all the time. Hard as I try to get the truth right before a story ever goes into print, folks have their own opinions about it. Sometimes they don't want it told."

It was hard to argue against that. Corrine would rather Bennett Solomon had not told the story of Emma's death or included her picture in it.

"What made you want to be a newspaperman?"

"I thought I was asking the questions."

Corrine smiled.

"Okay," he conceded. "I am one of my favorite subjects, so I might as well talk about me. Story is, my folks picked me up on this very trail somewhere. They came up on a young woman traveling with a rough group. She'd just given birth to two baby boys and didn't know how she was going to manage. So she offered one—me—to my folks. Said she could only bear to part with one. I've often wondered if I was the give-away boy, or the pick boy. My mother claimed she and my father were the ones who picked me, but I wonder if she was telling the truth."

Solomon played with the sock that was still in his hand, waiting to be repaired.

"Anyway, my folks never had any other children, and never picked up any more on the trail, so I was raised with my imagination for a playmate." He slipped his hand in the sock and held it up like a puppet. "We settled in Oregon City. My father was a preacher, and my mother a schoolteacher, so there were always books and stories around.

"I taught school for a while, but after they died—they were pretty old when they got me—I decided to come farther inland where I could meet settlers and hear their stories. I never tire of it. I guess having so many questions about my own life has made me curious about everyone else's."

Corrine finished darning the first sock, tied off the knot, cut the yarn and reached for the second one. "So you have a twin brother you've never met?"

"Don't know his name or even if he's still alive. I've dreamed up dozens of possibilities for how we might cross paths some day. Maybe I'll write a ten-cent novel about it." Solomon slipped his repaired sock back on. "How 'bout you, Miss Baldwyn? What's been the most exciting part of your life? What dreams are you storing up behind those blue eyes?" He peered closer. "Or are they gray?"

The questions, along with his smile, took Corrine off guard. She had never noticed how much Solomon's smile looked like James's. He even had nice teeth like James, plus there was that similar jawline. Could James be Bennett Solomon's brother? That seemed unlikely. James had said his grandmother raised him.

Solomon was still looking at her eyes.

"Everyone in my family has blue eyes." Corrine concentrated on the thread and needle, wishing he'd stop peering at her so closely. "I doubt my life so far would make a good ten-cent novel, but my mother's story might. The most exciting thing that ever happened to me was coming out here...and meeting Emma Austelle."

The worst thing was losing her. Corrine wondered what Emma would have said about Corrine sneaking off to follow James and Charlie.

"As for my dreams," she continued, "that's the question I keep asking myself. Do people really get to choose how they want their lives to be? Or is it all worked out in the heavens and we just live it day-by-day, not knowing what the predetermined outcome is?"

She tied off a knot, cut the yarn, and handed back Solomon's second mended sock.

He cocked his head as he took it from her. "Why, Miss Baldwyn...you're a philosopher."

"Is that good or bad?"

He looked down at the sock in his hand then flashed his James-like smile again. "Oh that's good. It's *very* good."

*   *   *

James and his crew followed the Snake River without incident to Fort Hall, a sparse fort set on flat plains of grass growing thin and meager in the hot June sun.

Charlie, having remained quiet and close-lipped during all five weeks of their travel, now pumped the soldiers full of questions. During their journey west the previous year, a man passing himself off as Charlie's father had kidnapped his mother. For a time, the man had been stationed at this fort.

"Did you know the man who called himself Robert Baldwyn? What was he like? Which bunkhouse was his? Did he leave anything behind?"

"Most of what he had was on him when he died," said a sergeant named Smith. "But we did find a box of letters. I was going to send them to your mother, but hadn't heard where your group settled."

"I'll take them." Charlie was as authoritative as James had ever heard him.

The box of letters was produced.

After that, Charlie grew quiet again as their group traveled on, reading and re-reading the letters by the light of evening campfires.

"I remember your mother writin' letters on the trip," James said to him one night. Chessor and Peters were already bedded down for the evening, away from the fire. James was on watch, leaning back on his horse's saddle, looking out over a thick blanket of stars that hung so low, it seemed he could almost reach up and scoop a fistful in his hand. Out here the land was flat and trees were rare, leaving little to obstruct one's view. He wondered what Corrine was doing and tried to remember if the stars looked this plentiful from her porch at night.

Charlie was close to him, propped on an elbow, reading by the dying embers. His eyes never left the page. "Those letters were to Mimi. Most of these letters, written to my father, were written earlier."

Michael Chessor, not much older than Charlie, started in his sleep. He grabbed the knife he always slept with, sat up, and looked blankly at James. Then he turned over and lay back down, cradling the knife to his chest like a baby.

James raised his brows. "Hope he don't hurt himself." He leaned forward and stirred the embers with a stick. "I haven't showed you how to throw a knife yet. Remind me and we'll do that tomorrow."

"All right." Charlie folded the letter and put it away, then propped himself up on his elbow again. "I feel a little funny reading my mother's private letters. But I've learned a lot about her. And learned some things about my father, too, by what she wrote him. Things I'm glad to know."

James broke the stick in two and flung the pieces into the darkness, throwing each one like a knife. The pieces were balanced, but too light to travel far. James liked throwing a well-balanced knife.

During the war soldiers often threw knives for sport. No one had ever bested James. Hoke said it was because James had long fingers, but James knew his secret was letting his forefinger slide down the knife handle. He never flicked it and made the blade spin. Instead, he cradled the handle lightly, gripping it just enough to keep it in his hand while putting force behind it, only letting go when the blade begged for release.

James looked out in the darkness to where the sticks had landed. "Life is a strange business, isn't it?"

"I've thought a lot about that letter I sent my Uncle Thad." Charlie followed James's gaze. "I wish I could chase it down. If he sends the ring back, I'll give it to Corrine. I think she'd like having it, knowing I was going to give it to Emma. She can use it for her wedding ring if the man she marries is agreeable."

"I'd be agreeable."

Charlie whipped his head around. "You planning to marry Corrine?"

"If she'll have me."

Charlie stared at him so long James began to squirm. Charlie Baldwyn was almighty serious—harder to read than his sister. It may have been unwise to tell the younger man his intentions. In the back of James's mind was the worrisome fear that Charlie blamed him for Emma's death. Would Charlie resent James's happiness when his own had been so badly affected by James's shortcomings?

"Why do you think you deserve her?" Charlie finally asked.

Worrisome fear or not, James met Charlie's eyes full on. "I don't. I won't ever deserve her. But I'd be good to her."

Charlie looked out over the far-reaching prairie that surrounded them, then up at the stars James had been studying a moment before. "How many men have you killed?"

James shook his head. *One too few…*

"Couldn't tell you. It's not a pretty business."

"You think you'll ever marshal again?"

"No."

"Why not?"

"Because it makes you lose count of how many men you've killed."

Charlie looked at him again, as direct as James had ever seen him. "I wanted to kill Hadley Wiles for hurting my mother. And if I ever see Duke Walden again, I'm killing him."

James scowled. "Charlie, I hate to hear you say that. Killing a man works on your mind."

"You and Hoke seem all right with it."

"Oh, no. Willing, maybe. Willing's not the same thing as all right. Willing is born of necessity. It's not vengeance. Vengeance causes men to do things they wouldn't do when they're thinking straight."

The light was low but James saw Charlie's jaw tighten. "Duke Walden is an outlaw and a murderer, James."

James nodded. He decided not to point out that Duke Walden hadn't been aiming for Emma when his bullet found her. Walden had a reputation as a murderer, but Emma's death had been an accident. James needed to believe that—was trying to believe that—because if it wasn't true, he was surely as responsible as Duke Walden.

"You have a valid point there, Charlie, and if Walden were to step out of the shadows right now I wouldn't hesitate to shoot him. A man's got to defend himself and the people he cares about. But when bullets start flying, the unexpected can happen, that's all I'm sayin'. And even when everything about it seems justified, it's never a satisfying feeling to know you took a life. Not if you got any kind of a conscience."

Charlie looked up at the stars again. "I saw you step out in the street that day."

James loosened his already loose collar that suddenly felt too tight. "Now, that's exactly what I mean, Charlie. See, if I could go back to that moment, I would never pull my gun this time."

Charlie seemed not to hear him. "We saw it from inside the post office—me and the clerk. We ran to the front window when we heard the shots. I saw Corrine and Emma dart from the café over to the side of the building, by Solomon's place, about the same time you palmed your gun. Then you stepped out in the street. The clerk said, 'He's going to stop 'em! Look, he's not afraid.' Everybody else was ducking into shops or hiding behind doors, including me. I thought the girls were safe."

Charlie looked James in the eye again. "And they *would* have been safe, James, but then Emma stepped out to see what was happening. I saw it. I saw Corrine pulling on her arm, as if telling her not to, but Emma must have been curious."

He squeezed his eyes with his fingers, but moistness seeped past them.

"Right before it happened, I thought about running out of the post office, back behind Solomon's, and going to the girls. But before I could get my feet to move, she was already falling into Corrine's arms. I stood there at the window thinking, 'This is not happening. This is a bad dream.'"

Charlie shook his head, rubbed his face with his hand, and looked back up at the blanket of stars. "I could hear the man's horse in the alley behind the post office. I could have run out and stopped him when you quit firing. But I didn't have a gun. I was too afraid to go after him without a gun, even after he shot the girl I wanted to marry."

Charlie looked back to James. "Remember when that buffalo charged Jacob, back when we were coming up the trail? I wonder now if it was really my bullet that brought it down. Hoke pumped it full of lead, too. I only got one shot off."

James nodded. "Hoke said it was *your* bullet that laid the killin' shot, Charlie. And if you'd been standing next to Emma back in Baker City, you might have made all the difference then, too—maybe convinced her not to step out—or you might not have. There's so much that's out of any one person's control. I froze up, too, when I realized she'd been hit. I blame myself for not running after that outlaw, and for not shooting him quick enough."

"But you at least had the courage to step out in the street, James."

"Well, I...I thought I could stop him," James admitted. "Just like you picking up that rifle with the buffalo: sometimes a person acts before putting much thought into it.

But I swear, if I'd known the girls—or anybody—was taking cover on the south side of Solomon's, I never would have thrown myself into that spot on the street."

Charlie swiped at his eyes. "If you're blaming yourself, you shouldn't."

Relief washed through James to hear Charlie say those words. It stunned him, though, to realize Charlie had been blaming himself for his own actions that day. "I'd say the same to you."

Charlie scooted down in his bedroll, closed his eyes, and lay quiet for a while.

James thought he had gone to sleep when Charlie said, "You'll make Corrine a good husband. If my Uncle Thad sends that ring? You should give it to her."

CHAPTER 11

Not the nervous type

From Fort Hall, James and his men turned away from the river and headed south. While they were coming up the trail last summer, Dotson had taken them through South Pass, a popular cut-through in the Rockies. But James's plan was to loop down to Fort Bridger and turn due east once they hit the trail left by the Mormons who'd come out of Missouri starting in '39. That trail should lead them straight to Silvertown, a mining boomtown nestled on the western side of the mountain chain where his grandmother currently resided.

At mid-day they stopped and James gave Charlie his first knife-throwing lesson. Afterward they rode on, loping along with relative ease, unaware that two groups were following them, gaining ground.

*   *   *

Harry Sims had known the route James planned to travel, so he advised Sheriff Eston to lead their group in a straighter line south to Fort Bridger, hoping to shave off time. They were riding harder than James's group, with a greater sense of purpose, and the pace was paying off. When Eston led them into Fort Bridger, they learned they'd missed Parker's group by only two days.

"We won't stay, then," barked Eston. "Mrs. Sims, Miss Baldwyn: get us some fresh food supplies. Solomon, see if the telegraph line is working between here and Baker City. If it is, let 'em know we're here and that we're closing in on Parker. Sims, how's your ammunition holding out?"

"Got plenty," said Harry.

Eston's eyes narrowed. "You sure? If we end up in a shoot-out, I don't need your religious convictions making you conservative."

Corrine laughed, remembering how Harry Sims had fought hand-to-hand with an Indian, using his Bowie knife, during the attack on their train coming west. "If we end up in a shoot-out," she said, "Harry's the one I'll be handing my rifle to."

Eston pointed at her suddenly. "That's right! We never have taught you to shoot." He took the rifle from her saddle holster. "Correction," he said to Tam and Harry. "Both you Simses can restock our food." He turned to Corrine. "You come with me, Miss Baldwyn."

Tam shook her head and Corrine scowled, but both did as the sheriff commanded.

After talking to a sentry at the gate, Eston had Corrine walk with him a half-mile from the fort, toward the only tree in sight. "Here, this looks good." He walked out several yards, took the bandana from his neck and wrapped it around a low-hanging branch.

"Show me what you know," he instructed when he got back to her.

Discomfort at being away from the fort alone with the sheriff crept up Corrine's back collar. "I don't really know anything."

Eston showed her how to load the rifle, a Henry. Then he took the cartridges out—all sixteen—reached for her hand, and laid them in her palm. Sixteen cartridges were a handful.

"Now you do it."

She did.

He took the gun back, removed the cartridges, and laid them in her palm once more.

"Do it again."

She did it again.

He reached for the gun. Sam Eston's hands weren't as long as James's, but they were masculine, the dark hair of his arms peeking from his shirtsleeves at the wrist. "One more time. Faster. You need to know how to load it in a hurry."

Corrine did it faster, the temperature of her blood rising with each new command he bellowed.

Eston pointed. "Now take aim on that bandana."

Corrine lifted the rifle to her shoulder.

He shook his head. "Here." He stepped behind her and put his arms around hers, reaching for the gun.

Her shoulders stiffened.

"Relax, Sweetheart. I'm just tryin' to show you how to shoot a rifle. If I wanted to seduce you, I'd have done it by now."

Corrine resisted the urge to turn her head and look him in the eye. His face was so near she could feel his breath on her neck. The heat of it heightened her nerves. She told herself he was a sheriff, sworn to uphold the law. Surely he wouldn't act unseemly.

"Look at your target, Miss Baldwyn. And put the butt of your rifle here." He ran his hand along her collarbone, until it hit her shoulder, and walked his fingers to the dip above her right breast. Then he moved the polished wood over to the spot. "Right there, away from any bones. It's going to kick some when you pull the trigger. You prepared for that?"

Why did he have to put his mouth so close to her ear?

"I can handle it."

"Let's see."

Steamed at the sheriff for breathing down her neck, for running his hand so familiarly along her collarbone, and for making her come out here with him in the first place, Corrine set the front sight in the notch and pulled the trigger. The gun roared and knocked her backward, but Eston was ready and caught her with his body. His hands slid over her waist and down her hips.

Corrine stepped from his embrace and pointed the rifle at the weathered soil in front of his boots. "Step back!"

His naturally dark face grew darker still. "Look, I'm doing you a favor here. Don't act like you don't appreciate it."

"I'd appreciate it if you'd step back! I believe I could hit the target better without you breathing down my neck."

Stepping to the side, he crossed his arms. "Do it, then."

Corrine worked the lever that pushed the spent cartridge out then loaded a new one. He didn't have to tell her how to do that. She'd seen it done. She lifted the rifle to her shoulder again. This time the bandana jerked in half, the part still tied to the tree kicking wildly from the branch.

As Corrine watched it with satisfaction, she bit her lip against the pain in her shoulder. The gun had kicked all right, but not bad. She doubted it would leave her shoulder as sore as her back and legs had been from sitting in a saddle all those hours on the trail.

"Again," Eston instructed.

She worked the lever. This time she blew off one small corner.

"Again. Faster."

She ejected the spent shell with a vengeance. This time she hit the knot and blew the branch off the tree.

Eston took the rifle from her hands. "You're a fast learner. You learn everything that fast?"

"Not everything." Corrine stepped away from him.

The line of Eston's lips tightened. "You seem mighty skittish to be alone with me. Do I make you nervous, Miss Baldwyn?"

Corrine felt a powerful urge to run, to put as much distance between herself and the handsome sheriff as she could. But she planted her boots in the dirt and held her ground. "Yes. Sometimes you make me nervous."

"You're not the nervous type. What do I do that makes you nervous?"

Corrine wasn't sure how to answer. No one had ever talked to her the way Sam Eston did. His words and behavior hadn't been *explicitly* suggestive, but his past offer to rub the soreness from her back, plus the way he slid his hands over her hips just now, sent her defenses up.

She had slept every night of this trip next to Tam. And more than once, Corrine had awakened to find Sheriff Eston staring at her over the glowing cinders of the campfire. To give him any encouragement might prove costly. James's warning about him kept ringing in her ears. *Don't ever encourage a man like Sam Eston.* What had James meant exactly? What kind of man did James think Sam Eston was?

"I'm used to it," Eston went on. "Making people nervous. Part of it is the badge, and part of it is just me, I guess." He took his hat off and sighed. "I'd like not to make you nervous, if you'll tell me how."

Once again, Corrine wasn't sure how to respond. The sheriff's moods could change so quickly!

"What am I doing wrong?" he asked again.

She groped for something to say. "You might listen to someone else's opinion every now and then. And..."

"And what?"

Not look at me that way. She shut her eyes so she could think.

Suddenly his mouth was on hers, pressing hard.

Corrine's eyes flew open. She pulled back, fighting an urge to slap him. "Why did you do that?" It hadn't been at all like kissing James. She had enjoyed kissing James. This was thievery, and she resented it.

"Just doing what any other man would do in my place. It's the first real opportunity we've had." He reached for her, but she dodged his arms.

"Sheriff Eston!"

"Look, I'm trying to go about this right. Don't you have feelings for me? Isn't that why I make you nervous?"

"No."

His head cocked. "You sure, Miss Baldwyn? You don't have to play coy."

"I'm not playing coy. Are we done here?"

It was a long, silent walk back to the fort. Corrine moved as fast as her laced up boots would carry her. Eston lagged a few steps behind. She could feel his eyes on her backside and wished mightily she had on a dress, instead of an old pair of Tam's more leg-defining bloomers.

Once they were back inside the walls, the sheriff stalked off. Tam pulled Corrine aside. "You think we can get him to stay the night and ride out in the morning?"

Corrine looked in the direction where Eston had rounded the corner of a log building. "We can ask. Why?"

Tam scrunched her face. "I probably should have told you this before we ever left. Harry and me are goin' to have a baby."

"Oh, Tam!" Corrine reached to hug her, then stopped. "Is everything alright?" Corrine had noticed Tam was putting on weight. Now that she looked closer at Tam's middle, the reason for the gain seemed obvious.

"I think so, but," Tam dropped her voice and sidled close, "I've lost some blood. It's got me worried."

"Should you go back? Is there a doctor here?"

"No doctor. I checked. And we're too close to reachin' 'em to turn back now. But I do think it would be good to get a full night's rest here. There's real beds."

The last thing Corrine wanted to do was have to face Eston again so soon. She spied him walking between two buildings in the distance and squared her shoulders. "I'll talk to him."

Eston was paying a soldier for a pint of whiskey when Corrine caught up to him. He raised the jar, half filled with amber liquid. "Now here's another mark you can log against me." He still carried the loaded rifle against his shoulder.

"I'm not logging marks against you."

The soldier selling the whiskey raked his eyes over Corrine. "You want to stay here and set up shop, Miss, you could make some good money."

It took Corrine a minute to realize he was speaking to her. "Pardon?"

"We got a couple doves here, following the railroad men layin' track to the south, but I guarantee if you stayed, you could out-earn 'em both. I'd be first in line."

Corrine stared blankly at the man. Then it dawned on her what he meant. Eston's fist flashed past her and blood splattered on her blouse.

"How dare you," Eston spat toward the ground where the man now lay. He looked at Corrine's blouse. "Sorry about that."

"It's fine." She looked down at the spatter of red, then back up again. Did the man say that to her because she was wearing Tam's bloomers? And now the stains on her chest gave the sheriff yet another reason to peer too closely. Corrine wanted to run screaming from this dirty fort overrun with men. She reminded herself that she was doing this for Charlie and James...to warn them.

"I'll get it out." She covered the stain with her hand. "Do you mind if we stay overnight?"

"Why?"

"We could all use the rest. Everybody's on edge."

He shifted the weight of the rifle, revealing a gash in his hand. "If I say yes will you acknowledge that I can take other people's suggestions?"

Without thinking, she reached for his hand. "You're cut."

Eston looked down at the soldier again, who was crawling away. "You might want to check for loose teeth."

Solomon came running toward them. "What happened here? You're bleeding, Eston. Is that your blood on Corrine's blouse?"

Corrine covered the stain with her hand again, wishing everyone would stop looking at it. The soldier's words and Sam Eston's earlier actions made her feel dirty.

"Sorry you missed the action, Solomon." Eston shook the cut hand. "If you want a story, go ask that man about the women here making money off the soldiers."

"Oh, I've already talked to the women. Interesting thing—"

"I don't think there's a doctor here," interrupted Corrine, "but you need stitches, Sheriff. Mr. Solomon, do you remember where I had my thread, in my saddlebags?"

"I do."

"Will you get them for me? The finer thread and smaller needle, not the ones I used on your socks."

"I will, but I need to talk to you when I get back." He started to leave then turned back to the sheriff. "Telegraph line to Baker City is still down, by the way."

"Appreciate you checking," said Eston.

Once Solomon was gone, Corrine turned back to Eston. "You trust me to sew you up?"

"I'd trust you with my life, Miss Baldwyn. I was just before trusting you with my heart."

Corrine didn't know what to think or how to feel. Sam Eston was confusing her. He was intense, commanding, and at times disturbing. But there were also moments he seemed as uncertain as a child.

"I'll be right back." Corrine needed a minute to clear her head, so she went to find Tam and told her they would stay the night.

"Good! One of the officers has offered us his room—me and you. The men can sleep in the barracks. Even better, I found where we can get us a private bath. Is that blood on your blouse?"

"It's Eston's. He cut his hand."

"Oh. Well, we can wash our clothes, too."

When Corrine got back to Eston, she found that Solomon had brought her whole saddlebag, not just the thread and needle, and left again. Eston was sitting on the ground beside it, his back against the nearest barracks, the rifle propped beside him. "Solomon seemed anxious to talk to you but said he had something to check on."

"All right." Corrine dug out the right needle and thread and set the bags between her and the sheriff, propped up to serve as a table.

"Or maybe he's just looking for a chance to steal *him* a kiss." Eston's words came slow and heavy.

Corrine reached for his right hand and laid it on the thick leather of the bags, then took the whiskey jar from his other hand. It had only been half full when he bought it, now it was half again.

He reached to take it back. "That's mine. I paid for it."

Corrine avoided his grasp then splashed a quick dab of whiskey on the cut hand and her needle. She expected him to jerk from the sting, but he never moved.

She handed the jar back, the acrid scent of the whiskey wafting up her nose. She didn't like the smell of liquor.

Corrine had watched Doc Isaacs stitch her mother up and knew it worked a lot like fabric. The more Eston drank, the slower his words became, but he never flinched as she moved the needle through his skin.

"Is it Parker?"

"What do you mean?"

"Now you *are* being coy."

"Are you asking me if I have feelings for James Parker?"

"That's why you came, isn't it?"

"My brother's with him, too."

"But you came because of *him*...because of Parker."

"Yes. I did." Moving a needle through skin was not exactly like moving it through fabric. Fabric didn't bleed. She didn't know how tight to pull the thread, worried it might tear and worried she was hurting him. But he still didn't flinch. His hazel eyes looked more heavy than pained.

"Do you two have an understanding?"

She nodded, trying not to flush at the memory of kissing James. She missed him. She was ready to see him again. "I believe so."

The sheriff stared hard at her. "If anything should happen to Parker, or happen to your understanding, would you consider me?"

Corrine tied off the knot and reached to take the jar again. "You need to keep these stitches greased. And I think you've had plenty of whiskey."

If anything should happen to James, Corrine would never forgive herself. The fear of something happening to him was what had spurred her to leave home and kept her moving forward to try to warn him...to convince him to come home, where he and Charlie belonged.

"I'll trade you." Eston leaned forward and stole another kiss as Corrine reached to take the whiskey from his hand. It left a lingering taste of fermented grain and oak on her lips.

"Liquor's always...done me this way. I shouldn't ought to drink it. Stay with me, Miss Baldwyn." He reached for her but she leaned away from his groping arms. "Stay with me while I go to sleep."

"I don't think that's a good idea."

By the time she found a blanket to cover him, he was out cold, stretched over her saddlebags. She picked up the rifle and unloaded the cartridges.

*   *   *

Marquis Walden was the first to pick up their trail. "Five horses, riding hard, only a day ahead of us. This one's tracks are lightest. It's probably the girl."

"They'll stop at Fort Bridger. Probably there now," said Duke. "If we're lucky they'll stay the night. Let's cut south and find a good place to lay for them on the other side."

CHAPTER 12

Living blind

Rain was falling hard.

Fort Bridger was a half day's ride behind them when shots rang out. Harry and Tam went right. Solomon followed them. Eston grabbed the dun's reins and led Corrine to the left. They dismounted under a clump of pine trees and waited. Nothing. An hour passed with no sign of the shots' source.

"We'll sit tight 'til this rain moves on," Eston said low in her ear. With the thick cloud cover overhead, it seemed night was falling early. He cut some branches and built them a crude shelter, settling the horses in the thicket nearby.

"Where are the others?" asked Corrine.

"They'll be looking for shelter, too. We'll find them in the morning. Try to get some rest. I'll keep watch."

Corrine laid out her bedroll and pulled a blanket up over her, shivering in the cold and damp. There was no point in trying to build a fire.

She eventually dozed, but woke in the night. Eston was beside her, pulling at her shirtwaist.

"What are you doing?" she asked.

"Trying to get warm. I'm freezing. Hold me."

His hands were like ice. She rubbed them between her own, trying to get the blood flowing.

"Turn around," he said.

"Why?"

"Put your back to me, so I can hold you."

She did as he instructed. He pulled at her shirtwaist again, freeing her blouse and camisole from their tuck inside her bloomers, his hands slipping up the bare skin of her back.

"Sam, don't." But his hands were fast and he knew how to work them. He massaged her back in circles, going lower…lower.

Lighting struck and then Hoke was there, bursting through the pine boughs, jerking Eston up by his collar and flinging him to the side.

Corrine cried tears of relief at seeing him, or were they tears of shame at having been caught in Eston's arms? Lightning flashed again. Hoke's eyes flared even brighter.

"You've put everybody in a tight spot, Corrine!"

"I'm sorry." She had always liked Hoke, but now she was afraid of him. She'd never seen him this angry. "You didn't have to come."

The flame of his eyes was worse than the lightning popping overhead. "What if I hadn't? What was about to happen?"

"I'm sorry, Hoke, but I had to come. My future lies with James."

And then she woke.

*   *   *

Tam was already up and dressed. She sat on the sole chair in the sparse room and bent over to lace her boots. "Felt good to sleep on a real bed, didn't it? Almost as good as that bath last night." She looked up and grinned. "I started to rub your back, then remembered you weren't Harry."

Corrine put her hand to her forehead. "I had a strange dream."

"Yeah?" Tam laced her second boot and stood.

"I'm just glad to know it wasn't real. How do you feel this morning?"

"Better. The bleeding has stopped." Tam reached into her pocket. "I meant to give this to you yesterday and forgot. A soldier gave it to Harry while you were gettin' your shootin' lesson. How'd that go? I never did ask you."

Corrine reached for the letter. "Sometimes Eston makes my skin crawl."

"He *always* makes my skin crawl. Men like that ought not to be given badges, but they're the first to volunteer for 'em. Solomon's nice enough. Still, I'm ready to catch these boys so we can get home."

Looking more closely at the letter, Corrine sat up. "It's from James!"

Tam smiled. "I'll go find Harry while you get dressed."

The letter was addressed to Miss Corrine Baldwyn at the Hoke Mathews homestead outside Baker City. James must have left it when he rode through and the postal rider hadn't picked it up yet. She tore the letter open and smoothed out the folded parchment.

Corrine,

I have never written your name before. Had to ask Charlie how to spell it. It looks nice on the page. Forgive my handwriting. It is not as smooth as your own.

We have been several weeks on this journey. I miss you even more than I thought I would. Yesterday, I woke to the cooing of a dove. I saw it take flight from the tree overhead — a lone juniper — and when the sun caught on its wings, it reminded me of you. Its feathers were the color of your eyes.

I wonder what you are doing today. I wonder that lots of days. I imagine you sitting at the table with your hands covered in dough like I have seen them lots of times and you flicking a stray hair off your face, or blowing it sideways like that way you have.

Each night as I watch the sun sink and the moon rise, I wonder if you are watching them, too, from the top of your hill.

A soldier at Fort Hall gave Charlie a box of letters your mother wrote. They have meant a great deal to him. He does not say much, but when he does, I sure enjoy his words.

Hoke gave me his father's Bible. Did you know Esther won a contest? She was considered the prettiest girl in all the land. But that is only because you were not born yet.

I look forward to the day I see you again. Keep your chin up where it belongs.

James

*   *   *

Sheriff Eston led the group out of the fort, with Harry and Tam behind him. Corrine and Solomon brought up the rear.

Solomon leaned out over his pinto toward her and spoke low. "I looked for you last evening and couldn't find you, Miss Baldwyn. I need to talk to you about something."

Corrine's heart still danced from reading James's letter. It had been a month now since she'd seen him. Having the opportunity on this trip to compare him closely to other men like Sam Eston and Solomon Bennett, combined with the way her heart had leapt over the ink of his words this morning, had convinced her she must be in love with him. There was but one thing gnawing at her memory.

"I wanted to talk to you, too, Mr. Solomon."

Solomon raised his brows expectantly. "Did you talk to that woman?"

Corrine's brow twisted. "What woman? What do you mean?"

"I thought maybe you talked to that woman who rode out yesterday. She was with those three men?"

Corrine shook her head. "I don't know what woman you're talking about."

"Oh." Solomon suddenly looked uncomfortable. "What were you going to ask me?"

"Back in Baker City, you hinted at having heard some disturbing things about Mr. Parker, but you didn't elaborate on them."

"Well...it's not an easy subject in mixed company."

"You alluded to that before, but I don't know what you mean by it."

Solomon repositioned himself on his horse and avoided her eyes. "I can tell you set store by Mr. Parker. I'm reluctant to say anything against his character that might cloud your opinion of him, and yet I feel compelled to reveal to you certain things that I have heard, some as recently as yesterday."

"Please stop talking in circles, Mr. Solomon. Speak plainly."

He looked embarrassed. "Will you call me Bennett if I do?"

"Yes. Now please tell me what you know about Mr. Parker. No matter what it is."

Solomon glanced up at the riders in front of them. He and Corrine had fallen behind but he seemed in no hurry to spur his pinto forward to close the gap. "Evidently—and you must forgive me, Miss Baldwyn, if any of this sounds like I'm personally disparaging Parker's name. I like the man, myself. But evidently he has a reputation for visiting with questionable women."

An image of the cook in Baker City flashed in Corrine's mind, the way she had laid her hand on James's arm at the D&J. "'Visiting'? What do you mean by visiting? And define 'questionable women.'"

Solomon leaned out over the side of his horse again and whispered, "He frequents bordellos."

His words had the same effect as if someone had just pumped cold water though her veins.

Corrine twisted part of the gray dun's mane in her fingers. "Bordellos? As in...?"

"Yes, ma'am. Brothels. I'm sure you're aware that there are many such establishments in the west. There are a high number of men in this area, and a low number of women, not nearly enough for every man to have his own bride. As is common in any developing part of the world, I'm sure you know this, there are those who seek opportunities where the opportunities present themselves. There are few ways for a woman on her own, with no family, to make a living in this part of the country."

The dun jerked its head back suddenly and Corrine let go of its mane, realizing she'd pulled it too tightly. "Mr. Solomon, surely you're not suggesting that James is the sort of man who would patronize and exploit women who find themselves working in such establishments."

Even as she said this, James's own words came back to her. He had said he'd made a study of women...that he'd gotten an early education...that he was an experienced man. Solomon's claim was plausible. But if James was the sort of man who had routinely patronized brothels, then he was *not* the sort of man she could marry. She did, after all, have principles!

Solomon continued, talking fast. "After I printed the story about Mr. Parker's heroism, I began to get letters from as far away as Texas, Miss Baldwyn. Several—all from women, I might add—agreed that Mr. Parker was a hero. They mentioned him as kind, gentlemanly, generous and selfless. Each one of those letters, upon investigation, originated from a bordello. I also got a couple of letters describing Mr. Parker as a vagabond—as a deceptive, underhanded cheat. Both of the latter were also from bordellos.

"I tried to ask Mr. Parker about it before he left," Solomon said, "but he wouldn't discuss the matter. In fact, he was surly when I brought it up." He repositioned himself on his horse, having leaned toward her so earnestly he'd been in danger of falling off.

"Miss Baldwyn, I feel terrible telling you this. Your face expresses shock and dismay. I admit, I feel a bit of that myself. Even at Fort Bridger, two women told me James Parker had called on them. It bothers me to know he spent time with them, especially if he has...well, an understanding with you."

"What did the two women say, exactly?" Corrine hoped her voice sounded more normal than she felt. Her temperature had risen several degrees while listening to Bennett Solomon. She fought the urge to twist the dun's mane in her hand again, and dug her fingernails into the hard leather of her saddle horn instead.

"They seemed rather fond of him. One used the word 'charming.'"

Corrine turned loose of the saddle horn, reached in her pocket and wadded James's letter into a ball. Oh yes, James Parker was charming all right. She felt like a fool for having told Tam and Eston—even Hoke, in a dream—that she belonged with James. For having said that they *did*, in fact, have an understanding.

She'd come all this way!

On second thought, she was glad she'd come all this way. Her anger would carry her the remaining distance. She would ride all the way to Mexico if necessary, just so she could punch James Parker in his hairy jaw when she saw him.

To think how he'd fooled her! How he'd fooled everyone. Or maybe Corrine was the only one who hadn't seen him for what he really was. What about Hoke? Did he visit brothels? Surely not. Hoke hardly even spoke to any woman besides her mother. James, on the other hand...James liked women. He always spoke to women.

Bennett Solomon leaned toward her again. "That's not all, Miss Baldwyn."

Corrine gripped the saddle horn again. *There was more?*

"That woman I mentioned at the start of our conversation? Yesterday, right after we arrived at the fort, while you were off learning to shoot with Sheriff Eston, I talked to a woman who claimed she'd had James Parker's child. Said he'd made her a promise of marriage, then left her. She had to give the child up, not having the money to feed it, but after reading that Parker had been awarded money from the government, she felt he owed it to her to help her get the child back. Claimed they'd known each other since they were children, themselves. Oh, Miss Baldwyn, I've dealt you a blow! I can see it from the white of your face. Do forgive me."

It was true. Corrine's body was betraying her. The breath moving in and out of her lungs felt thin, as if the altitude had changed. The dun, sensing something was wrong with its rider, slowed to a stop.

Solomon called nervously ahead to the others. "Hold up there!"

Tam rode back to them at a gallop and looked at Corrine with alarm. "What's wrong?"

Solomon turned apologetic eyes toward Tam. "I shared upsetting news with her."

Corrine waved her hands at Solomon to stop. "Don't...tell it. Nobody...needs to know. Don't. Don't say it."

Tam raised a fist and shook it at Solomon. "You told her about that woman? Bennett Solomon, I swear! I told you not to say anything about that, not until James has had a chance to answer for himself!"

Corrine's eyes bulged. "You mean you *knew*? And you kept it from me?"

Tam waved Solomon away. "Go on! We'll catch up to you directly." Dismounting, she motioned to Corrine. "Come here and sit with me a minute."

Numb, Corrine did as she was told.

Tam took their horses' leads and wrapped them loosely over a pile of rocks. Then she sat on one of the larger stones. "What did Solomon say to you, exactly?"

Corrine told her.

Tam shook her head. "It may not be what you think, Corrine."

"May not be what I *think*? I don't even know what to think, Tam. Could James really have fathered a child? If he's the kind of man who spends time with women like *that*, then he isn't a man *I* would be willing to marry."

Tam looked at her sharply. "Women like *that* may not be what you think they are."

"Any woman who would sell her body isn't Christian, Tam."

"Don't judge other women so hard, dearest. I took a turn at it myself. And Harry Sims was willing to marry *me*!"

Corrine looked out over the scrub brush as if she were seeing her surroundings for the first time. The way the ground sloped, the grass coming up, the rocks that lined the path…. *Tam?* As a woman who would sell herself? Had Corrine been living blind all her life?

Tam gave her a minute, then nudged the side of Corrine's boot with her own. "I'm sure this comes as a shock to you."

The feel of Tam's foot sent repulsion crawling up Corrine's leg. She jumped up and stepped away.

"Don't touch me with your boot. Don't touch me at all!" Corrine looked down at her bloomers. "Is it sinful for me to be wearing these?"

Tam rolled her eyes. "It's not the outfit of a soiled woman, if that's what you're worried about. Trust me. The profession calls for less."

"But I've felt the way men look at me since I've been wearing your clothes, Tam." The repulsion had reached Corrine's lips. She could hear it coming out in her voice.

Tam rose to face her. "I wore bloomers all the way from Independence to Oregon, Corrine. Are you telling me you thought I was a harlot all that time? If men are looking at you, dearest, it's because you're lovely! You stick out like a sore thumb, especially in forts and mining towns made mostly of men. They don't see a lot of women, especially not ones as attractive as you. I ought to have known better than to let you come out here with us."

Blood pumped hot through Corrine's veins. She'd begun this day in a blissful state. Clean from a bath, heart glowing with the belief that James Parker loved her—*only* her—and that she loved him back. There had been that disconcerting dream, yes, but she had pushed that cleanly from of her mind. Now, with the news that James had a past—and Tam, too—the dream flashed back briefly. She pushed it aside again. That had only been a dream, after all, and in it, Hoke had arrived before anyone could have accused her of sin.

But this wasn't about *her*; it was about Tam! And James!

Who were these people to whom she had been giving her heart and trust?

Corrine looked down to avoid looking at Tam. Her eyes fixed on the stain on her blouse. She had scrubbed the spot hard but had failed to turn it snowy white again. Why did everything have to be so hard? Corrine wanted to go home. Things were simpler there. Should she ride back to Fort Bridger and try to catch a wagon train when one came through? What kind of people might those strangers be?

The questions came nonstop then. Did Harry have a past, too? What about Sheriff Eston and Bennett Solomon? What might they have done? Did *they* visit brothels? Was it really any safer for her to stay with this group, with the people she had thought she knew? Or should she take her chances with others?

Corrine had never known anyone who did such things. She'd only ever heard whispers about people who lived on the fringes, not about people she lived in such close quarters with...people that she took for granted had always behaved and lived as she had.

Corrine looked back at Tam with a dark twist in her brow. She didn't know whether to be hurt or angry, but leaned toward the latter. "Why *did* you let me come out here?"

Tam's jaw dropped. "Because you begged me! There was all that talk of how James needed you! Listen, if you can't accept the realities of life, you ought not to have insisted on coming. I only let you come because you seemed so bound and determined. But don't you go pointing fingers at me or Harry just because you don't like how things are."

Corrine's chest felt tight. She'd never been on the receiving end of Tam's anger before, but she didn't care—she was mad, too! Corrine felt betrayed...lied to...and worst of all, ignorant. Now what was she supposed to do? She had been sleeping next to a sullied woman and chasing a sullied man. What did that make *her*?

A young, blind fool, that's what.

She wanted to bring the world back into its former focus, but couldn't make things slide back into place. Even their color hues had shifted.

"Does Harry know about your background?"

Tam nodded. "He does. And now you can appreciate why I love him so much. Harry Sims is a good man if ever there was one."

Corrine wasn't sure she agreed. Was Harry a fool, like her? *And Harry a preacher!* Tam was a preacher's wife. Surely there was a biblical law against such things. And now they were bringing a child into the world.

"Who else knows?" asked Corrine.

"Nobody, unless Harry's told 'em, and I don't think he has. I'd appreciate it if you don't tell."

Corrine looked at Tam—really looked at her. Tam's dark hair was pulled up in a loose knot, the first streaks of silver starting at her temples. Her warm brown eyes crinkled at the corners, the lines formed there by her normally ready smile...or had those crinkles been etched from pain?

Nothing about the woman who stood in front of Corrine shouted evidence of her past, not even the bloomers. Tam was right: she'd worn bloomers since Corrine had first met her, and Corrine had never suspected Tam of being anything but practical.

It hadn't occurred to Corrine that someone she liked—admired, even—could be guilty of having done things she'd always been taught were wrong.

"I won't tell," muttered Corrine.

"I'm sorry it's not a perfect world, dear." Tam shook her head and took up their horses' reins. "It's time we got back to the others."

CHAPTER 13
"Gunshots. Two."

The Waldens chose a spot behind a large rock formation at a point where the trail curved and rose. Then they waited. And they watched.

First three riders came into view below them, then one more, trailing behind.

"There were five riders before Fort Bridger," said Baron.

"Maybe one of 'em's laggin'...or stayed at the fort," said Viscount.

"That's the girl, in back," said Duke. "I'll get her. Shoot the others. Take good aim, now. I don't want her hit. We need her."

Baron pointed at the first man and indicated for Viscount to take the second. That left the third man for Marquis, who slipped off his horse and seemingly melted into the scrap land below.

Viscount shook his head. "Always prefers knives over bullets."

Duke held up a hand demanding silence, giving Marquis time to get into place. When he lowered his hand, Viscount and Baron fired and the front men toppled over. Over their gun sights they saw Marquis leap from the side of the trail and cleanly sweep his knife across the third man's throat.

Duke charged his horse toward the girl, who was trying to get her rifle raised from a side scabbard. She'd just cleared it when Duke kicked the side of her horse with his one good leg, knocking it from her hands.

She flew off her horse and hit the ground. Before she stopped rolling and could get her feet beneath her, Marquis put his boot in the middle of her back and shoved her down.

Baron checked the men they'd shot. "Two dead."

Viscount chuckled and turned over the one Marquis had cut. The man clawed wildly, trying to put his throat back together. "This one's not dead yet, but he will be, oh…there he goes."

The man stopped moving.

Favoring his shot leg, Duke dismounted and pulled the worn piece of newspaper from his jacket pocket. He held it next to the girl's face as she writhed on the ground, trying to get out from under Marquis' boot.

She turned her face toward him.

"You're not the girl we're looking for." Duke pointed to the three dead men on the ground around her. "Is this all your party?"

"Yes."

"Marquis, go see if there's another group coming."

Marquis mounted and disappeared down the trail.

Baron and Viscount stepped over to look at the girl as Duke took her arm and hauled her up.

"Please don't hurt me," she said. "Maybe I can be helpful to you. I can cook." She looked at Baron and Viscount. "I can keep you comp'ny."

Duke spat. "We're not looking for comp'ny. Who are you?"

"How old are you?" asked Viscount.

"Twenty-three."

"Don't talk to her!" said Duke. "Answer me, Miss."

"My name is Sairee...Sairee Adams."

"Who are these men we just killed, and where were you headed?"

"Just three men I met yesterday. I needed someone to travel with. I was headed to Baker City with another group, but at Fort Bridger I learned the man I was looking for had come down this way, toward Silvertown, so I threw in with these men."

"Who are you looking for?"

"A man I used to know. We were supposed to get married, but he ran out on me."

Duke thrust the torn newspaper under her nose. "We're looking for the light-haired girl in this picture. You seen her? You know her?"

Sairee shook her head, but her eyes registered surprise.

Duke slapped her across the face. "Don't you lie to me, Sairee Adams. You know her!"

Sairee Adams held her cheek. "No, I don't! I've never seen her before in my life. I swear. But I know *him*." She pointed.

"That's the man I was talking about, the man who ran out on me. James Parker."

*   *   *

Corrine and Tam had just caught up with the men when Sheriff Eston pulled back on his horse's reins. "You hear that?"

Harry nodded. "Gunshots. Two."

Solomon scanned the horizon. "I didn't hear a thing."

"Your senses are dull from working indoors," said Eston. "Sims, why don't you scout ahead? We'll swing due east, to be on the safe side."

"Hold up there, Eston," demanded Tam. She looked at her husband. "Harry, don't give me that look. I'm tired of him barkin' orders at us all the time." She pointed her finger at Eston. "Now, aren't you the sheriff? Shouldn't *you* go south and investigate those gunshots, and let Harry lead us east?"

Eston frowned. "I normally would. But if you want to know the truth, I had a little much to drink last night and think Harry is the better man for it."

"Humph," Tam grumbled. "I'm sure he *is* the better man for it. But it's not his problem you're not yourself this morning."

"Tam," said Harry quietly. "Go with the sheriff. We're wasting precious time arguing. I'll circle back around and join you soon enough."

Tam's brown eyes crinkled with worry. "I don't like it, Harry."

Harry stepped his horse over and laid a thick hand on his wife's arm. "It'll be all right. I know how to take care of myself."

"Don't take any chances, Harry. Promise me. I need you."

Harry's lips curled into a smile below his handlebar mustache. "I'll join you soon enough. Now go on. Stop giving the sheriff a hard time."

"Ain't no point in him barkin' orders at us all the time," Tam muttered as she fell in line behind Eston and Corrine, with Solomon taking the rear.

Tam continued to grumble as Harry spurred his horse in the direction of the gunshots. Corrine knew she was part of the cause; she had upset Tam by not receiving her news well. But Corrine didn't care. Her heart still smarted with disappointment. What was she doing out here, chasing a man she wasn't going to marry? She only longed to see Charlie now—to be with a member of her own family, someone she really knew...someone she could trust.

Tam kept looking over her shoulder, watching Harry get smaller and smaller on the horizon. "It's not our problem if he can't hold his liquor," she muttered. "Ought not to have been drinkin' in the first place."

"Tell her to keep quiet back there," Eston hissed to Corrine. "Until we know we're in the clear."

Corrine turned what she intended to be a pleading look on Tam, but suspected it came across more like fuming.

The memory of Corrine's dream came back to her and her heart began to beat wildly. Could this day—this month, this year—hold any more upheaval? Or was her whole world destined to slide crashing over a cliff?

*   *   *

Harry Sims was a preacher out West now, but that hadn't always been the case. He'd been raised in the swamps of Louisiana, where snakes and gators lurked in ankle-deep waters and up on nearby banks. Harry had learned early on to step light and careful, so as not to attract the attention of any man or beast that might seek to cut his life short.

He could tell there was something abnormal about the terrain just ahead of him…something out of place to the regular lay of the land. Then he came up on the bodies of two men who'd been shot, and another with his throat slit.

After waiting behind the cover of a mid-sized rock formation, wanting to be sure the force that had snuffed out the lives of these men had moved on, Harry eased in and inspected the bodies. Best he could tell by the signs left behind, the men had been ambushed by an equal number of riders. One horse, its rider lighter than the rest, had ridden up with the slain men, then ridden on with the ones who'd killed them.

Harry was just straightening up from studying the tracks when he heard the click of a hammer. Being more methodical than quick, Harry knew he couldn't get his weapon up fast enough to defend his life. So he waited.

He didn't want to die.

The will to live is naturally strong in most men, and it had grown stronger still in Harry since the day he met Tam Woodford. Harry had never expected to find a wife—not on the trip West, not anywhere. When he'd been called to ministry, Harry had fancied himself like the apostle Paul and prepared for a life of celibacy. It didn't seem a particular hardship, since no woman ever looked twice in his direction.

But then Tam Woodford did. She looked at him twice and looked at him hard, as if her eyes could see straight through to his soul.

God was surely watching over him. Harry didn't know what had made him join Colonel Dotson's wagon train back in April. He'd simply felt a call to go west and answered it, just like he'd felt a call to preach and answered that.

Tam had gotten eyes for him from the first night, evidently, from the first prayer he uttered over the group standing in a field in Independence. Tam had pursued him. If she hadn't, they'd both still be alone and that child growing in her womb right now would never have had the chance to be.

The thought of their child now, and his desire to know it and protect it, made Harry stretch his hands high, just as high as he could send them.

"Don't shoot."

The last thing Harry had told Tam was that he knew how to take care of himself, and here he'd let someone get the drop on him!

"Turn around slow," said a voice that seemed well practiced with the words.

As he did, a man with a silver badge came into sight.

"Who are you?" demanded the man. "And what are you doing here?"

"Name is Sims."

"Sims?" The man's brow furrowed. "From Baker City?"

He lowered the rifle and stuck a burly hand out. "Collin Mears. I been lookin' for you. Following the Waldens. You with Sheriff Eston?"

Harry nodded. "We heard shots."

"So did I."

"I came to see what I could learn while the others rode on toward Silvertown. That's where Parker's group is headed."

"The Waldens have been here all right." Marshal Mears pointed at the man with the throat wound. "That's the work of Marquis, the oldest. So this isn't your bunch?"

Harry shook his head.

"I was worried it was. Didn't know what any of you looked like, except the girl."

Harry looked closer at the faces of the slain. "Must be the group that left Fort Bridger ahead of us. I didn't talk to any of them myself, but I understand there was a woman with them." Harry pointed at the light horse tracks. "Looks like she went on, but I can't tell if she wanted to or not. Seems like she didn't put up much of a fuss."

"You know anything about her?"

"No. But my wife had a conversation with her."

Mears looked down at the bodies. "Mind helping me bury these men?"

Harry breathed with relief. He was just glad not to have been left on the ground himself.

Yes, he thought. God was surely watching over him.

CHAPTER 14
Until the world went black

Harry and Marshal Mears had traveled an hour when they heard voices being carried on the wind. Mears eased off his mustang, wrapped his bridle around a cedar branch and lifted the flap on his saddlebags, pulling out a pair of moccasins. He set his heavier boots by the base of the tree and continued on foot, motioning for Harry to follow. Harry slipped off his boots and followed in his sock feet, thinking how Tam would fuss if he wore holes in the wool.

Presently a camp came into focus. Harry and the marshal spied two young men arguing and a woman bent near the fire. An older man sat off to the side, peeling bandages from his leg. Harry could tell by the way Mears's eyes registered satisfaction that this had to be the Walden camp. He was looking at Duke Walden. And this was the woman from Fort Bridger who had been traveling with the slain men Harry and Mears had buried.

"What happened to your leg?" the woman asked Walden.

The old man scowled at her. "Nobody said you could talk."

When he went back to tending his leg the woman spit silently into the pot she was stirring. Harry and Mears looked at one another.

The woman hadn't gone willingly.

Her eyes cast around the camp, as if she was looking for a way of escape, and all at once landed on Mears. Harry saw her eyes widen in surprise. He looked over and saw Mears put a finger to his lips. The woman nodded. But then she reached for a rag.

Harry Sims didn't consider himself a prophetic man, but he knew what was going to happen seconds before it played out in front of him.

The woman wrapped the rag around the pot handle.

Mears held up a hand, shaking his head hard, signaling for her to wait. They hadn't yet accounted for Marquis.

But as soon as the woman had a good grip, she nodded at Mears again, ignoring his frantic motions. She lifted the pot and slung its contents behind her toward the two young men who were arguing.

Mears took aim on Duke Walden, but before he could get his shot off, one of the young men leapt forward and raised his gun while the other knocked the girl to the ground. Flat on his stomach several yards away from the marshal, Harry heard the shot and saw Mears's body jerk and his rifle fall. Then Harry felt a searing pain in his own shoulder.

He looked down and saw the handle of a knife, the blade buried to the hilt. A man was running toward him — Marquis!

Harry raised his rifle and shot, knowing he would miss. His eyes never really landed on Marquis. The man had materialized from nowhere and was moving fast.

But the shot was enough to make Marquis drop and roll away from Harry. As soon as he did, Harry jumped up and ran for his horse. He pulled the knife from his shoulder—it had bypassed the bone. He flung it away and felt something slam into his right leg but kept running, knowing he had to reach his horse if he was to ever see his wife again.

The image of Mears' body jerking on the ground loomed large in Harry's mind. *Lord, make me swift. Give me wings. Help me fly. Back to my wife and the child she carries.*

As Harry reached to pull his horse's bridle loose, he felt another slam, this one in his hip. He jerked the leather from the tree—stripping the branch, tearing off a large piece of cedar, freeing the reins of Mears' mount, too—as he threw himself over his own horse, swatting its rump with the branch as he charged away.

Harry kept swatting the steed's rump and riding, riding and losing blood, losing blood and swatting the rump, until the world went black.

*   *   *

Duke Walden, unable to put weight on his leg, used the barrel of his rifle like a crutch to hobble over and inspect the body. He poked at the man on the ground with the rifle once he reached him. The metal of the barrel clinked against the silver badge.

Baron spoke behind him. "I'll go after the other one, Pa!"

"No!" Duke stopped him. "We need to ride on to Silvertown. My leg's got hot." Duke turned from the body on the ground and looked at the girl. Viscount had dragged her over by the arm. "You try another stunt like that, and I'll put a bullet in *your* leg."

The woman looked down darkly at the man on the ground. "He was a lawman. He was going to help me."

"But you helped *him* instead," said Viscount.

"Helped him die," said Duke.

Pulling the girl awkwardly with him, Viscount reached down and wrested the neckerchief off the body on the ground. After using it to tie Sairee Adams's hands behind her back, he pulled her over to her horse and lifted her up on it.

"You best listen to him," Duke heard Viscount warn her. "He don't say things unless he means 'em."

Baron and Marquis packed the camp up.

Duke saw Sairee Adams lean down to Viscount from the back of her horse. She smiled at him and whispered. "Say, how 'bout me and you go our own way when we get to Silvertown? I could treat you real nice."

Viscount glanced at his father. "I bet you could. But you ain't a Walden. A Walden don't leave his own for nobody. I don't care how hard you bat your eyes. 'Sides, Baron done told me you already tried that on him. You might as well not bother with Marquis. I don't think he knows there's a difference in men and women."

Baron stepped his horse toward them. "Pa's only keepin' you alive for bargainin' power, Miss. I wouldn't cross him again if I was you."

Duke would have smiled if he had been a smiling man. He'd raised those boys right.

*   *   *

At midday, James, Charlie, Bart Peters and Michael Chessor stopped at a stream to rest a minute and let their horses drink.

"We should reach Silvertown in another couple days," announced James.

"I guess we know where you're goin' when we get there." Peters grinned at Chessor.

James ignored them and stepped upstream to refill his canteen. He got far enough away so he could only faintly hear their voices.

"One night and he made use of both their services," said Chessor. He and Peters exchanged grins.

"What are you talking about?" asked Charlie.

"You didn't hear about James making the rounds with the women at Fort Bridger?"

"What women?"

"You didn't hear about those two women?"

"No. What...some of the officers' wives or something?"

Peters and Chessor laughed.

"Doves, Charlie," said Chessor.

"'Doves'? What does that mean?"

James straightened and took a long drink from his canteen, only half paying attention to the conversation downstream.

"Women who sell their services, Charlie. Prairie doves."

Charlie's forehead didn't twist like his mother's and sister's; it shot together in a hard 'V'. "What does that have to do with James?"

Then the meaning of what they'd said finally registered. James knew it had, because as he wiped his mouth and put the cap back on his canteen, he turned and saw Charlie barreling down the hill at him.

James had never seen Charlie Baldwyn riled before. But now, the young man's neck veins popped below a red face, and his hands spread wide, reaching for James's throat.

Charlie lunged at him.

James sidestepped and threw his canteen on the bank.

From the middle of the stream, where he now stood, dripping, Charlie turned on James like an angry bear. "You spent time with low women? Don't you go near Corrine again! Hear me?"

James raised his hands to show Charlie he wasn't the enemy. "Charlie, I did spend time with 'em — "

"How *could* you, James?"

" — but I didn't make use of their services. I offered 'em enough money to give 'em a break, is all."

Charlie lunged again, this time catching James around the waist. They hit the bank with a hard thud and rolled. Charlie's head was like a boulder against James's stomach, pushing the wind out.

As they wrestled for the upper hand, James finally got Charlie's head out of his stomach. The wind rushed back in and filled his lungs. "Women..." James deflected Charlie's fist swinging wildly for his face. "...in those circumstances don't want to be...they just..." Charlie's knee found the same spot his head had recently vacated. James pushed it away with his elbow. "They just don't feel like they have any other choice."

Charlie's arm stretched up, his hand reaching to get James in a chokehold. James ducked and snaked his own arm around Charlie's neck. "How many men come along and give 'em money and don't require anything of 'em?"

James nudged Charlie over with his knee, then pinned the younger man's arms to his side and answered his own question. "Not many, that's how many."

Charlie's boots sprayed clods of earth as he kicked them on the ground, trying to get free of James's hold. Charlie was squirmier and even harder to handle than his sister had been the day Emma died.

"You expect me to believe you didn't take something in return? How gullible do you think I am, James?" Charlie twisted. James was hard-pressed to hold him.

"I don't care if you believe me or not!" He tightened his grip, suddenly mad. This wasn't the first time he'd had to defend himself against others' accusations. He was used to it. But it made him angry that Charlie didn't believe him. Charlie Baldwyn was the one young man whose good opinion meant something to James.

"It's God's honest truth," he snarled in Charlie's ear. "You can ask Hoke when you get home, or Harry Sims. If I know there's a brothel nearby, I go find it. I look for the girl who's the least tainted, the one who seems like she hasn't sold her entire soul to hopelessness yet, and I tell her to wash her paint off, put on a normal dress, and sit and talk with me about how she ended up there."

Charlie's twisting grew weaker. But James could see that the younger man still didn't fully believe him.

"It's God's honest truth," James said again. He released Charlie and pushed him away on the creek bank, spent from fighting.

Charlie stood up, his countenance low. But he didn't rush at James again. "And those women don't throw themselves on you? You telling me you don't take advantage of it?"

James stood and brushed himself off, keeping up his guard. He'd given Charlie a couple of knife throwing lessons, and hoped Charlie wouldn't practice what he'd learned on him.

"They do throw themselves on me...nearly every time. They can't believe I'm serious and don't want nothin' from 'em. They're used to men cryin' into their breasts, or throwin' their sick all over 'em from bein' drunk. Nobody ever looks a woman like that in the eye and says, 'How are you, Sweetheart?' 'What kind of life did you hope for when you were a little girl?' Or, 'When was the last time you had a night off?'"

Charlie's eyes widened. "You don't worry about your reputation, James?"

"Only family I've got is my grandmaw, Charlie, and she's the one that got me doin' it. I lived around sullied women all my life."

"Your *grandmother* was one?"

James shook his head. Convinced Charlie's temper had sufficiently cooled, he allowed himself to break eye contact and pick up the canteen he'd thrown on the ground.

"No. My grandmaw was a midwife. A lot of times, doctors and other midwives—so called respectable women— won't help a sullied woman if she gets with child. And they get with child all the time. Hazard of their profession. Some of 'em are real young when it happens, fourteen or fifteen...and scared to death."

Charlie sat down on the creek bank and held his head in his hands. "What is the matter with people?"

James sat next to him and waited for their breath to grow more even. "A lot of people have splintered lives, Charlie," he said. "Especially out here. And a splintered life can lead to ugly behavior. It doesn't have to, just often does. Part of what you're feeling is the pain of having your eyes stretched."

Charlie looked up at him darkly. "I buried the girl I loved, James, don't tell me I don't understand there's disappointment in life."

James held his palms up. "I mean no insult, Charlie. But my eyes got stretched early. I grew up around brothels, seeing the worst of humanity. It made me want to be different."

He lowered his hands and leaned back on them, taking a minute to enjoy the sound of the water gurgling in the creek and the cool grass on the bank beneath them. "When I met Hoke, I could tell he'd had a hard upbringing, too. We don't ever talk about it, but I knew he was searching for a future that was different from his past. I understand why he was drawn to your family. There's something fine and pure about every one of you. That's a credit to your mother. Your father, too. And anybody else who had a hand in raising you."

"Mimi."

"The woman who cooked for your family in Tennessee?"

Charlie nodded.

"If she helped raise you, she must be a good person."

"She is." Charlie looked at James now with less malice in his eyes. "How do you keep your heart from being bitter?"

James grinned. "That's a credit to the little bitty woman who raised me. She's not much bigger than a sack of cattle feed, but I never knew a woman with more spit and fire. She poured love into everybody around her. Sure poured a lot into me. I hear her voice in my head all the time, telling me what to do and what not to do."

"I hear Mimi's voice in my head, too." Charlie ran a hand through his hair, knocking out leaves that had stuck there as they tussled. "And I still remember a lot of things my father taught me. I feel bad Jacob didn't get to know him better before he died."

"I'd wager he has a pretty clear picture of your father...thanks to you."

Charlie looked at James again. The young man had had the clear blue eyes of a boy when James first met him.

Not anymore.

"We all help put voices, good or bad, in another person's head, Charlie. Never forget that."

Those blue eyes burned into him. "You can't be going to brothels if you marry my sister, James."

"I know." James nodded. "Hoke's given me plenty of lectures about that. That's why we're taking this route through Silvertown. I'm lookin' for a new way to help. I want to find my grandmaw and convince her to come to Baker City. If I can get her there, she'll spread her good like a medicine. You know the cook from the D&J?"

Charlie nodded.

"She wants to start her own café, and a home for women down on their luck, to teach them new skills, like cookin' and sewin'. She has some good ideas that remind me of things my grandmaw used to say. I was goin' to send my reward money to my grandmaw, but after hearing Hannah's plans, I decided I wanted to bring my grandmaw back to Baker City. I'd like to get the two of 'em together. I figure then I can focus on makin' me a family of my own. With your sister."

"Are we not going to Kansas, then?"

"Oh no, I still plan to go after that horse herd. I just want to find my grandmaw first." A soft wind blew down the creek bank and ruffled his hair. James looked up. Clouds were rolling in. "If I'm goin' to settle, I'd like to have her close by."

CHAPTER 15
Crumbled pieces all around

Sam Eston led Corrine, Tam and Solomon toward Silvertown for two more days. They kept waiting for Harry to rejoin them. But he never did.

Tam looked back over her shoulder so much, Corrine feared she would get a crick in her neck. When they stopped the evening of the second day to make camp, the worry lines in Tam's forehead etched so deep Corrine was sorry she'd ever been cross with her.

"At first light, I'm ridin' back to find Harry," Tam announced over their meager supper of beans and bacon. Solomon still had a pone of cornbread he'd been rationing since they'd left Fort Bridger. He handed out crumbled pieces all around. Tam refused hers and hardly touched her beans and bacon.

"You'll need your strength, Mrs. Sims," said Solomon.

Tam's eyes looked blankly at the newspaperman as she rubbed her growing abdomen. The bloomers were stretching tighter across her belly. Corrine hadn't thought about what Tam would do if she outgrew them. The skirt and petticoats

Corrine had been wearing when she got to Tam and Harry's were stuffed in the bottom of one of her saddlebags. She'd offer the fabric to Tam soon, and see if she couldn't use it to rework the waist of Tam's bloomers to accommodate her growing girth. Perhaps the gesture would help ease the tension between the two women, in addition to easing the tension in Tam's waistline.

"You can't be riding back to check on him by yourself." Eston's eyes swept over Tam's middle.

Tam stood up and clenched her fists to her sides. "I can, and I will!"

"If anybody goes to check on him, it'll be me," said Eston.

"Then do it!"

"What will the three of you do while I'm gone?"

"Wait right here. I'm not movin' another inch without my husband." From the way Tam crossed her arms and stood rooted, Corrine wondered if she intended to stay in that precise spot until Harry reappeared.

"But surely we're gaining ground on Parker's group!" said Solomon, ever the optimist. "We have to be close to 'em."

"If you want to ride on to catch him, you go ahead," said Tam. "Me? I'm not going any farther until I know Harry's safe. I never should have let him go investigate those gunshots. If anything's happened to him, Sam Eston, I'll have your hide!"

"Please," said Corrine. She didn't like the thought of Eston riding off in one direction and Solomon, in the other.

"Can't we talk about what's best without pointing fingers? Harry's a capable man, Tam. I'm sure he's fine. He's just gotten delayed somehow." Even as the words left her mouth, Corrine knew they sounded feeble.

Suddenly, it began to rain.

Tam's eyes flashed as she went and pulled a rain poncho from her saddlebags. "You think I don't know what a capable man my husband is? Of course I do! But he should have been back by now and you know it. The only reason I haven't ridden back to check on him already is you, Corrine. I don't feel like I ought to leave you unchaperoned. But nobody asked you to come on this trip. You insisted on it, going against your mother's wishes. The Bible says thou art to *honor* thy mother and father, and you didn't!"

Corrine wasn't one to weep lightly, but Tam's words pierced her. She had to work hard to hold back tears. If anything had happened to Harry, she knew Tam wouldn't only blame the sheriff.

Shame and worry closed her mouth. Corrine didn't say another word to Tam that evening as she huddled under her own rain slicker. In fact, hardly a word was spoken by anyone in the group. Moods were as damp as the evening.

Solomon threw Corrine several regretful glances, as if trying to tell her he was sorry she'd gotten a tongue-lashing. But Corrine turned away, unable to stomach his sympathy. She was determined not to spill the flood of tears that was still building behind her eyes. This meant staring hard at the rain soaked ground or off in the direction their party was headed. Meeting Solomon's or Eston's glance would prove her undoing if she saw any caring there. Staring at a raindrop hanging off the slicker near her eyes, she longed for her charcoal pencil so she could sketch it. The act of drawing might have brought her some relief.

She knew right where she had left the pencil and her drawing pad: in the hope chest James made for her. Should she keep the hope chest, now that she knew James was a scoundrel? Would she ever make it back home, where she'd have that option?

Thoughts of the warm dry cabin Hoke had built overtook her mind. She longed to be back there. She longed to have Lina curl up beside her on their quilt-covered bed. How hard the ground was every night when she laid her tired body on it! How wet and damp this evening promised to be, as the rain continued to fall on her oiled slicker and roll off the ends. Her arms were tired from holding it over her head.

As she dropped her arms and pulled the slicker tighter around her chin, she could almost smell her mother's biscuits. It didn't matter to her anymore that they weren't as good as Mimi's. They would have tasted like heaven compared to the stale pieces of Solomon's crumbled corn pone that now sat like stones in her near-empty stomach.

*   *   *

Abigail held a feathered quill in her hand but had trouble focusing on the blank parchment that lay before her on the table. The top of the inkwell was open but she had yet to fill her pen.

Where were Charlie and Corrine? Had they found one another yet? Were they safe? And would the telegraph line to Baker City *ever* get repaired? Hoke had ridden into town to check on it. Again.

She watched Lina and Jacob play on the other side of the room with the small figurines James had fashioned for them out of wood pieces and given them at Christmas.

She took a deep breath and dipped her quill into the ink.

June 10, 1867

Dearest Mimi,

My heart is heavy and looking for ease. Where shall I begin?

Abigail had resisted the urge to write to Mimi for weeks. Now that she was allowing herself to, she felt instant comfort in releasing her fears to the parchment. She might never see Mimi again this side of heaven, but at least she had the knowledge that the former slave she loved was thriving and happy back in Tennessee. And though letter writing was a slower process than unburdening herself in person, Abigail still had the means to pour out her heart to her friend.

She told Mimi about Emma's tragic death and Charlie and Corrine's leaving.

You and I did not raise these children to be impulsive, Mimi.
Hoke says you have to let children grow wings or they won't be strong to face their lives. But this not knowing, Mimi…this not

knowing may be the hardest challenge I have ever confronted as a mother.

It was hard to watch Robert go off to war. It was hard to see you ride off in Arlon's buckboard. It was hard to pack my family into two prairie schooners for a five-month journey into the unknown. It was hard to see Lina sick when she contracted fever on the trip. It was hard to be separated from the children, and to think I might not get the chance to finish raising them. But this? This is harder still.

This impulsiveness that has taken Charlie and Corrine from the safety of the roof Hoke provided — does it signal an abrupt end to my role in their lives? The swift, unexpected nature of these events has left me restless and offered a test to my faith like no other I have yet endured.

Hoke would go after them if I demanded it — would pluck them up from wherever they've gone and force them home. But I can't bring myself to insist upon it, knowing he believes it best to let them go.

To let them go.

I can hardly bear the pain of letting them go, Mimi.

What will happen to them? I close my eyes and try to hear what you might say to comfort me. I long for your words and prayers. Were it not so selfish a request, I would beg you to come to me. But you mustn't.

Mimi had her own life to live, and a husband. Her Thomas was her priority now.

Give Thomas my love.

All I ask is your prayers for Charlie and Corrine. Pray God keeps them safe and brings them home to me. I keep trying to make my family whole, and rips keep bursting in the seams of my fabric.

Abigail heard the hard, steady thud of a horse coming up the hill. She stood and went to the window. It was Hoke. Her heart never failed to quicken at the sight of him, even when she hurt...especially when she hurt.

Jacob jumped up. "Is that Pa?"

Abigail's already full heart grew fuller still at hearing Jacob call Hoke "Pa." She nodded. Jacob ran outside to meet him.

Abigail looked back down at her letter. She longed to share news of the coming baby with Mimi, too, but couldn't bring herself to do it. She'd never given birth without Mimi by her side. But she feared if she included that news, Mimi would indeed make the arduous journey west. Abigail didn't need one more person she loved putting herself at risk, certainly not on her account.

She picked up the letter, walked to the kitchen, then opened the lid to the stove and fed the letter to the flames.

It was too selfish to worry Mimi with her burdens.

*   *   *

Harry woke to the sound of rain falling, but no rain was soaking him. He opened his eyes and saw a dark-skinned woman tending to a fire. He lay on a straw bed in the corner of a cabin. When he tried to rise, the straw made a crunching noise and the woman rushed to his side.

"Don't you be gettin' up. José said you need to keep still."

Harry laid back down, the smell of a hot stew filling his nose. "Who is José?"

The woman spoke in quick low clips. "Never you mind. He'll be back here directly."

His shoulder burned. Harry remembered the knife blade and looked down. The knife was gone. Had he pulled it out himself? His shirt was off and a seeping bandage covered his wound. His leg and hip burned, too. His hands felt like blocks of wood as he tried to ease a worn quilt off his leg.

"You tryin' to see where all you was hit?"

The woman came back to stand beside the bed. She wore a blue cloth wrapped around her head and as she moved closer, James thought he caught a whiff of cornmeal. She pulled the quilt back to show him his wound sites, careful to respect that he was naked underneath.

"Both bullets are out. I've got your clothes. Mended 'em. Got the blood out with a paste. I make it with meal. Rub it, lay it in the sun to dry, then brush the paste off. That's the way I do it. Only works if the blood's still wet."

He put a thick hand on hers. "How long have I been here, Miss? Or is it Mrs.?"

"Humpf." She sniffed. "Ought to be Mrs., but it's not. You been here two days."

"How did I get here?"

"José brought you. You had nearly bled out when he found you. Lost a lot from that shoulder. Took two handfuls of meal to make the paste. José was on his way to Fort Bridger."

"Who is José?"

"I told you: never you mind." She tucked the quilt back in around his legs and torso, wrapping him tight, like a swaddled infant. "He's the master of this here dwellin', that's who."

Harry let his eyes roll over his surroundings. He was in a cabin, rough-hewn in the old style. Either José had built it crudely or he and this woman had found it, abandoned.

Harry tried to guess the woman's age, but her skin was so smooth, it was hard to tell. As he watched, she went back to the fire. "José killed the last chicken this mornin'," she said. "All for you. Said to cook you a broth. He'll make that trip to Fort Bridger soon enough for more. This one had quit layin' anyway. We need us a rooster, is what we need, so we can grow us more chickens. But José worries about folks hearin' it. He don't want anybody to know we're here. He don't want anybody to know *I'm* here."

She brought the steaming bowl over and sat beside James, on her knees. She had trapped his arms inside the tuck of the quilt. "If we tend you, you're not goin' to tell anyone we're here, are you?"

Harry felt as helpless as a babe. But it wasn't a bad feeling. If this woman and José had meant him harm, he wouldn't be lying in this cabin, smelling a broth from their last chicken. "No, ma'am. I won't if you don't want me to."

She softened her demeanor then. "José is a good man. He don't deserve what people would do to him if they knew he was livin' with me."

She spooned broth into Harry's mouth then. He could have fed himself. It was his left shoulder that was cut. But she had such an authoritative air he wasn't eager to question her.

Good Lord, that soup tasted good!

As his belly filled, Harry felt his eyelids droop. "Tell José thank you if I'm asleep when he gets back. That was the best stew I've ever had. You're a mighty fine cook, Mrs. José."

Harry saw the corners of her lips turn upward, revealing the whitest, straightest teeth he'd ever seen on a human.

Then he lost consciousness.

*   *   *

Hoke was splitting firewood with Jacob when he saw a rider coming up the hill, headed fast toward the cabin.

"Run and tell your mother Clyde Austelle is coming."

"How do you know it's Clyde?" asked Jacob, squinting. The rider was still a half-mile away.

"Because he wears a tan hat and the Austelles have a red horse with a white rear leg." It was a fine horse, as tall as the stallion.

"Oh." Jacob ran to the cabin.

Hoke met Clyde at the top of the trail as Abigail, Jacob and Lina all ran out to join him.

Clyde held up a paper, breathing hard. "Telegraph's repaired! This just came through—from Fort Bridger. Colonel Dotson said run it out to you quick."

Hoke reached for the paper.

BODY OF MARSHALL MEARS FOUND NEAR FT BRIDGER STOP WALDENS BELIEVED RESPONSIBLE STOP

Hoke stared at the telegram in his hand. Two nights ago, he had dreamed he was on the trail again. He hadn't told Abigail about the dream, not wanting to worry her. But now he knew.

It was time for him to go.

CHAPTER 16

An internal meter

When restlessness had fallen on Hoke two days before the telegram's arrival, he hadn't said anything to Abigail. But she knew him well enough to know his mind was not at ease.

"What is it?" she had asked the day after his dream.

"I don't know yet," he said. "I just feel bothered."

"How do you know to be bothered if you don't know what's bothering you?"

"I don't know," he admitted. "It might not be anything. If it *is* something, it'll show itself."

And it did, the next day, in the form of Clyde Austelle riding up their hill.

Ever since Hoke was a child he'd had an internal meter to warn him of danger. He never could explain it, and no one could explain it for him. But that meter had rarely failed him. He had learned to simply be grateful for the heightened awareness that so often kept him safe and moving in the right direction.

Hoke handed Abigail the note and looked up at Clyde, noting the worry on the young man's face. Clyde had been a good friend to Charlie, and if Hoke's gut served him right, Clyde would have made a play for Corrine if James's feelings for her hadn't been so obvious. Clyde was younger than Corrine, but he had all the makings of a solid man.

"Ma said for your family to come stay with us if you go."

Hoke's gut twisted the same way Abigail's brow did as she soaked in the meaning of the block letters in the telegram. The plea that hung in her eyes when she looked up at him…. If he hadn't already known he was supposed to go, that look would have been reason enough to decide it.

"Tell your Ma we'll be there directly." Hoke smacked the rear of Clyde's horse, sending him back down the hill.

As Abigail ran to the cabin to pack, Hoke went to the barn to harness the mules and wagon. He threw his saddle in the buckboard and tied the white filly and stallion to the back as the details began to work themselves out in his mind.

He'd leave his family, Rascal, the filly, and the mules with the Austelles. He'd take the stallion with him, of course.

He picked up the second saddle—the one James had brought back from town the day Emma died—and started to put it in the buckboard. If he took two horses, he could rotate between them and travel faster. But he didn't like the thought of taking the filly.

It would surely test the strength of the stallion to have to ride as hard as Hoke was going to push him. But Hoke didn't want to draw any unnecessary attention. The filly, being white, would make him more of a target. He would need to travel at night and the filly would draw the reflection of the moon.

Hoke set the second saddle back in the barn. The stallion would have to do the job, at least until Fort Bridger. Hoke could pick up a second horse there.

He ran his hand over the black horse's flanks and whispered, "May God give you strength — a double portion — and clothe your neck with thunder." He would keep uttering that prayer until he firmly believed in it.

I could use a double portion, too.

When Hoke yawed the mules into the Austelles' yard an hour later, several folks had gathered there: Colonel Dotson and Christine, along with Gerald and Josephine Jenkins. Doc Isaacs and Nelda had come with their new baby, and with Caroline and Will. Chancey, the saloon owner, was there, too, wearing the temporary badge Sam Eston had left him, and the freckle-faced cook from the D&J stood close beside him.

George Dotson, Gerald Jenkins, Charles and Clyde Austelle all looked prepared to go with Hoke. They circled up as Hoke jumped off the wagon and reached for Abigail.

The men's willingness touched him. "Gentlemen, I'm honored, really I am. But..."

"I told you he'd rather go alone," Jenkins said to Dotson.

Dotson nodded. "You sure, Hoke?"

Hoke's hands were reluctant to turn loose of his wife's waist. He let go only when she reached to help Lina from the wagon, his throat squeezing so tight he could hardly speak.

"Best service you can offer me is to look after my family," he said. "Abigail will have the harder job, having to wait for word."

Dotson clapped Hoke on the shoulder. "I've sent a telegraph to Silvertown, in case James's group gets there before the Waldens. No other major towns between it and Bridger."

Hoke nodded.

"The Austelles offered your family a place here," Dotson continued, "but we've got plenty of room at the hotel."

"Thank you," said Hoke. He knew his family would be well cared for with the Dotsons.

"And I'll ride out to your place and check on it every few days," added Dotson.

Hoke could see that Clyde Austelle, standing beside his father, Charles, itched to go with him. But Hoke knew his best chance was to go it alone. He didn't want anything or anybody to slow him down.

"Take our red horse." Clyde said, holding out its bridle. "There's a good saddle on him, and he's fast. Got legs as long as the stallion. Having two horses will get you there sooner."

It was a fine offer. After the stallion, there wasn't a better horse in Baker City. Hoke nodded to him. "I'll do my best to bring him back to you."

The Austelles had lost their daughter to a Walden bullet. Was Hoke being selfish not to let the Austelles come with him?

In his dream, he'd ridden alone. Hoke listened to his gut.

Women had gathered around Abigail, Jacob and Lina. Hoke took his wife's hand and led her off to the side. He pushed the brim of her straw hat up so he could look into her eyes. "Sweetheart…"

She put her hand to his lips and shook her head. "I know I asked you to never leave me, Hoke. But you're right to go. I'm asking you to go."

He started to speak again and she pressed her fingers against his lips. "And nothing—*nothing*—is going to keep you from coming back here to me." She pinched the bridge of her nose with her other hand. He was well familiar with the gesture—it was meant to stem the tide of her tears. She cradled his face in her hands then, and whispered, "If it should, God forbid, I won't hold it against you. I'll always be grateful to you for trying."

Tears sprang into her eyes then. When he saw them, he felt his own fill.

"But you *are* coming back to me," she whispered. She bit her lower lip to try to stop it from quivering and shook her head as if angry that her body was not cooperating. He could barely hear her now, her voice had dropped so low. "And you're going to bring my children home. Because you are David Hoke Mathews, and God gave you eyes to see and ears to hear, and a heart that knows things sometimes without knowing why it knows them. He brought you to me once, and He can bring you to me again."

Hoke put his forehead to hers and wiped her tears with his thumbs before pulling her in. The taste of her lips under his as her hat was knocked to the ground…that was a memory that would stay with him throughout the countless unknown miles ahead.

Finally, he released her, then bent down to kiss Lina on the forehead and muss Jacob's hair with his hand. "You're the man of the family 'til I get back, Jake."

"Yes, sir."

Jacob had taken aim on a buffalo once while sitting on a horse too big for him. The boy hadn't looked a bit worried then, and he didn't look worried now.

Good.

Hoke swung up on the stallion and took the reins of Clyde's horse, then tipped his hat to Dotson and the other men before letting his eyes feast on Abigail one last time.

"Go," she said. The tears were freely flowing now, but she was smiling.

He kicked the stallion forward with a "yah!"

*   *   *

Melinda Austelle came to stand with Abigail as she watched Hoke ride from her sight. Once he was gone, Abigail hooked her arm through Melinda's and turned to Colonel Dotson.

"How quickly can he get to Silvertown?"

"If he was an ordinary man on an ordinary horse I'd say two weeks. For Hoke? He might do it in eight days."

Abigail nodded and put a hand on her middle. Just then—at precisely the spot where she'd placed her hand—there came an unmistakable thump. It was the baby's first kick, and the kick was strong.

*   *   *

Bennett Solomon took first watch while Sam Eston whacked several evergreen limbs from a tree and built Corrine and Tam crude shelters. Still, Corrine barely slept that night as the wet seeped through her bedroll.

Up until their argument two days ago, Corrine had laid her bedroll next to Tam's every evening. But since the argument she'd put more distance between them. Even on this wet night, when it would have made sense to huddle together for warmth, Corrine didn't get the feeling Tam wanted her close. Neither had Tam protested when Eston went to the extra trouble of building two crude shelters instead of one.

Corrine's pride smarted. If Sam Eston had true feelings for Corrine, why hadn't he defended her against the onslaught of Tam's mean words? He had been quiet and brooding ever since they left Fort Bridger.

And Solomon! Corrine had found him lighthearted and witty at the start of their journey, with his James-like grin and sunny view of the world. But ever since he'd burst her hopeful outlook so completely with his revelations about James, his optimism had done nothing but irritate her.

Each time Corrine heard one of the horses nicker, or the splash of rain-filled puddles as the sheriff and Solomon changed watch in the dark, she worried Tam was leaving. If Tam left her, she'd be alone in the middle of the prairie with two grown men, men who weren't much more than strangers to her: one who had made unwelcome advances, and another who had revealed her own folly to her. But at morning's light Tam was still there, her mood as surly as the day before.

The rain had finally stopped. Sam Eston rode out at sun-up, as promised, to look for Harry.

At mid-day, just as the bedrolls they'd laid out in the sun had finally dried enough to roll back up, Tam said low to Solomon and Corrine, "Don't turn around. There's a group of men about to ride in to camp. Let me do the talkin.'"

Corrine tried to act normal but couldn't keep her heart from lurching with jagged beats that felt as hard against her chest as they were loud in her ears. "Are they Indians?"

"No. White men...white men bringing trouble."

Walking to her horse to tie her bedroll to her saddlebag, Corrine peeked over the gray dun's back. Three men...still a quarter of a mile out.

"Should we make a run for it?" Corrine asked.

"We can't outrun 'em," said Tam flatly.

"They're probably just passing through," said Solomon, his voice as upbeat as ever. "Maybe they can tell us how close we are to Silvertown. They look like they're coming from that direction. Should I put coffee on?"

Tam glared at him. "You do that, Solomon. Give 'em the last of our coffee. Be all neighborly, and see what kind of information you can learn from 'em. But don't you tell 'em anything about us. I'll do the talkin' about us." She turned, raking her eyes over Corrine, top to bottom. "We need to cover you up."

"What do you mean?"

"We need to try to make you ugly." She stepped over to Corrine's horse and dug in her saddlebag. "Here." She pulled out Corrine's old skirt. "Put this on over those bloomers." Corrine peered over the back of her horse again. The men were closer now, but still out of earshot.

"Stay behind the horse so they can't see you clear. And get your shawl out and cover your head," continued Tam. "Here." She stooped down, grabbed a handful of soft mud left from the night's rain and the mash of the horses' hooves, and smeared it on Corrine's cheeks and forehead.

"Tam!" Corrine jerked away from her.

"Hold still!" Tam slapped her across the face. "Do you want them to kill me and Solomon so they can have you?"

Corrine put a hand to her cheek. "Don't you think you're overreacting? They might be perfectly decent men."

Tam's look to Corrine was as pregnant with disdain as her belly was with child. "If they get here and they're upstandin' you can keep bein' mad at me, Corrine. If they get here and they aren't, and we both live through it? You can thank me later."

A mixture of anger and shame making her head hot, Corrine stepped into the wrinkled skirt and tied it on, careful to stay behind her horse as the three men rode toward their camp. Then she wrapped the gray shawl up over her head. The mud Tam had rubbed on Corrine's face felt heavy and stank.

"Here's our story." Tam pulled Corrine over to where Solomon stood, pulling at her blouse, rubbing more dirt on the sleeves and front, rumpling her up. They had only moments until the men arrived.

"Solomon, you're my husband, and Corrine, you're a girl we picked up on our way to Silvertown. You're sick. Hunker down and look sick, now. Sit over there. It wouldn't hurt to drool. Keep your rifle close to hand. We'll say you've got the clap."

Solomon made a face.

"What's that?" asked Corrine.

"I'll tell you later. Just stay covered and don't talk." Tam picked up her rifle and laid it over her arm.

The men were within earshot now. Corrine pulled the shawl down over her head and angled her face to the ground. She sat on a fallen log. Even with the ground still soft, she could feel the vibration of the horses' hooves through her boot soles and the tree stump beneath her.

Tensions thickened as the men rode closer. Corrine sensed that Tam was right. These men weren't upstanding. She kept her head down and didn't look up, but felt the air chill as the men came forward.

The vibrations from the horse's hooves stilled beneath Corrine's feet. Feeling the men's eyes peering around the camp, she chanced a peek from the corner of the shawl. Three men, six eyes: all of them locked on her. She looked back down at the ground.

Respectable men would have offered a greeting.

"Y'all come from Silvertown?" asked Solomon.

The man closest to where Corrine sat grunted affirmation.

"How far is it?"

"Hard day's ride," answered one of the other men. "Two, if you're travelin' with women. These both yours?"

"I'm his wife," said Tam.

One of the men must have indicated Corrine. She heard him say. "What about that one?"

"We picked her up a few days ago," said Tam. "She's sick with a fever. Brought on by clap."

The men snickered. "She a working girl, then?"

Tam shrugged. "She hadn't told us much. We're takin' her to Silvertown."

"There's Arapahoe around. We saw signs of 'em a few miles back. Huntin' party by the looks of it. You got coffee?"

"We're mighty low," said Tam. "But you should be well stocked if you just came from town."

"We'll share some with you then." The men dismounted. Corrine heard Tam huff under her breath in frustration. It would have been best if the men had moved on.

Solomon took a pot and filled it with water from his canteen. One of the men got coffee out as Solomon stoked the morning fire back up. He began to pump the men with questions, and they offered their answers readily.

The men were railroad surveyors. The Union Pacific was building from the east, they said, near Council Bluffs. The Central Pacific was coming from Sacramento.

"We got a contract with the Union Pacific," said a man with a deep voice. "We're riding out to see how far behind the Central Pacific got while they were blasting through the Sierra Mountains."

Corrine peeped out from her shawl again. The man talking had a thick black beard. "Word is, they brought in a bunch of Chinese workers."

"Dangled 'em out over the rocks to poke the dynamite in the crevices. Don't that beat all?" This came from a short stocky bald man.

"Limber as little monkeys," said the first man. "Hard workers, too. Who would have guessed that?"

Solomon seemed to warm up to the men. The third one had never spoken. He was thin-faced and sandy-haired.

As the men talked, Corrine began to breathe easier. They weren't asking questions about her anymore. These were men with jobs who might have families. She inched the shawl back from her eyes so she could study them. When Corrine's eyes fell on the third man, he was staring at her...hard.

She jerked her head down, but he stood up and walked toward her. "Hey, let me see your face." The man reached for her chin.

Tam stood up. "I wouldn't get too close to her if I was you." She tried to step between them, but the man moved too quickly.

Corrine ducked her head down, but the man's hand swept over her forehead and pulled the shawl off, causing her golden hair to spill out. The three men stared at her. Corrine tried to pull the shawl from the man's hand, but he held it fast.

"You don't have fever!" He felt for her forehead again. She pulled away, but he grabbed her arm.

"Hey!" Solomon stood up to intervene. The sandy-haired man's arm swung back, catching Solomon in the chest. He toppled backward.

Tam pointed her rifle in the air and fired. Everyone stopped. She readied for another shot, aiming the gun's barrel at the chest of the sandy-haired man. Corrine jerked her arm from the man's hand. He didn't move. Nobody moved.

Nervous chills shot up and down Corrine's spine. She hadn't felt such chills the whole journey, not even during the cold sweat that followed her nightmare or when Bennett Solomon shared his disappointing news. These were chills like the ones she'd felt when she stood in the dark on their homestead outside Baker City, saddling the dun, deciding to ride by moonlight to get to Tam and Harry's by dawn. She remembered how the air had felt like moist cotton brushing her face that morning, how the naked tree branches had stirred in the wind.

Had it all been a warning? Had the wind known she would come here, find herself in this moment? Had it known she would fall into company with rough men once she didn't have Sam Eston, Harry, Charlie, Hoke, or James Parker to protect her?

For the first time since Solomon had made his revelation about James, Corrine longed to be back in James's presence. His arms had felt so capable...so safe.

CHAPTER 17
What potion swirled

Corrine held her breath as the sandy-haired man looked down at her hair, then back up to the barrel of Tam's rifle.

The bald man jumped up and pointed at Corrine. "You were lying to us! She don't have the clap."

Tam held the rifle barrel steady. The sandy-haired man started to pull his sleeve down, as if he meant to use it to rub the mud from Corrine's face, but Tam stopped him with a shout.

"Hey! Keep your hands where I can see 'em! Don't you touch that girl." She looked at Corrine. "Get our horses saddled." Then she barked at Solomon. "Help these gentlemen off with their guns and boots."

"Now wait just a minute!" the bearded man protested. "You got no cause to—"

"Mister!" Tam interrupted, waving the gun. "I'm in no mood for conversation."

The men held their tongues after that.

Solomon gathered the men's weapons and their boots, offering them apologetic looks in exchange.

"Pat 'em down!" barked Tam to Solomon. "Make sure they ain't got knives in their belts or up their sleeves."

Corrine shivered. What *had* the man been doing with his sleeve? Did he have a knife hidden there?

Tam waved the rifle barrel. "Hands up, gentlemen! Get 'em where I can see 'em!"

Corrine hurried to pack up what remained of their camp. Once their horses were saddled and ready, Tam told Corrine to step out of her skirt.

"What?"

"Use it like a sack to collect the guns and boots!" Tam jerked her head toward the pile on the ground. "Solomon, grab the reins on their horses."

The bald man said, "You might as well shoot us if you're going to take our horses."

"Don't tempt me," Tam spat. "We'll leave your horses a few miles that way." She nodded her head. "Boots and rifles, too. But don't you come after us. We won't be so generous next time."

Corrine stepped out of her skirt and knotted the waist opening. She still had the bloomers on underneath, but felt as if she were disrobing.

She and Solomon quickly had the guns, knives and boots gathered inside the skirt she'd spread on the ground. She felt the men watching her as she worked.

The bearded man started to chuckle. As Corrine reached to pick up the last gun, the sandy-haired man lunged for her. Rough hands grabbed her waist. Corrine struggled to break free. The rifle boomed. Its reverberations rang loudly in her ears. The hands were off her waist now. The sandy-haired man was down.

Tam grabbed her arm. "Get up! Get on your horse!"

Tam was dragging her...flinging her forward. Solomon was already on his horse. The makeshift skirt bag was left lying on the ground. The other two men were reaching down for their guns. Tam was firing again. Corrine mounted. She grabbed the reins of Tam's horse and threw them back to Tam.

Tam pulled on the reins. Her foot was in the stirrup. One of the men was taking aim. Solomon kicked his pinto forward and hit the man's shoulder. The shot went wild. Tam swung her leg over the back of her horse. They rode.

Corrine put her head down and resisted the urge to look back.

*   *   *

The next time Harry opened his eyes, a large Hispanic man was watching him. Harry's hands felt less wooden now.

"Are you José?"

The man nodded. "Sí." One of his front teeth was missing, but its absence did nothing to spoil the man's smile. Harry's mind registered the irony: the woman had beautiful teeth and was slow to smile. The man was missing teeth, and he was quick to smile—so broadly, in fact, it threatened to split his face in half.

"*Mi esposa, Carlina.* " He pointed to the woman.

The woman's eyes dropped. "I already told him we weren't legally married, José."

"I can fix that," said Harry.

José's eyebrows popped up. "You are a holy man?" He slapped his hand on a generous thigh. "Do I tell you?" He started talking fast to the woman, too fast for Harry to keep up.

"He says he found a Bible in your saddlebags," explained the woman. "He wasn't trying to pry, he was just trying to—"

"I'm not offended," said Harry. "I owe you my life."

José waved the claim off. "*El Senor.*" He pointed heavenward, his face lit with joy. "He bring you to me."

With a wide smile stretching his cheeks, José shook his head and muttered something in Spanish about the goodness of the Lord as he walked out of the cabin with a big hand spread over his heart.

Carlina spooned more broth into Harry.

"Carlina's not my real name," she whispered confidentially. "That was José's mother's name. He likes it, so I let him call me that."

Harry wondered what potion swirled in her fabulous broth—surely some herb or ground up plant designed to bring on sleep. "What is your real name?"

"I better not say. You see, José found me when I ran off from where I was. After a bad beatin'. I would have died, too, if José hadn't found me. I was named for my small size when I was born."

"Did José kill a chicken for you?"

She flashed her teeth. "José done killed more'n a chicken for me."

"You know you're free now, don't you?" Harry wondered if his voice really sounded as groggy as it seemed, or if it was actually his ears that were working slow. "You don't have to hide. The war is over." He opened his mouth for another spoonful of broth.

"We heard that," Carlina said, putting the spoon to his lips. "But I killed the man who beat me. He's got family just as mean. They'd kill José and do worse to me if they ever found us."

His stomach full of broth, feeling warmed by the sunshine now streaming through the cracks of the logs, Harry couldn't help but close his eyes again.

The next time he opened them, Sam Eston was looking down on him.

"I need you to get dressed and come with me," the sheriff said. "Your wife's fit to be tied."

Carlina poked her wrapped head around the sheriff. "He's too weak to travel."

"No, I can ride." Harry sat up. His head spun. He waited until the world stopped moving and took a deep breath. "Will you bring me my Bible, José? And would you let me marry you and Carlina before I leave?"

"You going to put your clothes on first?" asked Eston as Harry threw his legs over the bed and started to stand. "I doubt they want to be married by a naked preacher."

*   *   *

James, Charlie, Michael Chessor and Bart Peters got their first look at Silvertown when they rode down the center of Main Street at mid-day.

"Silvertown is sizeable," said Chessor, nodding appreciatively at the array of brick and wooden storefronts.

"Where does your grandmother live, James?" asked Charlie.

"I don't know," James admitted. "She came here three years ago, after Denver flooded, to take care of women who were followin' the miners. I've never known her to have much of a place. Back room somewhere, more'n likely. One of the saloons...or maybe a church."

Bart Peters chuckled. "Those are quite different, James."

James shook his head. "The woman is a contradiction in more ways than one."

Chessor pointed his horse toward the largest sign on the street, which read "Saloon."

"Let's see if she lives here. If not, you go on looking for her, James." Chessor grinned. "You'll know where to find us when you're done."

*　　*　　*

Pearl Parker had only ever stood four feet, eleven inches tall in the vigor of her youth. Now, at seventy, she was only four foot, nine, her spine bowed from all the bending of her livelihood.

She had been born in the late 1700s in a cabin north of the Ohio River to parents whose faces she could hardly recall. Fever took them days apart when Pearl was twelve.

With the help of the family's single mule, Pearl threw her tiny frame into the effort of dragging first her mother's body, then her father's, out the cabin door and into a root cellar her father had dug. A heavy wagon wheel sat on top of a cellar door made of sticks, the pieces tied together with a horsehair rope. She pulled and tugged the iron wheel off, lifted up the stick door, and dug out the vegetables left in the root cellar before pulling the lifeless forms inside.

Days later, when the bodies began to smell, she made a thick mud paste and packed it around the edges and between the cracks of the stick door.

Pearl lived alone in the cabin another seven months and three days before another human found her. She was sure of her count because her father had taught her the months and days of the week. Her mother died on a Monday, her father the following Saturday. Seven months and three days later a Mormon with two wives and six children walked into her yard. All their possessions were piled in three handcarts.

The family took over the cabin. Pearl had been without human companionship so long, she'd nearly forgotten how to talk, much less protest.

One of the wives was expecting, her belly ripe with child. On a night when the moon shone bright and full overhead, the woman went into labor. The wives were bitter rivals, and the first wife refused to help the second. She took the children outside and left the pregnant woman alone wailing in the cabin. The man stood at the door and lifted up a prayer.

"A lot of good that'll do." Pearl went inside to see how she might offer more practical assistance.

That was the first baby she delivered: a fat, slick girl who slid right out of the second wife's body and into Pearl's tiny outstretched arms.

Pearl had never seen an infant before. She had no idea how the thing had gotten inside its mother's belly, but she intuitively knew to swipe the birth fluids from its mouth and to grab it by its flailing feet, so as not to drop its slippery body on the ground. The woman, already mother to two, talked Pearl through the process. She knew where best to cut the cord and warned Pearl to look for the after sac.

As soon as the baby girl found her voice, Pearl, too, began to cry. That Mormon's prayer had been effective after all, and Pearl, being the real-hands response to it, had witnessed something holy. How the others in the family, no matter how young, could opt to stay outside and not view the miracle would forever remain a mystery to Pearl.

When the Mormon family left the cabin, Pearl went with them. She sought out the doctor in the town where they settled, and began to work for him. She learned to stitch cut skin and set cracked bones and to perform all manner of other medical tasks. But what she lived for then, and what she lived for now, was the miracle of the birthing moments.

*   *   *

When Duke Walden, his three sons and Sairee Adams rode into Silvertown just before dusk, they rode past the biggest sign that read "Saloon" and straight toward a fancy blue sign instead, lettered in white script with the picture of a snake wrapped around a pole: "Tom G. Burleson, Physician. Animals Doctored When Time Permits."

*   *   *

Doc Burleson was just finishing the set of a patient's broken arm when a group burst into his front medical office. It was a rough looking crowd — an older man, three younger, and a woman — but he had grown used to rough-looking people. The cowpoke who sat on the table in front of him now was rough-looking, too.

The doctor could see that two of the younger men favored each other considerably, though one was stockier. They had to be twins.

The woman's hands were tied. The old man's leg was wrapped.

"I'll be finished in a minute." Doc Burleson reached for a piece of cloth to make the cowpoke, who had been kicked by a steer, a sling. In the corner of his vision he could see that one of the twins held the woman's elbow. She looked longingly at the doctor and the cowpoke. *Help me*, said her eyes.

"You might want to wait out—"

The men from the group crowded into the space around him, and before the doctor could finish his sentence, the cloth was yanked from his hands and the cowpoke jerked off the table by his injured arm.

The cowpoke howled, but not so loud that Doc Burleson couldn't hear the bone crack back out of place.

"What's the meaning of this?" He tried to rise from the wooden stool. "I just set that man's arm!" Rough hands pushed him down again.

The stocky twin led the cowpoke by the arm to the door, placed his foot on the man's backside and kicked him, sending him sprawling into the dusty street. Then he slammed the door shut. The doctor could hear the cowpoke's howls bouncing off the wood.

"He'll be all right." The older man raised his wrapped leg and set it on the table under the doctor's nose. "Fix this."

Doc Burleson looked at the three younger men who had each stationed themselves in a corner of his office, rifles in their hands. The leaner twin, who'd been holding the woman's elbow, now shoved her down on one of the two side chairs in the office. The stocky twin grabbed the other chair and thrust it under the front door's knob.

The lean twin untied the woman's hands, looped the bandana over the back rungs of the chair behind her, then retied them again. When he was done, he looked up at the doctor and smiled.

"Who *are* you?" Doc Burleson asked.

"Name's Duke Walden," answered the older man in a gravely voice. "Marquis, slip out the back and go tie our horses where we talked about. Get back in here before that cowpoke goes to the sheriff."

Duke Walden!

The story had been prominently featured in the Silvertown paper. The details swiftly rolled through the doctor's keen mind: The Waldens had robbed a bank in Baker City; Earl Walden had been killed by a former U.S. Marshall; the Waldens were wanted in several states and territories, from Nebraska to California, for robbing banks and stagecoaches and killing several men. Doc Burleson wondered if they had killed any doctors.

Recognition must have registered in his eyes.

"I see you heard of us." Duke nodded toward the stocky twin. "Baron." Then he jerked his head toward the leaner one. "Viscount." They were both shorter and heavier than the one Duke Walden had called "Marquis."

"This here's Sairee Adams." Duke pointed to the woman. "And you're Tom Burleson, physician, who doctors animals when time permits. Now that we're all acquainted and I've cleared your appointments for the day, I want you to heal this leg."

Doc Burleson resisted the temptation to tell Duke Walden that only time and God could heal. As a physician, all he could do was seek to remove the things that might delay or prevent healing, and administer those things that might help it along.

A physician practicing medicine in a western town in 1867 expected to see some things, and Tom Burleson had known before he came to Silvertown he might find himself in sticky situations. So he took a deep breath to ease the fear that was threatening to put a shake in his hands and began to pull the wrappings from Duke Walden's leg.

Walden set his rifle butt on the wooden floor and leaned a hand on the top of the barrel to steady himself.

"Would you like to lie down?" Doc Burleson peeled off the seeping bandage. The wound smelled, but wasn't rancid...a hopeful sign. He had a feeling Duke Walden wouldn't take it well if the leg needed to come off.

"I'll stand," said Duke.

"Where does this lead?" This question came from Baron who stood at the inside door.

"Living quarters," answered Marquis. Doc Burleson whipped his head around. He hadn't heard the tallest son come back in.

Marquis was right. Doc Burleson had the front office where he saw patients and a side room for those in need of overnight care, plus his own room and a small kitchen. The kitchen had a door that led out back to the outhouse...and to wherever Marquis had tied their horses.

Thankfully, there were no overnight patients at present.

"You the only one who lives here?" asked Marquis.

"Yes." The doctor's wife had died five years ago. That was what had driven him west: his need to flee the memories.

Now that the wound was free of its wrappings, the doctor could clearly see it: a gunshot hole in the upper thigh. By the position of it, Doc Burleson guessed the bullet had nicked the bone, but not shattered it. He lifted the leg to see where the bullet had exited the other side.

Guessing by the size of the hole, it'd been made by a .44 ball.

"Did you get this in Baker City?" Both the front and back of the leg were hot to the touch. In fact, now that the doctor had leaned in close to inspect it, he could feel that Duke Walden was burning with fever. Still, the leg wasn't as rotten as he'd feared. It might be saved.

"In March."

This was the middle of June. The doctor felt himself wince, then thought better of it. He summoned his best poker face, instead.

"If you read the paper you know a man named Parker gave me this. You're going to help me pay him back. You…" Duke pointed to the woman again, "and her."

Burleson decided to ignore the last part of Walden's statement. "We need to address your fever." He reached toward his medicine cabinet.

Baron drew a pistol from its holster and pointed it into the doctor's chest. Doc Burleson studied it. It was a Smith and Wesson that carried a .32 ball, and would tear quite a hole if discharged this close to flesh.

"You give him anything you shouldn't, it'll be the last thing you ever do."

The doctor had been in some tense situations, had even served as a Union medic during the war, but this was the first time anyone had ever stuck a gun to his chest.

Longing for a sip of whiskey, he took another deep breath to ease the fear that was threatening to put a shake in his hands.

CHAPTER 18

A hard day's ride

Once they'd ridden several miles, Tam pulled her horse up and pointed. "Tie those men's horses here, Solomon." Her voice was strained.

Swinging a long leg over the pinto, Solomon dismounted and did as he was instructed. Corrine had never seen his face so ashen.

As soon as he remounted, Tam kicked her horse and took off again. Corrine and Solomon followed mutely. The events that had just transpired kept replaying in Corrine's mind: the feel of her waist being grabbed, the blast of the rifle, a quick glance at the man as Tam threw Corrine toward her horse, the mud on the ground turned red.

Tam set the horses at a quick cantor and rode another two hours before pulling up again. "You think you can find your way on to Silvertown, Solomon?"

"I guess." His words came out labored. This was perhaps the closest Bennett Solomon had ever come to the actual news he published in his paper. Corrine wondered if his heart was pounding in his chest, like hers. Tam sounded strained, too.

"Why?" Solomon asked.

"You're going to have to ride on. I can't go any farther. Something's not right with me." She ran a hand across her middle. "I need you to get on to Silvertown—you heard 'em say we were within a hard day's ride of it. That's closer than I realized. Get a doctor and get back out here to me."

Bennett started to dismount. "What is it? What's wrong?"

"Dammit, Solomon, I ain't got time to elaborate! Get on to Silvertown now! Don't you stop until you get there. Ride that pinto into the ground if you have to. If he goes down, you run. Keep your head down and out of trouble."

"All right, all right. I'm going.'" Solomon looked apologetically at Corrine.

"We'll be fine." Corrine tried to keep her voice from quaking. The fear that had wrapped itself around her when the three men rode into their camp was back, and at twice its former size. She and Tam were about to be left alone and Corrine's nerves hadn't yet calmed. But she nodded her head all the same, trying to ease her pulse and sound convincing. "I'll see to Tam."

"Humph. *You'll* see to *me?*" muttered Tam.

When Solomon stalled and opened his mouth to argue, Tam said, "Of course she will! Would you *please* go to Silvertown, Solomon! Find a marker. There!" She pointed at a nearby stand of aspen trees. "We'll make camp right there.

Remember that stand of trees and how they form a circle. Now ride!"

"Wait!" called Corrine. "Take my horse instead." She quickly dismounted and stripped off her saddlebags. "The dun will be faster."

Tam eyed her appreciatively and nodded. "Take 'em both, Solomon! Switch your mounts."

Solomon transferred over to the dun and held onto the pinto's rein while Corrine adjusted the stirrups. As soon as they were set, she looked up at him. "Be safe."

He didn't like the situation he was being put in; Corrine could see it on his face. She didn't like it either.

He leaned over and brushed dried mud from Corrine's cheek. "I'll get back as fast as I can, Miss Baldwyn."

"I know you will." Corrine tried to sound more confident than she felt.

"Go, Mr. Solomon!" yelled Tam. "Ride as if the life of me and Harry's child depends on it!"

Solomon gripped the reins harder, his face registering alarm. He kicked the dun and rode.

The women watched his form grow smaller in the distance until he finally disappeared over a rise. Corrine's heart sank at the sight. Then it bubbled up hot with anger at the position she found herself in: no family, no friends, no skilled men to protect her, no horse. And Tam had *shot* a man! *Had that really been necessary?* Surely they could have reasoned with those men.

Corrine wheeled on Tam. "You're barking an awful lot of ord—"

She stopped and stared at a blood trail Tam was leaving behind as she slowly slid off her horse. Corrine's arms stretched out just in time to collect her as she fell.

* * *

Pearl Parker let herself into the back room of the church. She didn't have a lock on the door, so she wasn't surprised when it swung wide and revealed a tall man with a new growth of beard sitting in a corner in her only chair, waiting.

But she *was* surprised by who the thin shaft of light revealed. Dim as the room was, she knew him in an instant and hopped from foot to foot like a child. "Jimmy! My Jimmy! Come here to me!"

In two strides, James crossed the room and scooped her in his arms. "Lord, have mercy. I believe you've shrunk!"

He twirled her around and was tempted to throw her into the air like a sack of cornmeal, but feared he'd break her, plus the ceiling was low.

Placing her gently on the floor, he said, "What kind of tiny hole are you livin' in this time, Grandmaw? Took me an hour to find your place. And then I didn't think you'd ever come home. I've been waitin' on you another hour."

"Jimmy, Jimmy, Jimmy!" She sure hopped spryly for such a tiny, aged woman. "You didn't tell me you were coming! I would have cooked for you."

"How? I don't see no cookstove in here." James looked around the room again though he'd had plenty of time to study it. The space was mighty sparse. A bed, the chair, a chest, and that was all. Not even the wooden bowl he remembered was in sight. "Lord, woman, is that why you've gotten so small? Have you quit eatin'?"

"I eat just fine." She grinned. "Doesn't take much when a person's my size. What brings you to Silvertown?"

"You! This seems like a rough town, Granny. Aren't you ready to—"

Before James could finish his sentence, a man filled the open frame of her door.

"Granny Pearl? Can you come set a broken arm?"

She scrunched her nose. "Is Doc Burleson not available?"

"Doc's been taken hostage."

"Hostage?"

"Yes, ma'am. Bad bunch rode in a little while ago. One of 'em's wounded. They threw this man out of doc's place and locked the door. Say they aren't letting the doc out until he tends to the hurt man."

It was the same as James remembered: people coming to fetch Granny Pearl at all hours, day and night.

"Who's the man with the broken arm?" she asked.

The man at the door shrugged his shoulders. James wondered if he had drawn the short straw among those free to run and fetch someone. "A cattle puncher that was in the doctor's office when they rode in. The doc had just set his arm and they whacked it out of place again, pitching him out the door."

Granny Pearl turned to James. "I've got to go, Jimmy."

"You want me to come with you?" James reached for his hat.

"No," she took his hand and squeezed it as if wanting to feel of him, to make sure he was real. "You know I deal with this kind of thing all the time. Will you be here when I get back?"

"I need to check on the three men I rode in with. I've been gone longer than I meant to be. You mind if I bring 'em back here with me? I want you to meet 'em." He hugged her, then released her to go with the man who was growing more impatient at the door. "Don't worry about feedin' us. We'll eat at the café before we come back."

James ducked his head as he stepped out of her door. He watched her follow the man who'd fetched her until she turned a corner, and wondered briefly who the bad bunch might be. There were a lot of bad bunches in the West. All the more reason Granny Pearl should be in Baker City, where he could keep an eye on her as she lived out her final days.

Silvertown was larger than James had expected. Goldrushers discovered gold north of Pike's Peak, then in several other creeks coming off the Rockies, back in '59. At first they ignored the gray ore that testified to the presence of silver, hungry only for the gold. But once the value of silver was finally recognized, Goldtown was renamed Silvertown and began to grow. Folks had streamed in like ants to a picnic ever since, settling in beside the Arapahoe who were native to the land.

The town soon came to be prized not only for its ore, but for its picturesque setting near the base of the western side of the Rockies. Two creeks ran down the sides of the mountain, joining together at its edge, wrapping around the town like a living, moving ribbon, the water that sprayed over the large boulders as white and silver as the chipped rocks the men dug out from its mining operations.

The town had begun with nothing but tents and clapboard buildings, but now solid brick structures lined the main streets, and the side streets were dotted with still more brick buildings, some of them cut from stone. The Methodist Church where James's grandmaw was living even had a stately steeple reaching toward the sky.

James stared up at it for a moment, marveling at the wooden architecture, before turning and taking long strides down Main Street toward the saloon where he'd left his men.

When James swung open the saloon doors the first thing he saw was Charlie Baldwyn seated at a table, his eyes lolling upward, a scantily clad woman's bosoms thrust under his nose.

*   *   *

Tam put her face in Corrine's shoulder and mumbled as tears wet the fabric of Corrine's blouse. "I wanted this baby so bad, Corrine. James says it's a girl. A baby *girl*! I wanted her so bad."

Suddenly, none of what had happened between the two women mattered. It didn't matter that Tam hadn't told Corrine about her past before Corrine rode off on this trip with her. It didn't matter that Tam had been angry with her or barked so meanly. It didn't even matter that Tam had sent Bennett Solomon down the trail and left the two of them alone. All that mattered was that Corrine do everything she could to help Tam save her baby…if it wasn't too late.

A warm breeze swept into the clearing and ruffled Corrine's hair. She looked up. The sun shone in clear skies now, but clouds were rolling their way again from the west. Was more rain coming? Trees were scarce, but a few evergreens dotted the landscape. The leaves of the aspens Tam had pointed out to Solomon winked and waved at her in the wind.

"Tell me what you need," whispered Corrine, kissing the top of Tam's head. She remembered James's tears falling on her own head as he held her the day Emma died.

"Get me over to that stand of trees and let me rest a minute. And pray those men don't come after us. I hope I didn't kill that man. It'll be better for us if they need to tend to him. But if he's dead, they'll likely track us down out of vengeance."

Corrine looped the reins of Tam's horse over one arm, circled the other around Tam's middle, and started walking her toward the aspen grove. "You ever shot anyone before?"

"Lord, no." Tam's voice caught. "I hate to add any more to my conscience."

Corrine's eyes began to burn from unshed tears. Tam had done this for her—added another weight to her heart because of Corrine. She hoped to never learn whether Tam had killed that man or not. It was easier on her own conscience to believe Tam hadn't.

When they reached the aspens Corrine settled her against one of the gray trunks. Then she tied Tam's horse nearby and came back to her. "Tell me what you need. Tell me what to do."

Tam rolled over in a sudden heap. "Just let me die. If Harry's not coming back and I've lost this baby, I don't want to live."

Corrine stared at her. Was this the same hot-tempered woman she had ridden with the past two days?

Determination swelling in her, Corrine pulled on Tam's shoulder, forcing the older woman to look at her. "What kind of talk is that? Roll over on your back now so I can see where you're bleeding."

Tam did as she was instructed.

Blood had soaked through Tam's bloomers, but that was all Corrine could tell without looking beneath them. "I'm sorry to do this, but I need to see what's happened."

"No need to apologize," said Tam flatly. "And I know what's happened. I've killed a man and now the Lord's goin' to take my child as payment."

It was more terrible to see Tam docile and defeated than it had ever been to see her riled. Corrine smoothed Tam's hair back from her face and studied her brown eyes. She had never seen them look so sad. Tam refused to meet her gaze.

"I don't like that we've been at each other's throats, Tam." Corrine was doubly shamed to have been brought to a moment like this for her to confess it. If Tam lost her baby, or – *God forbid* – if Tam should die, Corrine would never forgive herself. Hadn't she been irritated with Emma just before Emma died? Was her anger some kind of curse?

Tam looked up at her then. "I'm not mad at you, Sweetheart. I'm mad at myself for my own stubborn nature. Harry told me not to come and he was right, as always." Tam's voice caught again. "If I lose this child, I'll know it was my fault forever."

Corrine shook her head. "Don't. My mother did that. She lost a baby before Lina, after riding horses with my uncle Seth. My father had begged her not to go, but she did. Then he blamed her for it. Or more likely, I think now, she blamed herself and just thought my father blamed her. I wasn't very old, but I was old enough to know it started tension between them."

She looked down at Tam's blood-soaked bloomers again, realizing for the first time how frightening that experience had to have been for her mother and Mimi, who tended to her. But Mimi and her mother survived it, and so would she and Tam.

"I feel at fault, too," Corrine said, "for insisting that I come with you on this trip. I've slowed you down and caused problems. I see now that if Harry and Sam Eston had come alone, they could have ridden faster and never would have had to split up for anything. It was selfish of me."

"It was selfish of us both."

Corrine lifted her chin. "But wallowing around in self pity doesn't help anything, Tam. We've got to do the best we can from this point forward."

A hint of a smile crossed Tam's face. "That sounds like the girl I saw on the wagon train. The one with gumption who stood in my yard and insisted she was coming on this trip."

A thin ray of peace entered Corrine's heart for the first time since she had read James's letter. With steady hands, she unknotted the string at Tam's waist and peeled off the blood-soaked bloomers.

What she saw filled her with hope. Tam had lost nothing but blood, and now that the bloomers were off, it didn't look like there had really been as much as she'd first feared. And the bleeding looked like it had stopped.

Corrine laid a hand on top of Tam's bare stomach, feeling around from place to place. Her skin was tight and warm. There was sudden movement under her fingers. Corrine pressed into the spot. There it came again. Unmistakable movement! As if a little elbow had sought out Corrine's fingers to nudge. A memory of Emma flashed through her mind as Corrine squealed, "She moved, Tam! She moved!"

"Lord, I know it!" Fresh tears hung in Tam's eyes but her voice had regained some it's natural fire. "If you think it felt big on top you ought to felt it inside. She's a strong one. I'll say that for her."

Tam let the tears fall then, but her laugh lines were widening in pure joy, bathed in relief. Like the sleigh ride over snow-covered hillsides, the cream in her coffee, and the click of her and Emma's boots on the boardwalk of Baker City, Corrine knew this was another holy moment that would live in her memory for the rest of her life. She didn't realize her own tears were flowing freely until she saw them dropping onto Tam.

Wiping her eyes with her sleeve, she vowed never again to judge another person on his or her past. *Never again.* It didn't make others foolish not to have thought or acted the same way she did. Corrine had taken excess pride in her own sensibilities and quickness of mind, she knew that now.

So what about James? Should she stop judging him, too, for all his past might hold? The unwelcome thought stabbed her heart with guilt.

That would have to be decided later.

"I think the bleeding has stopped," said Corrine. "And I don't see any tears or punctures. The blood had to have been coming from inside. Is that normal? Do you know?"

"I don't know. I spotted before, when we got to Fort Bridger, but this was heavier. I could feel it start about the time those men rode up. The longer we rode to get away from 'em, the stronger it got. Not a good time to be in a saddle, but what choice did I have?"

After inspecting and cleaning Tam as best she could, Corrine dug through their saddlebags for a light blanket with which to cover her. Corrine's gray shawl and skirt had been left back at the old campsite, but she still had her petticoats. She pulled them out and cut them into strips to use as washrags.

Finding a small pan and a bar of soap in Tam's saddlebags, Corrine went to the nearby creek to draw water so she could wash Tam's bloomers and get some supper started.

She found a small piece of bacon wrapped in oilskin in Tam's bags and knew a few tart apples rested in the bottom of her own, plucked from a tree two days ago. The apples hadn't seemed like much at the time, but they would be filling, along with the bacon.

After gathering twigs and sticks, she dug through the saddlebags again for matches.

Not wanting to give away their location to the men they had left behind, Corrine built the fire under the thickest overhang of the aspen branches, hoping it would help diffuse the smoke. She kept the fire small, just big enough to get water boiling and the bacon cooked. Would the smell of the food travel? Would it lead those men right to them? But what choice did she have? She could afford to wait, but Tam needed to eat.

Corrine fixed a plate for Tam and scooped what was left in the pan back into the now empty oilcloth so Tam would have something to eat tomorrow. She could go hungry easier than Tam could. Corrine went back to the creek to wash the pan and studied on how she might catch a fish in the stream.

After eating, Tam appeared to doze.

Next, Corrine scrubbed Tam's clothes. Once she had them clean, she laid them over a branch to dry. She turned her head often to stare in the distance, praying those men wouldn't come looking for them. What were her options, if they did? All she knew to do was keep her and Tam's rifles close by. Tam couldn't run and Corrine couldn't leave her.

Corrine inspected Tam's rifle. It was an older model, foreign to her. Tam was sleeping and Corrine didn't want to disturb her, so she set out what looked like the makings to reload it, and the rifle itself, on the ground within Tam's reach.

She kept her own rifle by her side.

Next, Corrine set about making camp. She scouted around for long sticks like Eston had used the night before. She stacked them by twos, pushing their ends into the ground—trying not to disturb Tam—and tying their tops together with string. Next, she took her scissors, walked to the nearest evergreen, and hacked off as many pine boughs as she could carry. Then she dragged them over, stacking them crossways over the frame.

Tam opened her eyes as Corrine laid pine boughs over her. She smiled, felt her belly, then went back to sleep.

Corrine took a minute to rest and think. If they were really just a hard day's ride from Silvertown, it would take Solomon another hard day's ride to get back to them. She didn't know when Eston might be back with Harry...or would he find Harry?

What would she do if Eston didn't return? Or if Solomon didn't return? What would she do if those men came after her and Tam again? Or if other men—say, those Arapahoe—happened upon them? What would she do if Tam took a turn for the worse?

All she knew to do was pray: for wisdom and courage, wisdom and fortitude, steady eyes and sharp ears...and a heart that resisted locking up with trembling.

Tam dozed most of the afternoon. Corrine let her. She sat by the smoldering fire working on the waist of Tam's bloomers, adding in some of the cut strips of petticoat, to give Tam's belly more growing room. Once Tam's other clothes had dried, Corrine folded them and laid them by her shelter.

As night began to fall, Corrine covered the remains of the fire with dirt. She didn't want to risk the smoke drawing attention against the backdrop of a darkened sky. She pulled her bedroll near Tam's shelter, but in a position that would give her the broadest view of the surrounding land.

As Corrine lay with her head propped up on her saddlebags, pulling the light blanket to her chin, she watched the sun slowly set. She wondered what her mother was doing back home. Her heart ached with a longing to be back in the cabin on Hoke's hill. She wondered what James and Charlie were doing and wished one of them was with her to make her feel safe. No, not James...she was mad at James.

Or was she?

Her eyes finally growing heavy, Corrine hugged Sam Eston's rifle closer to her side.

CHAPTER 19
Out of the horse trough

Charlie stared, fascinated by the rosy-cheeked woman who waved her ample chest from side to side in front of him. His mind felt strange, almost like it itched, only he couldn't figure out how to scratch it.

Shortly after James had left them in the saloon, Bart Peters and Michael Chessor ordered drinks. Chessor slapped Charlie on the back.

"You ever had a strong drink?"

Mimi had given Charlie whiskey mixed with honey when he had bad colds as a child. "It'll keep the infection from droppin' into your chest," she vowed. The liquor always burned going down. "That burn is lickin' up the poison like a flame in oil."

He had never liked it. But the way Chessor and Peters were grinning in anticipation of their hard drinks now, he hated to admit that fact. Charlie was acutely aware that he was the youngest in their group and had already felt himself the fool for not knowing James spent time with the women at

A Contradiction to His Pride/Leanne W. Smith

Fort Bridger. Charlie didn't want Chessor and Peters to think him naïve.

"I've had whiskey lots of times," he said.

"Well then, whiskey it is." Chessor nodded at the man behind the long wooden counter. Charlie and Bart Peters watched him pour the liquid. When Chessor raised his glass to his lips, so did they.

Had it been only one little glass of whiskey, Charlie's mind might not have grown so thick and scratchy...or was it itchy? But after the first, Chessor had insisted on ordering another...and another after that.

Charlie marveled at how the liquid, when it first slid down this throat, hardly had much impact. The taste was mighty sour, and it burned just like he remembered as a child — perhaps a little more, since this was a bigger dose and didn't have the honey mixed in. But then, something pulled at his mind the instant the alcohol dropped into his stomach. It was as if there was an invisible thread that ran from his stomach to his head. Every sip tugged on the cord. Now his mind seemed to be sitting farther down in his head than normal.

He didn't remember leaving the bar and sitting at the table. The room felt lighter than his mind. Perhaps the room had floated over.

He saw people opening their mouths and heard words in the air beside him. He smiled politely, but didn't really know what they were saying. It was pleasant here in this saloon. He had never been in one before. He wondered why church people thought saloons were bad. Everyone in this saloon was friendly...like the rosy-cheeked woman who was talking to him now.

Charlie had never seen paint on a woman's face before, or a feather in the stacked up hair on her head. He hadn't ever seen so much of a woman's legs, either, like the ones wrapped in black stockings that showed under this woman's skirt that was much, much shorter than any his mother and sisters wore. Neither had he seen a neckline so low that the round swell of a woman's bosoms sat exposed above the black lace of the edge. The woman's shoulders and arms were bare, too.

What kind of dress was that, anyway? Charlie had never seen a woman's arms naked all the way to where they joined her body at the shoulder.

He tried not to stare, having been taught it was not polite, but he didn't have good control over his eyes. They seemed drawn to the woman's creamy skin, and the front of his head was so heavy it kept bobbing toward her pillow-like bosoms. He could feel the corners of his lips lifting into an endless grin.

The lines around the woman's eyes were deep, deeper than his mother's. He wondered how old she was. Not that it mattered. It was nice to sit here with her. He had missed female company in the weeks he traveled with James. He had missed his mother and sisters. And Jacob. And Hoke. And James. No...James was with him.

James wasn't with him.

Where was James? Something about his grandmother....

The woman's mouth was moving but her words moved past his ear faster than he could make them out. She was pulling on his arm. She must want to show him something. Charlie tested his legs to see if they still worked. They did. He could stand. She took his arm again and they started up the stairs.

Suddenly James was there in front of them.

"James!" Charlie's voice still worked. How nice to see James again! Charlie smiled. Was James coming, too?

James reached down to take the woman's arm from Charlie's elbow.

"I believe you've got my riding partner there," said James.

Who was James talking about? Charlie looked around for Hoke. Hoke was James's riding partner. Or did he mean Peters and Chessor? Now where had they gone? Weren't they just sitting at the table with him?

The woman looked unhappy. Her bosoms heaved and her hands went to her hips as James took hold of Charlie.

She held to Charlie's other arm. "He's of age."

"Now how would you know that? Did you ask him how old he was?"

"If he's old enough to be in here, he's old enough to decide for himself if he wants to go with me."

"No ma'am. He's in no shape to make a solid decision just now. How many drinks did he have?"

"How would I know?"

James peeled the woman's hand off Charlie's other arm, took his elbow and led him back down the stairs.

"How many drinks did you have, Charlie?"

Was James talking to him? Or the woman? Was her name Charlie, too? Charlie looked over his shoulder for the woman. She was gone. He looked back to where James was leading him. The man behind the counter came into sight. "What did you serve him?" James asked.

"Whiskey."

"How many?"

Charlie held up three fingers. At least, he thought he did. Was that three? Or four? How many was three again?

"Seven or eight," said the man.

James leaned down close to Charlie's face. Charlie jerked back. Suddenly he didn't feel so good.

"Uh-oh." James grabbed Charlie under both armpits and steered him toward the door. But he was moving too fast. Charlie couldn't get his legs to work quickly enough. Now James was dragging him.

"Hey, James." The words tumbled out heavy and slurred. "What's your hurry? Slow down. I don't feel—"

James kicked the doors open and threw Charlie into the fading evening. The sun was setting. Charlie couldn't see well. His legs never had caught up. Torso-heavy, he pitched off the boardwalk into the dusty street.

Before he could collect himself, James was beside him, hauling him up. "Get up!" James was being rough. He was hurting Charlie's elbow.

"Hey," started Charlie again, but before he could get any more words out, James grabbed the back of his trousers at the waistline. Charlie felt himself lifted into the air, then he was sailing.

He landed with a slap in water.

Water covered him. He couldn't breathe. Charlie's arms and legs flailed wildly until he got a hold of what felt like the edges of a metal tub. Clawing, he sputtered up for air. The cold water stung his nose from going in wrong. The shock brought some focus to his mind as he coughed and gulped for breath.

Had James pitched him in a water trough? Or had he fallen?

Charlie stood shakily on his feet and raked water from his eyes. Who were all these people staring at him? Where was James? There he was. Charlie raised his fist. He'd show James! Just like he'd showed him on the creek bank!

But when Charlie took a step toward James his foot hit the side of the metal tub and he fell out of the horse trough into the dusty street again.

*   *   *

James looked down at Charlie, disgusted. Peters and Chessor were nowhere in sight. But he could guess where they were. Same place Charlie would have been if James had taken any longer getting back to the saloon. And the woman would have cleaned Charlie's pockets before she was finished with him. One had to deal carefully with older women in saloons. He ought to know. They could clean the pockets of a happy, drunken cowpoke faster than could any other kind of thief, and they'd have the upper hand when the man sobered up, with him feeling too red-faced to accuse them of it. James preferred dealing with the younger ones, tried to turn their hearts before they fully morphed into slick-palmed thieves.

James hauled Charlie up out of the street and tossed him back in the water trough. The boy looked like he needed at least one more good dousing.

Charlie would be mad at James when he came out of it. But his face had gone green. If James hadn't tossed him in the water trough, he'd be hunched over in a back alley tossing his whiskey there.

Hoke had done the same thing to James one time. In fact, that's how they met.

James hadn't been about to climb the stairs with a woman when he had gotten tossed; he had nearly gotten himself killed in a gunfight instead. He and Hoke happened to be in the same saloon in Fort Dodge, Kansas, when James started mouthing off. Seeing that James had had too much to drink, Hoke drug him out and tossed him in a horse trough. The next morning when he woke up in the clean hay pile of a livery stable, Hoke was chewing on a hickory stick, leaned over a wooden rail watching him.

"Brought you some breakfast."

That was all he'd said. Then he went back to reading a book he held in both hands. James would later learn it was Hoke's father's Bible.

Ignoring the taunts of the crowd calling for him to pitch Charlie in again, James hooked his hand on the back of the young man's sopping trousers one last time and hauled him out of the horse trough, then tossed the spent youth up over his shoulder. With all the hard work Charlie had been doing the past year, he'd bulked up and didn't toss lightly.

Cold water now dripping down through his own shirt and trousers, James carried Charlie to his grandmaw's room behind the Methodist Church. She wasn't back yet. He settled Charlie, who had passed out, in one corner, and looked for a quill to leave her a note before going off to find some food. Not finding one, he decided to go look for her first.

All James had wanted was a bath and a meal. He shook his head at Charlie one last time before going out the door. At least Charlie had had *his* bath.

*   *   *

Bennett Solomon had a poor sense of direction but an excellent recall of geography. He knew where Silvertown was on a map: knew it was to the east, knew this trail was supposed to lead right to it and that he should keep the afternoon sun to the back of his right shoulder. But by the time the sun went down, he'd lost his compass, his stomach was complaining, his eyes were fighting to stay open—and he'd begun to doubt everything he thought he knew.

All day he'd ridden hard. "A hard day's ride," the man had said. "A hard day's ride," Tam had instructed him. The words repeated themselves to him over and over. Just how far was 'a hard day's ride,' exactly?

A normal *hard day's ride* would happen during daylight hours. The sun was up by six this time of year. Or was it five-thirty? He ought to know, he included the sun's patterns in his newspaper. And the sun circled back down below the horizon around eight-thirty...or was it nine? That was fourteen hours of daylight. Of course, a normal traveler wouldn't push a single horse hard all that time. He had ridden at a hard gallop that first hour, noon to one. He had the gray dun and pinto to switch between, so he should have been moving faster than the average man.

A hard day's ride. He only had to go a hard day's ride and he would be there.

It was dark now and he continued on, studying the stars above, grateful they gave him markings—only, he didn't feel as confident about reading them as he had about keeping the sun behind his shoulder.

He was tired. He couldn't tell what time it was. The gray dun beneath him and the pinto beside him were both tired, too. The dun, smelling water, steered him to a creek. He decided to rest a minute, eat, and let the horses drink.

His eyes were so heavy.

*   *   *

James got his meal and bath after all.

His looked for his grandmaw but couldn't find her. She'd always been one to keep late hours. Charlie was still snoring in the corner of her room. And as far as James knew,

Chessor and Peters had never come down from the stairs of the saloon.

So...still hungry—having never eaten supper—James went to the nearest café and sweet-talked the owners who lived there into opening the door and cooking him a buffalo steak, which they served smothered in gravy, with a side of new potatoes. He told the woman not to bother scratching him up some biscuits, but she had a pan of leftover cornbread and offered him that. He slathered a generous piece with fresh butter and wrapped the rest in his neckerchief when he stood up to leave.

"You know anything about the town doctor being taken hostage?" he asked them. That piece of news had festered a bit in the back of his mind.

"The sheriff is looking into it," said the cook.

"He's a good sheriff," added the woman's husband.

Trusting then that the sheriff had the matter in hand, James asked directions to the nearest bathhouse. He went there next.

"I'm saving this cornbread for a friend whose sleeping off his first drinking binge," he told the Chinese couple who ran the bathhouse. "He'll wake up hungry."

The woman nodded, taking the parcel from him with care, then took his clothes to brush and iron while her husband, no taller than the woman and two heads shorter than James, filled a tub with steaming water.

The Chinese couple smiled and nodded several times to indicate that James should enjoy his bath. And he did.

Having grown accustomed to the absence of a beard before making this trip, he shaved while he was at it.

As James soaked in the tub he thought about Granny Pearl, Corrine, and the painted woman he'd found with Charlie on the stairs.

He surely did love women...always had. One of his earliest memories was of standing by a bedside, holding a woman's hand, as his grandmother pushed the woman's skirts to her waist.

"I can't." The woman squirmed.

"You'll have to, honey. You squeeze that boy's hand—he's got strong hands for his age—and you squeeze your body like you're emptyin' your insides. That's the way it works. You feel that pain roll in, you push through it by squeezin'.'"

James could still feel the hard clamp of that woman's hand, twenty-four years later. And he remembered how the arch of her back, the scream of her lungs, and the sack of baby and fluids that erupted from between her legs had awed him into silence.

He wondered just how many babies Pearl Parker had helped bring into the world. James himself had been witness to dozens. There had surely never lived a greater servant to downtrodden women than Granny Pearl. And the experience led her to form some opinions about the matter. She had filled James's youthful ears with her conclusions.

"Don't you ever strike a woman," she'd admonished him while tending to women's unearned bruises.

"Women are given special charge, Jimmy," she'd say when toting him along to the back room of a brothel. "They partner with God to bring life into the world. They deserve to be respected for it."

And there was another frequent comment, often muttered as they left a woman whose hands were wringing red over the prospect of caring for an unexpected child. "Men are selfish bastards," she said. "Not you, darlin', but some men. They have no idea the lengths to which a woman would go for them, if only they would treat her with a little kindness."

James smiled at finally being in the same town as his wee grandmaw again. She hadn't changed one bit—was older, of course. That, and he could have sworn she'd shrunk. Maybe she had.

Eight years ago when James had last seen her, she'd seemed ancient, tiny...frail. But nobody had ever told *her* that. Or if they had, she didn't believe them enough to slow down and play the part.

At least he'd found her in a private room at the church and not living in the tents out back with the town's drunk and homeless. Hoke thought *James* was bad, giving his money to questionable women. What would Hoke think about his seventy-year-old grandmaw sleeping in the back rooms of brothels, saloons, and the occasional church cot so she could be close at hand to the people who needed her?

Respectable folk often avoided her. But the underbelly, the night rovers, the painted women, the saloon dancers, the drunks who benefitted from her strong pots of coffee and the scraps from her table...no matter what town she was in, they always knew and loved her.

James had left her last in Dodge City. She followed the women. When gold was discovered in a new vein and men flocked to the area, so did the women. In a new town thrown up around a gold discovery or the building of the railroad, doctors were often slow to arrive, and when they did, they often didn't see the women Pearl Parker was willing to help.

Women down on their luck take the brunt of everything. How many times had James heard her say that? And she ought to know, what with all the hands she'd held and tears she'd wiped.

His bath water grown cold and his heart full of memories, James stepped from the metal tub and dried himself off.

*   *   *

Solomon's eyes flew open. A skunk! His eyes couldn't see it in the dark, but his nose told him it was close. The dun snorted, apparently as eager to get to another location as Solomon was himself. Solomon was grateful the skunk had roused him, otherwise he might have slept the night through on that bank.

He led the dun and pinto away from the creek and looked to the stars to get his bearings. There was Orion's Belt. Best he could calculate from its position in the sky, Solomon needed to ride for the bottom corner of Orion's bow. So that was the direction he headed.

Once he was moving again—at as solid a clip as he could muster in the moonlight, as the land rose and became more steep—he wondered how long he had slept. He kicked the dun to go faster, a new appreciation rising in him for how the Pony Express riders must have felt.

Good thing Corrine had offered her dun. Her horse was much stronger and faster than his pinto. He only swapped over every couple of hours to give the dun a break from carrying him.

He was on the dun now: a gelding that stepped light and sure over the rising land. A patchy string of clouds had broken up long enough for him to locate Orion, but currently blotted out the moon. Occasionally an opening in the cloud cover would appear and the way would grow clearer, then a moving patch would blot it out again.

Sometime in the night, the dun's pace picked up. The horse threw his head back, waking Solomon, who had fallen asleep again on his back. The pinto was gone. Solomon had dropped its reins.

Lights shone in the distance. A town…a sizable town. It had to be Silvertown. Relief surged through Solomon.

He kicked the dun and rode him in.

CHAPTER 20
Feeling clean and peaceful

Corrine woke with a start. It was dark, the evening cool. Had she heard something? Did Tam need her?

Her ears strained to listen; her eyes strained to see.

Rain had never come. A patch of clouds currently covered the moon. Corrine could just make out Tam's shelter.

The blanket over Corrine had grown heavy with damp from the air. Before crawling out of it, Corrine watched Tam's horse, standing nearby. Were its ears pricked? Was it watching something in the dark or was Corrine only imagining things? Perhaps Tam had called out and that's what the horse was hearing.

Corrine's nerves pinged with foreboding. When she didn't hear anything for several minutes, she told herself to calm down. But while she was awake, she ought to check on Tam.

Easing the blanket off, she stood, picked up a stick and reached to stir the dirt and ashes, even though she knew the fire was long gone. She had put it out herself. The stick, the ashes, and the dirt were all too moist with the evening's damp to produce any warmth or light.

As she tossed the stick aside, Tam's horse snorted in warning. Something lunged at Corrine, knocking her to her stomach on the ground. She didn't think to scream.

A man whispered with his mouth on her ear, "Keep quiet. There's a band of Arapahoe not half a mile from here. If they hear you, they'll come kill us both."

Fear surged through her. Corrine had heard that hostile Indians could do terrible things to white settlers. But being knocked to the ground by a strange man was terrible, too. What would he do to her?

"Who are you?" she asked. The man was crushing her with his weight. "Let me go, I can't breathe."

He rolled away, keeping her left side pinned down but freeing her right arm. Air rushed back into her lungs. Her heart lurched as if it might jump from her chest.

The clouds parted and revealed the moon. Corrine craned her neck to see the man's face. It was the bald man from earlier that day.

Corrine's terror turned to rage. Her right hand groped until it found the stick she had tossed. Turning the point toward the man and twisting, she tried to jab it in his neck but only grazed him.

He rolled off, yanking the stick from her hand, whispering loudly, "God sakes! What'd you try to gouge me for?"

Corrine was incredulous. "Why'd you attack me? What do you want?"

"I told you to keep your voice down," he hissed. "You trying to get us both killed?"

Both? Had the man not noticed Tam's shelter then?

"Looks like you been left behind. Looks like you're cold, the way you were shivering just now. Where's the man you took off with? And that woman? They left you, didn't they?" He leaned in to study her face in the moonlight. Corrine's cheeks were clean now. No mud. "And I know you don't have the clap."

Corrine still didn't know what that was. Tam had never told her. But by the way everyone said the word, she suspected it was a disease women working in brothels might get.

Her mind searched wildly for the best response.

The man pointed a finger in her face. "Don't you move, or try anything like that again. I'm lightin' enough of a fire so I can see you better." He cracked the stick he'd taken from her over his knee. "I'll start with this." He leaned down close to her face again. "I'm not lying about those Arapahoe. Keep quiet, now, and still. So's our bodies hides these flames."

Corrine couldn't let him build a fire. He might see Tam's shelter. She crawled toward the rifle she'd left lying on the ground.

"Come back here!" He grabbed her boot and pulled her back toward him. He was strong. "On second thought, I don't need no fire." He tossed away the stick pieces. "Too dangerous anyway with Indians about. I can see you just fine. I remember what pretty hair you had." He ran his fingers through it. "Gold as wheat."

Corrine tried to pull away, but he yanked her by the shoulder, his eyes peering into to her face. Was he alone? What had happened to the others?

"Did the other man die?" she asked.

"I'm sure he's dead by now. That woman blasted his arm off. We didn't stick around to watch him bleed out."

"What about the other one?"

"Tarkington?" he said. That must have been the bearded man's name. "I told you...there's Arapahoe not half a mile from here. They've got what's left of Tarkington strung up on a pole."

Corrine's heart missed a couple of beats.

"They had our horses when we got to 'em. I just barely got away." The man took Corrine's hand and put it to his scalp. She felt a long flesh wound running down the back. "They may be tracking me. If we make it through the night, you can ride out with me at daylight. I'm going to need that horse of yours." He put his face close to hers again. "Just lie still now. I won't have to hurt you if you keep quiet."

Corrine wondered if Tam had heard him whispering. Would she come to Corrine's aid? Was she able?

Poor Tam...Corrine had peeled her bloomers and underclothes off. Tam was covered with a blanket, but that was all. Corrine resisted the urge to look in the direction of the shelter, where Tam's clothes sat folded on the ground. She didn't want to give away Tam's location.

"What's your name?" The man ran his hands through her hair again.

His touch was like bugs crawling up her skin, but she resisted the urge to slap his hand away. "My name is Corrine."

He grinned suddenly, moonlight glinting off his teeth. "I like that you ain't afraid of me."

"I *am* afraid of you," she said.

"How come?" he sneered.

Corrine wondered if the man had been drinking. But she didn't smell any liquor on his breath. "Because you lunged at me in the dark, and you're holding me on the ground as we speak."

"I'm trying to keep you quiet, and keep you safe." A sudden earnestness in the man's voice made Corrine wonder if his head wound had caused him to become disoriented. That might be to Corrine's advantage…or it might not. "I saw how the horse snorted and got your attention. I been watching you for a while."

Corrine felt a chill run down her spine. *How long?*

"Did you know you make a little noise when you sleep?"

"What kind of noise?"

The man grinned. Moonlight bounced off his teeth again. "Reminded me of a little stream gurgling over rocks."

Corrine saw a flash of movement. The man must have seen the sudden change in her eyes, for he turned, but it was too late.

Tam brought her rifle butt down on the bald crown of his head.

*　　*　　*

The hour struck midnight as Bennett Solomon rode into Silvertown. He stopped the gray dun at the first sign of life — a set of half doors with just enough light spilling over the top for him to read the "Saloon" sign overhead. Peeling his lanky legs off the dun, he pushed the doors open and stumbled in.

Flickering oil lanterns mounted to the walls helped him take in the scene. A man dozed in a corner. Another had fallen asleep at a table. Three were awake, playing a hand of poker. A sixth man watched him from behind the bar while drying a glass.

Solomon stepped toward the counter as quickly as his worn out legs would carry him. "Where's the doctor?"

"Only one doctor in town. Has an office at the end of Baker Street. But he ain't available at the moment." The man set down the glass and reached for a bottle.

"Why not?" Solomon watched the man twist the cork from the bottle and pour amber liquid in the glass. He hoped the drink was for him...he needed one.

Sure enough, the man slid the glass toward him. "Outlaws rode in earlier today. They've taken him hostage. Holed up in his office. Bad bunch, from the sound of it."

"What's the sheriff doing about it?" Solomon eyed the glass.

"The sheriff knows they're in there, but he ain't been able to root 'em out."

"Is there anyone else who can help me? There's a pregnant woman a hard day's ride from here. She's hurt. Any midwives in town?"

"Granny Pearl."

"Where can I find her?" asked Solomon, tossing part of the amber liquid back, wincing at the burn. He wasn't a man who drank often.

"She keeps a room behind the Methodist church." The man lifted the bottle to see if he wanted more, but Solomon shook his head.

He downed the remaining contents of his glass, scraped a long finger through his pocket for a coin, and turned to leave. Then he stopped, the newspaperman in him clicking back in. "Wait. What are the outlaws' names?"

One of the men at the poker table answered. "Waldens. Duke Walden and his three sons. Wanted for several bank robberies."

As the shocking words slid slowly into Solomon's brain and settled, a noise at the top of the stairs drew his attention. First one cowboy, then a second, came into sight. They started down the stairs, hands resting on their belt buckles, looking well pleased.

Solomon peered closer at them. "Say...how do I know you?"

One of their faces registered recognition. The cowboy snapped his fingers. "You're that newsman from Baker City!"

*   *   *

James stepped out on the street sometime after midnight, feeling clean and peaceful. He stretched his arms up high, looking forward to a good night's sleep back at Granny

Pearl's. As he walked past the saloon he saw a horse tied at the rail. Something about the animal was familiar. He stepped closer to inspect it by the light that spilled out through the doors.

His heart went cold.

This was the Baldwyns' horse! The gray dun. What would the Baldwyns' horse be doing tied to the hitching rail outside a saloon in Silvertown? James instinctively checked the Walker at his hip.

A man came running toward him. "The doc's been taken hostage!" The man was excited with the news, but James had already heard it. As the man continued, though, his heart went colder still. "Bad criminal bunch has him. Rode in this afternoon. Duke Walden."

"Duke Walden!"

"Yeah. And they don't just have the doctor. They've got a woman, too. Young woman. They claim they'll kill her if James Parker doesn't hand himself over."

James looked at the horse again then grabbed the man by his shirtfront. "What are you talking about? Where are they?"

"The doc's office. On Baker Street." The man tried to pry James's hands from his shirtfront.

"Who's the woman?" demanded James.

"James Parker's fiancé."

The man fell to his knees, James released him so fast. This man could only be talking about Corrine. And her horse stood here at the hitching rail in front of his very eyes! How could that be? How had they gotten her? James looked at the gray dun again in disbelief.

"Where's Baker Street?" he growled down at the man. The man pointed. James ran in that direction.

*   *   *

A man stumbled through the saloon doors and announced, "They're demanding James Parker or they'll kill the woman!"

Solomon whipped his head around.

"What woman?" he asked. "Where's Parker?"

"Where's Charlie?" asked the second cowboy, looking around the saloon.

The man behind the counter said, "A man came and got the boy. It might have been Parker."

"It *was* Parker," said the man at the poker table.

"Where'd they go?" Solomon asked him.

"Don't know."

Solomon rushed to the man who'd just entered. "What woman are you talking about? Do you know where Parker is? I've got to find him!" Solomon turned to the bartender again. "And there's a hurt woman a hard day's ride from here I've got to get back to! That's why I need a midwife." He'd already told the bartender that, but felt the need to restate it.

"The Waldens had Parker's woman when they rode in," said the man who had come into the saloon. "They say they're going to kill her and the doc unless Parker hands himself over. Everybody's looking for Parker now."

Solomon's heart dropped. *The Waldens had Corrine?*

His newspaperman's mind went straight to work. They must have found her and Tam after he'd left them. He could see it all happening in his mind's closed eye. They knew what Corrine looked like, of course, because they would have seen her picture in the paper. Guilt stabbed at him; he was responsible for that.

But if they'd taken Corrine, then what had they done with Tam? Had she been left out there alone? Was she still alive?

Solomon had to make amends. He had to get back to Tam and find out what had happened.

CHAPTER 21
Situation dire

James was crouched in a dark alley across from Doc Burleson's office arguing with the Silvertown sheriff when Bennett Solomon, Michael Chessor and Bart Peters spilled around the corner. James recognized Solomon in the moonlight and grabbed him by the shoulders. "What are you doin' here?"

"We're looking for you! To warn you!" Why did Solomon's eyes look so guilt-ridden?

"Who's 'we,' Solomon?"

"Sheriff Eston. Harry and Tam Sims." His eyes dropped. "And Miss Baldwyn."

James's heart pulsed with physical pain as if someone had punched him in the chest. "Then it's true? The Waldens have Corrine?"

Solomon hung his head. "I'm sorry. I left Tam and Corrine earlier today. I don't know how they could have—"

James squeezed his anger into Solomon's shoulders and shook him. "Why? Why did you leave her, Solomon?"

"Mrs. Sims was sick. She—she made me ride on! Something happened to Harry and Eston went back to check on him. Three men came and Mrs. Sims shot one of them. We rode away, but—she's expecting! And something was wrong. She sent me for a doctor."

"What's wrong with her?"

"I don't know." Solomon twisted his shoulders to get out of James's grip. "The Waldens must have come along and taken Corrine after I left. But I don't know how they could have gotten past...." The look on his face changed. There was that hint of guilt again. "I fell asleep."

James had withheld his fist from Bennett Solomon several times in Baker City, but here in Silvertown he no longer saw the need. He knocked Solomon to the ground, hitting the man harder than he really meant to, but—somebody needed hitting! And Solomon was a satisfactory target.

The sheriff stepped in front of Solomon before James could haul him up and hit him again.

"Parker! That's not helping anything."

James ran his hands through his hair and looked wildly at the sheriff. "I can't stand here and wait on you to handle this." He spun around and walked toward the blue sign with the white lettering.

The sheriff and Chessor both reached for him, pulling at his arms. James thrashed from their hold, drew the Walker and cocked it. "Hold back!"

"Don't do it, James," Chessor pleaded.

James nodded toward Solomon, who was just getting his knees back underneath him. "Go with him, Chessor. Find out what's happened to Tam. I'll handle this."

Then he called out, "Walden! I hear you're looking for me!"

"You James Parker?" The voice was too young to be the old man's.

"I'm Parker. Is it true you have a woman in there?" called James.

"We got us a woman, all right. *Your* woman." This was a different voice, more sneering, but still not the old man's.

James's jaw clenched. "You better not have hurt her! I swear to God, I'll rip every one of you apart if you've hurt her!"

"Why don't you come in and check on her?" The knob twisted and the door opened a crack.

The Silvertown sheriff had released his hold on James, but he tried a final time to stop him. "They're lying, Parker. We haven't seen any evidence there's a girl in there."

A man standing in the shadows stepped forward. James could just make him out. It looked like his arm was in a sling. "There *is* a girl in there. I saw her. I was just coming to tell you, Sheriff Starnes."

James and the sheriff both turned to the man. "Who are you?" asked James.

"The man they pitched out when they rode in."

This was the man his grandmaw left to help. What had ever happened to Granny Pearl?

James gripped the man's shoulder with his free hand. "Was she okay? Blond woman? Young? Pretty?"

"Real pretty," said the man. "Her hair was up under a hat, but I could tell it was light-colored."

"What about the little woman that set your arm? Where'd she go?"

"She left to help someone else."

"She's not caught up in this?" James pointed to Doc Burleson's.

"No. I believe she went to the other end of town."

James released the man and called over his shoulder, "I'm comin' in, Walden!"

"James, don't!" hissed Bart Peters. "They'll kill you."

"She recognizes your voice!" It was the sneering man again. "Seems glad to hear from you!"

"Will you let her go if I come in?" James was in the middle of the street now.

"Glad to!"

"I want to see her!"

The front door of the doctor's office opened wide enough to reveal a woman, skirt flowing, with a hand clamped over her mouth. James's eyes searched hard, but the night was dark. A lamp was lit inside the doctor's office, but it didn't throw off enough light to see the woman's face. He could only tell it was a woman being shown to him.

He wondered if he could lay a bullet in the head of the man holding her fast enough to free her. James had always taken pride in the accuracy of his marksmanship...until the day Emma was shot and he'd failed to take Duke Walden down. This night was dark. He couldn't chance it.

James's blood boiled to think they had Corrine.

"Don't hurt her," he cried. "Let her go! Take me. I'm the one you want. Take me. Let her go."

"Leave your gun!" called the man holding her in the doorway.

James laid his Colt Walker in the dust of the Silvertown street and raised his hands in the air as he straightened back up.

"Don't hurt her! You hear me, Waldens?" His voice cracked. "Don't hurt her."

If he kept saying the words, maybe he could will them into action. It was all he could do; all he could think about. *Please, God, don't let them hurt her. They can do anything they want to me, just don't let them hurt her.*

James had felt so useless the day Emma was shot, then again on the day she was buried, not knowing anything to do to stop the ache inside his chest, a feeling made all the worse by knowing how many hearts around him were aching, too.

The sight of the woman in the doorway—struggling, a hand clamped over her mouth—did more than cause his heart to ache. Fear gouged through him, leaving every limb cold and abnormally weak. James's legs wanted to buckle, but he willed them to keep moving forward.

"Don't hurt her!" *Please, God. Don't let them hurt her.*

His arms were as high as he could lift them. They could have him. They could shoot him. "Just don't hurt *her*," he whispered.

He was almost close enough to see her face when the man backed away and moved her from view. She was struggling, trying to shake her head at James, trying to speak, but the man held her tight. James had held Corrine once himself, but not like that—never like that: forcing her head, clamping a hand down over her mouth. He wanted to rip the man's arm off for holding Corrine that way.

Let her breathe, for God's sake!

"Let her go, Walden! Take me. Shoot me. Ease up on her," begged James, stepping closer to the door. The woman was pulled farther back into the room.

James's boot was on the step. He reached the opening. Angry arms pulled him in, then he felt the swing of fists, clubs, and the butt of a rifle.

*   *   *

Bennett Solomon's heart raced wildly as he searched out the telegraph operator's house and rapped his knuckles on the man's door until they bled. Finally, he roused the man from sleep.

"I've got to send a telegraph!"

"But it's the middle of the night," complained the operator from behind his unopened door.

"I have to send one now! It's an emergency!"

Grumbling, the man turned the key in the lock and cracked the door. "What kind of emergency?"

"Life and death kind."

The man didn't appear to appreciate the nature of the emergency like Solomon thought he should have. It was Solomon's nature to be patient with anyone that moved more slowly than he, but this man was so deliberate to put on his boots, take out a large set of keys, and walk with Solomon to the telegraph station that Solomon actually pulled the man the final few feet.

"Unhand me if you want this telegram sent!" fussed the shorter-legged man.

Solomon unhanded him and switched to pumping him for information.

"Do you know anything about the Waldens taking over the doctor's office? Or them having James Parker's fiancée?"

As soon as Solomon said it, he knew Corrine wasn't really James Parker's fiancée. He was the one, after all, who had used that word in the paper, leading everyone to think they were engaged. The Waldens had gotten that idea from him. Guilt made him clench his fist and pound his own head to keep from hitting the short man in front of him.

The telegraph operator shook his head. "I heard they had the doctor in there, but I didn't know they had a woman. I warned the sheriff that the Waldens were headed this way, but they slipped in past him, all the same."

"How did you know they were coming?"

"A warning came by telegraph from Baker City a few days ago."

The operator unlocked the station door, reached for a clean paper and charcoal pencil, and slid them toward

Solomon. "What's your message? What do you have to do with the Waldens coming, anyway?"

Solomon groaned. "I may have started all this. Can I see that telegram?"

The clerk felt around on the desk, his hand finally landing on the paper. He squinted at the message and shook his head. "It was for a fella named James Parker. I didn't know if he'd ever arrived in town, so I showed it to Buford — that's Sheriff Starnes."

The telegraph was from Colonel Dotson.

WALDENS ON YOUR TRAIL STOP ESTON PARTY TRYING TO WARN YOU OF DANGER STOP

Solomon considered this new information for a moment. He had roused the telegraph operator from sleep, thinking he needed to send news back to Baker City, informing them that the Waldens were here and had taken Corrine captive. But now that he knew Baker City was already aware that the Waldens were after James Parker, he rethought the wisdom of this plan.

Sharing these new developments would only cause worry. Hard as it was for a newspaperman to admit, sometimes news was better left untold. After all the missteps he had taken, putting Miss Baldwyn in such danger, he needed to get things right from here on out.

"Never mind," said Solomon,

"'Never mind'?" Solomon hadn't thought the man could grow any more disgruntled, but he did. "You got me out of my bed!"

"I'm sorry." He handed Dotson's message back to the operator. "Where can I find Granny Pearl, the midwife?"

The operator made a face. "Why should I help you?"

"*Please!* Tell me where I can find her."

The clerk began to close the telegraph office back down. "Last I heard she was living near the mission, in the basement of the Methodist Church."

"'The mission'?"

"Yeah, you know: they help the drunks. She bounces back and forth between the drunks and the harlots."

Solomon's brow pinched. "What kind of midwife is she?"

"The kind that gives all her money away to people who don't deserve it."

The irritated clerk shoved Solomon out of the station, locked the door behind them and pointed out the steeple of the Methodist church, then went tersely back in the direction of his home.

Before Solomon had roused the man, he'd sent Chessor off to ready their horses. The church was on the way to where Chessor was waiting, so Solomon headed quickly in that direction, wondering what was happening with James and where Charlie Baldwyn might have gone.

A candle burned in the window of the sanctuary upstairs. Perhaps he should offer a quick prayer before taking back off. He pushed open the heavy oak door and stepped inside the church.

The most undersized woman he had ever seen was kneeling beside the altar. As soon as he entered, she jumped up and stepped down the aisle toward him. Solomon was surprised at her spritely movements, given the whiteness of the bun on her head.

"Is that you, Jimmy?" Her voice wasn't much louder than the squeak of a mouse.

Solomon turned to see if she was talking to someone else, but they were the only two people in the room. "No ma'am. My name's Solomon."

"Like the king?"

"Why, yes ma'am. Like the king."

"You're tall, like my Jimmy. I thought you were him. Can't see as good as I used to. What brings you to the church, Solomon?"

"I'm looking for a midwife named—"

"Oh!" The woman gave a hop and clapped her hand. "Is someone having a baby? Let me get my bag. It's downstairs." He followed her outside and around the building to a small door that opened in the back. She went inside and emerged a moment later hugging a tapestry bag to her chest. "Where is she?" Little round glasses sat on the end of her nose.

"You're Granny Pearl? If you don't mind me asking ma'am, how old are you?"

"Seventy. Why? Do I look it?"

"Well," hesitated Solomon, "I did expect you to be older, with a name like 'Granny.' But...."

"But not this old?" She snaked a small hand around his elbow and squeezed his arm. "The good thing about my age, son, is that I've seen it all. Take me to your woman."

"She's not *my* woman. She's Harry's woman. And she's a hard day's ride from here."

"Oh. Will we need a wagon, then? To bring her back?"

"Yes, ma'am, but...should we wait? 'Til it's daylight?"

The woman lowered her white head and looked at him over the rim of her glasses. Even in the dim light of the moon, he could see her eyes were the clearest blue.

"Son, you don't have to keep callin' me 'ma'am.' You're welcome to call me 'Granny Pearl,' like everybody else does. Do *you* need sleep? Is that why you're waiting until first light? Or do you think I can't handle it?"

Solomon didn't mean to be insulting, but if he'd known the woman was this old, he would have asked if there was someone else. He'd ridden hard to get here and doubted this woman was up to taking that kind of ride back out to where Tam was waiting. "It just seems safer to wait until daylight."

She cocked her head up and peered at him through the round spheres of her spectacles. "Safer for who, son? Is it safer for the woman out there having a baby?"

Solomon dropped his eyes, ashamed—as if he hadn't felt enough shame that evening. "Well...no."

"Come on, then." She slapped him in the seat of his pants. "I know where to get us a wagon if you've got a horse."

CHAPTER 22

Soft spot for preachers

"I didn't think I popped him that hard," said Tam. "Do you suppose something else could be wrong with him, like maybe his heart locked up from shock or fear?"

The patchy cloud cover had rolled east and now the sun poked its head over the horizon, beaming at Tam and Corrine. The two women sat back-to-back so they could keep watch over the motionless bald man on one side of them and the open land on the other. Tam had her bloomers back on, their waistline widened with patches of Corrine's old petticoats.

Corrine leaned over and lay her hand on the man's chest, which continued to rise and fall. "His heart is still beating."

"Wonder why he's never woke up then."

"I don't know." Corrine studied his head. "But it looks like you hit him right in the spot where he'd already been wounded."

"The head can be delicate. You ever known anyone got kicked in the head by a horse?" Before Corrine could answer,

Tam went on. "I knew a man once that got kicked in the head by a horse. He never was the same after."

Tam must be feeling guilty. This might be the second man she had killed in so many days. Corrine didn't know whether to feel guilty, relieved or frightened that she and Tam were still alone in an unknown land. She knew she was glad to be alive and grateful to have the sun back.

Corrine stood and stretched her stiff limbs. Her eyes scanned the horizon again. She and Tam kept talking about the bald man, but what Corrine really wondered was *if* and *when* someone else would come. And when they did, would it be someone who could help them…or someone who would bring them harm?

"He said a band of Arapahoe Indians were nearby." Corrine went to her saddlebag, pulled out the oilskin with the leftover bacon and apples, and held it out to Tam. "Here, eat this."

"What about you?"

"I'm not hungry."

As Tam began to eat, Corrine had a sudden thought and went back to her saddlebags. Taking out the cotton fabric left from her petticoats, she unzipped one of her boots, removed her scissors, and found a spool of thread. Then she sat down behind Tam again and began to make a sock-like tube.

"What are you doing?" asked Tam over her shoulder.

Corrine tied a knot in the thread. "I've been trying to figure out how to catch a fish. This might let me scoop one."

Tam nodded appreciatively, putting the last bite of
bacon and apples into her mouth. "I thought you weren't
hungry."

Corrine smiled. She was glad Tam was eating, and glad
Tam seemed more peaceful today than she had been the day
before.

"I lied," she admitted. "Besides, we can't sit here
passively waiting for the men to come back and feed us."

The cotton scoop worked. Over the next hour, Corrine
managed to collect three small fish inside the tube. Mindful
that the bald man was likely telling the truth about the
Indians, she resisted the urge to cheer. But it felt good to
have survived the attack of a man in the night, and it felt
good to know she and Tam might not starve while they were
figuring out what their next move should be.

Corrine built a small fire under the thickest branches of
the aspens while Tam skinned and deboned the fish.

"How far does smell travel?" Corrine rubbed the pan
with what little grease could be salvaged from the oilcloth
before laying it down for Tam to put the edible fish parts on.
The fish looked much smaller now than they had at the
creek. Corrine wished she had caught more, as her stomach
loudly voiced its displeasure at having been left unfed.

"I don't know...a little ways, anyway. How far off did he
say those Indians were?"

"A half-mile. That's awfully close. But they might have
been upwind instead of down, and...surely they've moved on
by now."

"Let's hope they're not moving in this direction."

Tam transferred the naked fish from the oilcloth to the heated pan, there being no meal, flour, or salt with which to coat them.

Corrine pointed to the man. "What will we do if he doesn't make it?"

"Bury him."

Tam said it so matter-of-factly, it startled her. She searched Tam's eyes for an explanation, but the older woman didn't offer any more information...not at first.

"Old Man Tate was bald," she finally said. "That was a man who took up with my mama after my father died. Old Man Tate." She stared hard at the fish. "I never knew my real father. My mother and Old Man Tate had three babies. Buried every one of 'em. After the last one, my mother went crazy in her mind. Tate said it was a blessin' when she died. I think he might have poisoned her."

Tam shook her head. "But it weren't no blessin' for me. I was thirteen years old, and once I saw how it was gonna be with him, I lit out. By the time I got to the nearest town, I was hungry. Begged for food. I don't even know how many days I begged before a woman in nice clothes came and found me. She said she knew how I could make enough money to eat. So that's what I did. I worked for that woman seven years, until a preacher in that town convinced me I could have a different life."

Corrine stared at the fish. The last time Tam offered revelations of her past, Corrine had received them badly. But she hadn't known this part of Tam's story.

Tam smiled weakly. "Did you know Jacob in the Bible worked for Rachel seven years? I know exactly how long that feels. Anyway, that's why I had a soft spot for preachers when I met Harry. I pray I haven't lost him, Corrine. He's the only man who has ever treated me so well."

Tam wiped at tears that slid down her cheeks. "Harry Sims acts like he don't deserve me. But it's me who don't deserve Harry Sims." Tam looked over at the bald man again, then off in the distance. "That's why I love him so much."

A memory suddenly popped into Corrine's mind of a young woman from Marston County, Tennessee, a girl who had shown up there pregnant, with no husband. She had lost the child during childbirth. At first she told people there had been a husband, but they later found out it wasn't true. Corrine hadn't realized such a thing could happen before the woman had come. When she was young, she'd just assumed marriage was a prerequisite for having children.

Corrine had been young then, but she was old enough to understand that something about the woman's situation caused people to be upset and whisper. Corrine's father had helped the woman, in his role as an attorney.

Now Corrine re-examined the incident in her mind, wondering what hardship that woman had faced prior to her arrival in Marston. Corrine didn't like knowing that people could take a sacred thing—something designed by God and meant to be holy—and brandish it like a weapon, or use it as a means of power over someone else.

Corrine was feeling the fine line between ignorance and innocence. She didn't want to be ignorant, but realized she had enjoyed being innocent. That innocence was slipping away as a result of holding a dying friend in her arms, being told she could make money by selling her body, and learning that the preacher's wife she thought she knew, and who she fully trusted, had done just that in a former life. How many things had floated past her, in her innocence, that would upset her now if she knew the truth about them?

"I'm sorry I judged you, Tam," Corrine said softly, turning the fish over with a stick.

"I don't hold it against you, Dearest. And I know you've dealt with some hard realities, but I don't think you've ever had to wonder where your next meal was coming from. Today, maybe—but not before this trip." Corrine could feel Tam looking at her, but she kept her eyes on the fish.

"I don't say this to hurt your feelin's," continued Tam, "that's not my intention—especially not with you bein' good to me right now and considerin' how much I love your family. But you can be a little high and mighty at times. You never know how bad some other people have had to claw their way in the world, Corrine. Everybody don't get dealt the same kind of hand."

Conviction coursed through Corrine. Tam had just whacked her right at the source of her embarrassment, same as she'd whacked the bald man in the spot where he had already been hit.

It was true that her first inclination was to point out to Tam all the other ways she might have gotten food at thirteen years old, besides selling her body and a piece of her soul. Corrine couldn't imagine that she would ever have sunk to doing such a thing. No...she would have died of starvation first! But it was awfully convenient to think that way, wasn't it, since she had never had to make that choice?

Corrine wrapped a piece of cloth around the pan's handle and lifted it from the flames. Tam was right and it shamed her. Pride had long stood in the way of her compassion.

Setting the pan on a rock so the fish could cool, Corrine asked, "Can I tell you something else I'm ashamed of, Tam? Since we're exposing my sins?"

Tam put her hand under Corrine's chin and lifted it. "I'm not tryin' to make you feel bad, Dearest. And you've seen me fully exposed now, both my past and my body. I reckon you can tell me anything."

Corrine smiled, but tears welled in her eyes as she swallowed. Shame bit her hard.

"The day Emma died, I was short with her. We had been to the D&J and the sheriff came in. He was all Emma talked about on the way to the mercantile. She was supposed to be in love with Charlie. So why would she go on and on about Sam Eston being so handsome? As if being *handsome* was the only quality in a man that mattered."

"I know what you mean," said Tam. "That big mustache Harry's got? That really don't help his appearance, and gave me pause at first. But his heart shone so beautiful, I decided it didn't matter."

Corrine laughed as she wiped her eyes. Why had she allowed herself to be so mad at Tam? If Tam could see the humor in life after all that she'd been through, why couldn't

Corrine be a little more light-hearted? But Corrine quickly grew serious again.

"When Emma and I heard the gunshots, I pulled her into the alley beside the newspaper office. She said, 'I bet that sheriff is out there!' and she stepped out to see. I pulled her arm and told her not to be such a silly goat, but she jerked loose and stepped out. I had never spoken to her like that before. Then she fell. I caught her just before she hit the snow."

Hard as it was to let the words out, their release brought Corrine instant relief. Still, she had to bite her lip to keep from sobbing. "When she died, my guilt broke all over her. My last words to her were condescending, like I thought I was smarter than she was." Now Corrine had gotten down to the festering thorn that had most bothered her. "I *did* think I was smarter than she was."

"Well, Sweetheart, maybe you were! Nothin' wrong with admittin' that. There's no question Emma was acting silly. Emma *could* be silly. The Lord's not going to strike you down for recognizing it. It's true! But being smarter don't make you better. God gives us all what He gives us, crosses to bear and talents to use, and no two of us are the same."

Tam wrapped an arm around her. "Emma's the one put herself out there, Corrine. Not you. If you're worried that she died knowing you were mad at her seconds prior, stop it. Because you'll never know what ran through her mind. I imagine she saw pretty clear she'd done a foolish thing. Kindest thing you can do for her now is remember the good.

All the laughter you shared together. Treasure that. Just treasure that."

Tam released her and looked out over the land again. "That's what I try to do with the memory of my mother: Just treasure the good. Not be bitter at her for leaving me with Old Man Tate."

She looked back down at the bald man. "Bury the bad memories down in the soil and walk away from 'em. That's what I say."

Later that day Tam and Corrine were sitting back to back again when two moving dots appeared on the horizon...two men on horseback.

Corrine lifted her rifle.

"Oh, Lord," whispered Tam as the moving mirages began to take shape. "Is that who I hope it is?"

When the men got within earshot, one of them stood in his stirrups and called out, "Who taught you how to shoot that rifle?"

Before Corrine could answer, Tam, who had hardly stood for two days, was up off the ground and running.

"Harry! Harry! Good Lord above!" As the men stopped and dismounted she threw herself on Harry. They rolled to the ground.

"Careful, woman!" warned Eston. "He's been shot."

But Harry didn't seem to mind. Tam covered his head and neck with such kisses that Corrine saw Sam Eston's cheeks color under his two-day growth of beard.

Eston looked at Corrine like he wanted to say something, but then Tam pulled herself from Harry and came barreling toward him next. "Sam Eston, I could kiss you!" She did kiss him—on both cheeks—and threw her arms around him, hugging him tight. "I didn't think I'd ever see you again. But you brought him back. I regret every mean thing I ever thought about you."

Smiling, she ran back to Harry.

Eston looked awkwardly at Corrine again. Then he opened his arms to her.

Corrine was so relieved to see him and Harry that she let him wrap her in his arms. It felt so good to be held!

Eston kissed her on the forehead, then pulled back to study her face. "You alright?"

She nodded.

All the tension, all the fear, all the worry of the last several days melted away as she stood safely inside the sheriff's arms.

CHAPTER 23
A man ashamed

With considerable effort, James opened his eyes. Both lids hung heavy and thick. One of them was pressed against something wet...the left eye, closest to the floor. It burned and didn't open as wide as the other. He reached back in his mind for an explanation.

Corrine!

The Waldens had Corrine.

James flexed his right hand. It still worked. He laid it palm down beside his head and pushed to rise up. It was dark, but a shaft of light snuck into the room from a source beyond.

His face lifted off the wooden plank with a soft smack from the suction caused by blood having pooled and hardened between it and the floor. He felt for the wellspring of the blood...a gash over his left eye. That explained his blurred vision and the burn. The wound was hot to his fingers, and swollen.

As his mind worked to piece together what had put him on the floor, James's hands explored the rest of his body.

Nearly every surface he touched was tender. His hand rested against the smooth grain of the wood floor. He wondered what kind it was...pine maybe? Pine was a soft wood, but still felt hard against his pummeled body.

He rolled over on his back, pains shooting up his left side, and continued to run his hands along his limbs to assess all that had been left in working order.

Shirt torn. Chest and torso bruised. A rib or two likely broken on the left side from the way it sucked his breath each time his lungs filled. A knee wrenched, like it had been kicked and twisted, and the ankle below it sore. But other than the open gash in his head and the cracked ribs, nothing else appeared to be broken or leaking.

Wait a minute—*shirt torn*. He felt in his pocket for the tintype of Corrine. It was gone! He swore. Had it fallen out when they'd beaten him? His hands groped the floor hunting for it. He treasured that picture. It had captured the last good smile he'd seen on her face.

He tried to sit up. The room spun. Muffled voices came from the next room. He looked around for something he could use to stop the bleeding of his head. A small bed stood in the corner, opposite him. A woman was curled on it, sleeping.

James stared at her. Even in dim light, with blurred vision and a knocked head, he knew it wasn't Corrine. But he did recognize the woman.

He got to his knees and dragged himself with effort to the side of the bed. "Sairee," he whispered. She didn't move. He nudged her shoulder. "Sairee."

Her eyes flew open. First joy, then shame, and next horror washed over her features. He must look rough. She glanced at the doorway, then back to James's cuts and bruises.

"You're bleeding," she said. The look of horror deepened.

It was probably a good thing the room was dim and she didn't have a clear view of the pool his face had left on the floor.

"What are you doing here?" he hissed.

She reached toward his head with trembling hands. Her wrists were tied together in a faded kerchief. "Jimmy, I'm sorry. I was lookin' for you and these men took me."

James pushed her hands away, not to be mean or angry. He just knew blood was hard for her and his mind was trying to piece things together. He didn't want to be distracted.

"Where's Corrine, Sairee?"

Her face changed. "Who's Corrine?" Sairee always had that cute nose. It wrinkled now, as if she smelled something irksome. "Wait. Is that the girl from the paper? What does she have to do with you, Jimmy? These men showed me her picture, but no one would say what she has to do with you."

Sairee Adams and Corrine Baldwyn certainly were a contrast. One could hear evidence of Sairee's hard life the minute they heard her raspy voice. James hadn't seen Sairee in what...eight years? That would make her twenty-three. Lines around her eyes now made her look older.

The cowpoke hadn't lied about her looks. Sairee was always easy on the eyes. Flighty, too...talked non-stop—

under normal circumstances, of course—and was impulsive. It had broken his grandmaw's heart when Sairee Adams ran off with a man at age fifteen, two years younger than Corrine was now. How had Sairee come to be in this room?

"Are you the only woman here, Sairee?"

She nodded. James couldn't keep himself from smiling. Relief flowed over him like a wash of welcome rain.

Sairee's eyes flew to the door. James's back was to it, but he could tell by the way the dim light diminished that a body had filled the frame.

He tried to turn but was slow in the effort. Boots clunked against the wooden floor as someone walked into the room. The air stirred behind him—from a leg swinging, he realized, as a sharp pain struck him. Lights exploded in his head. The tip of a boot had slammed his back.

James fell to the floor, grabbing his left side with one hand, slapping the ground with the other as he tried to reach the boot. The way that pain seared, there was no doubt his ribs were cracked. He gulped for air, but could only handle short intakes.

"Get up!" Rough hands pulled Sairee off the bed.

"What's goin' to happen to me?" she cried as a young man pulled her from the room.

"Fix us something to eat. Then you're needed to assist. Soon as it's daylight, the doc's takin' Pa's leg off."

The thin young man dragging Sairee looked down at James. "We'll be takin' your leg off next."

James got a good look. He was a Walden all right—same cold eyes James had seen on the boardwalk in Baker City.

"Leg for a leg," said the man with a sneer. "Then life for a life."

*   *   *

Tam, Harry, Corrine and Sam Eston were all staring down at the bald man, trying to decide what to do with him, when another dot appeared on the horizon, coming from the direction of Silvertown this time.

Corrine didn't recognize Michael Chessor until he rode into their camp.

Chessor looked from his horse down to the man, whose color had grayed. "What happened to him?"

"Michael Chessor!" cried Tam, smacking his leg. They pelted him with questions.

"How did you get here?" asked Eston.

"Where are the others?" Corrine wanted to know. She started to ask about James, but caught herself. "Where's Charlie?"

"Have you seen Bennett Solomon?" asked Tam.

Chessor raised his hands. He had plenty of questions of his own. "Who's this man on the ground?" He leaned toward Harry, "And what happened to you?" Then to Corrine, "How is it you're not in Silvertown?"

Corrine twisted her brow. This last question made no sense.

"James gave himself over to the Waldens because he thought they had you." Chessor looked as confused as Corrine felt.

"*Had* me?" What did Chessor mean by that? "No," she said, stating the obvious. "They don't have me."

Chessor's eyes glanced over the group, lingered on Tam's stomach, then returned to Harry. "You look awful."

It was true. Harry had been in no shape to ride back to them, but he had done it.

Corrine pulled at Chessor's arm. "What are you saying about James? And where's Charlie?"

Chessor shuffled his feet. "We got into Silvertown yesterday. The Waldens rode in sometime later and took a doctor hostage. They're camped out in his office. And they had a woman with them. I saw her. It was dark, but they said it was James Parker's fiancé. Everyone thought it was you. Bennett Solomon was there. He even thought it was you."

"It must be that woman from Fort Bridger," said Tam grimacing.

Harry had told them about Mears's death before Chessor rode up, and about the woman the Waldens had taken captive. He also said Duke Walden was still tending the hole James put in his leg.

"Where's Solomon?" asked Tam again.

"He's coming, with Granny Pearl," Chessor told her. "She's a midwife. They're a few miles back with a wagon to take you into Silvertown. I rode on ahead."

Eston assumed command. "Chessor, Miss Baldwyn and I will ride back with you now." He nodded to Corrine. "You can take Tam's horse." He pointed to the bald man on the ground and said to Harry, "That wagon should be big enough to get all three of you back to Silvertown."

Before anyone had time to question or protest, he had helped Corrine mount Tam's horse and they were riding out with Michael Chessor at a fast clip.

Two hours later they passed Bennett Solomon and Granny Pearl going the other way.

Solomon stood in the buckboard as they passed, his face lit up with relief to see Corrine. "Miss Baldwyn! I thought they had you!"

Eston waved Corrine and Chessor on and barked at Solomon, "Nope. I've got her. Now you get the others. We'll see to Parker."

*   *   *

As Sam Eston rode out of view, Granny Pearl squeezed Bennett Solomon's arm.

"What did that man say?" Her voice was no louder than a chipmunk's. Solomon marveled at her stamina. His own body was bone weary from the events of yesterday and from riding through the remainder of the night on this buckboard. When he'd stood in shock and pleasure to see Miss Baldwyn ride by, he had all but toppled out.

Solomon bent down toward the tiny woman. "He told us to get the others and said he'd see to Parker."

Her face scrunched beneath her spectacles. "What Parker? Me?"

"Why, no ma'am." Solomon didn't want to be condescending, so he reminded her gently, "Your name's Granny Pearl."

She swatted his arm as fast as she'd swatted his rump back at the church. "Pearl Parker, son. Pearl Parker!"

Solomon's eyebrows raised. "He was talking about James Parker."

She peered up through her round spectacles into his eyes, squeezing his arm again. "Jimmy? *My* Jimmy?"

"Wait a minute! You called me Jimmy when you first saw me."

"That's because he came to see me yesterday. When I saw you, I thought you were Jimmy, because you're tall like him."

Solomon studied her. "Are you telling me you're related to James Parker?"

Granny Pearl slapped his arm again. She was surprisingly strong. "He's my grandson!"

"Well, I'll be damned. Oh, forgive me, ma'am."

Instead of slapping or squeezing his arm, this time she laid a hand on it warmly. "Son, I've heard it all. I've seen it all. And I've doctored it all. Now, you need to tell me who you are and what this has to do with my Jimmy."

*   *   *

Charlie woke and sat up. His head spun. Where was he? What had happened?

He was in a small room with sparse supplies. He got himself to his feet, his body swaying. There were no windows in the room, but faint light shone around an ill-fitting door.

He stumbled toward it and threw the door open as his last meal came up to greet him.

Standing in an alley, Charlie heaved until there was nothing left in his stomach to lose.

Though dawn was just breaking, the sudden brightness of it felt harsh to his eyes. He wondered if he should go back inside the room and lie down on the bed. What was this place, anyway?

Then he remembered. This was Silvertown. They'd ridden in yesterday...stopped at the saloon. Charlie looked around. Overhead, a steeple rose from the top of the building he'd just exited, into the brightening sky. A church? James said his grandmother sometimes kept a room at a church.

Wiping his mouth, Charlie made his way to the wider street he spied between the buildings. Where was his hat? Gone. He felt his pockets to see if he still had his money. He did. And the knife Hoke had given him was still in its sheath on his belt. His clothes were somewhere between wet and damp.

What about his gun? Was it still on his horse? Was his horse still tied in front of the saloon? And where were James, Chessor and Peters?

Charlie was lurching down the boardwalk when Bart Peters came running out of a café.

"Charlie! Charlie Baldwyn! Where were you?"

Charlie's mind was still moving slow. Head pounding, he focused on Peters. "I don't know, exactly. Where were you?"

"I spent the night in the hotel. Was just having breakfast." The Peterses had plenty of money. They owned the mercantile back in Baker City. "The Waldens have James. Chessor rode back with Solomon to look for Tam. And I couldn't find you."

Charlie blinked, trying to make out Bart Peters's words. "What are you saying?"

"You must have been drunk, Charlie. I knew you were having too much whiskey yesterday."

The finer details were coming back now: the saloon, the whiskey, the rose-cheeked woman, James…the horse trough.

Charlie groaned. He'd made an ass of himself, he was sure of it.

Shaking the humiliation from his head, Charlie replayed the man's words in his mind. "Back up, Peters. Who did you say had James?"

"The Waldens. James gave himself up to the Waldens last night to save your sister."

The last bit of fog fled Charlie's mind. "My *sister?*"

"The Waldens have Corrine, Charlie! Haven't you heard?"

Charlie swayed on his feet. "That's not possible."

"I don't know how, but they've got Corrine. Her horse was tied to the hitching rail in front of the saloon."

Charlie steeled his jaw. "Show me."

Peters led Charlie back to the saloon and Charlie saw his brown horse still tied to the hitching rail. Behind it was a large pile of dung. The gray dun was nowhere in sight.

"It was here last night." Peters pulled Charlie toward two men talking on the boardwalk near the saloon. They told them Bennett Solomon had left town with Michael Chessor to go look for Tam Sims.

"I knew that already," said Peters. "And the midwife went with them."

"They took the horse Solomon rode in on," one of the men said. "The gray one. Word is, Parker's still at Doc Burleson's. The Waldens haven't let the doctor or the woman go yet. The sheriff has been trying to talk to them, but things apparently aren't going well."

"We need to get down there." Charlie turned to leave.

"You look terrible," said Peters. "Shouldn't you eat something first?"

Charlie grabbed Peters by the shirtfront. "The Waldens have my sister!"

"Right." Peters dropped his chin. "We should get down there."

Peters led Charlie to the spot where the sheriff was crouched, across the street from Doc Burleson's. The Silvertown sheriff proved to be a short, stocky man who reminded Charlie of Harry Sims, minus the mustache.

"We were hoping they would release the girl when Parker handed himself over," said the sheriff. "But they didn't. I thought they might do it at daylight, but they haven't yet. Nothing we can do but wait."

"'Nothing we can do but *wait*'?" Charlie gave him a dark look. Hoke Mathews wouldn't have waited. And James Parker wouldn't have waited, either. "We can't sit here and do nothing, Sheriff! Let's take action while they're distracted. My sister's in there!"

"If we storm in, son, they may kill your sister. They're going to be on edge as it is. One of my men already got hit trying to work his way around to the back door."

Charlie's eyes narrowed. He'd be damned if he just sat here! He turned away.

"Where are you going?" demanded the sheriff.

"What do you care?" said Charlie hotly.

"Now don't you go off half-cocked! I told you, I've already had one man hit. They can't leave that office without us seeing them. They're not going to get away. Patience, son, and we'll get this thing worked out."

Charlie brushed the sheriff's hand off his arm. "I'm not going off half-cocked." He had never gone off half-cocked in his life. Well...maybe that one time he rushed at James on the creek bank.

"Your eyes are bloodshot and you reek of vomit," said the sheriff evenly. "Go cool off! Stay down and out of their line of fire, so's you don't get yourself killed."

Crouching, trembling with anger, and seething at the "half-cocked" accusation, Charlie walked off down the side of the building. Peters followed him. "What are you going to do, Charlie?"

"I'm going to get my gun. Somebody's got to take this situation in hand."

Charlie ran back to his horse and retrieved both his rifle and handgun. He felt bad when he thought about how long his horse had been standing there. Hoke would have been disappointed in him for that. And his mother would have been disappointed in him for drinking that whiskey and talking to the painted woman.

But that wasn't the worst of it. How could Charlie ever face his mother again, or Hoke, if anything happened to Corrine? How did she come to be in Silvertown, anyway? What happened after Charlie left home? Had his family not been safe in Baker City? Had the Waldens taken Corrine right off the homestead? Why hadn't Hoke prevented it from happening?

Filled with worry and the fear that he had somehow let everyone down or contributed to this alarming situation by leaving home, Charlie untied his horse and handed the reins to Peters.

"Do something for me. Take my horse to the nearest livery and brush him down and see that he gets fed." Charlie reached in his vest pocket, fished out one of the few coins he'd brought on the trip, and handed it to Peters.

Peters shook his head. "No, let me, Charlie. But promise you won't do anything stupid. Just stay with the sheriff and follow his lead until I get back."

He seemed to take it as agreement when Charlie didn't answer. But Charlie didn't have any faith in the Silvertown sheriff. Somebody needed to get his sister out of that doctor's office.

When he got back to Baker Street, he slipped past the alley where the sheriff and a small group of onlookers were positioned, turned down the next one, and moved to the street corner to study the lay of the land.

A rooster crowed somewhere. The sun was nearly above the horizon now. It made Charlie think about the apostle, Peter. Now *there* was a man ashamed. But unlike Judas, Peter didn't wallow in his mortification. Charlie felt bolstered by the thought.

Harnessing his courage, he plotted quickly. The doctor's office sat directly across the dusty street. Light shone from within, but curtains covered the two front windows and Charlie couldn't see inside. The offices on either side of Doc Burleson's were dark. Charlie wondered if the sheriff had cleared everyone out of them.

He raised his gaze. On this side of the street, the buildings were taller. In fact, the one he stood next to appeared to have the highest windows. If he could get up to the top floor and get himself into position, he could watch for a chance to shoot through the windows of the doctor's office. He'd pick the Waldens off, one by one.

He tried the doorknob of the building. It was locked. Fine. The sheriff thought Charlie couldn't be patient? He'd show him patient. Charlie figured he'd wait thirty more minutes for someone to come and unlock this door.

And if they didn't, he'd charge it and break it down with his fists.

CHAPTER 24
The splinter of bone

Tom Burleson held his tongue and wished once again for a shot of whiskey. He had one half bottle left, in the lower right cupboard, behind his back. The Walden sons had searched all through the kitchen, taking stock of the food and drink supply, but they hadn't yet thought to search the cupboards in the front office. And for this, Doc Burleson was grateful.

It was hard enough work taking a man's leg off without having to do it with a wailing woman and angry men all around him. A shot of whiskey would have helped. But he didn't want them to know it was there. Its existence felt like one small ace in his pocket.

Truth was, it wasn't the only ace in the room. There were also several instruments and treatments that, if used wisely, might get him out of this predicament.

Stay calm. Pay attention. Don't make anybody mad. The voice in his mind sounded a lot like his long-dead wife's. *Hold every possible ace in your pocket.* He needed to focus and ration his waning strength. Stressful situations had a way of draining a man of both.

He thought back over the events of the tense morning. He had held off as long as he could, hoping to stop the spread of Duke Walden's infection. But it had become clear: the man would die if they didn't get his rotting leg off. Chances were pretty good he'd die even if they did. Still...the voice kept telling him it was important to buy time. Taking the leg off was his best shot at that.

Duke Walden never should have traveled with that gun wound in his leg. His hatred for James Parker had to be strong.

Doc Burleson didn't tell the Walden boys, or Duke himself, that the old man might not pull through, even with the amputation. But he could tell the old man knew. He could read it in his eyes. So it surprised him when Walden agreed to go through with it.

Doctors saw some strange things. It wasn't possible to always predict what a patient would want, or what the outcome of a medical procedure might be. Doctors stood with people in tense moments, and tense moments had a way of revealing the truth. Truth was in the eyes, so Doc Burleson had learned to watch the eyes...to notice how eyes took news.

When Doc Burleson told the Walden boys it was Duke's leg or his death, their eyes revealed neither tears nor pain. Just anger.

Viscount circled the room, holding his rifle. Suddenly, he let out a volley of cursing. Doc Burleson braced himself for the man to shoot them all.

"How long will it take him to recover?" Baron wanted to know. "We can't stay holed up in here forever!"

"Shut up, Baron." Duke grabbed the doctor's shirtfront and pulled him down close to his mouth. "Do right by me or these boys will make you wish you had."

As soon as Duke released Burleson, he grabbed hold of Baron.

"I want Parker to suffer," he said hoarsely. "Don't kill him 'til I wake back up. That'll give me reason to do it. I want to see his last breath. Get those other two if you can, that boy and girl from the picture. That'll make Parker suffer more. When the time's right, get yourself out of here. You got plenty of shells?"

Burleson readied his saw and instruments and watched Baron check for ammunition.

Duke Walden could have recovered from this wound. But when he chose to strain it and expose it to the elements, just so he could kill a man, he had selected his own coffin's first nail.

Baron looked at the doctor. Once again, the doctor thought he saw more venom than hurt in the younger man's eyes.

"You got any weapons or shells?" Baron grabbed Burleson off the stool. Burleson considered the instruments he had just prepared. His Gemrig saw, with the open frame and removable blade, was especially sharp. In that moment, Burleson would have liked to use it on Baron's arm.

"Any guns?" demanded Baron.

Just one. Another ace the doctor had been hoping to keep tucked in his sleeve. But it might prove a better strategy to give up the obvious weapons in order to hold onto the less apparent ones. He pointed to the cabinet where he kept the gun. Baron released him and emptied the cabinet of weapon and shells.

Duke reached for Viscount. "Make sure Parker suffers," he said, holding onto his son's arm. "If this doctor does me wrong, make him suffer, too."

It didn't surprise Burleson to hear him say it. He doubted the sons needed to be told. Retribution obviously ran in their blood.

Marquis stepped up when Duke released Viscount, but Duke apparently didn't have any instructions for Marquis. Instead he looked back at the doctor. "Don't hold back on that ether or I'll come up off this table, slashing."

Doc Burleson didn't correct him. He used chloroform, not ether.

"Marquis!" Duke barked suddenly.

Marquis, who had turned to leave the room, came back. His eyes were flat. No feeling in them at all, that the doctor could see. "Put a knife in my hand, boy," Duke said. "Sharpest you got."

Marquis hesitated, then reached into his boot and pulled out a long, thin blade. He looked at it, turned it in the first shafts of light coming through the window, then held it over the old man's face as if considering something.

"That'll do." Duke reached for the knife.

Marquis gave it to him then left the room. As he walked away, the doctor noticed Marquis had several knives on him. One on his gun belt, one tied to his leg, and another slung in a casing on a loose string down his back.

"I need assistance," Doc Burleson told the others then. He had removed a lot of limbs during the war. Minie balls were slow and heavy and most often hit a man's extremities, shattering bones beyond repair. The scalpel cuts and sawing of bone wouldn't take him long—ten, maybe twelve, minutes. First he'd cut through the skin and muscle—top, side and bottom—down to the bone, leaving one side of the flesh long to form a flap over the stump. But he needed extra hands for wiping blood and holding pressure on the arteries until he could tie them off and sew down the flap.

"Go get the girl," said Baron.

But when Viscount did, all Sairee Adams did was wince and wail.

Because of where the wound was located, the amputation had to be made high on Walden's leg. It had been Doc Burleson's experience that the higher the amputation, the worse a man's chances for survival, but he kept that information to himself.

First, Doc Burleson wet the rag with chloroform and held it over Duke's nose. As he waited for it to work its effect, he lifted Duke Walden's leg to get a feel for the density and width of the bone. The leg felt heavy. The limbs of the unconscious were always heavy. His own arms felt heavy, too. He was tired.

Tapping several spots on the old man, he waited to see if there was any reaction. There was none. The chloroform had taken full effect.

He set the scalpel against the skin, hoping the woman might prove helpful after all. But at the first sight of red,

Sairee Adams set to screaming like the blade was slicing through her own flesh and bone.

Doc Burleson nearly dropped his knife when a gun suddenly boomed in the room. Looking up, he saw that Marquis had shot at someone outside.

Really! he thought in frustration. These were worse conditions than he'd had to operate under in the war.

*　　　*　　　*

James woke to the sound of screaming. The sun was fully over the horizon. When he lifted his head, the dried blood didn't stick to the floor as bad this time. He lay in the same room as before. As he looked around, his gaze landed on a loose board under the bed. Reaching with his right arm— even *that* caused his left side to throb—he pulled at the board, but he lacked the strength to yank it loose.

That was concerning. James prized his strength and had always depended on it. But the board held fast.

The screaming was coming from Sairee. He was certain of it. James remembered when the thin man took her away earlier, he had said she was needed to help take off Duke's leg. James could have told the Waldens she didn't tolerate the sight of blood well, but they hadn't asked him. He prized that, too: his knowledge of things.

Would either his strength or knowledge be sufficient to free them from their current circumstances?

Suddenly worried the Waldens were torturing Sairee, and not just working on Walden's leg, James pulled himself up from the floor, his ribs exploding with pain. As he stumbled toward the door, he heard the sudden sound of a shot from the next room. A stockier man than the one James saw before, but with a similar face, stepped up to block the doorway.

"What are you doin' to her?" asked James thickly. He tried to see into the other room, but the man's bulk made it impossible.

"She's fine. Just not liking the sight of pa's leg coming off."

Sairee was still screaming but James could hear it now: a sawing sound behind her cries, and the splinter of bone.

Sairee's screams reached a fever pitch.

"Hold pressure on that artery!" yelled a voice James didn't recognize. That had to be the doctor.

The man in the doorway turned to see what was happening in the front room. He winced.

Feet clattered against the wooden floorboards. Men cursed. There was a sound like medical instruments clanging against a metal table.

"Get her out of here! I'll do it myself!" yelled a young man's angry voice. "Baron, get over here!"

"I'm watching Parker," said the man in the doorway. "He woke up."

"Marquis can watch Parker if he's through shootin' at people. Marquis, there's a window in that other room where you can keep an eye out. Tie those two to opposite ends of the bed, then keep watch. Baron! Get in here and help with Pa's leg!"

The sounds from the next room were bad, but the smell was truly awful. James had been by his grandmaw's side lots of times when the smells of the sick and wounded filled his nose. This was worse than anything he remembered.

There came more shuffling of feet and rattling of metal, the sounds of boots tromping and a thud from the other side of the wall. Baron disappeared from the doorway but before James could step forward, it was filled again by Sairee and the man who must have been Marquis. They knocked into James, who was already unsteady on his feet, causing him to pitch backward.

The last thing he felt was the crack of his skull landing again on the soft pine of the floor.

*   *   *

When Charlie heard screams coming from inside the doctor's office, he lost his head and went charging for the door where Corrine and James were being held. Men tackled him before he had crossed the street.

As he writhed on the ground, listening to the cries of anguish reach a fever pitch, a shot rang out, kicking up Silvertown dirt inches from his head.

"Get him up and over here!" called the sheriff. "Before the Waldens put a bullet in him."

Strong arms grabbed Charlie on either side and lifted him from the street, then dragged him to where the sheriff and onlookers huddled.

"Take him to the jail and lock him up," the sheriff told the other men. Two men who appeared to be deputies each took one of Charlie's arms and hauled him in the direction of the jail.

"You can't arrest me!" called Charlie over his shoulder, kicking at the street. "I haven't done anything illegal!"

"It's for your own good, son," said one of the deputies. He couldn't have been much older than Charlie.

"Don't call me 'son,'" spat Charlie. "I'm not your son. You're not my elder." It wasn't Charlie's nature to be insolent, but these were extreme times, after all.

The deputies rounded the corner and pulled Charlie into the jail. The first cell held an old man who appeared to be sleeping off a drunk. The men threw Charlie into the second cell. The iron door clanged shut behind him—the sound of finality.

Charlie pushed off the back wall he'd fallen against and threw his body at the bars. "You can't arrest me!"

"No?" The older deputy cocked his head. "Sure looks like we just did."

"I want a lawyer." Charlie tested the iron with his hands. He was so mad he almost believed he could bend the bars. "Who are the attorneys in this town?"

Both deputies laughed.

"Harold Pickens is your best bet," said the younger deputy.

"And the closest," said the older.

"All right then," said Charlie. "Someone go get Harold Pickens. He'll tell you that you can't arrest me. He'll tell you that you have no right to hold me."

The deputies chuckled as if they found this amusing. They started to leave.

"That's right!" Charlie called. "Go get Mr. Pickens. He'll tell you!"

"No need," answered the youngest deputy.

"What do you mean? I've got legal rights!"

"No need to get Harold Pickens." The older deputy opened the door. "He's already here." The deputies stepped out onto the boardwalk. Charlie watched the door swing shut.

He looked around. There were three cells. The third one was unoccupied. The old man he had taken for a drunk raised a hand, never opening his eyes.

"Harold Pickens."

*　　　*　　　*

The rush of adrenaline Corrine had felt when Sam Eston and Harry Sims rode into camp earlier that day was wearing off as she, Eston and Chessor pushed hard toward Silvertown. The knowledge that James was in danger, the fitful night she'd spent, her worry over whether the bald man would live or die, her hunger…it was all taking its toll.

Emotions broke through her in waves. She was filled with dread for James and a longing to see Charlie, and was afraid of what they'd find when they arrived. She felt nervous at having ridden off with two men, but was relieved not to be the person in charge of making decisions. No sooner did her heart swell with one emotion than another elbowed in to take its place.

They traveled at a good clip, side by side with Corrine in the middle, but not so fast that Eston couldn't lob a barrage of questions past her to Michael Chessor.

"Any problems before you got to Silvertown?"

"We crossed some signs of Indians, and Charlie and James got into a tussle."

"What about?"

Chessor cut his eyes to Corrine then back to Eston. "Oh…man stuff. They smoothed things over."

"What's the town like?" Eston asked.

"Silvertown?" Chessor thought a minute. "Bigger than I expected. A creek runs behind it, coming down from the mountain. That's where they first found gold, then silver. Truth is, I hadn't seen much of it yet."

The landscape around them now was turning picturesque, a snow-capped mountain range appearing in the distance.

"Why didn't Charlie come with you?" asked Corrine.

Chessor refused to look over at her. "The barkeep said James came and got Charlie. I'm not sure where they went. James told me to stick with Solomon and check on Mrs. Sims, so that's what I did."

"What did you mean exactly when you said James gave himself over?" Corrine pressed. "Did you see him? Is he all right? Is Charlie all right? And where were you when James came and got Charlie?"

Her questions appeared to make Chessor uncomfortable.

"I'm sure the men were drinking, Miss Baldwyn," said Eston. "That's probably where Charlie was, sleeping off his drink."

She glared over at him, remembering well that Eston himself had needed time to sleep off his drink. Eston looked away. When she looked back at Chessor, he wouldn't meet her eyes either.

What was it with men and liquor?

"Not Charlie," she said. "Charlie doesn't drink."

Chessor lifted a finger, as if to say something, but then he must have changed his mind. He concentrated on the trail in front of them.

"What happened when you saw Solomon, exactly?" Eston asked Chessor.

"Peters and I were coming down the stairs from...." He shot a furtive glance at Corrine. "From...upstairs, and right about the same time I noticed this tall man at the bar looking at us, close like. I recognized him as the newsman from Baker City. He said he'd been traveling with you and the Simses. About that time a man ran in from the street and said the Waldens had a woman. Said they were going to kill her if James Parker didn't hand himself over."

It began to fully dawn on Corrine what James had done, exactly...and why.

The realization horrified her. Had it only been weeks ago that Corrine had longed for adventure? She'd had plenty now. If she ever made it back to the safety of Hoke's cabin on the hill, she didn't believe she would ever again feel the need to leave it.

"We ran down to where the sheriff was, across from the doctor's office," Chessor was saying. "Me, Solomon and Peters. James was there. He told the Waldens he was coming in and begged them to let the woman go."

Fear had shot up Corrine's spine again and was clawing at her throat. Fear and guilt. She felt responsible. "So the Waldens have James? That's what you're saying?"

Another furtive glance from Chessor. "Peters and I told him not to."

"He's in the doctor's office?" clarified Eston.

"He was when we left."

"Did they turn the woman loose?"

"They might have by now, but they hadn't done it yet when we left."

"Does the Silvertown sheriff have the situation in hand?" asked Eston.

Chessor shrugged. "He was standing outside the doctor's office trying to reason with them. He didn't want James to give himself up to them, but then James turned his gun on us. Said he had to try to save the girl."

The girl….

"He must have known it was that other woman," said Corrine, trying to break loose from the tentacles of guilt.

"No, we all thought it was you, Miss."

"Why?" Corrine's frustration and sense of helplessness mounted. "Why would they think that? James didn't even know I was headed this way!"

Chessor looked squarely at her this time. "Solomon was there. He knew you were headed this way. He thought the Waldens had come along and taken you after he left."

Corrine was having trouble breathing...and trouble thinking straight. The Waldens had James. How had the force of that not fully struck her until now? *The Waldens had James.* And the Waldens might kill him.

They were riding at a pretty good clip already, but Corrine kicked the flanks of Tam's horse to make it go faster. Silvertown lay nestled inside the mountain chain ahead. Tired or not, they needed to get there, and fast.

The men kicked their horses and followed.

CHAPTER 25

In an iron box

Charlie felt sick again. His head pounded. He needed water.
He hated being caged in an iron box, powerless to help his
sister.

Bart Peters showed up at the jail mid-morning with a
steaming cup of coffee. A steaming cup of coffee had never
tasted so good. Charlie felt certain his body had been near
collapse from worry and dehydration.

"Woman at the hotel let me bring that out to you," said
Peters, "but said I better get the cup back to her." He reached
in his pocket and pulled out a biscuit, slipping it through the
bars.

Charlie saw Harold Pickens peep at them from the next
cell through the crack of an eye. His suit was wrinkled and
dusty. Charlie couldn't decide if he'd been in a fight or
pulled from a ditch.

Charlie took his time chewing the biscuit and drinking
the coffee. He handed the empty cup back to Peters. The
biscuit had still been warm. No food had ever tasted better,

not even Mimi's cooking, but it barely filled one edge in the hole of Charlie's hunger.

"What's happening out there?" Charlie asked Peters. The two deputies were back in the front room. Charlie had tried to catch snatches of their conversation, but wasn't able to piece much together.

"Chessor isn't back yet," said Peters. "He rode out with Solomon last night. Things have been quiet in the doctor's office. The sheriff found where the Waldens tied their horses and he put some men on watching them. He's got others watching the back of the house. That's all they're doing right now, Charlie...watching."

Charlie banged his head against the bars. It was torture to be stuck in here!

"Any more screams?" He hated to ask the question, not sure he could bear it if there had been.

"No."

Charlie considered this. What did it mean? Had they hurt Corrine? "How can the sheriff just stand by and not take some sort of action? Can't he bargain with them somehow?"

"He's waiting to hear the Waldens' demands." This came from Harold Pickens, who still lay on his cot with his eyes closed. "They haven't given them yet."

"What do you know about it?" Charlie studied the man in the cell next to him. "You've been in here the whole time it's been going on."

"Because I have experience negotiating, Charles. And I listen. You should try it."

Charlie hadn't spoken to Pickens while the deputies were gone. He didn't like feeling that he was the brunt of their joke. Harold Pickens couldn't be a lawyer! It seemed obvious to Charlie that he was a drunk or a nutcase who'd only claimed to be an attorney. But the man couldn't be one. Charlie's father had been a lawyer. Charlie knew what kind of man it took. Not this kind of man.

Peters looked Harold Pickens over. "Why are you in here?"

"I showed contempt in court."

"Why'd you do that?" asked Peters.

Pickens opened his eyes and sat up. From an upright angle, he looked more sane. "Judge Wainright and I have a little game going. He's mad because I know the law better than he does, so he throws me in jail for contempt of court every chance he gets. They'll let me out this afternoon."

"How do you know?" asked Peters.

"Because that's as long as he can legally hold me."

Charlie grabbed the bars. "So you really *are* an attorney?"

"I really am."

"Then why didn't you say something when they were hauling me in here? Help get me out!"

"First: you didn't ask," said Pickens. "Second: you needed to cool off—still do—just like they said. And third: you keep looking at me with haughty eyes. I don't like haughty eyes, Charles. There's a scripture about that. You thought I was a drunk, didn't you?"

Charlie felt unfairly judged. But as soon as the thought flitted through his mind, he realized he was guilty of exactly the thing Pickens claimed. He wasn't proud of the fact. It was just that...lately...his pride had taken more blows than he was used to.

Charlie couldn't keep himself from asking, "Why is your suit so dusty if you were thrown in here straight from court?"

Harold Pickens grinned. "Go on. What else have you observed? And what do you know about the law? You talked like you had some familiarity with it."

"My father was an attorney."

"How did you know they didn't have a legal right to hold you?"

"I was just guessing about that."

"You were wrong," Pickens said. "But you *did* sound convincing, which is a good skill for a lawyer. They do have a legal right to hold you for your own safety: if they have a reasonable right to believe your life is in danger, or if you're obstructing the sheriff's efforts to do his job."

Charlie sighed. "That no longer applies. I've cooled off. So how can I get out of here? They have my sister, Mr. Pickens."

Harold Pickens softened then. "What is she like?"

"What does it matter?"

"Well, if you're going to accurately assess the situation, Charles, you need to have a good handle on all the variables. What do you have to work with? Is your sister flighty or smart?"

"Smart."

"Smarter than you, I hope. Is she pretty?"

"Very."

"Hmm," Pickens mused. "That's a problem."

"Why?"

"How many men are in there?"

Pickens let that sink in. As Charlie's face hardened, he continued. "What are their ages? How many women? Who's got the upper hand? Word is, the oldest Walden came after Parker. He's got three sons. He's injured, but as far as we know the sons are not. The doctor's pretty savvy...I've met him. What about Parker? Is he a western man? Seasoned?"

Charlie nodded.

"Good. I imagine they've beaten him pretty bad. You need to prepare yourself for the fact that they may have hurt your sister, too. The Waldens aren't going to kill them, at least not right away. They need them to escape. You've got to think like they think. Put yourself in their shoes. They're mad at Parker. They will have seen a picture of him with you and your sister. I've seen that picture. Your sister *is* pretty. Now, what would swing the variables? What would reshuffle the deck? You ever gamble, Charles?"

Charlie and Peters looked at one another and shook their heads. Charlie, especially, was fully invested in Harold Pickens' logic now.

"Gambling and practicing law are similar," Pickens said with a nod of his head. "Both are about gaining the upper hand and keeping it. You have to act like you don't want anything. Right? Because the moment you let someone else know what you want is the moment you lose the upper hand.

I'll get out of here when I'm supposed to, in part because they think I don't care if I get out."

Charlie had to admit the man didn't look like he cared if he got out. "I did think you were a drunk," he confessed.

"Aren't we all, on occasion?" Harold Pickens sighed. "I actually did get drunk."

"So you lied."

Pickens grinned. "First rule of law, son: the truth is a slippery thing. The way one man sees it may not be the way the other man sees it, and they may have witnessed the same event. But they will not have witnessed it with the same motives and level of interest. Is it the law's job to ferret out the truth? If it is, then *which* man's truth?"

Pickens answered his own question. "No. The law's job is to administer a just ruling." He leveled his hands out like they were a balancing set of scales. "In a just ruling, the truth will often out. Remember King Solomon and the babies? His just ruling revealed the truth. What is *just*, you may ask?"

Charlie didn't ask, but of course he wanted to know.

"That, Charles, is the question with which anyone in a profession of law must grapple. Before you can grapple, however, you need to assemble the facts—*all* the facts."

Charlie stared hard at Harold Pickens' dusty suit. The truth dawned on him. "You were drunk before you went into court? That's why the judge ruled you in contempt?"

Pickens nodded. "I was."

"Why?"

"Now you're asking the right question, Charles." Harold Pickens smiled. "There's hope for you, yet."

*   *   *

It was deep in the night. Corrine's will to stay in the saddle and her eyelids' desire to drop were engaged in a mighty battle. Her will was near defeat when Eston pulled up sharply.

Chessor and Corrine stopped and watched him as he turned his head, listening.

"I thought I heard something," the sheriff whispered. "Over there." He pointed.

The foliage was thick here, but there was still a clear path open before them.

"I'll check." Chessor nudged his horse in that direction.

Corrine lay over the neck of her horse, thinking she'd just rest her eyes until Chessor returned. Next thing she knew, Sam was pulling her from the horse and holding her in his arms. When she opened her eyes, his were close.

"You alright?"

"I'm fine." She twisted to free herself from his embrace, but in the weak, slow effort, lost her balance and fell to her knees.

Eston dropped next to her and ran a hand over her shoulder. "You're not alright. We need to let you rest."

"No!" She pushed away his hand. "Please, we have to keep going. It can't be much farther."

Corrine didn't want to stop. She needed to get to James—James was in danger. And she needed to be in a town again, with people, away from where strangers could sneak up on her in the night. It spooked her to think of one more person having a chance to watch her sleep.

She stood to show him that she could. "Please," she said again.

Chessor reappeared, looking spooked. "I saw a horse, a small one. Looked like he was saddled, but no rider. He ran off. I didn't think I should take the time to go after him."

"He may be following us, if he's lost his rider." Eston looked up at the moon. "It'll be daylight in a couple of hours. Will we be to Silvertown by then?"

"We should hit it right about sunrise."

"Let's go then," said Corrine. "I can make it."

With reluctance, Eston helped her back into the saddle.

Chessor was right: they rode into Silvertown shortly after the sun broke. As they did, it was all Corrine could do to stay on her horse. She could see it was a lovely town, just as Chessor had said, but was having trouble focusing on anything beyond her horse's mane.

Eston said, "Point us to the nearest hotel, Chessor."

"No!" cried Corrine.

"Yes." His tone didn't allow for argument this time. "You need rest and a meal. After we get you settled, I'll go find out what's happening."

Chessor must have seen how tired she was, too. He didn't ask questions, just rode them down the middle of the street. They stopped in front of the first hotel they came to, and as soon as they did, Bart Peters came running from an eatery beside it.

"Miss Baldwyn! Sheriff Eston! Chessor!"

Eston dismounted and reached for Corrine. She tried to swing her leg over but was clumsy about it, so he pulled her into his arms again. As he carried her up the steps of the boardwalk to the hotel, she heard Peters say, "How is this possible? I thought she was bein' held by the Waldens."

"Different girl." Chessor jumped up on the boardwalk to open the hotel's front door. "She was with Tam Sims...." His voice faded off as Sam carried her inside and Chessor closed the door behind them.

"Put me down," she said weakly. "I need to find Charlie and get to James." But she knew she might lack the strength to stand. Her head felt strange and the room was spinning.

A matronly woman sat behind a desk. Sam said something about a room. Then she was being carried again…up a staircase…laid out on a bed. *A real bed!* All that rain, the bald man's attack, days and one long night of riding hard. After the misery of the last three nights, a real bed felt like heaven.

Corrine felt her head being lifted and someone spooning a hot broth past her lips. She was so tired, she wondered if her body might be too spent to keep breathing. Did anyone ever die from exhaustion?

Then there was silence.

Blissful rest.

*   *   *

Charlie was sitting with his head in his hands when Sam Eston walked in. Harold Pickens had been released the previous afternoon, just as he'd predicted. Charlie jumped up and grabbed the bars of his cage. "Sheriff! You've got to help my sister!"

"Relax, son. Your sister's fine. She's at the hotel, sleeping."

"What? What happened? Is James there, too? How did they escape?" Charlie hadn't heard the sound of gunshots through the windows.

"The Waldens never had her. They've got some other girl." Eston flashed his badge at the youngest deputy and motioned for him to open Charlie's door. The deputy did so, albeit reluctantly.

"Sheriff Starnes is releasing you into my care."

Charlie grabbed Eston's shoulders. "Where is she? Where's Corrine?"

Eston shook Charlie's hands off and took him by the arm. "Hotel. I'll take you."

*   *   *

Corrine woke to the sight of bright mid-day sunlight streaming into the room. The window was open and she heard the sound of running water in the distance. Charlie sat beside her bed. She didn't mind if Charlie watched her sleep. For a moment she thought they were back home, in Marston. No, it must be Baker City.

Wait, where were they? Those places didn't include the sound of running water. She looked around. The room was unfamiliar.

Charlie leaned forward on his elbows, the legs of his wooden chair complaining. "Hey, Sis."

Corrine studied him. He looked older. How long had it been since she'd seen him? Only two months, but longer than she'd ever been away from him. New hair grew on his chin. He looked rough, like he hadn't washed or slept in days.

"Happy birthday late," she said.

He grinned. "Happy birthday late to you, too." He raked a hand over his face. "Ma would have a fit about those bloomers. But you know what? They suit you."

Corrine looked down. She hadn't been tucked beneath the sheets of the bed. Someone had laid a light blanket over her, but she had kicked most of it off.

Charlie stood. "You need to eat."

"Don't leave!"

"I won't, but Mrs. Spencer said to let her know when you woke. She promised to bring up a hot meal. I'm hungry, too."

Corrine's stomach growled angrily. "How long did I sleep, Charlie?"

"A couple of days."

"What?" Corrine started to rise but Charlie reached to stop her.

"Slow down, Corrine. There's no rush. In fact, everybody's trying to stall for time."

"Why? I don't understand. Please explain what's happened. Where's James? And Tam?"

There was a knock on the door. Charlie opened it and Sam Eston strode in. He sported a clean new shirt, had a fresh haircut, and a new trim to his mustache.

Self-consciousness washed over Corrine. She knew she must look a mess — worse than Charlie, even. She still wore her stained white blouse and Tam's bloomers that she had been wearing for days…in the rain, as she was getting attacked, while riding through the night.

Her body felt weak. Was it because she hadn't eaten in so long? As Charlie ducked out of the room to tell Mrs. Spencer she was awake, Corrine thought of the three small fish she'd caught in the stream. How long ago had that been? She'd only eaten one and given the other two to Tam, and she'd missed a meal or two before that, and then done all that riding. Corrine remembered what Tam said about being hungry as a child. How long had Tam gone without eating before she was finally offered a chance for food?

Corrine's self-consciousness grew as Eston studied her. "How're you feeling?" he asked.

"Fine." Corrine felt her cheeks flush. As Charlie came back into the room, she was certain he would notice the warmth in Eston's eyes.

"They're all here now," announced Eston to Charlie. "Solomon, Harry, Tam and the midwife. They're staying at the other hotel since this one was full. It slowed them some to have to stop and bury the bald man," Eston explained. "He died before they got here."

Corrine felt a stab of guilt. Eston must have read it in her eyes, because he changed the subject. "Solomon found

his pinto. Brought it on in. That must have been the horse
Chessor saw."

"I told her she needs to eat," said Charlie, nodding
toward Corrine. "Mrs. Spencer promised to bring lunch up.
Any change at the doctor's office?"

Sam cut his eyes at Corrine and shook his head.
"Sheriff's been trying to talk to them, but they're not saying
much. They did say they might release the girl in exchange
for food."

"And James?" Corrine was fearful of what they might
say, but she had to know. "Any news on James?"

Both men avoided making eye contact with her.

"Still alive as far as we know," said Eston. "The Waldens
claim he is. They know they won't ever get out of here
without some bargaining power. If they turn the girl loose for
food, that only leaves 'em James and the doctor, so I don't
think they'll kill them, at least not while they're still holding
them in town."

Kill them?

No. James couldn't die. James was so strong…so
capable. When she had snuck out of the cabin to help come
warn him, Corrine had fully expected to reach James before
the Waldens ever did. And she'd felt certain that, should any
kind of showdown take place, James, Harry, and Sam Eston
would take the thing in hand. Chessor and Peters were also
capable, as was Tam. Charlie could shoot well. Didn't their
own group outnumber the Waldens?

"I told you what our best leverage is," said Charlie. "Just
say the word."

Sam dropped his voice, but it was impossible not to hear his response. "Let's discuss it in the hall." He smiled at Corrine then.

Remembering how gently Eston had pulled her from her horse, she felt her cheeks grow warm again. Back at Fort Bridger the sheriff had asked if Corrine would consider him should anything happen to James, or to her and James's understanding.

Had her understanding with James been altered? Yes...no. She didn't know. She just knew they had to get James free from the Waldens. James couldn't die...he couldn't. Because she loved James, whether he was ever to be her husband or not.

Corrine's eyes watered. She didn't quite feel like herself. She hadn't regained control of her body and emotions. She wanted to know why Charlie said they were stalling. Who, exactly, was stalling?

The sound of footsteps came from the stairs, followed by a knock on the door. This time when Charlie opened it, a matronly woman poked her head in. She carried a tray laden with food. "I brought you a hot lunch."

Corrine pulled her legs up so Mrs. Spencer could set the tray on the end of the bed. Charlie glanced at the tray longingly, but stepped out into the hall with Sam Eston. Corrine could hear them talking low but she could no longer make out their words.

"You must be Mrs. Spencer. Thank you." Corrine's mouth watered as she breathed in the smell of the warm food. Beef stew and cornbread!

The woman leaned in to pat her arm. "Honey, I'm so happy to do it. It's good to see you awake! I never saw a girl so worn out." She dropped her voice to a whisper. "I hate to know all you've been through."

Corrine looked down at her wrinkled clothes and ran a hand over the messy braid of her hair.

Mrs. Spencer noticed. "Would you like a bath, Miss? There's the nicest bath house run by a sweet Chinese couple just across the street."

"Oh, yes! And I'd dearly love to wash these clothes I'm wearing. Do you have anything I could wear while they're cleaned?"

The woman's eyes brightened. "Why, of course. I'll help find you something suitable. Don't you worry about a thing."

She must have seen Corrine's furtive glances toward the door, for she added, "You should go ahead and eat, miss. I doubt your brother will mind."

"Alright." Corrine didn't need convincing. She tried not to gulp the food down, but oh! It tasted good. Between bites she said, "I don't know how I can ever repay you for your kindness."

Mrs. Spencer smiled and leaned in again. "Honey, that nice-looking man out there has paid for everything." Then, in a more confidential tone: "I don't mean to give unsolicited advice, Miss, but if that gentleman is unmarried...well, I don't know how a girl could do better."

This woman obviously hadn't met James Parker.

Charlie came back into the room as Mrs. Spencer left. Corrine heard her talking to Sam Eston in the hallway. Then

Eston briefly stuck his head in the door and nodded before taking his own leave. "I'll be back soon."

Charlie ate as though he was as hungry as she was. "Your sheriff is pretty capable," he said. "He's been reminding me of Hoke."

Corrine's brow twisted. "He's not *my* sheriff."

"He's pretty fond of you."

Corrine didn't say anything. Mrs. Spencer had left a tureen with more soup on the tray. She ladled a second helping into both her and Charlie's bowls.

"I met an interesting attorney when I was in jail," said Charlie.

"You were in *jail?*"

"Not for long. The lawyer was in the cell beside me...contempt of court. You ever remember Pa getting jailed for contempt of court?"

Corrine shook her head.

"I'm pretty sure he was once. I want to ask Ma about it. And she may not be happy to hear it, but being in jail isn't half as bad as sneaking off like *you* did! Ma must be worried sick."

"I know. I feel terrible. It was foolish of me. To tell you the truth, I'm surprised Hoke didn't come after me."

"He's coming now." Charlie grinned. "That's why we're stalling."

"What?" Corrine dropped the ladle. It clanged against the porcelain bowl.

"Eston sent a telegram to Baker City to let them know you had arrived. Dotson sent one back saying Hoke was already headed this way. Evidently he left as soon as they heard about the U.S. Marshall the Waldens killed. That was seven days ago." Charlie looked toward the window. "He could be here as early as tomorrow."

CHAPTER 26

His only solace from the pain

James woke to his body flailing. No...that was wrong. He was being shaken. Cold water hit his face. He could tell from the way everything hurt that he'd been beaten again. What day was it? How long had he been here? Was this how life would end—wake up, get beaten, pass out from pain or lack of food in his belly, until the body that had never failed him wore out and refused to draw another breath?

He could hear Sairee whimpering on the bed behind him. How long could this go on?

"Get up," a voice said.

Was the command for him or Sairee? James was shaken and water had been thrown at him, but now the boots moved away.

James and Sairee had been tied to opposite ends of the bed for two days—her up on it and him on the floor. Or had it been three days? It was getting harder to keep track of things. James had stopped trying to have conversation with her. Each time he tried, the Waldens overheard and stepped back in to let him feel their disapproval.

He had run out of ways to turn his body so his cracked ribs didn't hurt. But if James kept real still, laying on his right side, the pain sliced less sharp and, eventually, sleep would come. Sleep was his only solace from the pain.

The Waldens circled in slow patterns, like vultures. If Bennett Solomon thought James had worn holes in the street back in Baker City, he ought to see the rotations made by the Waldens here in this house.

Marquis, who spoke least, had grown the most restless. It might not have seemed so to the casual observer, but James was no casual observer. For hours he lay with his eyes closed...listening...memorizing the sound of each Walden's paces.

James knew the breadth and depth of the rooms by listening and feeling the vibrations of the Waldens' footfalls on the floors. The one time he had gotten near the door, he was quickly pushed back in the room, then tied. But he knew there was a room to the right, the front office. It was the long, narrow room he had first been pulled into. There was also a room to the left, where they'd carried the old man after the surgery on his leg.

When they walked the hallway between the doors and around the kitchen table, it formed the loose shape of a cross. It was a mighty small space for the seven people it held.

James didn't have a pocket watch. He'd always relied on the sun and moon to know the time. And now he couldn't see them — the single window in this room being shrouded by a curtain. It didn't leave a beat down man lying on the floor much to go on.

A man could go mad in a closed-in space like this one, even without having his body battered. Doubly so with no ability to see the clouds in the day or the stars at night, no chance to feel the sun or wind on his face, or to breathe in the smells of the land...no view of doves lighting on branches in the trees to remind him of Corrine Baldwyn's eyes. James had never been inside a closed-up space so long.

The confinement had given him plenty of time to think about how Corrine had felt in his arms: the warmth of her lips, her hair cascading down when he pulled on the pins.... Corrine had gorgeous hair. She would age into a beauty. She already had.

James hoped she would have a long and happy life. He wished he could have been there to bounce her children on his knees as he watched her cooking in the kitchen. He had faulted Hoke for watching Abigail with a silly grin. He wouldn't do it again. If by some miracle he lived through this, he suspected he would do more than grin at the chance to feast his eyes on Corrine one more time, and he wouldn't care squat if anyone thought him foolish for it.

"Get up." The voice came again from the doorway. The Waldens often stood in that spot, directly in line with the window. James hoped the Silvertown sheriff was thinking of that, and posting a shooter on the roof of the building across the street. Though, of course, no one could see in past that curtain.

It was Baron in the doorway. James was familiar with each voice now. Had this command directly followed the other? Or had a span of time passed?

James's body was half twisted under the bed, his hands tied to the foot of the bedpost with strips of cloth. The cloth wasn't as strong as a rope. If he hadn't lost so much strength in his arms, he believed he could have broken it.

James heard footsteps. Baron's boots came into focus. His eyes traced upward from them, past worn trousers, all the way up to the stockier twin's face. The pounding in his head echoed in his ears.

"Get up."

The words were more forceful this time. But they weren't directed at him – Baron's head wasn't facing him.

"And stop your whimperin'. We're turnin' you loose."

Sairee gave a cry of joy.

Baron flashed a knife, cut through the bandana that held Sairee's wrists, and pulled her to a standing position.

"God, you smell," he said meanly as he took her from the room. Sairee cried some more, whether from the harshness of the words or relief at the prospect of her freedom, James wasn't sure.

If he could have swung his feet out in time, he would have tripped Baron Walden for saying that to her. What was one more beating? Men could relieve themselves easier than women could. Sairee had wet herself the day they made her help with Duke Walden's leg. James knew it better than anyone, having been holed up in this room with her. But it was probably a good thing she had wet herself. James was sure this had worked to her advantage.

Men were selfish bastards. That thought ran through his mind a lot lately. The Walden men were evidence to it. No doubt Sairee had learned this fact long before the Waldens ever snatched her.

James struggled to find a new position, one in which his pain might ease. They were releasing her. Good. He knew he wouldn't be released. This was the end of the road for him. So far the Waldens had kept him alive and left him both his legs, but for how much longer? Until Duke Walden was well enough for them to make their break? How long would that be?

James wondered what it felt like to die. Death would likely be a welcome reprieve by the time they finished with him.

Thoughts of Corrine kept returning to his mind. There was no doubt his affections had been real. At least one of his goals had been accomplished—that of gaining clarity about his feelings. And he had seen his grandmaw one last time. He need not worry about her. She was scrappy. She probably would have outlived him, anyway. Lord, the woman might outlive them all!

James didn't know how the Baldwyns' horse had come to be tied outside the saloon, all he knew was that Bennett Solomon said Corrine was coming this way. Why would she do that? Why would she travel out here, if not to help warn him? She had to have felt *something* akin to love.

The thought traveled through his busted ribcage and settled in his heart like a soothing salve. A lump formed in his throat. Or had she come only for Charlie?

No. It was for him...he needed to believe it was for him.

Thank God the Waldens didn't have her. *Thank God!* Sairee could handle the rough treatment better than a girl like Corrine. Sairee had been born to rough treatment.

They had been children together, James and Sairee—for a while anyway. Her mother had been a saloon girl—young, and pretty like Sairee. James was eight when they showed up in Fort Smith, Arkansas, where he and his grandmaw lived then. Sairee was five. Her mother stayed there two years, pushing Sairee out most evenings. James and his grandmaw lived in the back of a Catholic mission there. His grandmaw saw that Sairee was fed and bathed and often tucked her into the bed with them at night.

It made both him and Granny Pearl sad when Sairee's mother left for Sacramento in '49, after gold was discovered in the Sierras. James tried to get Sairee's mother to leave her with them, but the woman had refused.

They came back three years later. Sairee was ten by then, and James thirteen. That time, Sairee and her mother only stayed a year. Then Sairee showed up one last time, when she was fifteen. Her mother had died and Sairee didn't have anyone else, so she sought out James and Granny Pearl, because they had treated her the kindest. But she didn't stay long. A gambler in Fort Smith took notice of her, and made her a promise he'd take her back to the East. Granny Pearl got one letter. Sairee had made it as far as the Mississippi. James hadn't heard news of her since.

He strained his ears at the sound of calls coming from outside, voices he didn't recognize, as Sairee was handed over. He wondered why the Waldens had decided to do it.

That afternoon, he learned why.

This time James woke to the smell of food. He heard someone pad softly into the room and he rolled to get up, pain shooting through him as he fought to pull himself to a sitting position. His arms tingled painfully as normal blood flow returned to them.

A small man he'd never seen, graying at his temples, untied James's hands and handed him a cup of water. James gulped it down then licked the cup, his tongue searching out every precious drop. How long had his body gone without water?

"We've got food," said the man. James couldn't believe they were letting the doctor care for him.

As Burleson disappeared back into the kitchen, Viscount took a step forward. He stood in the doorway and glared. James backed himself up to the wall and glared back. The smell of food teased his empty stomach—and there was the sound of bacon sizzling!

Soon the doctor returned with a plate piled with eggs, bacon and griddle cakes. *Griddle cakes!* He even held a jar of molasses in his other hand.

James could have wept.

He reached for the plate and made quick work of its contents, first shoveling the hot eggs into his mouth, then wrapping a griddle cake around the bacon, pouring molasses down the middle, and dragging the eggs and the cakes through the molasses that spilled back onto the plate.

Burleson and Viscount stood watching him eat. When James had the plate wiped clean he handed it back up to the doctor. "You Burleson?"

Burleson nodded. He left with the plate and returned with another cup of water. And coffee! "Now that you've eaten, I'd like to look at that head wound." Burleson cut his eyes back to Viscount.

Sam Eston, back in Baker City, had been the first to speak the Waldens' names. Bennett Solomon's articles repeated them. Add to that a snatch of conversation overheard here and there, and it hadn't taken James long to put each face with a name.

Viscount had taken the most pleasure in initially cracking James's ribcage, but it was Baron's sharp-toed boots that had kicked him on the floor. James couldn't decide which one was meaner. Marquis now...Marquis was the oddity. Something about Marquis Walden was off. James filed that fact away, in case it proved beneficial to him later...before they killed him.

Why were they bothering to feed him if they intended to kill him?

Viscount stepped away from the doorway. James could hear him talking low to someone in the kitchen as James drank the glorious coffee down.

Warm coffee did his insides good!

Dr. Burleson left for a moment and came back with water and rags. When he leaned down next to James, James could see in his eyes that the man was tired.

"They let the girl go," he whispered.

James nodded.

"Traded her for two week's worth of food. I told them that was the earliest the old man could ride of out here." Dr. Burleson bathed and inspected James's head wound as he talked. "I've been trying to convince them to let me treat you. Having food to eat, and some whiskey, has helped them relax a little."

"You took the leg off?" asked James. Just how much whiskey had the Waldens been given? Under the right circumstances, whiskey could be weapon. But whiskey or no whiskey, James was surprised they were letting him and the doctor talk.

"Three days ago," the doctor said. "Just below the hip. It was his only chance to live. But…"

"I've been here three days?"

The doctor nodded. "Walden may have suffered a stroke during the procedure. He's not responding. I haven't said anything about it to his sons." James could barely hear the doctor, the man was talking so low. He slathered some kind of ointment on James's head. It stung like the dickens, but James was grateful to get it. "They're starting to get restless, though. I don't know yet if the whiskey is going to make that better or worse."

Every few seconds, one of the twins would step into the doorway to check on James and the doctor. The two men tried to time their conversation accordingly.

"If the old man dies," Burleson said, wrapping James's head with a bandage, "I'm not sure how the sons will take it."

"Are you helping him along?"

"No. I figure it won't go well for me if he dies. I was keeping him heavily sedated at first—I always do after an amputation—but I started cutting back on the chloroform yesterday afternoon. He should have awakened by now."

James knew exactly what would happen to *him* if the old man died...same thing that would happen if the old man lived. The Waldens were going to kill him. He had surrendered himself to this inevitability the moment he laid down his gun and walked through the door. But if Duke Walden pulled through...well, the doctor might have a chance.

"Can you look at my ribs?" James asked once his head wound was patched. "I believe those boys' boots have cracked a couple."

Viscount hovered in the doorway for a moment, then went back to the kitchen.

James said in a low voice, "You're right. Your best chance at livin' is keepin' the old man alive."

"But I can't work miracles."

"Anyone outside who might be prayin' you one up?"

Doc Burleson grinned, then his eyes grew sad. "I used to have someone like that. If this thing ends with me going to meet my wife, I won't mind. Sometimes I think life is sorely overrated."

"That's not a comfort, coming from a doctor. I'd have preferred to live, myself."

James thought again of the way Corrine had melted in his arms, the hunger of her unchecked mouth. The memory had been his to cherish all along the trail, and now it might prove his final comfort. Would she have waited for him? Did she already love him? He liked to think she did, and that was why she'd traveled out here.

He swallowed hard. Part of him hoped the news of his death would break her heart, but the better part of him didn't want her to suffer. She would end up marrying Sam Eston. He knew Clyde Austelle was crazy about her, too, but Sam Eston with his charcoal duster and black mustache would likely win out in the end.

Damn…damn it all to hell and back.

Boots scraped against wood. James and the doctor looked up to see Baron frowning down on them. "You done enough for him. Get back to Pa."

The doctor collected his things. James hated to see him go. After both men were gone, he listened to the sounds outside his room. Something had changed. There were fewer footsteps. One of the Waldens had left.

But where had he gone?

CHAPTER 27
Born from adversity

The day Hoke had ridden out of Baker City, he'd squeezed his thighs against the sides of the horse's flanks and rested his palm against the largest vein of its neck, breathing in the power of the stallion. He felt for the right rhythm, knowing it lay somewhere between a lope and a trot.

Every horse had four speeds: walk, trot, lope and gallop. At a gallop, the stallion could outpace any other horse Hoke had ever mounted. But not even the stallion — seventeen hands tall and powerful of limb — could maintain a gallop for more than a few miles. A lope, also called a canter, was just under a gallop and set on a three-beat rhythm, rather than four. Hoke had used it often in the cavalry to cover long distances and knew it was his best pace, so he nudged the stallion to a lope and held it there.

Having Clyde's horse along, fully saddled so he could switch between mounts, allowed Hoke to push the horses harder.

Keeping them hydrated was his biggest challenge.

It was luck he'd just come up this route and was familiar with the streams and rivers. He fell into a rhythm: lope two hours, trot for thirty minutes, rest and water, switch horses and do it again.

He held the rhythm four days, stopping to sleep only when the moon was high, and starting again the next morning well before it set. Hoke shot a rabbit the first day and a squirrel, the third. Abigail had stuffed one of his saddlebags with cornmeal cakes and dried jerky—food he didn't need to cook—and he gathered a few nuts and berries on the trail.

Hoke had brought along a bag of oats and fed his mounts each a handful, along with an apple, when they made their light camp at night. He knew the plump, lush grass his stallion liked best. So if he saw a good place for grazing, he stopped and encouraged the horses to take a few bites.

Hilly, wooded terrain gradually became flat and open. Hoke preferred hilly and treed because it provided more cover, but the horses' hooves ate up the ground faster on the open flatland they came to at the southwest tip of Wyoming. Riding without cover made the hairs on the back of Hoke's neck stand tall. He didn't like the feeling that he might be watched. There were pockets of natives and pilgrims, individual trappers and outlaws, living all over this land. So Hoke pushed the horses hard through the flatlands, urging them on toward the hills and trees he knew were coming on the western side of the Rocky Mountain chain.

The Pony Express had come through this land, only a brief nineteen months before telegraphs lines rendered it pointless. Hoke was too stout to have ever qualified as a rider, but he felt like one now as he raced to get to Silvertown.

Riding allowed a man time to think, even when he was riding fast. This ride was going to cost him something. Hoke could feel it in his gut. He didn't know yet what the payment would be, but he felt it come closer with every steady rotation of his horses' feet.

Love always had a price...both losses and gains.

Hoke thought of how his father had cared for his mother as she lay dying. Soon after, his father had fallen ill. His father had paid a price for love, one that left Hoke on his own at ten. Meeting Abigail finally helped Hoke understand that love. He would do the same for her if it ever came to that, just as willingly as he had conceded his independence shortly after meeting her. She hadn't asked him to...he'd just done it.

Watching James ride off without him, feeling the bittersweet change in his own priorities, Hoke had been reminded of love's cost and payments.

What would be the final cost of this trip he was making now? He had vowed he would never leave Abigail, because her first husband had done just that. The price of that husband's love for civic duty had cost her much. But when Hoke had felt the scales tip—when he'd realized that *not* doing all he could to bring Abigail's children home might prove costlier than going back on his word—it changed the level of his restraint.

What dangers lay ahead now? Or behind? All the threat to Hoke's family might not be ahead of him on the trail. It was Hoke's job to protect Abigail and her children. With them spread out like this, he'd had to make choices. But by God, he wanted to be back home for the birth and raising of his own child. To know and to hold that babe in her womb— to be a force and influence in its life—meant more to Hoke with each passing day.

For twenty years Hoke led a nomadic life, and now he had a family. How it had ripped him in the gut to leave Abigail standing in the Austelles yard! But he was doing this for her. He knew that. She knew that. Charlie and Corrine might be nearly grown, but Abigail's heart was still wrapped up in them.

James was on his mind, too. James needed him.

James Parker was the closest thing he'd ever had to a brother—a brother born from adversity. Six years they'd watched each other's backs, shared each other's meals, and watched the smoke curling up from campfires they built on the trail.

Hoke had been twenty-nine and James just twenty when Hoke first heard him talking. James couldn't even make him a good growth of beard then.

Hoke had just stepped into a saloon at Fort Dodge in Kansas for a drink. It had been his practice to allow himself one when he first landed in a town—just one, to settle his nerves and enjoy the pleasure of being alive. Then on to a hot meal, bath and shave, if those were available options, and a quiet place to rest and read until he hit the trail again.

As he'd stood at the rough hewn bar in Fort Dodge— filled with rowdy men playing poker and women draped over their shoulders—one voice bellowed above them all: the voice of a tall young man whose tongue Hoke could tell was naturally loose, made all the more so by the liquor in his throat.

James was arguing with another man at his table. Hoke was only half paying attention but gathered the disagreement had something to do with a woman. Hoke did notice, however, that the other man worked his gun loose from its holster under the table. That man was about to let James know he didn't appreciate what he was saying, and didn't care whether the liquor was causing him to say it or not.

Hating to see a man die—particularly a young one, at an unfair advantage—Hoke stepped over, hauled James up by the scruff of his neck, and helped him to the door. Not sure what else to do with him, Hoke pitched him into the nearest horse trough.

James was a big guy...strong and bull headed. He came up spewing water, ready for a fight. But the liquor had done its job. It was an easy enough feat to grab James's head and dunk it back in the water until he simmered down. And simmer down he did. One thing Hoke could say for James Parker: the man did not hold a grudge.

By the time Hoke had helped him get his long legs out of the trough, James was all but hugging his neck. Hoke smiled now, remembering. The next morning Hoke watched him over the stall door in a livery as he woke up lying in a pile of hay. Not one ounce of resentment. He smiled up at Hoke like they'd been pals forever. Hoke tossed him something to eat and when he rode out of town later that day, James Parker rode beside him.

The younger man's company had proven a nice change, for Hoke had grown lonelier than he realized.

In southern Colorado Territory, after foiling an attempt to rob a group of travelers, they were offered jobs as U.S. Marshals. That's what they were doing when the Civil War started. The outbreak of war didn't have the impact out West that it did in the South, but they turned in their badges to join a Union regiment just the same. Between their year of marshaling and four years of riding scout together during the war, Hoke had learned much about the character of the man whose life he'd saved. And James had returned the favor more times than Hoke could count.

Hoke knew James was capable. James was seasoned. James could face up to a scoundrel like Duke Walden as well as any man could. But Hoke also felt protective of him. If a man was hunting James down and wanting to take his life, it kindled resentment in Hoke that was difficult to swallow.

Hoke pushed the horses as hard as he dared. Under prime conditions, it would take him eight days to reach Silvertown.

The first four were uneventful. Hoke cut as straight a line to the town as he knew how. Whenever he saw signs of other riders, he swung wide—not wide enough to slow him down, just wide enough to avoid them. He hardly stopped to eat or rest, and the brutal pace began to take its toll.

Late on day four, with his head heavy and his mind not working as well as it ought, a dark cloud rolled up. The wind stirred the trees. He'd just found himself back on hilly, treed land.

Hoke finally had to stop the horses. Sheltering under an aspen, he stripped the mounts of their saddles, rubbed them down with a brush, then huddled under an oilskin slicker near them, feeling bad about their meager shelter.

The wind picked up. Lightning flash above them. The stallion tolerated it well, but Clyde Austelle's horse began to pitch. Hoke worried the horse was going to kick the stallion. He was out from under his slicker, trying to move the horse farther away, when a clap of thunder boomed overhead. The vibrations were so strong it felt like Hoke had been pushed. He was suddenly filled with an overwhelming desire to get away from that aspen tree.

Clyde's horse continued to pitch as Hoke tried to untie him, and got its neck tangled in its bridle. As Hoke worked to free him, lighting flashed again. The horse, wild with terror, jerked and broke the line, taking off.

Hoke watched him go, regret washing over him with the rain. The stallion was now upset and pulling. Hoke flung off his slicker, threw his saddlebags and the best of the saddles over his shoulder, and untied the stallion. He would walk them out of the storm. He hated to leave the second saddle on the ground, but couldn't carry both and didn't expect to see Clyde's horse again.

Night fell. Every few minutes, the sky lit up. Hoke figured they walked five miles before the storm began to weaken. As the lightning moved off to the east, Hoke searched again for a suitable tree under which to make shelter. That night he slept fitfully, waking just before the dawn.

There was no point in wasting time looking for Clyde's horse. Hoke saddled the stallion and got back on the trail.

*   *   *

By the time Hoke reached Fort Bridger late on day five, both he and the stallion were pretty well spent. He thought to leave his horse and acquire two more to take his place. But after a night's rest and quick survey of his options—and after noticing the way an unsavory looking man at the livery was eyeing his horse—Hoke decided to purchase a second mount and keep the stallion on a lead. Riding the second mount for a day or two would give his horse a welcome reprieve.

Hoke couldn't bear to part with the stallion and didn't want to take the chance the horse might be gone when he returned.

Late the next day, on the back of the new horse, Hoke was riding weary again, when the stallion suddenly jerked on its line. Hoke whipped his head up, his hand poised to unhook the safety strap on his pistol. At first he didn't see anything. Then just as he relaxed his knees on his mount, the stallion jerked once more, squalling in a way Hoke had never heard before. Fear shot up Hoke's spine as a bear rose on its hind legs off the trail in front of them.

The horse pitched and Hoke fell backward, dropping the reins on both horses. He rolled, then clawed his way up into a standing position. The bear lumbered after the new horse, but then, as Hoke ran to catch the stallion, the bear turned. Hoke threw himself over the stallion's bare back. The bear charged, and with the swing of a paw, gashed the stallion's flank and Hoke's right shoulder. The stallion squalled again and shot off, Hoke clinging to its back, leaving the bear behind them. He could see the blood pouring from the stallion's side, could feel his own seeping out to join the flow.

The stallion ran until he was completely spent. Once the horse slowed, Hoke lowered his feet to the ground. His saddle and bags had been on the new horse. So had his rifle. All Hoke had left was the Colt Army pistol in his hip holster and the knife strapped to his thigh. No food. No oil slicker. No oats for the stallion. But that part didn't matter.

He could see in the stallion's eyes that the horse was going to die.

Hoke inspected the gash on the stallion's side. It was deep. Blood poured down the horse's back flank and over the ground they'd covered. If the bear—wolves, coyotes or men—decided to track them, the trail of blood would lead right to them. Hoke's shoulder wound was a minor scratch by comparison. The bear's claw had only caught it by the tip, before sinking deep into the horse's flank.

It had happened so fast. Thinking back on it, Hoke thought he remembered seeing red when the bear threw out its paw. Had the bear been wounded? It must have been. That would explain its aggressive behavior.

The stallion's front legs buckled. Hoke's heart caught as he laid a hand on his holster. No, he couldn't afford to attract any undue attention. He unsheathed his knife instead—an

"Arkansas toothpick," the blade kept razor sharp. The stallion wanted to lie down but was having trouble. Hoke helped him bend his legs.

The horse was on his good side now, with the wounded flank turned up to the sky. Hoke rubbed the horse's forehead, between his big, brown eyes.

It was his fault. Hoke had been groggy and not paying attention. The stallion had been the first to notice the bear. He had tried to warn Hoke by pulling on the line. But Hoke was so spent, his reaction had been slow. If he had been on the stallion's back, he would have felt the horse's warnings sooner.

Damn the luck!

The stallion was just a horse. Hoke told himself this: *Just a horse.* But in truth, there had never been another like him, and never would be again. Hoke loved horses. Always had. He'd seen a lot of them, had ridden more than a few. The stallion had been one-of-a-kind. The horse could have lived if Hoke had left him back at Fort Bridger...but if he had, Hoke realized, the stallion wouldn't have been there to warn him about the bear.

Damn.

The animal's eyes kept looking into his...knowing. Begging.

Hoke couldn't stand to see any horse suffer, certainly not the stallion. He looked into the horse's fading eyes and nodded, his own eyes wet now. Gripping the knife, he slid it quick across the stallion's neck, through the largest artery, the same one he'd laid his head against at the start of this journey, while breathing in the horse's strength.

He laid a hand above the cut on the stallion's neck—a neck that had been clothed with thunder—until the horse bled out and breathed his last. Then Hoke stood, wiped the blade and his eyes, and started walking south.

Here had been his cost...the cost of laying a great horse upon the altar. He prayed this would be the entirety of this day's payment...and this journey's.

Sometime in the night—closer to morning, according to the position of the moon—Hoke smelled wood smoke.

He looked up and saw its thin line in the distance.

*   *   *

Hoke found a spot within sight of the cabin and slept. He needed rest and he wanted to give the inhabitants of the cabin a chance to stir before he walked up on them. The smoke had come from a smokehouse near the larger cabin, the remnant of a night fire burning out. It was a miracle he had smelled it and was able to make out its line.

At daybreak Hoke's eyes flew open as he heard a sound in the distance. Someone stepped from the cabin. The figure moved like a woman and went straight to the smokehouse. The thin line of smoke that had petered out while Hoke slept now widened again, its smell growing stronger.

The woman walked back to the cabin carrying something in her arms. Eggs, Hoke thought, and a slab of whatever meat she was smoking. Hoke's stomach rumbled.

He let the woman get back inside the cabin before he approached the house. Once he was within shouting distance, he yelled, "Man approaching!" careful to hold his hands out from his sides so as not to look threatening.

"What do you want?" This was not a woman's voice, but the boom of someone large. A man...with an accent.

"Name's Hoke Mathews. On my way to Silvertown but lost my horse."

"You alone?" The accent was Mexican.

"I am."

The door opened. The man waved him forward but kept his gun at hand.

Hoke knew he looked a sight. "My horse's blood," he explained as he entered the cabin. A rotund man and dark-skinned woman looked him over. "I had two horses. Bear raised up. One horse with my saddle took off and the bear took a swipe at my other one."

"Where?" asked the man.

Hoke described the location. The man nodded. He appeared to believe him.

The man offered a large hand and smiled. "José. Mi esposa, Carlina. See?" He reached for a folded piece of paper from a crude cabinet near the table and showed it with pride. "Mi esposa."

Hoke read the note: *I, Harold T. Sims of Baker City, Oregon, record this day of June 4, 1867, that I married José Hernandez and Carlina (given name of Bitty, last name unknown) in Colorado Territory. Samuel Eston of Baker City, Oregon signs here as witness.*

Hoke was fed, mounted and riding again within the hour.

As he rode, he marveled at the kind turn of events. While the man's Spanish was stronger than Hoke's English, the two had managed to piece things together quickly.

Hernandez owned one donkey. But two days before, when he was tracking a bear that he shot—a bear that had left marks on his smokehouse door—he found a horse with its saddle and supplies still on it. Hernandez didn't know it had once belonged to U.S. Marshal Collin Mears, but Hoke did when he saw it. He never forgot a horse, especially not a good one. And the man offered the horse freely—happily—claiming any friend of Harry Sims who needed it, would honor him in taking it.

As Hoke shook hands with José, he promised, "I'll do my best to get this horse back to you." Hoke couldn't help but feel like Abraham. He'd been required to lay the stallion on an alter of sorts, but had been given the spotted mustang of a dead man in its place—a mustang that virtually flew over the land.

CHAPTER 28

Slivers of birch

James listened to the sound of footsteps walking in patterns around the rooms. Signs of restlessness were growing. James would have sworn Marquis had left earlier, but he heard him now, so maybe he had only imagined it.

The sound stopped as the three brothers congregated in the kitchen. It was the first time James had heard them talking this clearly. He didn't know where the doctor was. They hadn't let him back into to James's room.

"When the hell is he going to wake up?" This was Viscount.

"You heard the doc. He's keeping him under chloroform," said Baron.

"No, he's not." This was one of the only times James had heard Marquis speak. "The doc cut back on the chloroform two days ago."

There was the sound of a scuffle. "Is that true?" James guessed one of them had grabbed Burleson.

What day was this?

He wished he could get audience with the doctor again. He'd been thinking...a doctor's office was sure to have several lethal items on hand.

"Why isn't he waking up?" demanded Baron.

There was a pause. "Your father might have had a small stroke."

Whap! James winced on Burleson's behalf.

"Easy, Baron," said Viscount. "Have you forgotten he's Duke Walden? And made of pure meanness? He'll wake up. He wants to see Parker die."

"Yeah, well...what if he don't?"

"I bet you my cut of that last robbery he will."

"A lot of good that'll do me if we get shot. What if they burn us out? I don't like being stuck in a cage like this. We ain't never been caged like this before."

"They ain't gonna burn this place, Baron." This was Viscount again. "Not as long as the doctor and Parker are in here."

As Marquis started to walk into the room, James closed his eyes to make it look like he was sleeping. After checking him over, Marquis stepped back into the kitchen and said something in a low voice to the others.

James turned his head to study on that loose board under the bed again. He tried to pull at it with the toe of his boot. There were only three Waldens who were conscious at the moment, and the doc seemed savvy. James could have whacked all three brothers if he possessed his usual strength. He felt of the cloth that held his hands. The knot didn't seem as tight since the last time they tied him.

James was sleeping less, but trying to make it look like he was sleeping more. It would have been nice to have Hoke's Bible from his saddlebags. James had enjoyed reading it as he traveled. He liked to bounce from interesting story to interesting story, rather than reading straight through, concentrating on the pages Hoke marked for him with thin slivers of birch. He thought about Samson growing his hair and getting his strength back, right there at the end of his life. Took his enemies down with him.

Maybe God would open up a chance like that for James.

*   *   *

Corrine lay in the warm bath trying to process all that had happened. She was grateful for the sweet-smelling soap and for the kindness of the Chinese couple who had poured the water and fussed over her. But her mind wouldn't allow her to fully relax.

Hoke was on his way; Charlie said so. But when would he arrive? The telegram was seven days old. How long would it really take him to get there? And how much difference could he make when he did? There were already two sheriffs and several townspeople trying to manage things.

Corrine looked to the wall beside her where a new skirt and blouse hung from a nail…gifts from Sam Eston…lovely gifts. Corrine was excited to try them on. She dipped her head back to wet her hair so she could lather it with the soap.

How would this situation resolve itself? Would James come out alive? What was happening in the doctor's office right now?

It had felt so good to see Charlie again. Tam, Harry and Bennett Solomon were back in Silvertown, too. Everyone was safe...everyone but James. And Hoke.

Corrine stepped out of the bath and dried herself off, thinking how nice the cotton towels were. She first donned her new undergarments—delighted to have them, yet embarrassed by who had provided them—then the blouse and skirt. Mrs. Simpson knew a seamstress and, with Sam Eston's help, had done an accurate job of guessing at Corrine's measurements. The undergarments and white blouse with eyelet trim all fit nicely, while the skirt, striped with alternating bands of navy and plum, was only a little loose in the waist.

Corrine had never owned such a full skirt with bold colors. She usually wore ginghams. *This* was a grown-up skirt. When she smoothed her hand down over the fabric, she felt she must resemble her mother. The skirt seemed especially elegant after wearing Tam's bloomers.

The Chinese woman came through the curtain and inspected the fit of her clothes. Before Corrine could get her boots laced the woman had taken up a needle and thread and was working to take in the waist, with Corrine still in the skirt. Corrine considered asking her to make a pocket. She had tied the scissors back on her left leg, under the boot, because she had nowhere else to put them.

But the woman was so fast and finished so quickly, Corrine didn't get the chance.

"Better," the woman said. So she did know some English!

"Thank you."

The woman looked pleased. Corrine wanted to offer her a coin for her services but didn't have any money. Sam Eston was paying for everything. But Hoke was on his way. Hoke would repay her debts. Perhaps after he arrived, she could come back and offer this woman an extra coin for her kindness.

Corrine saw Sam leaned against the railing of the boardwalk outside the bathhouse, waiting to escort her to where Charlie and the town sheriff waited. As she thanked the couple one last time, the gentleman pushed something into Corrine's hand. It was the tintype of her, James, Charlie and Emma.

"How did you come to have this?" she asked.

After many gestures, she understood that they had found it on the bathhouse floor. James had been here, days ago, and it must have fallen from his pocket. They had recognized Corrine.

Corrine asked if she could keep the picture. They insisted on it. She had left her own tintype back at the cabin and hadn't looked at the image in a long time. Seeing James in it now filled her with both hope and dread. He had to come out of this alive. He *had* to.

Corrine promised them she would do her best to return it to the tall, jovial man they kept describing to her. She wondered if they knew he was currently being held against his will in a doctor's office at the other end of town.

When she stepped from the bathhouse, Eston took a long, measured look at her, appreciation thick in his eyes. Corrine held out the sides of the skirt and curtsied. "You pick out nice fabric."

He handed her a straw hat. Her old one had been lost during her, Tam's and Solomon's mad dash of escape. "You look nice in that skirt."

The Chinese woman had given Corrine pins to put her hair up. Before she settled the hat on top, she tucked the tintype inside its inner band.

Eston frowned. "Are you sure you feel well enough to go down there?"

"Yes. I slept for two days, I've eaten, and now I'm clean and wearing lovely new clothes. I want to know what's going on."

Eston offered his arm. Corrine took it. They walked down the street and turned behind several buildings, then turned again. There they found several people standing in the narrow space between the buildings.

Charlie was there, and Bennett Solomon, and the tiny older woman who'd been sitting on the wagon seat with Solomon when Corrine rode past. A younger woman was talking to someone she called "Granny Pearl." Wasn't that what Michael Chessor had called the midwife?

As Eston stopped to talk to Buford Starnes, Corrine turned loose of his arm and took Charlie's. "Nice skirt," he whispered, laying a protective hand over hers.

"The bath house is really nice, Charlie."

He nodded but she could tell he didn't really hear her. He was straining to listen to the conversation between Eston and Sheriff Starnes. Corrine was interested in it, too, but she was even more curious about the conversation happening between the two women. Leaving Charlie, she walked toward them.

"Sairee, after all I did for you, I can't believe you've repaid me like this!"

"I'm sorry, Granny Pearl."

The women looked at Corrine. She looked back. Was this younger woman the one who'd claimed to have had a child with James?

"Is it true?" asked Corrine.

"Is what true?"

She was pretty, with darker hair than Corrine's and a pert little nose like Emma's. But her eyes held a shadow of suspicion. Corrine could tell this woman had been hardened by life in a way that Emma hadn't been, and now never would be.

"Is it true that James is the father of your child?" Corrine knew it was rude to just come right out and ask such a question, but it had burned in her from the moment she first heard the news. The words jumped past her lips before she thought better of it.

Granny Pearl's jaw dropped. "Lord, help, Sairee! Is that what you told people?"

Sairee looked down at the ground.

It wasn't true. Corrine could tell it from her face. Relief surged through her, as palpable as the relief she'd felt when Harry and Sam Eston rode back into her and Tam's camp.

"I saw in the paper that Jimmy got all that reward money," said Sairee, facing Granny Pearl's anger. Her speech sounded raw, uneducated...earthy. "I just thought...."

"You thought he'd share it with you, did you?" Granny Pearl fairly hopped with anger. "Sairee Adams! Of all the ungrateful things!"

Quick tears poured from Sairee's eyes. Her emotions seemed as raw as her voice. What's more, she smelled like urine. Corrine only now realized it. She suddenly felt guilty for exposing the woman's lie to Granny Pearl and causing her more embarrassment.

"I'm sorry, Granny Pearl!" wailed Sairee.

But Granny Pearl wasn't pricked by Sairee's tears. "Jimmy was like a brother to you! And now look at the predicament he is in."

"Wait," said Corrine. "How do you know each other?" She looked at Granny Pearl more closely. "How do you know James?"

"Jimmy's my grandson!" Granny Pearl turned back to Sairee, "And he was just as good to you as I raised him to be. You haven't seen him in years. Do you even have a child?"

Sairee nodded.

"Where's the child now? Being raised by somebody like me, who takes in girls like you?"

"He's a boy. I left him with a farmin' couple in Fort Smith. I went back there and you and Jimmy was gone. They

said you'd come out here. I was on my way to you when I saw
the article about Jimmy, so I latched on to some travelers
goin' to Oregon. I got as far as Fort Bridger when I learned
he come through there, so I follered him."

Granny Pearl shook her head and began to pace in a
circle. She mumbled as she walked.

"Lord, so many babies left behind. So many babies!"
She put her hands to her head. "My own daughter...twin
boys. Then Jimmy. Least *his* mother didn't leave him on
purpose.... My *own* daughter left with hers! I would have
raised those boys. Would have raised them both. Would have
taken Sairee, too, if her ma would've let me. Now look at her.
Just like my own girl. Leaving her baby! Did I teach her
nothing when she was with me?"

Granny Pearl stopped in front of Corrine. Her anger
abated. "Who are you, dearest?"

"Corrine Baldwyn."

Her eyes lit up. "The girl Jimmy thought he was giving
himself up for?"

Sairee Adams' eyes narrowed and her lower lip flung
out. Her eyes fell down the broad stripes of Corrine's pretty
new skirt and back up again.

"Yes, ma'am." Corrine tried not to puff herself up in
front of Sairee. After all, it was only by the grace of God and
the kindness of others that she had these nice clothes.

Corrine saw Granny Pearl sizing her up, too—not so
much the clothing, but her eyes. "Tell me this, Miss
Baldwyn." She pointed a small bent finger at Corrine.

"Would you ever ride off and leave your baby? Or hand one over to strangers on a trail?"

Of course Corrine wasn't a mother so she really didn't know how to answer that question. But then she thought of her own.

There was nothing Abigail Baldwyn Mathews would not do for her children, even if it meant risking her own joy. Corrine knew how much Hoke's love and protection meant to her mother, and wasn't Hoke on his way out to her and Charlie right now? He wouldn't be making that ride without her mother's approval.

"I hope I'll be the kind of mother who would give my life for my children," she said. "That's the kind my mother has been."

Granny Pearl's grimace softened. "I like you."

"What about *me*, Granny Pearl?" wailed Sairee.

The grimace returned. "Have I not shown my love for you, Sairee? That don't mean I always *like* you."

Sairee turned on her heel and stomped away.

Granny Pearl shook her head. "She won't stay mad. That's one thing she and Jimmy have in common. She'll pout like the dickens for a while, but she'll get over it. They were easy children, that way."

Something Granny Pearl had said nagged at Corrine.

"Mrs. Parker, may I ask you something? You said your daughter had twins and gave one away on the trail. Can you tell me more about that?"

Granny Pearl sighed. "Jimmy's not my real grandson. His mother died in Arkansas. 1840. I didn't know anything about her. Died in childbirth. Don't know anything about his father, either, or whether the woman was ever married."

Corrine studied the older woman as she spoke, marveling at how tiny she was. Here stood the source of James's raising. How had she, like the smallest of acorns, nurtured such a mighty oak?

"I helped with a lot of children over the years, children neglected by their mothers, like Sairee, but they were in and out of my kitchens. Jimmy was the only boy I ever had from birth on up to manhood. I named him James after my own father."

"Does he know you're not his real grandmother?" Corrine suddenly burned to know everything she could about Pearl Parker. Every detail would be some clue to James.

"Of course! Why I never told that boy anything but the truth. He was such a help to me...and company, too. Truth was, he helped heal me. I've always been small. I went straight from looking like a child to looking like a drawed-up old woman, so men have left me alone for the most part. Except one. Oh, he was slick, that one. And handsome. He made me a promise then ran. I shouldn't have been surprised when the girl who came out of my own stupidity did the same thing. I met that slick man when I lived in Ohio. And let me tell you, I saw how mean folks can treat an unmarried woman with a growing belly."

Guilt reared its head at Corrine then. She realized she likely would have thought low of Granny Pearl had she been one of the people in that town. Once again, she remembered the girl who had shown up in Marston.

"Honey, I've lived long enough to see—to know—that some children come into being in less than ideal ways. But that don't mean that child itself is not a miracle. Every birth of *every* child is a miracle. God taught me that when I was young."

Granny Pearl shook her head. "I guess He was preparing me for my role in life: taking care of unfortunate women. And every now and then, their children."

Corrine's admiration for Granny Pearl rose like yeast. What some women like she and Tam had lived through! And they not only refused to let the past destroy them, they let it gird them with strength and compassion for others.

"I went to Fort Smith after Evie was born," the older woman said. "And when she was *sixteen years old*—least I was older, but she was about your age, I'd say—she ran off with another slick man. She wrote me one letter. Said they were headed west when she gave birth to twins and the man got himself scalped by the Indians. A group of travelers helped her. She gave one of the boys to an older couple in that group. I guess she was doing her best in trying to keep one, but after that she took up with *another* man."

Granny Pearl turned and pointed her bent finger at the blue sign across the street with the white lettering. "*Duke Walden!* Imagine how I felt when I learned it was Duke Walden who had rode into this town and now has my Jimmy! Walden let her keep the boy she had left. That's how she put it in her one letter to me, said he let her *keep* her own child. She wrote to tell me what had happened since they were my grandsons."

Corrine must have been staring at her strangely because Granny Pearl stopped then and asked, "What is it, dearest?"

"I think I know who your grandson is."

"Well, I know who he is, too! He's that oldest Walden boy in that doctor's office, threatening to kill my Jimmy! Now you tell me that's not a terrible coincidence! My flesh-and-blood grandson threatening to kill the child of my heart! Why, I had Jimmy with me longer than I had my own daughter! And those other boys are my grandsons, too! Word is, my girl died giving birth to the younger pair."

"No," said Corrine. "I mean, yes!"

The Walden boys had to be Granny Pearl's grandsons, which was absolutely remarkable. But...Corrine smiled at the older woman.

"I think I know who the missing one is, too."

CHAPTER 29
In her marrow

Charlie was trying hard to convince Eston and Starnes his proposal had merit.

"Once I get inside, the distraction will create an opportunity for the doctor and James. If I know James, he's sitting on a plan, just waiting for the chance to use it."

"But you don't know what kind of shape Parker is in, Son," said Sheriff Starnes. "Or the doc. The Waldens could have killed one or both of them, for all we know."

"They wouldn't have done it on purpose," Charlie argued. "Those men are their collateral."

"Even so, we don't know what all's been going on inside that office," said Starnes.

Eston crossed his arms, looking Charlie over. "A lot of men carry knives on their bodies, Charlie. They'll search you."

"Not under my belt strap, they won't! They'll think it's just the leather."

"I still say we wait until something happens," said Starnes.

Charlie groaned. He considered himself a patient man, but that Silvertown sheriff beat all he ever saw for waiting!

"What's your hurry to get in there, Charlie?" asked Eston. "You know they don't have Corrine. I thought we agreed to wait until Mathews arrived."

It surprised Charlie that Eston, who had taken such forceful action to get him out of jail, was doing so little to rescue James. It didn't make sense...unless Eston didn't want James to make it out of this ordeal.

Eston's admiration for Corrine was obvious. Was he secretly hoping this showdown might reduce his competition? It was hard to understand why the man had come all this way to warn James, then so quickly pulled the brake handle.

As Charlie watched, Eston shot a furtive glance at Corrine. Was he reading Charlie's suspicions and squirming uncomfortably beneath them? Well...Eston wasn't the law here, Sheriff Starnes was. So Charlie concentrated his persuasive skills on Starnes.

"You station one of your best shooters, or Michael Chessor, in that room up there...." He pointed to the building he'd had his eye on for days "And I'll work from the inside to get that curtain off the window and a Walden in his line of fire. As soon as that happens, we can surely take the other two down inside while you rush the doors, front and back."

"I don't know."

Starnes was the least decisive sheriff Charlie had ever seen.

"We can outwit these men!" insisted Charlie. "I'll be the Trojan Horse!"

Meeting Harold Pickens had reminded Charlie of the power of logic. He was convinced the key to solving their problem was changing the variables. Before leaving for the war, his father had consistently cultivated and relied on his reasoning skills as an attorney. Now Charlie was eager to do the same—to put his revitalized passion for logic to the test. He was tired of waiting. Who knew when Hoke would arrive, or *if* Hoke would arrive? Charlie knew he could outwit the Waldens if given the chance!

"Let's get Chessor up in that room before you do anything," said Starnes, his resolve bending.

Charlie was thrilled. He looked for Corrine, wanting to assure her there was no need to worry. She wasn't going to like his plan.

The last time he'd seen her, Corrine was talking to Granny Pearl. The white-haired midwife was talking to Bennett Solomon now, Solomon bent low to hear her, listening with rapt attention, his face filled with joy. What could the little woman possibly be saying that would make Solomon so happy...make him look like he wanted to reach down and hug the little woman to his chest?

"Where's Corrine?" Charlie asked Eston.

Eston's eyes searched the crowd. This had been the congregating place since the ordeal had started: an alley across the street and one building over from Doctor Burleson's office, behind a brick wall that provided good cover from gunfire.

"I don't know. She was just over there." Eston stepped toward Granny Pearl. Charlie followed. "Excuse me, ma'am. Where did Miss Baldwyn go?"

Granny Pearl released her hold on Bennett Solomon and looked around, blinking. "She went with that man."

"What man?" Eston asked.

"The man from the telegraph. He said he had a telegram for her."

Solomon's face screwed up. "That man wasn't from the telegraph. I know what he looks like and he hasn't been here. Did that man say he was from the telegraph office?"

"Yes. He said he had a message for her, from Baker City."

"Why didn't he say anything to me?" asked Charlie.

"I don't know. You were deep in conversation with the sheriff and I was excited to learn that Bennett is my grandson—"

"Grandson?" said Eston.

"Yes! He has to be! He's twenty-eight years old, and—"

"I want to hear it," Eston cut her off. "I do. But right now we need to find Miss Baldwyn. What else did the man say? Starnes!" Eston waved the local sheriff over.

"What did the man look like?" asked Charlie.

"He was tall," said Granny Pearl.

"About my height," added Solomon.

"You saw him, too?" Charlie scanned the nearby crowd for tall men.

Solomon nodded. "I didn't hear what he said, but I saw what he looked like. Skinny fella. Bearded. Dark hair."

"About the same color as Bennett's," added Granny Pearl. Her face froze and she grabbed Solomon's arm. "Oh, no. One of those boys in that office is your full brother—the oldest one. You don't think...."

The confidence that had lifted Charlie's heart only a moment ago now fled, leaving a cold, low feeling in its place.

"Solomon, run to the telegraph station and see if Corrine is there. Charlie, search the immediate area. Starnes! Send someone to the hotel to see if there's any chance Miss Baldwyn went back there to see Harry or Tam."

Eston barked the orders so fast, everyone just stood and looked at him for a moment, fear settling over the alley like a mist.

"Now!" he demanded. "Run!"

They ran.

*   *   *

Corrine had been so thrilled to introduce Granny Pearl to Bennett Solomon that when a tall thin man touched her elbow and said quietly, "A telegram's just come in, Miss, from Baker City. I believe you'll want to see it," she smiled and took his arm, eager for more potential good news.

It seemed such a good omen. Suddenly she knew—she just *knew*—things were going to work out.

She glanced over at Charlie, who was talking to Sam Eston and Buford Starnes, and almost tapped Charlie's elbow, but he was talking to the men with such passion she hated to interrupt him. So she slipped on through the crowd with the man until they came to the back of the alley and turned the corner.

The man spun around. Corrine suddenly felt a knife against her throat.

"Come with me," was all he said.

This was the second time a stranger had gotten her in his grip.

This time was worse. Corrine sensed it in her marrow, just as surely as she had believed only a moment ago that all would be fine. The bald man could never have pulled off such a feat, walking her right out of a crowd like that, at the very moment she and the others had let their guards down. Corrine hadn't even looked closely at the man before allowing him to lead her away.

She did now, as he took her arm and propelled her forward. They slipped behind several buildings then through a growth of dense underbrush at the end of town.

Had her present circumstances been different, Corrine would have thought the area beautiful, once they got past the wildest of the underbrush. She was getting her first look at Silvertown's setting. Day had only been breaking when she had ridden in. She'd noticed it was hilly and wooded, but saw now that the buildings were set in a scenic valley near a large creek, or was it a river? The sound of rushing water played like tinkling music in the background.

As they walked, the music grew louder. Corrine marveled at the man's ability to step so lightly through the wooded forest. When they came out of the underbrush he stopped. There it was: a river thick with boulders, water rushing around them in white sprays. Two separate falls in the distance merged and fed into one thick stream.

The man hadn't spoken again. Neither had Corrine. She studied him. Tall...thin. Eyes and hair the same color as Bennett Solomon's.

"You're Marquis." It wasn't a question.

He didn't answer. How had he slipped out of the doctor's office undetected? He had certainly not walked out the front, and Sheriff Starnes was supposed to have men watching in the back.

Corrine felt surprisingly calm. On the one hand, this man was like a coiled rattlesnake...sure on his feet, quiet in his demeanor...willing and ready to strike if needed. So different than the lanky awkwardness of Bennett Solomon! But there was something else about him that *did* resemble Solomon. She got the feeling he hadn't set out to be a snake. Maybe his natural inclination had been to sit back and watch his prey before deciding what to do with them.

Marquis lifted the straw hat off her head. Her hands groped the air, pawing to get it back. The tintype was in the band!

"Take your outer clothes off." He threw the hat to the ground.

Corrine put a hand to her chest. "I will not!"

"Take them off or I'll cut them off." He spoke calmly, but raised the knife.

He did just say *outer clothes*, after all....

Trembling, Corrine bent down to unlace her boots. She pulled off the right one, then the left, careful as she did so to push the cloth that held her scissors higher on her leg, under the drape of her new petticoats. She considered grabbing the scissors, threatening him with a weapon of her own, but she didn't think she could pull the act off with the current tremor in her hands.

Next she unfastened the waist of her skirt and stepped out of it. This was the second time she had stepped out of a skirt with an audience—she didn't like it any more now than she had the first time.

"The blouse."

Corrine unbuttoned the eyelet blouse and dropped it beside the skirt. The petticoats covered as much of her body as Tam's bloomers had, so she didn't feel entirely naked; still, the camisole lacked sleeves. She had sometimes worn regency dresses when she was younger, but had since grown used to her arms being covered.

Marquis pointed with the knife. "This way."

When she turned she saw the sharp corners of the tracks her boots had left behind. Then she understood: bare feet would be harder to follow. Marquis wanted to confuse the people who came looking for them—make them wonder if she had gone for a swim or been murdered and thrown into the river. They might be fooled into searching the water downstream.

Marquis moved her upstream, in the opposite direction. She noticed he wore moccasins.

Corrine tried to think. Tam wouldn't save her this time. How quickly would others realize she was gone? How much time might searchers waste scouring the river?

Marquis had a pistol on his hip and one knife that she could see. She had thought nothing of him wearing a gun when he had approached her in the crowd. All the men around her were armed, some more heavily than others.

Corrine took a deep breath and prayed for wisdom. Something told her this time wisdom—not force, luck, or the jabbing of sticks, but real *wisdom*—would be the key to her survival.

CHAPTER 30
A Sharps

José Hernandez had insisted Hoke take not only the mustang, but his rifle, too—a Sharps. Hoke had traded his old Sharps for a Winchester just before leaving Independence last year, so he was well familiar with the model and the make. It was a fine weapon, oiled and well cared for.

As Mears's horse ate up the miles between José's cabin and Silvertown, Hoke took aim on several targets, getting used to the weight and feel of the gun. It shot low, and a little to the left of the sight.

He no longer rode at a lope, sensing the stakes had grown higher...James and Corrine were in danger. So he pushed the mustang to an open gallop, thinking on every four-beat rhythm: *Damn you, Walden...Damn you, Walden*...for causing him to lose the finest horse that had ever lived.

And Hoke would not let that man rob him of one thing more.

*　　*　　*

Harry had been at the hotel with Tam all day. Granny Pearl had given Tam strict orders of bed rest. But she hadn't told Harry *he* had to stay in bed.

"I want to go see what's happening." Harry kissed Tam on the forehead.

"All right. But don't get caught up in anything, Harry. Just get the news and get on back here. Promise?"

He promised.

*   *   *

Marquis guided Corrine back through the underbrush, following the river until it took them behind the buildings on the opposite side of town. The sun had just begun its descent, causing the shadows to lengthen. A breeze blew in over the water. The evenings were cooler here than they had been out on the trail.

As they drew closer to the buildings, before leaving the brush, they stepped over a pair of legs. Corrine felt sick. Her hands shook. If she had been thinking to break away and run—and she had—she knew it was time to lay those thoughts aside.

Hadn't Sheriff Starnes stationed more than one man on the back side of Doctor Burleson's offices? Had Marquis killed them all? Wasn't the sheriff checking on the men?

Marquis pointed to a door with the sharp point of his knife and motioned for Corrine to run toward it. With the vision of the two legs still fresh in her mind, she did as he instructed. He followed.

When they got to the door, it opened and they stepped inside.

* * *

Charlie stood on the riverbank with Corrine's clothes in his hands. It didn't make any sense. Corrine would never have come out here on her own, and she wouldn't have disrobed in front of a stranger.

One of the men who'd come to help search said, "Looks like she went for a swim." But that was a ridiculous conclusion. Corrine just had a bath.

When Eston saw the pile of clothes, he immediately run downstream, his eyes combing the water. Charlie saw him now peeling off his boots and shirt, to jump in and look for her. If Charlie had wondered if Eston was crazy about Corrine before, he didn't now. The truth was obvious. Eston was losing his composure.

But Corrine had never gone in that water. Charlie would have bet his life on it. So then, *Why?* He was asking that question more and more. Why had they found her clothes lying here?

* * *

A man shorter than Marquis, but with meaner eyes and a stockier build, grinned at Corrine, his eyes running up and down her underclothes.

"You beat all I ever saw, Marquis. Got her here and barely clothed to boot. Come here, Sweetheart." He grabbed her wrist and pulled her toward him, then whistled. "You really are pretty! The picture in the paper didn't lie. And you smell better than the last girl we had in here. Hey, Vis!"

A third man stepped in the room—this man's twin, but leaner—and glanced at her. "Good timing. Tie her in there, Baron. Marquis, you take the front watch." He jerked his head at the doorway behind him. "Pa's wakin' up."

Corrine could hear a man talking low in the room to her right. She took stock of the one she stood in. It was a kitchen with a stove and two cupboards: one pie safe and a glass-door cabinet with shelves and a few dishes inside. Most of the dishes, dirty from use, covered a small table near the door.

Baron pulled her into the other room. It was dim, with a heavy curtain on the window, but Corrine had no trouble making out the heap on the floor.

James!

She bit her lip as Baron ripped off part of a top sheet and used it to tie her hands to the headboard. "I'll be back," he vowed. Then he left the room.

Corrine could hear the men talking on the other side of the wall, but she only caught pieces of their conversation.

"Pa!" one of them said. "We got the girl!"

Corrine was more interested in *this* room...in that heap on the floor.

They hadn't tied her feet. James's were tied, and his hands pulled up to the foot of the frame. She nudged him with her toes. No response. She nudged him harder. Panic set in. What if they had killed him?

Straining one leg forward, she put her foot between his, caught it on the cloth that tied them, and tried to pull him toward her. His body was heavy, but he looked thinner than she had ever seen him.

Corrine strained and pulled. Slowly, his body slid toward her. He groaned. She stopped, relief shooting through her. He was alive! But she didn't want to hurt him.

She nudged him with her foot again. "James," she hissed. "James. Wake up." How much time did they have before the men came back? Corrine watched the door. She shoved his foot harder.

Suddenly he twisted, quicker than she would have thought possible, lashing out in anger with his feet. Corrine's heart caught as it occurred to her how many times he must have awakened to a kick.

"James, it's me. Corrine. Wake up!"

*   *   *

"Charlie!" Bennett Solomon came running toward him. "I talked to the telegraph operator. He says he's the only one who works there, and he never talked to Corrine."

Solomon's eyes flew to Eston down in the water and the clothes in Charlie's hands. "Oh, no! Does Eston think someone killed her and threw her in the river?"

Was it the newspaperman in Solomon that made him fly straight to the most sensational conclusion?

Charlie shook his head. Corrine had not been killed and thrown in the river. That made no more sense than the swimming theory. There was no sign of a struggle here and he liked to think Corrine would have fought harder for her life than this calm scene would have indicated.

This was staged.

It had to have been Marquis Walden who had taken her. And they had all been standing there! The man had walked right past every one of them and plucked her from their hands.

"Are there not any photographs of the Waldens?" Charlie asked Solomon.

"None that I could find when I ran my story." He looked pained. "You really think I could be related to them? They've done such awful things!"

"I don't know what to think." Charlie handed Corrine's clothes and boots to Solomon. "But I'm not waiting on Sheriff Starnes anymore."

Charlie ran back to get Chessor and Peters.

If the door of that building across the street from the doctor's office was still locked, he might need help breaking it down.

*　　　*　　　*

James raised his head and looked at Corrine, his eyes flat, as if he didn't know her. Had they beaten him so badly they'd damaged his brain? Corrine thought of Tam mentioning the man who had been kicked by a horse...the head was a delicate thing.

James's head was bandaged, but blood had seeped through. Blood was even smeared in strange patterns on the floor. It looked like his head had lain in a pool of it for days.

Her throat closed and tears sprang to her eyes.

"Corrine," he said weakly.

Oh! He knew her!

*   *   *

They had her – the Waldens had Corrine.

No!

James could hardly wrap his mind around it. But there she was, tied to the bed. Was this some kind of nightmare?

Where were her clothes if this was real? She looked too good without them. He didn't want the Waldens to see her without her clothes. And James hated that she was seeing *him*. He *never* wanted Corrine to see him like this: down on the floor, busted and weak.

James wanted to die. But... *No!* He couldn't die. He had to get her out of here! He couldn't depend on the doctor to do it, or expect the Waldens to grow a conscience.

"James," she was whispering. Was that love in her voice? Were those tears slipping down her cheeks? "James. It's me!"

Of course it was *her*! He could see her plainly. Did it look like he didn't see her? Her hair was pinned up. And he could smell her clean body.

What was she doing here?

"Can you see that loose board under the bed?" he asked hoarsely.

She twisted to look. It wasn't easy, the way she was tied. "Yes."

"I need a weapon. I think I know how to get that board loose." If Corrine could only lift the bed and slam the foot of it down on the right spot of that plank of wood, he believed he could yank it loose from the other side. That would give him something to whack the Waldens with next time they came at him...or at her. The critical moment had come—he had to have an instrument for whacking.

"I've got scissors," she whispered.

"Where?"

"Tied to my leg. I think I can get them."

She hiked her left leg on the bed, putting it close to her hands.

He watched in awe as she raised the hem of her bloomers to reveal a long pair of scissors...and a beautiful leg.

"Say you'll marry me."

Corrine had been turned to the wall, working to get the scissors out, but turned back to him now with a twisted brow.

"What?"

"Say you'll marry me. If I die, I want to know you said yes."

She stared at him. Lord, he knew he looked a sight! This wasn't how he had pictured asking her—he wasn't even sure this moment was real. Nothing, from his first plans to woo her until now, had gone the way he tried to orchestrate it—so to hell with orchestrated plans! Perhaps he would just take life as it came to him, from here on out.

Not that he meant to lay there and let the Waldens take him lightly. He needed the strength to surge back in his arms like Samson's had...so he could save her.

Her brow twisted harder. "Is this what you call 'official'?"

"Yes!" Then he restated for emphasis, "By God, yes!"

Corrine's brow twist was just like her mother's. She looked at him with a dropped jaw, not answering, then went back to freeing her scissors.

Lord, help a man! Even here on the floor—his death surely imminent—he couldn't get the upper hand with her.

*   *   *

Think, Corrine, think! Really...why would James ask her to marry him at a moment like this? She had the scissors free. Now she needed to prop them in such a way that she could slice the cloth with the point.

She glanced back at the door then at James. He turned his head to listen. He looked terrible, his beard grown out with dried blood in it.

"Something's coming," he whispered.

Corrine had raised both her legs up on the bed to prop the scissors. She stopped and looked at the door. The scissors were between her knees. The Waldens would see.

But no one was coming. She could still hear them talking in the next room. No footfalls.

"They're not coming, James." She secured the scissors.

"Outside. Something's coming. A horse. Hear it?"

Corrine strained to listen. She didn't hear a horse. Maybe James's ears had been damaged. Maybe he was hearing some kind of a ringing in his head. She looked at the window. A curtain covered it. That needed to come off.

"Hurry," he said.

"Almost there." Then she heard it...the sure, steady clop of a horse's hooves coming toward them.

CHAPTER 31
The rise of the Rockies

Harry had just approached the alley where a small crowd was gathered across from the doctor's office. He couldn't find Charlie, Corrine, or Sam Eston anywhere. But there were Granny Pearl, Michael Chessor and Bart Peters.

"What's happening?" he asked. Excitement charged the air.

"They may have gotten Miss Baldwyn," said Peters.

"What? Who got her?"

"The Waldens," said Chessor. They all looked distraught.

"How?"

"Walked right up here and took her," said Granny Pearl, wringing her tiny hands. "My own grandson!" She began to walk in circles, mumbling. "More women done wrong by a man than I know how to count. A few done right, it's true. There's some good men out there. Lord, I hope I raised mine to be, and even then sometimes a woman is too blind to see it. Oh, you get to be my age, you just wish people would treat one another with decency. Common decency." She stopped in front of Harry. "Why is that so hard?"

Before Harry could answer, he heard the sound of running feet approaching and turned.

"Charlie! What is it?" called Peters.

"Come with me!" Charlie pulled his rifle from Chessor's hands and ran toward the door of a building down the street.

"Where are you going?" called Chessor, running after him.

But Charlie didn't answer. As he and Chessor disappeared from sight, Peters said, "What's that sound?"

Harry and Granny Pearl listened. It was the sound of a horse. Someone was coming right up the center of town, racing a horse at top speed.

*   *   *

Hoke had found Corrine's shawl the day after leaving José's cabin—day seven of his ride. It was weathered and torn, but he knew it was hers. Dried blood and a dead man's remains, scattered by animals, lay on the ground nearby. He found tracks leading from the body to a spot where some horses had been tied. Indians had since crossed the path. The remains of another man had been left on a pole. He also found a camp, the skin and bones of fish...and ruts from a wagon.

Hoke read each sign then kicked the sides of the mustang, feeling the urgency of his mission tightening in his soul.

Hoke pushed the mustang as hard as he could without killing him.

He slowed some in the night, but knew he couldn't afford to tarry. As morning broke he could see the rise of the Rockies against the sky. At Fort Bridger, they had given him a good description of the land and the route. Silvertown was this side of the mountains. So Hoke pushed, pushed, *pushed* the mustang forward, testing the animal's limits and his own.

When the town came into focus, just as the sun began its descent overhead, he squeezed the horse's flanks with his legs and pointed him in, straight to the center of town.

A group of people on the left...the point of a rifle in a window overhead, aimed at the door across the street...a blue sign with white lettering over the door: *"Animals Doctored...."*

The mustang knew it had entered a town and wanted to slow, but Hoke was filled with too much fury. He saw his Arkansas toothpick sliding over the vein of his beautiful stallion's neck and charged straight for the door under the blue sign.

* * *

It all happened slower than seconds, but faster than minutes, like twenty clustered clicks of a clock's moving hand...

That's how Solomon decided he would write it after he had a chance to interview witnesses and persons involved. And he would, of course, assemble the facts into chronological order. Any good newspaperman worth his salt knew when he had the makings of a great dime novel on his hands—all the more remarkable considering the facts of this one were true.

First, Duke Walden had rallied. Many patients did just before they breathed their last. And his brief recovery could not have come at a more convenient time.

Doc Burleson had been expecting Walden to rouse or die. For two days Burleson planted medical instruments and potions around the office so that when the moment arrived, he might swing it toward opportune.

Burleson had been allowed to check on James one more time after he bandaged his head. James was passed out from a beating, so he didn't see Burleson slip the removable blade of his bone saw under the mattress, over James's head. Burleson could only hope James would see it next time he woke. The blade should be easy enough to spot from the floor, but wasn't visible to anyone standing.

Burleson had also slipped a smaller knife in the front of his own waistband, hidden a bottle of arsenic in the kitchen, and stashed extra chloroform by Duke Walden's bed. After that, he waited...for that opportune moment.

Duke's rally was the first tick on the proverbial clock.

Click one.

The old man opened his eyes, asked for water, and Viscount rushed to his side. This happened as Marquis brought Corrine in the door.

Two.

Baron tied Corrine and joined Viscount at his father's side.

Three.

As the twins told their father they had the girl, Marquis stood alone in the front room, at the window.

Doc Burleson would later say he thought it odd Marquis didn't come to the bedside. It was as if Marquis was still the family whipping post, even after capturing Corrine, which was the very thing his father had wanted.

Doc Burleson stepped to the kitchen to get Duke a cup of water—*four*—and added a healthy dose of arsenic—*five*.

Then he stepped back in and held it to the old man's lips. This was a violation of the Hippocratic Oath, of course, but after nearly a week of this ordeal, Doc Burleson had decided, to hell with the oath, and to hell with this man. Last rally or not, he was ready for Duke Walden to meet his destiny, and was done taking chances.

As Duke began to sputter, the arsenic taking its effect, he mumbled, "That boy is only your half brother."

Click six.

His words sat in the air as if not knowing where they ought to land.

Click seven.

Burleson stood with the remaining arsenic water in his hands, wondering for a moment who Duke Walden meant. He could only mean Marquis, since the other boys were twins.

The twins looked at one another then at Marquis, who now stood peering at them from the bedroom door. He had to have heard the pronouncement, too, but no emotion crossed his face.

Click eight.

Marquis took the cup from Burleson's hand, drank the water, and stepped back to the office.

Nine.

Duke Walden breathed his last—*ten*—giving one final shudder, then his body went still.

No tears from the twins, but they did look stunned—whether by Duke's words or his death, the doctor said he couldn't be sure.

Corrine got the point of her scissors through the fabric—*eleven*—and sliced. Her hands free, she reached to jerk the curtain off the window.

Twelve.

The yank of it pulling a nail from the wood made a noise. Baron heard it.

Thirteen.

Corrine grabbed the scissors that had fallen to the bed and reached for James. As she cut the tie from his ankles—*fourteen*—James spied the blade beneath the mattress.

Corrine cut James's hands loose—*fifteen*—just before Baron came into the room.

A bullet shattered the window—*sixteen*—and Baron's head jerked back. His body hit the wall then slid to the floor.

Seventeen.

As James pulled the blade from the bed, Viscount stepped in the doorway and looked down at his slain brother.

Then a blast came from the front office.

Eighteen.

Marquis had opened the door as a horse came charging toward it. Hoke shot high and a little to the right as Marquis dropped and rolled back through the office, into the kitchen, and past the table.

He jerked the back door open and ran out as Viscount — *nineteen* — pointed his gun at James.

But James had already flung the blade into Viscount's belly.

Click twenty.

And it stuck.

Viscount looked down. Then Hoke, who had jumped from the mustang's back just before it charged the door, shot him in the head. The twin's body jerked back like his brother's, then fell down beside him on the floor.

Maybe that was twenty-one clustered clicks, rather than twenty — Solomon would have to work that out — but at any rate, Doc Burleson had then held his hands up to show Hoke he wasn't the enemy.

Hoke strode forward

Corrine, who spied him through the door, called, "In here!"

Hoke put his hand first on Corrine's head, then James's, his eyes raking over them. "You hurt?"

They both shook their heads, but it was obvious James had taken several beatings.

"I'll see to them," said Burleson.

"You the doctor?" asked Hoke.

James waved him on. "We're fine. Don't let him get away, Hoke! We don't need to be lookin' over our shoulders."

Burleson smiled and put a hand on Hoke's arm. "Marquis won't get far."

"How do you know?" asked Hoke.

Burleson offered a grim smile. "I just know."

*   *   *

Sam Eston was the last one to leave the riverbank. He swam across it and back, then across once more, searching for the body he feared was in the water.

Solomon later learned that Eston's first wife had not died from fever, as he had told Corrine, but from drowning. Eston told people it was fever because he didn't want anyone to think she might have taken her own life. There was no explanation for her drowning that day, no reason for it. She had only gone to the creek to wash. Her death apparently haunted Eston. Thinking a similar fate might have happened to Corrine must have rattled him in a deep, unwelcome place.

Eston was coming up the bank of the river just as Marquis went running down it. Eston tackled him and the two men went rolling.

When Harry Sims and Bennett Solomon found them, Marquis was rolled over on his back, a trickle of foam coming from his mouth. Eston sat nearby, his hair and clothes wet, with his head in his hands.

"What happened?" Harry asked Eston.

Solomon bent down to inspect the man who had been his twin brother.

"He would have killed me. Got the drop on me. But all at once something took hold of him. He started shaking." Eston ran his hands through his hair. "It was spookier than having a knife at my throat!"

Solomon bent down and stared into Marquis' face, so similar to his own. All at once he began to unlace the slain man's moccasins.

"What are you doing?" asked Eston.

"I want to check his toes." Sure enough, the last two were fused together...both feet.

"I'll be!" said Solomon, scratching at his jaw. "Biggest question of my life. And now I almost wish I didn't know."

He realized with a guilty pang that whether he had been the pick boy no longer mattered. Either way, he had been the lucky one.

CHAPTER 32

Neatly into place

Standing in the lobby of the D&J Hotel in Baker City, Abigail put the telegram to her lips and kissed the paper with relief. God had been merciful. Corrine, Charlie, Hoke, James, Tam and Harry...all safe. She held her hands to her growing stomach.

She used to think that if she worked hard enough and did what was right, a time would come when all of life fell neatly into place. But she didn't believe that any more. Life was full of both beauty and challenge. The best thing one could do was enjoy the beauty when it showed itself, and weather the challenges as they came...until the next rainbow appeared.

Mimi used to say that. "Just you wait for that next rainbow, Miz Abigail. It's comin'! The Lord, He done whispered it in my ear."

Abigail smiled. She could finally write that letter to Mimi.

*   *   *

Doctor Burleson's office and bedrooms had been cleared of the Waldens' bodies, scrubbed of blood and swept of its broken glass and splinters of wood, and the disheveled medical instruments all set aright. But James still refused to go back there to recover. In fact, he declined to recover inside a building of any kind. Not even—and especially— Granny Pearl's basement room at the church.

"No, thank you. That's quite the hovel, down under a building like that. I can't even stand up straight in there. No windows...I got my fill of not seeing the sky!"

He and Hoke made friends with the livery owner and slept there in the hay at night. During the day, he would go inside only to eat at the café—and did he eat! Corrine had seen him eat many times, but he went at his food with extra vigor during the four weeks they stayed in Silvertown. After eating, it was right back to the livery to read Hoke's Bible or relax within sight of the river as he healed.

Although James refused an indoor recovery, he was happy to let Granny Pearl, Tam, Doc Burleson, and every cook in town fuss over him. He loved being fussed over. Granny Pearl was to thank for that. If Corrine was expected to match the level of attentiveness Granny Pearl heaped on James, Corrine wasn't sure how things would work between them.

The excitement the Waldens had brought to Silvertown slowly turned down to a simmer, but Corrine suspected the story would be retold in the saloons and around dinner tables for years to come. Hoke was elevated to the status of a hero.

Charlie's marksmanship was praised. Granny Pearl was celebrated for producing such amiable grandsons as James and Bennett Solomon (she quit trying to explain they weren't related by birth) and she was pitied for having a daughter that took up with the likes of Duke Walden. Harry was offered a job preaching at the Methodist church after he offered a few redemptive comments at the burials of the Walden clan: Duke, Marquis, Baron and Viscount.

He turned them down, of course, with his arm around Tam, "Our home is in Baker City."

*   *   *

"When we get married," James said to Corrine as they sat by the river's edge one afternoon, "let's just say I've been out working with one of the horses, and it kicks me a good one. How bad are you going to suffer to see me wounded?"

Corrine suspected James wanted her to croon over him, to lean in close and run her hand along his jaw. He would likely kiss her if she did, since they were sitting alone on the riverbank. But she wasn't giving in that easily. She could tell James liked working his charms. He had just begun to get his confidence back, starting every other sentence with "when we get married" and "after we're married." But she held out a little longer, letting him work the muscles of his cleverness.

James hadn't wanted Corrine to come around him first the two weeks of his recovery. That hurt her feelings. He was quick to let anyone else flutter around him, but refused to see Corrine. She'd begun to think it was because she hadn't given him a resounding 'yes' when he made his proposal of marriage official. But she still couldn't get over the untimeliness of the offer.

Hoke, Harry, and Charlie all told her James was keeping her at arm's length because a man didn't like a woman to see him when he was down. But he certainly let everyone else fuss over him...just not Corrine.

"Give him a chance to get his strength back," Charlie had said. "And to restore his manhood. His pride's a little wounded because you saw him at his lowest. He said you were the one who cut him free, not the other way around."

"Yes, but if he hadn't thrown that knife, and if you hadn't shot through the window...."

"And if you hadn't pulled the curtain down, and if Hoke hadn't come charging through town just then and shot through the door....." Then Charlie took her hand. "Let's just be thankful things worked out as they did."

Finally, one morning James was sitting at the table when she came to the café to meet Hoke for breakfast. His scars still looked deep, but they appeared to be healing. Now he was flirting with her again, taking walks, sitting on the bank of the river next to her. She didn't want to say anything to scare him off, but...she had something on her mind.

Patience.

Raising her brows and feigning innocence she said, "If a horse kicks you after we're married and you're injured, I will weep and tear my clothing."

James narrowed his eyes. "I don't know how I feel about marryin' a liar."

He put his hand on her striped skirt, spread across the grass beside him. His wrists were still chaffed; his head still bruised. Doctor Burleson and Granny Pearl couldn't agree on whether it would take his ribs six or eight weeks to fully mend.

"Speaking of clothing," said James, "you're welcome to tear this thing up. I don't like you wearing the skirt Sam Eston had made for you. If I get you a skirt made, will you switch to wearing mine?"

"There's no need for that. I'll wear Tam's bloomers again when we make the trip home. Can we talk about something more serious?"

"What could be more serious than you wearing the clothes I have made for you, instead of Sam Eston's? And just how close fittin' are those bloomers? Did he see you in those?"

"James." She laid her hand on his forehead. "You needn't worry about Sam Eston."

James was quick to cover her hand with his, moving it down to his lips for a kiss before letting it go. "I'm glad he's gone. I've never liked him. He should get him a job somewhere else. When we're married, he better not be lookin' at you the way I've seen him do."

Sam Eston had already ridden out and was headed back to Baker City. When he came to say good-bye to Corrine, he hadn't so much as shaken her hand or hugged her. In fact, he would hardly look her in the eye.

Men and their pride... Corrine wasn't sure she would ever be good at appeasing them.

Of course, Hoke had been standing nearby when Eston came to say good-bye. Hoke was waiting outside the hotel every morning when Corrine woke, and he walked her there every night after supper. He hardly let her out of his sight during the day. She suspected he wasn't far from her and James now, since it was his job to guard his wife's most sacred treasures.

After Eston left Silvertown, Bennett Solomon told Corrine what he'd learned about the sheriff's first wife. She felt sorry for his loss. "Why are you so rough on Sam Eston, James? He rode all the way out here to warn you."

"Well, he didn't do it quick enough. Tam told me about him drinking too much at Fort Bridger and that's how Harry ended up getting shot. I appreciate him doing right by Tam and fetchin' Harry back, but I told you before, he's selfish. He mostly takes care of Sam Eston."

Corrine liked it when James scowled. He was lighthearted by nature; few things caused him irritation. When something did, it was almost fun to sit back and watch him stew.

"Stop lookin' at me that way," he said.

"Looking at you how?"

"Like you got me figured out already. I prefer to be a man of mystery."

"You're full of mystery, alright. Take that Sairee Adams…"

"I told you, Sairee and I were kids together. She's like a sister."

"She says you kissed her."

James shrugged a shoulder. "I might have pecked her on the cheek."

"She says you slept in the same bed."

"As *children*, Corrine! Because, bless that girl's heart, her ma hardly paid any attention to her! She'd have been curled up on the street somewhere if Granny Pearl hadn't put her in the bed with us. I slept with Granny Pearl in them days, too. You fault me for that?"

Of course she didn't fault him for that, but…she wanted to know how many other girls he might have kissed. "Are there other Sairees out there?"

*   *   *

James stretched out on the grass after releasing her hand. The fuller he stretched his body out, the better it felt to his ribs. Not liking where this talk was headed, he raised back up on an elbow.

"Now, wait just a minute. I know Sam Eston kissed you. Tam saw it when he and Harry rode back. And you didn't slap his face for it, neither. When were you going to tell me about that?"

Corrine's brow twisted. "I was relieved to see him. I'd had a frightening night."

James reached for her hand again. "You shouldn't have come out here, Corrine. It's nothin' short of a miracle somethin' worse didn't happen."

Her eyes and chin fell. "I thought you would be glad to see me." She looked so gloomy he couldn't stand it.

A Contradiction to His Pride/Leanne W. Smith

"Let's call it even. I won't kiss anybody else if you won't." He winked at her.

"You promise?" she asked.

"'Course I promise!"

"And about visiting brothels...."

James held a hand up. "I know. I won't do that anymore. I'll try to take more care with my reputation. We don't want anybody to think you're marryin' a scoundrel."

If any man was a scoundrel, it was Sam Eston. It heated James's blood to think Eston kissed her. Frankly, he could have done without Tam telling him that. But part of him was glad to know it. And he knew it had happened at a vulnerable moment for Corrine. When Tam first told him, though, it set James back. He held off from spending time with Corrine until after Eston left, wanting to see for himself if Corrine would seek Eston out if James gave her a cold shoulder.

She didn't.

He wasn't trying to punish her, exactly. Mostly his pride was wounded by Tam's disclosure—as if Corrine seeing him weak and down on the floor hadn't been bad enough! Awakening to find that the Waldens had her, while he was tied and unable to protect her from them, had been nearly as bad as the day Emma was shot.

James's heart was filled with grief and sorrow that day, but not shame. He'd still had the strength to hold Corrine that tragic day. And he took some comfort in knowing how pure his motives had been in trying to do the right thing. But this...this was hard to shake. He was supposed to be

402

Corrine's protector. How could he be sure of his ability to do that now?

James had killed fourteen men in total. That didn't count Viscount Walden. Hoke was the one who put the final shot through Viscount's head. James knew exactly how many men he had killed. He didn't tell Charlie that night on the trail because he took no pride in the number. But he *had* taken pride in his ability to do what was called for in a critical moment. And he wasn't sure if he had that anymore.

*   *   *

James looked so serious, Corrine ruffled his hair. "I like that you don't stay mad about things. Granny Pearl says you've always been that way."

"Maybe our children will get all our better qualities." James stretched back out on the grass.

Their children.... Corrine couldn't keep from smiling. "Why are you still determined to go to Kansas for that horse herd?"

He raised back up on his elbow and reached for her hand. "I told you, darlin'. It's something I need to do."

To restore his manhood....

"Let's not argue about it in the week we have left," he said.

"I'm not trying to argue, but it can't be good to break horses if your ribs have been cracked, James."

James sat all the way up now, and reached for her. He grimaced at the strain of pulling her curled knees toward him. She felt guilty for upsetting him...for causing him more discomfort.

"That's just it, Corrine. I won't have you looking at me like I'm not strong to tackle the hardships in front of me. This is nothin' but a few cracked ribs. Cracked ribs heal. Now, I set out to get a herd of horses, and by God, I intend to do it. Yes, it'll be hard, maybe dangerous, but it'll also be profitable, and I'd like a chance to earn both your respect and my own by doin' what I set out to do."

Corrine's throat was full. She couldn't speak, so she nodded. She tried to push back the tears she felt rising to the surface, but wasn't successful. Her tears embarrassed her. What was wrong with her? Why had she been crying at the drop of a hat ever since Emma's death?

James grimaced. He looked more pained than he had when he pulled her knees closer to him. "Please don't cry," he whispered. "It kills me to see you cry."

She laid her fingers on his lips. "I'm not upset, James. I'm proud. Proud to be loved by someone like you."

He hugged her long and held her close. "I can't tell you the good it does me to hear you say that."

Corrine hadn't told this to Charlie or Tam or Granny Pearl or Hoke, but there had actually been some benefit to seeing James lying on the floor of the doctor's office. As awful as it was to see him suffering, that was the moment she knew she loved him. He was just James then...not a man of charming pronouncements or procurer of romantic sleigh rides. Not the man with a clean-shaven jaw. Just himself.

He had been willing to sacrifice his life for hers, with no reason to expect that he would come out of the ordeal alive. She had never seen him so unguarded...so *vulnerable* before. And yet his eyes had held no self-pity or resentment.

Even when James learned that Bennett Solomon was Granny Pearl's real grandson (and knowing that *he* was not), James didn't act worried it would take anything from him. He simply said to Bennett with a laugh, "You goin' to change your name to Parker? I know you like that 'king' part on the Solomon."

James pulled back to look at Corrine. He had the warmest brown eyes, with laugh lines at the corners, and he was clean-shaven again. She liked him clean-shaven. She liked him bearded, too.

He kissed her. He kissed her a long time...until Hoke's voice at the top of the hill behind them said, "That's enough now."

"Ignore him," mumbled James.

*   *   *

Tam was still mad that James, Chessor, Peters and Charlie weren't coming back to Baker City with them.

"It would give you time to heal, James! You could ride in the wagon with me and Harry. And we've got Granny Pearl to take care of us!"

"I've got to get that herd. These boys'll be disappointed if I don't take 'em, I've talked it up so much." James winked at Corrine.

They loaded up. Corrine, Hoke, Bennett Solomon—who had not changed his name—Tam, Harry and Granny Pearl were all headed back to Baker City. James and his crew would ride on to Kansas. Sairee Adams had already left on the stage, headed back to her son in Fort Smith, Arkansas. Corrine suspected James had paid her fare.

Hoke looked over Charlie's horse and supplies, making sure he was well set.

"You sure about this, Charlie?"

"I'm sure. Thank you for coming, Hoke." Corrine watched them embrace, marveling at how much Hoke was starting to feel like a father.

Charlie hugged Corrine next. She was determined not to cry. She understood his and James's need to go, but it still hurt to part ways with the two men she cared about most in the world.

But it was only temporary. They would come back to her. They would come home.

"I'll be praying for you, Charlie," she said. "Every night. And if you're not back by our birthdays, I'll wait to make the cake when you get there."

Charlie pulled her to the side. "If that ring comes, I told James I wanted you to have it. I didn't tell you that part before, but you should know I've told him about it, and I've told him he can give it to you for your wedding ring if you want."

"I remember Grandmother's ring. If it comes, I'll save it, and wear it with pride after James gives it to me." They hugged again. She tried to memorize the feel of her brother's arms.

Everyone hugged and cried, or tried not to cry. Everyone but Hoke. After hugging Charlie, Hoke stood by looking like he'd had about all he could take of their fussing. Corrine knew it had been hard for Hoke to wait a full month to get back on the trail toward home.

Hoke didn't hug James; he slapped him twice on his clean-shaven jaw instead.

"You just like feelin' my face because it's so smooth," cracked James. He winked at Corrine again.

"Stay out of trouble this time," Hoke told him. Then Hoke swung up on the mustang and glared down at the others until everyone was either mounted or in the wagon.

* * *

James kissed Corrine on the forehead and helped her onto the dun. Solomon was on Tam's horse since Tam was in the wagon. Hoke had purchased the wagon and a pair of mules to pull it. Harry flipped the reins and they started moving off.

It was strange to see Hoke on the mustang that had belonged to Collin Mears. He had bought a second horse in Silvertown and it was tied to the back of the wagon now, but neither it nor the mustang compared to the stallion.

"We need to find him a better horse," James said to Charlie.

They stood in the middle of the street and watched the group get smaller and smaller as Corrine turned in her saddle and waved. Then the wagon turned the corner and she was gone.

James realized Charlie was watching him. Was it a fool's errand to think he could still find that horse herd in Kansas? What perils lay between this day and the moment he would hold Corrine again?

Charlie continued to study him.

"What?" asked James finally.

Charlie shook his head. "You can marry my sister."

"Oh, I plan to."

"I'm just letting you know I don't have a problem with it. I told her to watch for that ring."

"Mighty generous of you." They turned to their horses, checking the stirrups, preparing to ride. "You better not give me any more problems between here and Kansas."

"Me give *you* problems? Ha! Just try to throw me in a horse trough again and you'll see what kind of problems I give you."

"I'll throw you in again if I have to. I'm ready to throw you in one right now."

"I'd like to see you try with those bum ribs you got."

"I don't have bum ribs. Doc Burleson says they're healing fine. Be like new long before we get to Kansas."

"I'm just saying, I know where to hit next time I have to take you down on a creek bank."

"That's not the way I remember it."

Michael Chessor shook his head, cutting his eyes to Bart Peters. "Y'all plan to bicker all the way to Kansas and back?"

Charlie looked at James with a gleam in his eye. At James's nod, Charlie dove for Chessor's legs while James hooked him under the arms. They dragged him to the nearest horse trough and, with Bart Peters looking on and laughing, they pitched Chessor in.

*   *   *

Abigail tucked the covers in around Lina and Jacob. Hearing voices in the hotel lobby below, she stepped out on the landing and looked down from the top of the stairs.

There stood Hoke, with Corrine beside him.

Relief flooded her heart so fast she had to grab the railing to keep from dropping to her knees. Hoke had come back to her, and he brought the daughter she feared she might have lost.

He took the stairs by threes. She had grown larger with child...his child. Abigail could see the wonder in his eyes.

Hoke laid his hand on her middle and buried his face in her hair. "What do you say we go home now?"

Abigail wrapped her arms around him and nodded.

Home.

A Contradiction to His Pride/Leanne W. Smith

EPILOGUE

Clyde Austelle delivered the letter. It's from Charlie!" announced Abigail, waving it in the air, opening it quickly.

Dear Ma,

Give my love to Hoke, Corrine, Jacob and Lina, and everyone in Baker City. Mimi sends her love, too. That's right, Ma. I'm back in Tennessee, in Marston.

I left James, Bart and Chessor with the horse herd in Kansas. We finally found it. James said it would take several weeks to get the herd ready to drive north. They were mighty wild and skittish. Chessor got thrown, which sent me and him into town. About the time he got patched up, I had a strong urge to take the train east. Those boys didn't really need me anymore, so I did it.

I first thought only to visit. I wanted to see the house again. I wanted to hug Mimi's neck and visit Grandfather's land. On my way through Independence, I stopped to see Mrs. Helton. She insisted I take Pa's law books. I started reading them.

When I first got into Marston I saw Buck Dale who offered me a job working on his farm. Isn't it a small world, Ma? Back at Laramie, when we got that letter from Uncle Thad telling us how the Dale family had been reunited, I never imagined I'd be back in Marston helping Buck Dale get his farm in working order. But that's exactly what has happened.

That was two weeks ago. I only planned to work long enough to earn money for the trip home, but having time to think while working on a farm during the day, and time in the evenings to read through Pa's law books, makes me hungry to get a law degree. So I'd like to work here long enough to earn money for school in the East, Ma. Don't you think Pa would have liked that?

In Silvertown, when James was being held by the Waldens, I realized what power there is in knowing the law. I think I'd be good at it. Once I get my degree, I'll be back. I promise. Baker City will need attorneys.

I love you, Ma. I miss you. But know that in time, I'll be home.

Charlie

NOTES & ACKNOWLEDGEMENTS

I've had many book ideas, but only a few with staying power. For years I've been cultivating a few of these. *Contradiction* was not one of them.

My initial vision was to write seven books, all connected to the fictional county of Marston, Tennessee. I didn't see these as a series in the traditional sense, but as individual tales all bubbling up from a common place. *Hope* and *home* are important themes to me, as are the women and men who dig deep into the soil to find and build them.

It doesn't make a lot of sense to have a patchwork quilt in mind with no firm pattern, just the hope that in the end the separate squares will all fit together in some artful way. But that describes my writing...both the larger quilt that may constitute my catalog some day, and the individual squares that represent each novel. My only explanation for why I think I'm supposed to do it this way is simply, "This is what I feel called to do."

Even though I didn't expect to write a follow-up to *Leaving Independence*, I did. And I have to say, the spiritual high I felt at the conclusion of *Contradiction* tops my list of writer highs to date. There is much about the act of writing and the art of storytelling that remains a mystery to me. And while I am certain I have fallen short in writing and telling this story, I *loved* trying. If you read this book and enjoy it, then we will have shared something, you and I...and I'll be deeply honored.

Thank you Stan, Jordan, Shelby, Lincoln, and Joan for being my closest circle of support. My daughter, Shelby Mick, designed the gorgeous book cover. The good-looking man on front, who is far more handsome than the James of my mind, is John King, my former student and now friend. The photograph was taken by Falk Neumann, who didn't have to make it so graciously available to me, but did. And Melissa Wilson helped sketch the vision. Without each of their contributions, and the love of a daughter willing to use her talents so tirelessly to serve those around her, this beautiful cover would not have been.

There are many others to whom I owe debts on this book, these in particular:

Julie Gwinn, my agent, who represents a warm and supportive group of authors, of which I'm proud to be a part.

Ami McConnell, fellow writer, who listened at a time when I hungered for it, and introduced me to Kerri Potts. I've long feared the ocean called social media. Kerri has taught me to swim and fish. If sales on this book are healthy, it will be in large part due to Kerri, with a straight line drawn back to Ami's friendship.

Dana Chamblee Carpenter is my several-years-running critique partner. She's the one I call when the censor has jumped on my shoulder and sneered that I'll never be good enough and don't know what I'm doing.

Finally, Shari MacDonald Strong deserves an award for editing two books and one short story for me now. She's gained an intimate look at my quirks and foibles, and rather than throwing my own books back at me, has become a voice of reason I value as highly as my own.

When I think of the book club members who have so graciously invited me into their homes, of the many people who have written kind reviews, of the folks at HHCC and Lipscomb and the extended family members who have asked about the status of this follow-up book every week for the past two years, of my launch team and a growing list of friends in the writing community, along with the book and publishing events I've been blessed to participate in...well...it's humbling.

A great cloud of witnesses has surrounded me, and I am grateful to every member.

ABOUT THE AUTHOR

Photo © 2015 Shelby M'lynn Mick

A Contradiction to His Pride is Leanne W. Smith's exciting follow-up story to the Amazon bestseller, *Leaving Independence*. In addition to writing, she teaches for a university in Nashville, Tennessee, where she lives with her husband, two daughters, and son-in-law. Visit her website at www.leannewsmith.com for information about her books, and for inspiration in pursuing personal and career-related dreams.

CPSIA information can be obtained
at www.ICGtesting.com
Printed in the USA
LVHW03s0720110618
580296LV00001B/103/P